T0036799

From the Longing Orchard

From the
Longing Orchard

a novel

Jessica Jopp

🐓 Red Hen Press | *Pasadena, CA*

From the Longing Orchard
Copyright © 2023 by Jessica Jopp
All Rights Reserved

No part of this book may be used or reproduced in any manner whatsoever without the prior written permission of both the publisher and the copyright owner.

Book design by Mark E. Cull

Library of Congress Cataloging-in-Publication Data

Names: Jopp, Jessica, 1961– author.
Title: From the longing orchard: a novel / Jessica Jopp.
Description: First edition. | Pasadena: Red Hen Press, [2023]
Identifiers: LCCN 2022027781 (print) | LCCN 2022027782 (ebook) | ISBN 9781597099295 (paperback) | ISBN 9781597099301 (ebook)
Subjects: LCGFT: Bildungsromans. | Novels.
Classification: LCC PS3610.O646 F76 2023 (print) | LCC PS3610.O646 (ebook) | DDC 813/.6—dc23/eng/20220702
LC record available at https://lccn.loc.gov/2022027781
LC ebook record available at https://lccn.loc.gov/2022027782

The National Endowment for the Arts, the Los Angeles County Arts Commission, the Ahmanson Foundation, the Dwight Stuart Youth Fund, the Max Factor Family Foundation, the Pasadena Tournament of Roses Foundation, the Pasadena Arts & Culture Commission and the City of Pasadena Cultural Affairs Division, the City of Los Angeles Department of Cultural Affairs, the Audrey & Sydney Irmas Charitable Foundation, the Kinder Morgan Foundation, the Meta & George Rosenberg Foundation, the Allergan Foundation, the Riordan Foundation, Amazon Literary Partnership, and the Mara W. Breech Foundation partially support Red Hen Press.

First Edition
Published by Red Hen Press
www.redhen.org

Acknowledgments

There are many people to whom I owe much gratitude for assistance of various kinds during the long process of writing this novel:

To Tony Eprile and Claire Messud, who read drafts of this novel at the New York State Summer Writers Institute at Skidmore and provided incisive feedback and essential encouragement.

To the amazing staff at Red Hen, who have been wonderful every step of the way.

To friends who read early drafts and offered suggestions and encouragement that kept me going: Barb Baird, Kate Miller, and Judith Villa.

To Scott S., whose tale of debilitating fear and courage overcoming it informed this narrative.

To Moyra Evans, whose dear friendship over many years has helped keep me steady.

To Susan Comfort, who provided companionship and support during much of the writing of this book.

To my sisters, Jennifer Jopp and Judith Jopp, and my wonderful family, for being who they are.

My profound gratitude and deepest appreciation to all for helping to bring this dream to life.

To the memory of two remarkable women, my mother, Madeleine Hart, and my aunt, Nancy Jopp Churchill, this novel is dedicated. Their humor, love of life, and sense of justice guide me every day.

Contents

From the Longing Orchard

1

Where Was *Field*?

hen, they lived in a third-floor walkup in Putnamton, on the south side of the city. When her mother held her in the chair on the side porch, gray paint chipping off the floor, the wood soft and slightly tilted, she smelled her mother's skin. Her father glued shims under the front legs of the chair, so when Sonya Hudson sat with her mother in the sun the world did not feel slanted.

Then there were shadows of the oak beyond her bedroom window and, along with the earlier smell of her mother's skin, there were scents to be absorbed by daylight and by darkness, textures to be noticed. Then, there was sunlight on her arm or on a chair, before it was *sunlight.* There were voices in her ear, singing whatever they were saying, one of the many mysteries. Even after language came, it wasn't this way; there was the summer porch just at dusk, and she knew as *red* the weighted globes of the cherry tree, draping themselves over the edge of the roof. And beyond that with the orange-pink sky of sunset, she knew the word *wide.* There were the warm fields she walked with her father, and the sidewalks in town, huge trees lining them, dusting down their shadows in the summer. She knew *field* and *tree.* Veined leaf and bumpy pinecone texture, frog-skin texture, night-bug sounds beyond the screen. She knew water her parents took her to, and, while her mother held her hand, both of them leaned into its blue well of scent. The faint green speckled rounds of stone worn smooth, damp in her hands. Each new word, *lake, stone,* came lifted, dripping, shimmering. With each new word, mysteries deepening.

But here she was at eighteen unable to live for those scents and textures or to leave her house, surrounded in her room by half-sketches, a pile of pencils chipped and broken behind her on the floor amid dirty clothes, plates of old food. There were sketches tacked to the wall above her desk, and notes written on the wall, marked in detail with the underlined heading <u>Don't Forget</u>; so that she wouldn't forget what to do next, she told herself.

The range of things she could do included starting a new sketch, working on one begun, finishing another. Or lying on the floor, looking up, and thinking about circular images—a constancy in her drawings that Elinor had pointed out—or opening the door to let Lois or her mother in, or walking downstairs to briefly join them for a meal. It did not include driving into town with them or going for a walk with Elinor or riding her bike out the path away from the suburbs and past the shoots of summer green pasture, this summer, the summer of her eighteenth year. It did not even include pulling back the curtains and unlocking and opening the windows, both of them, or, especially, leaving them unlocked at night, or looking at stars netted in them, or sleeping out in the yard as she and Lois did as kids sometimes, or thinking about next year or about any others after this one. Her list of things to do, so that she wouldn't forget, did not include putting her pillow and sheet on the floor by the open window on a clear night and sleeping in the spill of moonlight coming in her room. She lived in a room in a house with her mother and her sister and beyond them others ordered the world of Harpur Springs, kept the buses running on time, the newspapers delivered. The world was filled with people like Norma Rae who worked hard, spoke up for others, who could stand on a table, hold up a sign, and make life better. When she and Elinor saw the film at the mall that spring, they had been moved to tears by it. Sonya found comfort now, in her room, in recalling such people. All she could do was get up in the morning, sit at her desk, and live in that one moment. The small rolltop had cubbyholes, supplies had their designated place. So that she would not forget which charcoal or sharpened colored pencil to pick up next.

Her mother came in, as she often did lately, and sat down in the rocking chair. "You haven't been out of this house, this room actually, in weeks and weeks. And I can no longer—I just hate to think of your nightmares about them." When Sonya was still venturing outside, going about a day, Marie had said she couldn't bear to see Sonya avoid the animals outside. And then her daughter had said, "I'm fine, Mom, really. I can handle that." Staying in, she could reduce the risk further, and not even have to avoid one.

Now the direct mention of her nightmares made Sonya cast her eyes away from her mother, down to the bits of scrap paper on her cluttered desk. She felt sweat forming on the back of her neck. Just last night they had been in the trees, hanging above her as she walked the path. She lifted her head briefly and saw their arms and tails loping down, their eyes cast down, watching her. There might have been fifty of them, and they took naturally to the trees. They leapt from one to the next as she walked. They were traveling her way, keeping an eye on her, above her and behind her, and they seemed at any instant about to slip from the mossy gray branches and drape themselves over her. If she were to look at them close-up, as she was sometimes forced to do in her waking life—chancing across one in the neighborhood—they would have yet another chance to threaten with their eyes, taunt with the shredded flesh wedged between their teeth. She had to hurry. When she began to run, the animals moved faster through the trees, and the end of the path, the clearing, moved further from her reach. It was the sweat of running that she had felt on her neck when she woke. But she did not tell her mother any of this. She shrugged.

Instead of saying again that she was fine, she said, "I'm used to them." It had been five years since her fear began, five going on six, five, with each day infused with it, each day holding its minutes stretched out almost to snapping by the blinding white of fear.

Across the room her mother sighed as she took off her straw garden cap, leaned forward with her elbows on her legs, and covered her face with her hands.

In the very beginning, when Sonya's parents lived in their first apartment in Putnamton, Connecticut, which they rented for fifty-five dollars a month, a special evening for them was a twenty-nine-cent quart of beer and the cheapest piece of meat her father could get at the Thirty-Fourth Street grocery store on his walk home from work. Her mother fried onions, peppers, and the pieces of liver, and they ate this over spaghetti with a loaf of bread. She had quit her job in the fabric store when her pregnancy started to show.

Born from the old sadness of each, and into their joined promise, was first Sonya and then, eighteen months later, Lois. Since they could not afford to go to the movies or to get a babysitter, Mitchell and Marie Hudson spent every evening with the girls, reading stories or, when their daughters were a little older, drawing with crayons on large sheets of rough scrap paper Mitchell brought home from his job at the paper mill. Sometimes the girls spread the paper out on the black and white checked linoleum floor of the kitchen, and sometimes their mother taped sheets of it to the refrigerator, and they stood up and drew, as if at an easel. They made houses, animals, and cities peopled with specks, the kitchen always wiped clean by supper-time and drawn on fire with color by the next afternoon.

When they moved out of the city, they pulled all their belongings in a U-Haul trailer behind the station wagon with fake wood strips along the sides. Sonya's parents had bought the car for the move for fifty dollars. Her father had also given the owner as part of the deal two clay birds he had made, finely detailed and carried in one hand. By the time they reached the central farmland of New York State, night had fallen. When her father got out to see why the trailer had slid off the road into a ditch, Sonya was awakened by the inside car light. Her sister was still asleep beside her. She heard her father urinate against a hubcap, then pace back and forth on the dark road cursing. The headlights cast their wobbly beam down the county road. Summer, and night bugs scritched in the cornfields on either side of them. Her mother reached her hand back, touched her knee and said, "We'll be there soon, Honey." Sonya slept while her father, with the generous help of a passerby, maneuvered the trailer back onto the road. And, though exhausted, he stayed alert the rest of the trip.

Their arrival in the town of Laconius, where Mitchell had gotten a job as a shop teacher, raised the population to three hundred fifty-six. A town this size had but a couple of stone churches, a corner grocery store, post office, and a filling station. Of special notice for those passing through were the handful of Greek Revival houses, here and there, set back from the road, among the mostly typical two-story wood frame houses, the farmhouses on the outskirts of town. Otherwise, fields all around the town stretching for miles, dairy farms plotted among them.

For a month they lived at The Bluebell, a motel a few miles out of town, at the intersection of a town road and a county highway that led to the interstate. The town's remoteness was somewhat compensated for by a party phone line, an intimate mode of communication that made possible the occasional inadvertent sharing of private information, and thus occasionally the subsequent intentional disseminating of it. In fact, this is how one party discovered that the Hudsons needed an apartment, and how, eventually, they found one available at the other end of Main Street.

There was not so much fear as wonder then, in the new place they rented when they moved out of the city. The upstairs floor of a house was theirs. Sonya and Lois watched, over the windowsill in the sun porch, as a strange machine carved neat rows in the field beside the house. When their mother taught them the word *combine*, for days it lay on their tongues like a piece of translucent yellow candy. In this kitchen too, the girls used the refrigerator like an easel.

Now she lived in her imagination, but didn't everyone, she might have asked herself. She told her mother she was fine. And she was; everyone lived that way. There were colors, textures, and sounds right in her room, and it was all familiar. Sonya didn't really need to leave her room for anything; after all, there wasn't anything else she needed. She could wear her clothes the right way, then inside-out awhile, then right-side out again. Food was not far away—downstairs in the kitchen. Her pencils and paper would last, and she had so much work to do that there just wasn't time to spend with Elinor or Lois anyway. They could come to talk with her, which they did. Her mother, too. But usually that was brief, her mother looking worried or trying to talk with her about getting out to check the garbage can lids or to carry a planter outside for her. Sometimes Sonya could manage these things.

Or her mother appeared otherwise pained, though tall, assured, asking her daughter to venture into the world with her, to the store or to an event of some kind, as if she could merely step beyond the threshold and carry herself among all those details, all those people going about their days. All that movement to absorb, sound to hear and make note of. When she declined the offers, she saw the gray of Marie's eyes turn inward, retreat a shade to that reserve of strength in times of disappointment. Even so, Sonya couldn't help but decline; far better to stay inside where she could take care of things herself, keep track of the path of light across her room during the day, the sounds of the neighborhood heard faintly through the closed windows, recall the efficiency of others beyond her street and let them keep that up, keep everything running smoothly. She had artwork to do and did not want to forget what to do next.

Or her mother was quiet, sitting in the chair in Sonya's room, turning the silver ring on her finger while looking down at it, and hesitating. The quiet accentuated her musk oil perfume. In that pause Sonya could go elsewhere, the weight of the present too much to take in; with no deliberate figuring on her part, she was back in the summer kitchen, the checked linoleum cool to her feet, her mother braiding Lois's hair, when her father came up the back steps, face contorted in worry, reddish-brown eyebrows knitted nearly into one. His thick red-brown hair, though short, a little wild, from his hands running through it in distress.

"It's Lloyd Duncan's son," he had said to Sonya's mother, referring to the fifteen-year-old who lived in the house on the other side of the field. "He and the Mancini boy were making an explosive of some kind, and it blew up in his face. He ran from their barn to the house. Collapsed on the kitchen floor, he lost so much blood. Blew off half his face. Stupid kid. He could have died."

Sonya's mother had put her hand over her mouth and closed her eyes, then opened them with the same look of concern that was evident now. "My God," she had said.

The word *collapse* had been new to Sonya and so full of significance she could hardly absorb the information. She imagined Andy Duncan, a teenager and thin, collapsing onto their kitchen floor. Blood would fill the tiny cracks and blur the squares. Her mother, father, sister, and she herself, would lean over him. They would fall into him, into the gape in his face, become part of his pain. Collapse must mean the rest of the world falls too, falls into the wounded person.

It had been just a few days earlier that she and Lois were sitting on the back steps in the sun sorting chalk for the sidewalk when he walked across the field, hands cupped in front of him. The girls looked up as he approached and asked them if they wanted to see what he and his friends had found that morning on the side of the road.

Sonya noticed his short dark hair combed back, a few freckles on his face matching the ones on his arms. He seemed almost grown up, with his white T-shirt, marked by a sweat patch here and there, hanging over his khaki shorts.

The girls looked at each other. "OK," they said.

"Here it is, in this box." With one hand Andy carefully lifted the top of the earring box, the name of a department store, Murphy's, slanted across it, which was in his other hand. Resting on the square of cotton was a finger, red apparent bloodstain at its base, which seemed to be absorbed by the fibers around it. The finger had dust and dirt embedded in its dried blood.

He saw their horror-stricken look and launched into embellished details. "There it was, lying there in the dirt by itself, not even wriggling anymore, and we stopped to pick it up and it was cold. The tip was almost purple."

The girls could hardly breathe, struggled to find air to form a word. "But whose is it?" Sonya asked. "Won't someone be looking for it?"

"Well, finders keepers," Andy said, putting the lid back in place. "It's mine now."

Lois grabbed her sister's arm. Sonya said, "We have to go in now."

"Any time you want to see it again, just let me know," Andy said, smiling as he turned to cross the field and head home.

When they had run in and told Marie about it, she sat them down and explained that it was not possible that he had found a finger.

"But we saw it."

"It was in the box."

"But how could a person lose one finger like that?" Marie tried to pacify their stupor. "It doesn't make any sense, girls. He must have played a trick on you."

Though they were inclined to believe her, the nauseated feeling they had had at seeing it lingered with them the rest of that day and into the next.

Now came the news of his accident. Thinking about his freckled cheek, Sonya tried to imagine his face blown apart but could not. "Will he be able to talk?" she asked her mother.

"Probably when his mouth heals, yes," she said. "Finish your peach." Sonya imagined his mouth healed, back in place.

She picked up the half-eaten peach she had set aside to better hear her parents' conversation. Her father went back outside. Eating the peach slowly, thinking about her teeth and about the fuzzy skin and sweet juice, she watched her mother braid her sister's reddish-brown hair. She couldn't imagine not being able to open and close her mouth around a peach. The phrase *could have died* hung in the air like a bat.

"What is heaven?" The linoleum floor was cool to her bare feet. Her mother's hands paused in her sister's hair as she looked at Sonya, the gray of her eyes, as usual, earnest, intent on her daughter's question.

"Some people believe it is the place a soul goes after a person dies."

Sonya held her peach in her left hand, wiped the juice from her right hand onto the front of her blue flowered cotton sundress, took the peach again in her right hand, and asked, "If Andy Duncan died, would his soul go to heaven?"

"Yes, I think it would," said her mother, braiding Lois's hair again.

"Could he feel pain in heaven?"

"No, he would feel peace there, Sonya."

"Would his mouth be healed so he could eat?"

"People don't eat in heaven."

"Can they smell anything?"

"No."

"Can they hear?"

"No."

"Can they see?"

"Sonya." She watched her mother wrap a rubber band around Lois's braid and brush the end, careful not to pull it. The girls were beginning to experiment with her hair, too. Hers was short though, so with limited styling options this meant that they stood on a chair on either side of her and combed her dark hair sometimes all forward, then all back, sometimes from one side to the other. Barrettes and other accessories were likely to come soon. Occasionally she let them help her tease it up.

"They don't play no games?" Lois asked, a puzzled look on her face, its usual hint of round wonder, openness about it, subdued.

"They don't play *any* games," her mother corrected.

"They don't play *any* games?" There was a note of alarm in Lois's voice.

"What *can* they do?" Sonya asked.

"They are souls. They don't exist in the world as we know it, but in a different world."

Sonya sucked on the peach pit to get the last hairy strands of fruit.

"Please don't suck on the pit, Honey."

She spit it out on a plate.

"Souls understand more than we can ever imagine. They don't need our senses. They have their own, more precise and better than ours. They are happy. It isn't something you girls should be worrying about."

Sonya did not know what *precise* meant, but she knew *happy*. She was five.

Later that afternoon when the girls spread huge sheets of paper out on the floor of the sun porch, Sonya drew Andy Duncan fallen on the floor. She gave him pots and cups and peaches around his body. She took a magic marker, double red, and drew all of his blood streaming back into his body through a sprawling gap where his mouth should have been. Then she asked her mother to write out the title, *Andy Duncan Collapsed in the Kitchen*, at the top in purple crayon.

That night Sonya dreamed that she hovered in the air with a winged woman dressed in white. Far below them in the black landscape someone sat holding his face together. The woman said to Sonya, "He almost died."

Every night for the next few weeks she listened in bed to Lois breathe and watched shadows the streetlights made. The rest of the house was quiet. A stately oak tree in the front yard stood between the house and a streetlight, and animals took shape on the walls. Their mouths seemed to move as if speaking, but she could not make out what they were saying. Sometimes a car drove down Main Street and cast its headlight beam through the room like a flashlight. Their room was sunk in ghostly shadowed light that was familiar to Sonya, and sometimes she felt as though she was on a ship that had sunk years ago. Perhaps the other world her mother spoke of was like this. She and Lois were not in air or water exactly. They might never again be up walking around in the clear light of the yard or of the kitchen. When she had to use the bathroom, she woke Lois to walk down the long hallway with her. The porcelain toothbrush holder with a neat red, blue, and two smaller pink brushes in it jutting out from the wall told her that the world was safe and that morning would come.

On the way to Andy Duncan's house with her mother and Lois, two weeks later, when he was out of the hospital, Sonya thought more about the word *collapse*. Walking across the warm summer field she wondered, was he still collapsed, was he going to look collapsed, or was it something a person did once and then was finished doing?

"Is he still collapsed?"

"No, that was just at first. He is recovering now."

"Can he talk yet?"

"I'm not sure. We'll see, girls. And if he seems very tired we won't stay more than a few minutes. He probably needs a lot of rest as his face heals."

They reached the gravel driveway and crossed to the back screen door of the two-story wood frame house. As Marie was about to knock, Lloyd Duncan approached from the kitchen and opened the door.

"Hello, Marie, girls." He nodded toward them. He was stockier than their father, *thick* was the word that came to Sonya from close-up, his shoulders broad, face almost square, his dark hair short and brushed flat on top like the hair of most of the men in town.

"The girls thought it would be nice to see how Andy is doing."

"Come on in. He's in the living room now on the couch. Not good for much help with the summer work, but what are you going to do?" He directed the question toward Marie, though it didn't need an answer. "If my wife was here, she'd get you a glass of water or make you some iced tea, but she's run off to the store."

"That's all right," Marie said. "We're fine."

As he led the way from the kitchen, Sonya noticed that the bare metal table had its matching chairs all pushed in. From the next room came a sound the girls recognized but hadn't heard too often, the midday game show chatter. They followed Mr. Duncan into the living room, where he walked over to the large wood-grain box with the doily and the plastic plant on top of it and snapped it off, the picture fading from the edges and disappearing through a spot of silver light in the center, until the screen was completely black.

Then they all turned toward the couch, where Andy reclined on his side facing the TV, wearing shorts and a T-shirt. The bandage wrapped around his head seemed to nearly swallow him, a small space for his eyes and an opening for his mouth, his hair matted and stuck to him in sweat. As he lifted an arm and gestured hello, Sonya noticed a glass of water on a table beside him with a straw in it.

"Hi, Andy," Marie said. "The girls wanted to come over and see how you are doing." Sonya and Lois said hi, and he looked at them and nodded.

"Well, there he is," his father said. "You are welcome to sit and have a chat."

Marie and the girls sat down in armchairs, all covered with thick plastic.

His father remained standing. "There is Mr. Explosive of 1966. Good thing you didn't come over to see *what* he is doing, because all he is doing is lounging there like a beauty queen. That's it, you see it! Probably couldn't even mow the lawn."

The girls, wearing shorts, shifted in their seats, peeling their legs from the hot plastic.

"Christ, when I was his age I had half the county lit up from explosives I'd made with my buddies out in some field. That's what we knew how to do—hunt, fish, torch crap up. You girls wouldn't know about that. I figured he'd like trying it too, but this one couldn't make a goddamn—excuse me—firecracker without nearly doing himself in! Isn't that right?" He glanced down at his son. "That army better hope to hell it don't draft you down the line. You might blow up your own unit before you get halfway over there to Vietnam."

Andy looked up at him and nodded.

"Good for I don't know what. Hey, he's all yours, girls. I've got work to do if you'll excuse me."

"Sure, Lloyd," Marie said. "We'll see ourselves out. Thanks." He walked back through the kitchen and out the door.

The brunt of what he had said, the weight of it, bore down on them in the hot living room.

Then Marie turned to Andy. "Will the bandage be on much longer?"

He nodded that it would be.

"Does it hurt to talk?" Sonya thought that it might but wondered if he could.

He nodded, then slowly sat up and reached toward the table to pick up a pad and pencil beside the water glass. He jotted for a minute or two and handed the note to Marie.

She read it out loud. "The doctor said it will take longer to heal if I try to talk now. It could be another couple weeks before I can open it more so it will be easy to talk and eat. But now I can eat soft food."

"It's good you can eat," Sonya said. Andy nodded that it was.

He picked the pencil up again and wrote a bit more, handing the page to Marie, who again read.

"There is a hole in the bottom of the box. We didn't really find the finger, it was one of my fingers. It was a trick my friend got from a book. I'm sorry if I scared you."

The girls watched him closely as he held up his hands and motioned the way his middle finger slipped through the hole so that it nestled on the cotton in the box.

Then Sonya asked, "It was really just a trick?"

When he nodded, each of them let out a breath of relief.

Marie smiled at him. "I'm taking the girls to the Five-and-Dime later. Can we get you anything?"

He shook his head.

"Girls, Andy probably needs to get some rest now. We should go."

They stood up, legs peeling off the plastic, and stepped toward the couch.

"I hope your mouth gets better," Sonya said, as Lois leaned toward him and more closely inspected the bandage.

Andy looked up and whispered, "Thanks for coming," his mouth barely moving.

Marie rested her hand briefly on his shoulder and smiled at him again.

Then they walked into the kitchen. Sonya peeked over her shoulder into the living room and saw Andy still sitting up, glancing through the doorway at them. When she caught his eye, he eased himself down, reclining, and gazed toward the blank television. They let themselves out the screen door and headed back across the field toward their apartment.

"Why is his father mean?" Sonya asked.

"It might be because he is upset that Andy has been hurt."

She thought about her mother's explanation. Maybe that was it. Yet there was something strange about his father.

When they reached their own back steps, Marie paused before leading the girls up the stairway to the second floor. She bent down and hugged each of them.

"I love you two."

They slipped their arms around her neck and held onto the scent of her summer heat.

And at times during her childhood the earth felt wide and smelled warm to her, and, this day, her father's hand up above leading her, with Lois on his other side, seemed to say: *I am up here among the tall things, closer to the tops of trees, closer to the sky, walking this round earth longer, come this way, I will show you.* They walked out across the playing fields, stepped into the lengthening sun of late day, stepping blade over blade over blade through sun, their own shadows stretching down to the warm grass. They stooped now and then to pluck a white puff whose name she learned that day and drop it in a brown grocery bag, treasure left behind, the field scattered with such finds that her father exclaimed with great joy, "Look, here's another one! Today must be our lucky day!" at each earth-smelling round. After the length of the field, they walked back home, in his hand a bag of the round discovered things that no one else had found and called his own. The luck of another day in which she and Lois learned a word.

When they got home and he poured them out on the kitchen table, his wife hugged him and said, "They look delicious, Mitchell." That evening she rinsed them in the sink, took out a frying pan, and soon their kitchen was filled with the earthy smell of the cooking slices.

But where was *mushroom* now? That place of damp wonder had had rain in it, the cool exhilarating kind someone could linger in. Or a deserted county road perhaps, that she had seen from the car window, the fields in rain, the day in mushroom. Now, at eighteen, if she thought about it, the word would remind her of her no-wandering. In a word like mushroom was a hint of what was lost. She had not fallen, though, to the summer floor in pain, her body damaged by recklessness, the place where a mouth had been now floating in spilled blood, its absence unimaginable to the psyche that was likewise diminished. Who was that boy from her early childhood? Had he recovered? If she tried to, she could not recall. Hers was not a physical scar; no shredded flesh dangled, unhealed. She can talk, she can, she does. She'll show her mother that she can.

"I'm fine, Mom," Sonya tried again. She spoke loudly in her dreams; she screamed in them sometimes. "Please don't worry." Where was *field*? She'll feel the damp joy of mushroom again, the wonder of starlight caught in a night window, melted to waves in the glass, the abandon of a summer storm moving across the reservoir.

Glenda had gotten out of it. Surely she could. But her grandmother was still confined by depression to some degree; she herself wouldn't be. There was nothing *that* wrong; recovery wouldn't be very dramatic. She would simply get up and go about her day. One day she would do that, and she would sleep through a night. One day soon, but for now she needed to focus on the notations in pencil above her desk with the heading <u>Don't Forget</u>; so that she wouldn't forget what to do next, she told herself.

She started to say "Don't worry" again, but when she looked away from the wall above her desk and back to where her mother had been sitting, Sonya realized that she had already left the room. When had she left? Had she walked over and rested her hand on her daughter's shoulder? Had she walked over and kissed the top of her head? Sonya did not know how long she had been sitting there, contemplating the notes above her desk.

2

Desert Candle And Blazing Star

Sonya got up from her desk, cleared a space on the floor and lay down. With her windows closed, she thought about the smells of summer, its tight closed hands, some of its heat and scent caught in her closed room. In the warm molecular wanderings of summer, some things could move, particles of sound moved, muffled, outside her window, and somewhere else curtains and blinds were open as light moved across a wall—an outdoor stucco wall of a cafe, where people sat to talk, their arms lifting their painted teacups to their lips, while ephemeral smells drifted from the kitchen in the rear, and they could get up, pay their bill, stretch toward the sky as their shoes clicked down the stone walk, without any thought or deliberation. She liked to imagine them, somewhere or other, the people for whom living was a word sung from their lip, summer, a ticket in their pocket. But not for her.

What had been for her were rich smells in the old clubhouse at the end of that year.

When the Hudsons left that apartment with the window from which the girls had seen the combine, the place in which they had first rolled words on their tongues like incandescent sweets, they rented a house on a side street in Laconius. This move did not involve a trailer but required many trips through town in the gray-and-white VW bus they had acquired in a swap of the station wagon. Sonya and Lois agreed that though there was a front porch, the best thing about the place was the small red wooden structure out back beside the barn. It had two floors, one room above the other, and downstairs there were moldy overstuffed chairs and a row of built-in drawers along one wall that had dead mice and cobwebs in them. A line of poplars bordered the yard.

In the summer, the girls' mother told them not to wander off by themselves. In the evening, after suppertime, they could stay in the yard until the bats and barn swallows lunged and spun in the air. They heard the leaves of the poplars stirring. Sometimes their father sat out in one of the green Adirondack chairs and drank beer, his flip-flops tossed aside in the grass. His frame filled the chair, and he eased, reclining, as if he'd just won the race, downed his draught with glory in his throat. But their father, athletically graceful, wasn't interested in competitive sports, had never, in fact, won any ribbon, medal, or cup of any kind. His body, though, those satiated moments, was in about the best place it knew. When he drank beer in the evenings, he exuded a confidence, an expansiveness, such that the god of summer backyards, whoever that might be, could have studied him from behind the willow tree and taken voluminous notes. Their mother read the newspaper with him or worked in the barn scraping paint off an old chair or another piece she had found and decided to salvage. Sometimes, when she stayed inside, Sonya and Lois would look up, close to their bedtime, and see their mother standing at the screened door of the lighted kitchen, calling them in.

While they lived in the city a friend of their father's had given the family an old television set. It was in the apartment a week, when, one afternoon, their mother saw Lois sitting mesmerized three inches away from the screen. "Mitchell," she said to her husband, "please take it back tomorrow." So the next day he returned it. Now in the summer evenings, when the town was quiet and living rooms up and down the street cast the blue glow of TV sets into the still air, the clink of dishes after supper drifting through open windows, Sonya and Lois leaned against their mother, arms bare in her sleeveless print shirt, and listened to a story. The girls could not get close enough to her, each straining to better see the pages. When it was time for bed, their father came over, down on all fours. Sometimes he nibbled their mother's toes or chewed on her sandal strap, and she laughed, brushed her hand over his hair, then pushed his head away. The girls climbed onto his back, and he rode them into their bedroom. Though their bath had washed out bits of grass, twigs, and dirt, it had not washed out the sun. Later, as Sonya fell asleep, she smelled the warmth of the day's heat on the back of her hands.

On summer mornings Sonya and Lois often took half-empty jars of old cold cream they thought their mother had forgotten behind some others on the bathroom shelf, brought these outside and gathered petals from rose bushes, pine needles, and fresh grass. They took all their supplies to their clubhouse, which they had cleaned out the first week of summer, and spent the day opening a store. They soaked rose petals in water in the hot sun until the water clouded pink, and mixed powder and cream until they had a thick base. These two mixed became a perfumed skin cream, whose exact ingredients and preparation time they meticulously recorded in a black speckled ledger from the Five-and-Dime. All their mixtures were named, and all the jars labeled: Rose Slips I and II, Pine Patch Cream, Essence of Grass. With their items displayed on the windowsill, many people came in from distant countries and after traveling for months on ships to purchase their goods.

Lois stood at the open window wearing a pair of Marie's pedal-pushers that on her fell as trousers, and Sonya walked up. "I am tired from my travels."

"We have what you need here," her eyebrows, reddish-brown like their father's, curving up to match a storekeeper's welcoming gesture.

Sonya took off her felt hat and nodded to her sister, who had a scarf around her head, tied on the side. She took from her pocket two smooth flat stones, a pinecone, and a chip from a robin's egg she found under the willow, and handed these to Lois. Her sister handed her a jar of cream for sore muscles.

"You are too kind," Sonya said.

"Not at all," Lois said, with a wave of her hand, in a voice new for that day.

Their mother's childhood had been vastly different from the girls'. As the only child of Herbert and Glenda Blasion, Marie had spent many hours alone in the warm corridors of the greenhouses that her father managed. She wanted her daughters to know that place, too. Now, on the nine-hour drive to Mercy Hill, in New Hampshire, Sonya tried to remember the greenhouses from the previous summer.

"Did we walk through them?" she asked her mother.

"Yes. Your grandfather took you girls on a walk to show you the greenhouse plants and the evergreens outside. Then you helped him tie up a vine. Do you remember?" She passed a banana over the seat to each of the girls. "It was tall, wild, and green, with orange blossoms in the shape of trumpets. You'll see it again."

But Sonya could not recall any specific plants, though she remembered a warm green haze with shimmering light above it, her grandfather lifting a wooden tub, his muscly arms, and a smell like the inside of a mountain. She peeled the banana and ate it slowly. Maybe she would remember more after this trip.

The girls were restless by the time they saw the sloping hills on the outskirts of town, twilight still illuminating the clusters of cows here and there in the distance. They turned down the familiar road to their grandparents' house, a modest white wood-frame set several yards from the road. This not forgotten.

They pulled in the driveway behind their automobile, the tan Rambler, and even that seemed to be in exactly the same spot it was in the last time they had visited. As the girls saw their grandfather come out to greet them, they sprung themselves loose. He lifted each girl up and kissed her, arms tight around. When he picked up Sonya, she remembered that she liked his smell, which she would come later to think of as what cured tobacco leaves probably smelled like, drying in a cool darkened shed in the middle of a field. Now, she just liked it. Then he stood back and beheld them, lovingly absorbing the details of their changed appearance. "My, you girls have grown. Look at you. Lois, you're going to be tall like your mother and me. Sonya, your hair has gotten so long."

The girls stood beside each other and giggled, looked up at his tall thin frame, graying hair, eyes that nearly matched his hair color. His face was smooth, as if he had an underground spring somewhere deep inside him, and it welled up now and then to wash away any lines of trouble on his face. "When can we see your plants?" they asked.

"Do I have work for you two! Tomorrow you can work with me. Your grandfather sure needs some help." Then he led them up the back steps and inside.

"Hi, Grandma," they said.

"Wipe your feet," their grandmother said. They wiped their sneakers against the bristly mat, then stepped into the kitchen. When Sonya saw the houseplant with the cluster of purple flowers centered on the table, she remembered sitting there with Lois eating powdered donuts and trying to keep the sugar from getting on the shiny surface. After eating, they had run their fingers along the grooved metal edges of the table, and their grandmother had wiped the dusty prints off after they had walked once around it.

Now she called the girls over to the sink to drink a glass of water. "Stand here," she said. She did not embrace them when they came over, but she stood with them while they drank their water, watched them closely. Her antiseptic smell was mixed up with the cleanser scent inside Sonya's glass; while she drank, she noticed her grandmother's hands at her waist, holding a dish towel, waiting to catch a spill. Her body was muscular with tension that the girls might have sensed, even if they couldn't name it. Though she was a small woman, she was still taller than they were, and Sonya felt her eyes cast down on them, measuring, monitoring. They were blue, but a pale blue, as if some of the color had been rinsed out of them. If the girls could lean close in, or look at her from above, they might be able to glimpse the residue of the color, somewhere near the bottom, but they never got that close.

The next day in the greenhouses, out behind their house, the smell and the high panels of glass came, familiar, to Sonya. Their grandfather gave each of the girls a copper watering can and helped them fill it at a spigot. As he led them down the rows, he pointed to plants to his left and his right that needed water. "That's good," he told the girls each time.

"Look," he would say suddenly, and point to a blossom bobbing on a slender stem, or to a tight bud, its swirl of color barely begun. "Coreopsis," he would say, and it sounded to Sonya like he was announcing the name of a city they had just arrived at after a long journey.

Or he seemed to introduce them. "This is Lemon Verbena." The girls watched him pinch the leaves and then smelled his fingers, shady with its scent. But every one had the title "Look" before it; if they had not already known what that word meant, they might think it was the name of something, too.

Outside again, he said to the girls, "See how our vine is doing," pointing to a tall vine of trumpet flowers growing up the end of one of the greenhouses and hanging over its roof. "It wants to be a giraffe." He told them it would not have been so strong if they had not helped him tie it up the summer before.

For the next several days, while their parents finished a few projects around the house, they worked outside with him, watering and walking between the rows, checking on seedlings, moving plants, and most of all, talking with him. Their grandmother stayed in most days, but in the evenings after the girls were in bed on cots in the living room she and their grandfather sat out in the yard with their parents. Sonya heard the murmur of their voices in the still warm air as she drifted to sleep, once her grandmother's voice rippling up in laughter, not a sound she had heard often. As she listened, Sonya wondered if her grandmother had a pastel mint in her mouth. She had noticed that her grandmother lined up a few in her hand and sucked on them in the evenings, and that sometimes it was after she had put her teeth in the glass in the bathroom. When it was before, she and Lois could hear her teeth slip around a bit. The mints were nickel-sized, ridged on the bottom, smooth on top, and came in pink, green, yellow. Sonya imagined them now, outside in her grandmother's hand, pale moons in a row waiting their turn to disappear in the dark of her mouth. While Glenda had these, the girls' parents enjoyed a cup of coffee, and Herbert may have been chewing on a bit of coffee ground, as he often did when he discovered it at the bottom of his cup, the same way he sometimes savored an apple peel or an orange rind, rolled it around his mouth awhile.

Toward the end of the week the girls' parents drove into town for an afternoon of errands. The girls were outside with their grandfather when Sonya went in for a glass of water. Distrustful as she already knew to be of her grandmother's temperament, and thinking she might be asleep, she tried to move quietly to the cupboard for a glass and bring it to the sink.

When her grandmother called abruptly from the other room, "What are you doing in there?" Sonya was startled and the glass slipped from her hand, shattering in the sink. She stood still as she heard her grandmother's feet stride across the living room floor, and she turned nervously to see her come fully into the kitchen yelling, "Do you know what a glass costs?" And then, "Stay right here."

Sonya stood rooted to the rubber mat in front of the sink while her grandmother walked out the back door, down the steps, and onto the gravel driveway. Then her feet stopped. Half a minute later Sonya heard her climb up the steps and turned to see her walk through the door with one hand in the pocket of her print housedress. Her grandmother stepped slowly toward her, as if underwater, taking hours to reach her.

She grabbed Sonya's hand and led her to a corner of the kitchen. Then she took from her pocket some dusty driveway pebbles and, bending down, spread them on the floor, arranging them into two flat circles a couple of inches across. She stood up. "Kneel on these," she said, wiping the dust on one hand off with the other. Sonya looked up at her short gray hair bound tight off her face, the cheek that she had seldom kissed. Her grandmother's eyes pierced back, an anger igniting the blue in them like flame.

Sonya hesitated, bewildered, and her grandmother gestured toward the floor. "If you can stay there for an hour, you will have made up the price of the glass." Sonya knelt, and as she glanced over to notice that her grandmother wasn't wearing stockings, she contemplated the skin of her legs, her strong calf muscles. Then she faced the corner and heard her grandmother walk across the kitchen to the sink, take a towel from a drawer, and methodically wipe out the glass, shaking the fragments into the garbage can after every wipe. She tried to imagine when her back was turned, so she could quickly lift a knee to rub away the pain and then kneel again, and managed to do this once with each.

"It has been only a couple of minutes," her grandmother said when she was finished cleaning out the sink. "I'm going into the living room and I'm trusting you to stay there."

Sonya heard her walk away. Her brain scrambled to figure things out, tangling itself on several questions that she had no answer for. She wondered whether her mother had ever had to do this and if it was in the same corner. And whether Lois ever did and had not said anything or maybe told their parents but Sonya herself had not known. Would her parents return before the hour was up and what would happen if they did, what would they say? And why would an hour pay for a glass? How much did that glass cost? Didn't people buy them in sets? She wondered how a price could be related to time, anyway.

With all of her questioning it was difficult to determine how much time had passed. It felt as if her kneecaps were splintering, the round hardnesses below them, her own weight above, pressing. There were burning rods in the back of her thighs. She tried to stretch the edge of her culottes down to cover her knees, but it didn't quite reach. Then to briefly shift her weight from one leg to the other for relief, but this made the weighted one feel sharper.

She heard footsteps up the stairs and turned as her grandfather came in the room, calling her name.

"I'm over here."

An expression she had never seen crossed his face, his eyebrows grappling each other in dismay, and in one swift movement he leaped around the table, lifted her up and held her. Then he said, "Go outside with Lois. I'll be right there." He put her down.

Sonya walked out the back door and halfway down the stairs, then stopped as she heard, for the first time, her grandfather's raised voice. "Never Glenda. My God, please." Then, after a pause, a louder, "*Penance*? My God, she's a child!" Then she heard subdued sobbing and heard him say, more quietly, "All right. All right."

She continued down the steps and ran into a greenhouse looking for Lois, finding her stirring dirt and water together in a clay pot.

"Hey, your knees are red."

Sonya bent over and touched the indentations in her skin, then rubbed her knees until they were smooth again. "I fell on the driveway just now running." She stood up.

"Where's Grandpa?"

"He'll be right out. What are you doing with this dirt?"

"I'm mixing it up. Want to mix some, too?"

"OK." Sonya found another pot, dumped dirt in it, and then poured water in it from a bucket Lois had filled. Stirring it with her hand, she felt the cool water mud and watched the dirt darken and change. She squirt it through her fingers, scooped and molded it, what was *penance?*, smoothed, cupped, and swirled it. She did this over and over, flecks flying up and falling down slow motion into their pots, with Lois beside her talking about her dirt, afternoon sunlight coming through the high glass warming their arms, warming their hair and their backs, finally feeling calm again.

When their grandfather came back outside, he asked, "What are my best workers up to?" He walked over and stood beside them and, as Lois explained their dirt project, he rested his hand on the top of Sonya's head.

A while later, hearing their parents' car pull in the driveway, the girls started for the door, but their grandfather said, "Why don't you kids stay here? I'll help them carry stuff inside. I'll be right back, and we can drop in on those tomatoes."

Sonya did not know how the incident was explained to them, but that evening at supper, though the conversation was casual, she could tell that her parents were distracted. And her grandfather was rubbing his ear scar more than usual. It was a cord of skin, slightly twisted like a rope, emerging from his left ear and appearing to slide past his lobe and part way down his neck. Sometimes when he tipped his head a certain way, it seemed to twist a little tighter. He told the girls that he had gotten the mark in a bar fight, but they knew this couldn't be true. Partly they knew it because he laughed as he said it, and partly they knew it because they loved him and couldn't imagine him fighting.

Sonya noticed that sometimes he rubbed the scar when he was trying to think of a word, and she thought of him pulling it down and out, and it would spiral down, twisted, from his ear. At the end would be the one perfect word, hooked and shining, that he'd been trying to think of. It would be magical, like a beanstalk or a rope made out of hair. Tonight, though, he wasn't saying very much, not enough to have to rub his ear to find another word. He was just rubbing it.

"Marie, did you see that we now have a Penney's?" Their grandmother detailed some of the bargains she had recently gotten at the store's opening, but their mother did not seem interested.

Instead she said to Sonya, "Have another ear of corn, Honey."

"No thanks."

She wasn't thinking about food, she had had enough for dinner. Instead, she was concentrating on the pair of wooden hands in the center of the table, with napkins between them. They were carved and upright, pressing toward each other. They would touch when the napkins were gone, move further apart when her grandmother put some more between them. There was a similar pair on the dashboard of her grandparents' car, but that set was much smaller. The wooden figure of the man with hair grown past his shoulders and a beard was almost the same size, beside the dashboard hands, but he was a whole body. Didn't her grandmother say once that men shouldn't have long hair and beards? But why did she bring him home from the store? His hands were the smallest, a whisper nearly tucked into the carved fold of cloth draping him. What were they all praying for?

"More macaroni salad?"

She shook her head. She wasn't quite at an age to realize that her mother's look of concern was not over whether she was eating enough.

That night putting the girls to bed on the fold-out cots, their mother told them they would be leaving in the morning, two days earlier than they had planned. "Your grandmother needs some rest. She's not feeling well."

"We'll be good," Lois said.

"It's not your fault. She's very tired, and it's better for her if we're not here."

The next morning, as usual on these trips, their grandmother stayed inside while her husband walked out with them. This time though, standing at the back door, she addressed Sonya by name followed with, "I'm sorry," but she did not hug the girls.

Seeing tears in her eyes, Sonya looked at her grandfather, who said, "Come on, I'll see you out," and headed down the back stairs carrying as much of their luggage as he could manage. Then he embraced them and got everyone settled into the car.

As they pulled out of town, Lois asked her sister, "Why did Grandma tell you she was sorry?"

"I guess she was sorry she was tired." Sonya, ashamed of lying, offered to buy her some gum the next day with the dollar their grandfather had given them.

"I want bubble gum," Lois said. They enjoyed poring over the many brightly colored gum packs, the cigars, wads, sticks, and balls, displayed on several shelves at the Five-and-Dime their mother sometimes walked them to in the afternoon.

On the ride home, Sonya concentrated on the greenhouses' warm damp mountain smell and tilted shimmering roofs and on the vine with orange blossoms, so that this time she would remember these during the year.

The next morning, when Lois had already begun playing outside, their mother sat Sonya down and said she wanted to talk with her.

"Your grandmother has some problems. She used to be terribly unkind, but she hasn't been in several years, and I thought she was better."

"How come?"

"It's difficult to understand. I think something hurt her when she was young, and sometimes she is still angry about it."

"Was she mean to you?"

"She did not know how to be a good parent like your grandfather did. I think he hoped that he could teach her how." Realizing that this was more information than her daughter had asked for, Marie said, "Your father and I will do everything we can to make sure that this doesn't happen again."

"I still want to see Grandpa."

"Of course. Don't worry about that." Marie wrapped her arms around her. After a few minutes she said, "OK. Lois is waiting for us outside. Let's go see what she is up to."

Near the end of that summer, one evening their mother sat at the dining room table looking at a bulb catalogue. She called the girls over and asked their advice about what to order, saying each could pick out a couple. It was difficult for them to know whether to choose by the picture or by the name, bright were the pictures and new were the names.

Once school started that September Sonya and Lois didn't get much dirt on their clothes, except when they occasionally lay on their backs in the yard and lifted their shirts to let caterpillars crawl over them. Or they stretched on the front porch on their stomachs clutching brown tree toads and counting to three before releasing and watching them, dazed, hop across the porch. So when the bulbs finally arrived in the mail in October, they were happy to spend a few cool cloudless afternoons helping their mother dig in the dirt, planting rows of bulbs along the barn, in a patch near the grapevines, and in a border along the side yard. During the day in school Sonya daydreamed about the Apricot Beauty tulip and the sun-yellow Desert Candle that would explode in spring. When she closed her eyes at night, she rolled the word *Holland* on her tongue and imagined fields of tulips bordered by a deep blue sea.

This image was what she thought of when their father told the girls he would make them lunchboxes. He bought a few sheets of thin plywood, measured, cut, and hammered together one evening, in the dust and turpentine smell of the barn, wooden boxes with brass handles, hinges and a clasp. He asked what pictures they wanted. Most of the kids in school had lunchboxes adorned with scenes from *Get Smart* or with *The Monkees*, images from a distant television that didn't mean much to them. On Lois's he painted a castle with her peeking out from a tower, across a meadow, and on Sonya's he painted a field of tulips and a bay. In the bay was a ship with a pirate on it, and the pirate, surprised by the field of flowers, held his mouth wide open in wonder, forever saying *O*. Though a few of the kids at school asked if they were poor, since they had homemade lunchboxes, and one of the boys, who was known for eating worms when dared to after pulling them in half, told Sonya hers was a boy's since it had a pirate on it, the girls brought them to school every day.

One evening the following March their parents told the girls during supper that since their father had found a better job elsewhere, they would soon be moving away from Laconius. They had lived in that house nearly three years.

Two days before the U-Haul truck was packed and the house completely empty, Sonya took one of her lucky stones, a round flat gray one with a pink quartz streak in it, out of her box of stones and shells. The rectangular wooden box was one her grandfather had used to store seeds in, and he had given it to her on one of their summer visits. She walked out behind the structure she and Lois had for a playhouse, knelt, and dug up a clump of muddy grass. She put the stone in the ground, pressing it down as far as she could with her thumb, then covered it up and patted in place the edges of grass.

Their father drove the truck, and the girls and their mother followed behind in the VW Bug that they had traded for the aging bus. They drove out of town four years after driving in in their station wagon with the paneled sides. As they drove down Main Street and out toward the county road that would lead them to the highway, Sonya and Lois each blinked out a window, poised on the edge of the seat, and neither of them spoke. When they passed the place they used to live, Sonya looked, too, at Andy Duncan's house across the field. She had seen him around town a few times with his father, and she knew that his mouth had since healed, though it pulled to one side a bit as he spoke. She felt in her stomach an unnamed and queasy worry. Then her throat became dry and tight as she thought of all the bulbs buried beneath March dirt that would soon come up in what had been their yard. She thought of Blazing Star and Double Hollyhock, and she wondered what lucky family would move into such a place of fire and light.

The summer heat of now was metallic in her mouth, strained rivulets of ore down the back of her wordless throat as she imagined the dissipating smells and sounds of the outdoor cafe, the people who could come and go effortlessly. If she had tried, if that time were not irretrievably distant and she wanted to dwell in it now, at eighteen, savor it, hold it in that pause before the present, before one more minute passed, she would not have been able to recall the flower names that she and Lois had selected from the catalogue. The names had stayed awake with her at night then, their letters, dazzling and bright, keeping her on this side of sleep awhile. But now they were lost to her, as constellation names were lost, and the names of cities she had never been to but that sounded magnificent. If she had tried, it would have comforted her to think that the names provided companionship for each other, in the glittering realm that on a better day she believed in just beyond the edge of her tongue. And perhaps sometime the strained rivulets in her throat would pulse out humming and with them would spill forth all the names of things she could not now recall, if she had tried.

3

Letters Worn Indecipherable By Rain

While Sonya and Lois had marveled one day, the summer before their move, at the bands of morning sun strutting across their drawing of *The Day Something Fell Out of the Sky*, its yellow globe drifting down the side of the paper and settling, finally, on a square frame remarkably similar to their front porch, a few streets away, back across Laconius, that is, Andy Duncan had matched prices to refrigerators and sofas with his mother during their usual round of weekday game shows.

The bursts of his laughter with her, his Broyhill guess a full fifty dollars off the mark, some of the contestants' clothes too "wild" for his mother's liking, she mistook for lightheartedness, a continuation of the joy she had always seen in her youngest son. The joy he had at ordering his matchbox configuration, each metallic car a glorious shade of color to him, a shade of color to hope for, long for, the wheels just a shade removed from another life. The joy he felt when his other brother came home, mature in work clothes and talking about paychecks from the garage he worked at in the next town, but not so mature that Ben couldn't step into the living room, move the coffee table aside, and buckle Andy's legs under him to throw him on the carpet wrestling, as they had for years, the older boy pinning the younger in such complete sweaty delight that Andy, if he had articulated the importance of that muscular, sweeping, movement to himself, might have said: this is what I live for.

Now his mother saw in him what she did not know was only disguised as joy, though it had genuinely, when he was younger, been such. Nor did she, or anyone, know for what purpose he had recently slipped out during the night.

Stepping as quietly as he could, he put on jeans and a T-shirt, sneakers, crept downstairs, across the living room, and slowly retrieved his father's key ring from the hook by the back door. Andy squeezed the ring together as he wedged it into his front pocket. He turned the skeleton in the door fixture and slid out into the warm summer night.

Walking down the driveway, he recalled helping his mother one summer put in a bed of begonias along the side of the house, his father disparaging them as "messy" plants, (but weren't they all, throwing around equally their spent leaves and their shafts of color?) questioning, as was typical, his wife's choice. She and Andy planted them anyway.

Turning onto Main Street all he heard was his sneakers against the slate squares of sidewalk, no one else around, no light even in any house, no sound of trucks from either the county road, or, farther, the interstate. He had been on that road only once, with his brother, to join him with friends on a three-day camping and fishing trip. He had first tried beer with them, Schmidt's, he remembered, though he could barely finish a whole can. The older boys could smoke and not cough, could blow rings, could flick the still-burning nub with just their thumb and middle finger into a nearby field. They could straddle one another in the thick grass, punching erratically. They talked about the quickest way to unhook a bra, and they unzipped their flies, strained their penises, impressively larger than his, and, running, tried to slap each other. Andy had returned from that trip with Ben bewildered, excited, exhausted by the prospects of what lay ahead for him.

Occasionally a slight breeze sifted the streetlight shadows of the trees, transposing the shapes of the leaves and the contours of his body and his clothes, on which the shadows fell. A tracing of him was left behind as he stepped through the filtered leaves, the slowly moving mysterious figures, feeling the absolute darkness around the edges of town and beyond those, the other more absolute darkness around coming as a weight pressing in on him, not articulated, but enough for him to sigh relief when he finally rounded the corner of Maple, walked past sleeping houses for another block, then came upon the outline of the two-story rectangular brick school at the end of the street.

The time Ben snuck out at night, or the only time their father caught him, he had wandered off to drink in a field with his buddies for a couple of hours, his return not quite quiet enough, their father already sitting at the kitchen table in the dark. Andy watched from the stairway as he bent the older boy, then thirteen, over the table and lashed him several times with a belt. Now his stomach churned a bit as he imagined what his father might do if he were to discover his betrayal of the household, and other, rules.

As he crossed the parking lot, urging himself onward, he rehearsed the route he would take to the second-floor supply closet where, stopping in the crowded hall one afternoon that spring to talk with his father at work, he happened to notice a rope on a shelf, coiled among huge packs of toilet paper rolls, industrial-sized bottles of cleanser, replacement mop heads, and cleaning uniforms. He imagined all of these now.

Though there was an outside overhead light at the entrance, he did not fear anyone seeing him at this hour. He removed the ring from his pocket, tilted it slightly in the light, and separated the main door key from the others. Turning the key, he pushed open the heavy door, then let it close gently behind him. As his eyes adjusted to the dark, he could make out here and there red lights on the walls indicating the emergency fire pulls and their nearby extinguishers. Knowing the layout of the school well, he found the staircase easily and walked up to the second floor. Even now, he thought, the school smelled of linoleum dusted from shoes, faintly of chalk and glue, even now in its summer emptiness. The closed classrooms, not the immense hallways, made him somewhat nervous, as if something were conducted behind their doors that had to be done in secret.

Though that unnerved him, Andy walked past several more closed classrooms and restrooms and came upon the supply closet. Parking lot lights gave that end of the hallway enough visibility through the stairwell window that he could study the key ring and find the few marked "supply" on a piece of tape. He recognized his father's handwriting. On the third try the bolt slipped aside, he turned the knob, opened the door, and ran his hand along the wall until he found the switch to the overhead bulb. The rope was exactly where he remembered it being, and he stepped in to retrieve it. It was a tangled mess, so he took a few minutes to unravel it, then lift one end up and turn it around and around his crooked arm like a garden hose. Wound, it was heavier than he anticipated it would be, but he had no difficulty in hoisting it up on one shoulder as he flipped the light off, stepped out, and then relocked the door.

Making his return down the darkened hall, aware of his pounding heart, he envisioned himself on a mission of some sort, secret, dangerous, in a way unlike anything else that had happened in his life up to that point, and it was with a mixture of dread and anticipation that he retraced his way down the steps, the downstairs hallway, and back out the main entrance, pausing to relock it, the weight of the coiled rope on his slender shoulder like a river-bottom stone, or a marker whose inscription has been worn indecipherable by rain, wind, and snow, though it still marks a place where something was lost.

He walked more slowly back. The shadows were heavier, more ominous now, their platted dimensions out to find him, expose his thievery. Stepping more slowly, more quietly than the night bugs he now heard stitching in the yards, though he hadn't heard them on the way there, he hoped they would not reveal him. Nor the shadows changing with his passage in and out of them on the sidewalk, give him away, nor the slates of sidewalk themselves, his sneaker imprints passing imperceptibly over them, give him away, nor his quickened breaths trailing out into the street's, the town's still air and drifting up over the trees to join the air outside of town, heavy with thunderstorms to come in other summers, give him away.

He tried to calm himself as he approached his house, headed down his driveway, stepped to the back door, pushed it open slowly, closed it behind him quietly, turned the skeleton key again, and replaced the ring of keys on their waiting hook. He crossed carefully through the kitchen, then into the living room, paused to catch his breath.

As he paused in the living room, he heard his father's footsteps in the upstairs hall, heard him stride into the bathroom, heard, even, standing in the center of the room, his father urinate, that and the ticking of the kitchen wall clock, a daisy with copper swirls spinning out from its sunny face, the sounds magnified in the house's otherwise quiet. He held completely still for several minutes, the television screen in its gray blankness suddenly offering him Maxwell House, or was it a cleanser, the woman scrubbing her toilet, the jingle in the background, after he heard his father walk down the hall again, close his bedroom door, after he knew his father was probably back asleep already. The gray blankness accompanying him in the still of the living room, several minutes longer.

He removed his sneakers, carried them upstairs, and returned to bed in his clothes, no noise of undressing to worry about, and slid the rope under the covers, pushed it down to the bottom with his feet. The next day he would have a chance to find its place, maybe in a box shoved under his bed, or maybe at the rear of his closet, behind the boxes of shiny metallic cars he would never part with.

He lay awake awhile recalling the time Ben was caught sneaking out at night. If he could have, he might have slipped himself between them, thin as a shadow, his skin grafting onto his brother's, taking half the pain. He cried as he thought of how he would have let his life slip into his brother's, the two of them together enough, would have let Ben carry him, if it came to that, then cried for other carrying, his mother carrying a basket of vegetables from the garden, turning at the back door to make sure he was still behind her, his father with a friend's help carrying an automobile engine to the barn, his brother once carrying a girl injured at recess from the playing fields to the counselor's car waiting to drive her to the clinic. He would have gladly taken Ben's splintering skin, felt the swell of knotted bruises pushing beneath his skin, carried, if he could, half the pain.

When he watched the morning shows with his mother, occasionally having a glass of punch while viewing the universe coming from that gray box, vibrant for others, their laughter mixed with the warm summer air. She turned to him sometimes, saw his face flushed with heat, and recognized in him what she would have no other name for but joy, no reason for her to figure it otherwise.

By now, a few streets across Laconius, Sonya and Lois might have eaten a peanut butter sandwich or drawn an array of shapes, some resembling people walking along with swinging limbs, others unspecified orbs, dropping from the sky or rolling along its edge, held fast to the page with enough brilliant yellow transit to punctuate an ordinary day.

4

The Lunar Eclipse

She had spoken, and spoken her wonder easily then, as her parents had when the world began for them. For Sonya and Lois, wonder was the stream discovered, on the third day after they moved in, deep in the woods behind the stone house on the side of the sloping mountain. They began finding stones etched with fossils to add to their growing collection. Though this new place, Bridgeville, was half a state away, they liked it immediately because of the mountains and valleys around it.

It was days like the one in mid-June when their father carried Sonya on his shoulders as they walked through the stream. Lois, already taller than her sister, walked beside them holding his hand. In his other hand he carried their sneakers, three pairs, laces tied together. Sonya saw tiny bright heartbeats of fish flickering in the shallow water. "Look!" their father said suddenly and pointed toward the water's edge at something round and beige moving sluggishly up the sandy bank. He put Sonya down and they walked over to it. He picked the turtle up, his hand spread across its back, and they watched its legs move as if it were still maneuvering the mud. "Touch it," he said. Sonya reached over slowly and rubbed its bony shell, while Lois touched one of its bumpy legs, and her eyebrows arched up in surprise as they all withdrew. They studied its orange belly and methodically blinking eyes.

It was days wandering the mossy streambank with her sister, bringing stones home, and nights like the night Sonya sat up in her bed, lifted the nearby window, and smelled the outside air. She saw stars glancing down on them from behind the trees in the front of the house and listened to the stream. Once the MacGraths, who had lived across the street from them in Laconius, heard that there was an adult snapping turtle plodding, dazed and lost, by the firehouse. They drove into town and hoisted the animal into the bed of their tan pickup. By the time they drove it back to their house everyone on the street had heard about it. All the kids in the neighborhood ran over to see the animal. When Sonya and Lois got there, Mr. Mac-Grath had just cut its head off, now in a large mason jar in the garage. His son, two years ahead of Sonya in school, took the hunting knife and stuck it repeatedly into the jar, laughing each time the turtle's jaw snapped to catch it. From out of the shadow of the garage the body of the turtle stepped, slowly and dripping blood down the driveway. All of the kids squealed and jumped out of its path. When Sonya watched it wobble directionless across the hot pavement, she felt the dull ache of horror thud in her stomach, the bottom drop out like a trap door, opening into endless dark. She and Lois went home. After supper that evening she drew a picture called *Turtle's Head in Jar*, in which its dull eyes sorrowfully watched its body float up into the sky. For days, whenever she closed her eyes or heard the neighbors talking about the turtle soup, she saw its head, mouth snapping hopelessly at the knife.

Now, sitting up in bed and listening to the stream, she remembered the snapping turtle. She wondered how long its body had wandered around the driveway. And she wondered if, after all the MacGraths had gone to sleep that night, the turtle's mouth continued to snap and if its eyes continued to blink in the cool cement dark of the closed garage.

On this July visit with her grandparents, Sonya noticed that her parents did not drive into town by themselves on errands but took the girls with them. And though their stay was briefer than usual this year, the girls had a couple of days to spend with their grandfather organizing pots, checking on seedlings, and walking through a field. Their grandmother, though, stayed in the house and did not talk with the girls very much.

It was a day late in that summer, the early afternoon humid, and dense clouds swam over the mountain. When the sky finally opened, Sonya and Lois took all their clothes off and ran out in the backyard, a narrow stretch between the house and the slope of the woods. Since they had no neighbors close by in Bridgeville, their parents let them run naked in the warm rain, the heavier the downpour the better, as they held hands and spun each other, ran up and down the soggy grass, pounding through puddles. Their hair covered their eyes, stuck to their faces, hung down their backs and whipped as they ran. When they were tired, they slid on their backs, opened their mouths wide, then sputtered the water with incoherent sounds, laughter, and fatigue. This time, too, they could smell worms and salamanders, the once-dry ground absorbing the rain. They thought they could also smell the sky opening, its relentless giving and turning in gray a reason to stop running, stop talking, to watch, and to catch their breath. They stayed silent for about fifteen minutes, then Sonya looked over at her sister. They rolled on their sides and faced each other.

Lois looked down at herself, touching first one of her nipples, then the other. "Want to touch them?"

"OK," Sonya said. She reached over and touched a nipple with her index finger. "Does it hurt?"

"A little bit. How come it hurts?"

"I don't know. You want to touch mine?"

"OK." Her sister reached out her hand and touched one of Sonya's nipples. Then Sonya touched it, too.

"Does it hurt?" Lois asked.

"Not too much," said Sonya.

She reached down, pulled up some grass, and threw it at her sister. Lois dug up a handful and tossed it at her head, then rubbed the muddy grass around in her hair while Sonya screamed. Sonya reached for a handful of dirt as her sister stood up and ran, then flung it at her back, and Lois turned and stomped the ground hard enough for bits of mud to fly up and splatter her.

When their mother heard their screams, she leaned out the kitchen window and yelled, "Girls, that's enough."

They tromped inside covered with mud and grass, making a trail of footprints to the bathroom. Even though the rain had been warm, they took hot baths, leaving a ring of grass around the tub. By the time they got out the storm had passed, and the air had cooled. They put on jeans and sweatshirts, and fell asleep on the living room floor. They might have dreamed about yards wheeling glistening after rain, or about suns spinning and burning, or planets. They might have dreamed about the smell of new shoes, or perhaps about grass. Then they woke for supper.

From the first time the girls heard their parents mention the lunar eclipse it sounded like a majestic event. And based on the picture of a previous one in the newspaper spread out before their father on the kitchen table, cleared after the meal, they concluded it was very much filled with mystery and beauty.

"We'll see it," he said, pointing at the paper, with Sonya standing on the rungs of his chair, arms around his neck, looking down at the paper over his shoulder. "Friday night, right here from the yard."

The girls were restless Friday evening and took turns running out to check the sky. "We won't be able to see anything for a couple of hours. Sit down and finish your pizza. I'll tell you when," their father said.

They switched the house lights off and went out at about nine thirty. The moon, just above the hill of trees, was already partially covered by the earth's shadow. Their father handed them the binoculars and explained the process by which the moon would be gradually covered, would seem to disappear, and then, just as magically, would emerge from the shadow of the earth as if from its skin.

The air was cool, no sound except a slight breeze rippling through the trees and an occasional animal noise coming from the woods. When she held the binoculars up and studied the moon, Sonya felt like they were out on the deck of a ship, their feet planted firmly on the wooden slats, with the huge night sky washed clear as it was, like the sky over the ocean, feeling the water's tilt. The moon had the same vastness and beauty it did other times she viewed it through the binoculars, but this time she experienced something else, another dimension, maybe from the feeling of her family standing around her in the dark, all of them looking in the same direction, heads back, part of the world's quiet. She remembered a nature magazine's photos of a comet and descriptions of people out on their front porches or in their vast yards at night, heads arched toward the sky. Maybe children were allowed to stay up, all of them searching the cool dark for the first flash of light. Wind rustled the cornfield, swept the hay with its invisible comb. Long ago, and the people were in a far-off place, like the Midwest, in black and white. They looked up through tunnels of space, past bright stars, and had no words except, "There it is." Then they were very quiet. When they turned back toward their houses, the comet was probably already sweeping thousands of acres away, leaving its trail arched over days, over many countries. With her family in that quiet came the enormous sadness, her parents' tears and other tears she saw in the newspaper for the two men who had been shot where will we find the likes of them again she heard the adults ask people crying in the streets and now they were all standing beneath that emptiness that found them in the yard. And that night Sonya would sleep with no words for such vastness, as those people had slept years before her, eyes closed under the same dome of black, and dream of night stones, hard and clear, stitched to the cloth of sky above them, washed clean, impenetrable, plotted down the avenues of space, down the boulevards of sleep. She would wake, as they had the next day, to the tangible sounds of others moving about the house, a voice calling from one room to the next, the clatter of dishes. They would wake to the inescapable fumbling about of days, and a feeling that the world was slightly changed.

They took turns, each seeing a glimpse of the shadow's passage, until the moon was completely covered in deep red shadow, then went inside. Settled in bed with the lights out, the girls talked in great detail about whether there was life on other planets, whether there would be mountains and streams, cities or smaller neighborhoods, similar food, before finally lulling into sleep.

Sonya tried the following day to draw in pencil the stages of the eclipse, but none of them seemed blurred or mysterious enough. She decided she would save the title, *The Lunar Eclipse*, for something else.

For her parents, too, the world had begun in wonder, but for each that was quickly complicated by circumstance. Sonya's mother grew up in the rural outskirts of Mercy Hill, the mill town in New Hampshire where her father managed greenhouses. When, at twenty, she packed two matching suitcases and boarded a bus for the five-hour ride south, she took with her the dusty warmth of geraniums in summer and the aisles of speckled colors under the glass greenhouse roofs. She took her rosary and the gold-embossed photo album her parents had given her for her high school graduation. She also brought childhood images of her mother on sunny afternoons rocking in the living room in silence, shades drawn, while her father worked outside. In her second year of college the man Marie had planned to marry had died. Then she lost her scholarship at the Catholic women's school because, after two years of dorm life, she wanted to live on her own, and the nuns were of the opinion that if she did so, she would set an untoward example for the other girls. She could stay on campus under their supervision or lose their financial support. It was after both these events happened that she decided to leave behind the brick mills, the Five-and-Dime store with its warped wooden floor, and the verdant countryside around the town. Marie had been not just the only one in her family to pursue an education (her father had left school in sixth grade, her mother in eighth, each needed for work at home); she had been the sole member of her high school graduating class of twenty-six to attend college. When packing her suitcases, she made sure she took her chemistry and botany books.

She moved to Putnamton, the Connecticut city of 175,000, to live with a friend, Ruth, from school and to get a job, finding one as a clerk at Fanci Fabrics. At first it had been her survival to look at the store wall clock and exist among the tape measures and bolts of cloth, hourly in the morning, then after lunch the same, until 2:00, 3:00, then 4:00, and then the next day begin again the hourly struggle by attending to the minutiae of mundane commerce. She was contained by textures, by the full roundness of each wooden disc, a thousand times wound in color, and by reading on the top of the spool in her hand the dark "MacMillan" or cursive "mercerized" against its pale paper label.

Then gradually, after months of this, it had become a sad kind of relief to concern herself with such insignificant detail, while missing the life she had imagined, missing the imagining of it. Eventually her grief, with no sloping hills to prod it, coming up against the steel of buildings taller than any she had seen in her childhood and the congested hum of wheels and concrete, folded itself deep inside her, distracted. She wore his watch though, which he had inadvertently left behind that day, its silvery round covering her wrist with delicate sweeping hands that were still moving.

One Sunday morning, several months after her arrival, she met Mitchell Hudson, someone Ruth knew. He was wearing an old blue bathrobe and, though it was still well before noon, drinking whiskey with his coffee. She learned that he was in the city to get a teaching degree, working as a sweeper at a paper mill and attending school in the evening. Within a week, she knew that his hands smelled like moist clay and that he could make her laugh.

Sonya's father had one home, until he was seven, in the Midwestern city of Wikeegee, and it had green-and-white striped awnings over the windows in the summer and an extravagant trimmed lawn. When his father took pictures of him and his older brother in their mother's arms out in the yard, the younger boy usually squinted from the sun and smiled, not so much because his picture was being taken, but because his mother's arm was around his waist and he was pressed against her. Six months after she died from heart disease his father sold the house and moved his sons to the South. Mitchell would stay awake at night until he heard his father come home, his mind drifting in an amber glaze of brandy, hands sliding up the stairway wall for balance, and fall onto his bed. He did not remarry. Instead he kept moving, taking various sales jobs, trying to stay ahead of his grief. But at each place, it settled in with him, and when it was too much, he packed up his sons and went to a new area. No longer able, finally, to live within the confines of four walls, a roof, rooms without his wife, however many windows, when his sons finished high school, he bought an old bread truck to live in. He built shelves in it, found a roll-out mat to sleep on, and painted over the rear windows. He did not mind the faded green lettering, Nickel's—Fresh Every Day, visible along the sides. Mobility was what he cared about.

And though Mitchell had lived with his brother and his father in many different cities and in many different houses, years later he could still hear the front door of the house at 1042 Woodlawn Avenue close behind the ambulance attendants when they carried his mother out.

When he met Marie, the sound of that door began to fade, and it was soon muted almost entirely by the joyous sounds of two young girls. Theirs became the voices in his head, the ones he hummed to, coaxing them into language. But behind that joy and under it, and around it and about it, close-in beneath it, and onto it, was seared indelibly the stark negative of his grief, through which he saw all else.

And for Marie, meeting Mitchell meant that one evening, eventually, she took off the watch that had been her beloved's and, rather than put it on her dresser top, tucked it inside a cedar box of photographs and slid the box back up on the top shelf of their bedroom closet. There it stayed, face up and, by the next morning, unwound. She got up and went about her day; she did not need to know at what time it would permanently stay.

One night when Sonya was awakened by voices, she sat near the window and again searched the sky, this time for stars behind the trees in front of the house. She heard her parents in the kitchen. She knew her father had been drinking because his voice made one blurred streak of words stumbling over each other, losing their way. But she heard *Portugal* float loose above the others, snap out like a filled sail, and then her mother said, "The girls have had to adjust to new schools. Now you want to ask them to start over in a new country? For shit's sake. And get there by *boat*? I just don't know."

Marie enjoyed using curse words, what she called "mouthy bits," because such language guaranteed a tangible, immediate way for her to repudiate, symbolically, at least, some of the confines of the religion in which she had been raised and which she had found increasingly repressive. She could announce, without announcing in specifics, that she had broken free from some of the strictures of the church most offensive to women. Particularly effective when she was wearing a skirt. It wasn't solely for the startle of the surprised stranger, the taken-aback clerk who had offended her or who had told her how to do something in a voice she found condescending, (the mechanic, now blanching, who had first suggested that the overheated engine needed water and whose explanation of what a radiator did was cut dramatically short with "I know what the hell the radiator is for"), though that part of it, the public aspect of the subversive language coming from her elegance, was gratifying to her. It was also, perhaps more importantly, in that briefest moment it took to announce a four-letter word or colorful, fresh phrase, a chance for her to feel as if she had physically yanked the weighted doors open to daylight and cast them back on their tight-lipped rust-bound hinges. Every little moment of a word ripping the air briefly asunder provided Marie with reverie at having found a way to propel herself forward.

And though the bits were occasionally addressed to him, Mitchell admired her adept use of them.

"It's an exceptionally gorgeous place."

"What's wrong with this place, with Bridgeville? With you, it always has to be the day before a journey." Sonya had often heard her parents say they liked the place, especially the emphasis on art, visible in the several pottery shops, which hosted a tour of studios each year; the furniture maker's storefront, featuring a few spare gleaming pieces rotated each month; even—and this was rarer—an instrument maker's gallery. Everything, it seemed, made by hand.

Her father said something about work there, in another country, and then their voices fell back down into the blend of murmur. Though she didn't know the significance completely, Sonya knew that her mother was going to school part-time and that she would soon finish a degree. How could she take her courses if they went to Portugal? Sonya got out her flashlight and her atlas. Portugal was far away. She decided not to mention it to her sister and went to sleep.

The next morning on their way out to the bus, they saw their mother hosing off the front steps. "What are you doing?" they asked, stopping to look at the dried bits stuck to the door and steps.

"Your father got sick last night. Probably something he ate took a wrong turn, but he's fine, girls." She shut the hose off briefly to kiss them goodbye. "Go catch your bus."

On the walk down the steep curved driveway and then out the road to reach the bus stop, Sonya thought about the conversation she overheard between her parents that morning. Her father had asked her mother what he did, and when she told him he had been sick, he had sounded surprised. How could he not remember throwing up? As she contemplated this, Lois said she hoped Tommy Hendricks would sit next to her again for their geography project so that they could work together on their plaster of Paris topographical state maps.

"I picked Massachusetts last year. It looks like an arm."

"I'm thinking about Montana or Texas," Lois said.

"Montana would be fun. You'd get some mountains."

Spring had come again. The grass smelled like cucumbers. The slice of moon hanging in the morning sky made Sonya think of round places away from the earth, turning in their own fluids, living and breathing apart from humans. It also made her think of the sound of their shoes along the road, and wonder how far away the sound echoed and whether or not anyone looked at the earth the way they looked at the moon. It hung above the mountain and the nearby fields in its place, the exact right distance away. Ultramarine. Could that mean distance? She thought of Portugal. She did not know how any place could be more beautiful than where they lived. She turned to her sister, lost in thought about the boy.

"Maybe he will sit next to you."

On a Saturday afternoon in May the girls took out sheets of heavyweight paper and packets of bright markers. They spread these out on the floor of their bedroom. Lois drew a picture of a boy with giant daggers slicing through his body from every direction.

"Who is that?"

"Tommy Hendricks."

"What happened to him?"

"He's a jerk and I hate him," Lois explained. She drew black clouds all around the edges of the paper. She titled it *The Boy with Daggers*. Sonya, having never liked a boy well enough to have to hate him later, puzzled over it, trying to imagine how her sister felt.

While Lois was drawing her picture, Sonya was drawing a girl with dark curls blossoming out of her head. She called it *The Dark-Haired Girl on the Bus*. She didn't know her name.

"Why are you drawing her?"

"She has pretty hair," Sonya said. She did not tell her sister that every day she looked for the girl, three or four rows ahead, and that since the girl got off first, Sonya watched her cross the road with her brother and walk up the hill to their house. She did not tell her either that if they were moving to Portugal, she planned to give her box of lucky stones to the girl, since they would probably have to be selective about how much they could bring on the boat.

When they left the following August, since the move was merely to another town in another part of New York State and not to Portugal, Sonya had no reason to give the girl her box of stones. Instead she drew a picture of her standing in a field of cucumber grass with a sliver of moon above. She titled it, in burnt sienna, *Here Under the Moon is Beautiful* and slipped it in the black metal mailbox at the end of the driveway of the girl's house.

The day before the Hudsons drove the U-Haul, which her mother had begun to call the "U-Sweat," down the driveway and out of the woods, Sonya took from her box a snail shell with a brush of pale green barely visible inside it that she had found at a lake. She brought it to the stream. She dug a hole about five inches deep in a shady spot on the bank, put the shell in, and carefully covered it up.

Here had been one place of wonder, here the musky cool shadows on the streambank, the unwavering starlight, the turtle's patterned shell. Not in this place nor in any other had her head been lobbed off and stuck in a jar, mouth tormented by a knife and a prodding boy. She had not been severed, jabbed, encased in glass to be humiliated by scrutiny, looking from a distance at her body, wandering in its own blood. No terror here, no terror then. Where all animals were wondrous. When a day was about getting out, getting dirt on her shoes or in her hair, tracking the day, leggy and green, back in with her after supper. Where night was amorphous sleep cooled by the woods, and spent dreaming of day. A nightmare now and then, but so few that they served to occasionally remind her of how peaceful her ordinary dreams were. Certainly no recurring ones, to haunt, as she had now, at eighteen.

Though she had not yet learned how to drive, she was behind the wheel of a pickup. In its bed were several old and broken television sets that she needed to drop at the landfill. As she approached a checkpoint at the entrance, she glanced ahead to see acres of rusted wreckage. But more noticeable to her than the tires, washers, soiled bags and ripped recliners, were those animals perched on top of many of the scrapped items. Their ears were outlined against the backdrop of the summer sky, as they were, every one, facing the entrance, as if they had a say in who was allowed to drop off refuse. If she drove any closer, the black and yellow of their eyes would bore through her, as they did, and they would vent their rotted mouths and dangle what they'd found in the cellar corner, what they'd clawed out of the trunk, decades covered. If she got any closer, she would smell their matted wet fur. She would see, from a frantic sideways search, the edge of their fur, the edge of someone's head visible in the dark mirror at night, the accidental glimpse revealing only the hair of whoever was there, the face not visible. Sonya's hands sweat on the steering wheel and her heart pounded as she quickly braked and, with great effort since there were already no fewer than ten vehicles lined up behind her with loads to dump, maneuvered to back up and turn around. The gate-keeper expressed bewilderment, but Sonya had no time or way to explain herself. She did, though, try to scream "Get them away from me" to no one in particular as she struggled to free the truck's tires from the rutted crowded road of the junkyard, their eyes worming into the back of her neck. As she woke, the road out became much more congested, the exit surely blocked. She snapped the desk lamp on and sat awake for a few hours with the contours of abandoned furniture and of the watching animals behind her eyes every time she closed them.

5

Baked Earth

The next time Marie came in to talk with her daughter, the following day, the previous conversation's discouragement showed as exhaustion in her eyes. She was tired of urging. Tired of trying to make an errand sound enticing, an event outside of any kind exciting—a flea market, a garden show, an estate sale. Had they not been in so dire a circumstance, her daughter's refusal could have been shrugged off as typical for an eighteen-year-old. Who at that age wants to spend leisure time meandering around with one's mother? But Marie knew nothing here was typical. This time, she sat down on the floor of the bedroom, having cleared a space, and asked Sonya about a drawing, on card-stock paper, leaned amongst others against the closet door. It appeared to her, from the swath of ultramarine colored pencil spilling the length of the paper, to be of a stream, though there were no distinct lines delineating the water from its bank; there were oblong shapes in the water but no obvious fish or stones.

"I think I was thinking about water, imagining it, but not thinking carefully about the shape of a particular place. I guess that's what I was imagining."

"You're not sure?" Her daughter's vagueness irritated her, though she wished it didn't.

"Sometimes I'm not deliberately thinking about anything when I draw. I just move the pencil and see what happens, where it goes."

"Oh. It seems like a stream to me. Does it—does it to you now?"

"Yes, actually, it does."

Marie picked up another drawing and asked about that one, too.

❧

In the new place they lived there was no stream. There was a low flat house in a sparse dusty town. There was the smell of hot gravel and tar in the late summer and early fall, and later in the fall the smell of the tall weedy field beside the house. When Sonya and Lois climbed on the bus in the morning, the other kids stared and pointed at their bead bracelets and the clay peace sign necklaces they had made the year before in art class, and they felt homesick through most of the school day. The attention drawn to them as new kids was compounded by the fact that they were the only students to wear bellbottoms. They thought that maybe since their father had been hired to begin a shop program for the Norwich district, and they would see him sometimes at school, they would eventually like the place.

However, the girls soon catalogued what the town didn't have. Their list was long: namely, everything they had liked about Bridgeville. But it did have one thing new to them.

Norwich had a quarry. There were a few signs around town for it: Norwich Quarry—A Stone's Throw Away, which Sonya imagined, based on the desolate billboard image, as a vast pit at the edge of town where men in overalls labored bent over, and now and then looked up to see a whole vehicle or a barn sailing overhead, blown into the abyss by an unexpected wind. She had seen as much in a magazine her grandfather had, *Natural Disasters: A Pictorial History*, which she found at the bottom of a stack on the living room end table. She knew it was possible for objects to be swallowed whole like that, for people and places to disappear. Maybe the Norwich quarry held such secrets.

At night now Sonya would often sit near the open window and listen to trucks in the distance out on the highway. Or, closer, she would hear the fall wind in the tall weeds and smell the dust and heat of summer leaving them, leaving the lanky clumps of Queen Anne's lace along the edge of the field beside the house, the color draining out of them, smell the ground, covered with dead leaves and twigs, hardening for winter. She thought of the curly-haired girl on the bus and wondered if she noticed Sonya's absence and if she kept the picture.

Closer even than the sound the dry weeds and emptying sky made at night was the sound of her parents' voices in the kitchen. She recognized now not only the slurred words of drunkenness but the other sounds of it as well: her father's usually graceful feet made clumsy, his hand occasionally brushing a wall for balance. She sometimes heard him in the bathroom stumbling and groaning, sounding like an agitated animal coiled in a cave, in the seeping veins of ore, where it was most comfortable, didn't have to find food or climb steep grassy slopes.

Sometimes his voice was brittle or on the edge of something, Sonya didn't know what. Once she heard him say he would rather be in Australia, with more sheep than people, and beautiful landscapes. Her mother said, "All right. If you can find work there, we'll go. The girls will adjust." Sonya decided not to look Australia up in the atlas until her mother told her they were moving there. Hers was the word of truth. But her mother never mentioned it.

One evening when Sonya heard her father ask her mother, "Do you think we should tell the kids?" she assumed at first that they were discussing additional travel plans. But it soon became apparent, as she listened from the bedroom, though afraid to hear, that they were talking about Andy Duncan. There was something they had just then found out.

"I'd rather they don't know about it right now. Maybe when they are a little older."

"Lloyd Duncan must be devastated," her father said.

"Well, he may have driven him to it." Her mother hesitated, then added, "I know that's a terrible thing to say. But I heard his yelling that summer. My God, what a wretched parent he was, you remember."

"No doubt about it. That aspect doesn't surprise me." There were other words in the kitchen and sounds out her window. "How tough. But to actually get a rope and—and from the banister?"

There was a pause in their words, and Sonya imagined them sitting at the kitchen table, their eyes cast down at their hands.

"More than a year already his parents have lived with it. I can't imagine how." Then, quietly, "Do you think that earlier, with the explosives?"

"I don't know, Marie. It's too awful."

"Remember when his brother stayed with them for a week to do that work? The two of them tore up that side yard and put in a hedge for their mother. Andy explained it to me several days later, when he brought tomatoes over. He told me that they were from her and said that if I wanted a hedge too, I should let him know and he would put one in. Then he laughed and said, 'She told me to say that last part, but it's true.' Remember that?"

Then Sonya heard what she thought was her father crying, a sound she seldom heard. There was an endlessness to it, though her mother's calm words and reassuring tone may have been some comfort to him. She felt a hollow in the bottom of her stomach, the day emptied out of her and some vast terror in its place, a gray sweep of nothing, her mind rendered blank with despair. Struggling with the information, she wanted to rush to her parents, to fill in that blankness with their love, but she knew that they did not want her to know what had happened. When she closed her eyes, she saw a disembodied finger first, then other parts suspended in gray air. So what about the finger trick, she kept thinking, so what; he hadn't meant any harm. She was sure Lois would agree but decided not to talk with her sister about it.

When she couldn't sleep that night, Sonya imagined the sound of the stream in Bridgeville, the steady flow of loose bank grass and the tumble of speckled pebbles. She imagined, too, the golden brown slant of moist mud, the soft bank glinting in sunlight through the trees, and the cool dirt in her hands and toes. Then she slept.

During the day, too, she thought of the stream. In late October Sonya came home from school one afternoon and sat out on the back steps. The sky was deep blue and the air still smelled like summer. Fall paused to remind them that, though winter was on its way, summer would come again. Marie came out and sat beside her. Sonya leaned against her arm, felt the warmth of her skin through her cotton shirt. She missed the stream, seeing the girl on the bus.

"What is it? You are sad these days. You don't like school here?"

"It's not too bad, but the other kids think we're weird because we don't have a television."

"Do you think we're weird?"

"No, we're just us."

"That's right. I think you and Lois are wonderful as you are." Her mother put her arms around her, rocked her. Sonya closed her eyes to feel it better.

"They think it's weird that I like art class."

Marie gathered her daughter's thick brown hair and loosely braided it. "Sonya, you have to be you first. Otherwise how will you know who you are? You like art class? So, you like art class. Don't worry." The dense knot in Sonya's stomach began to dissolve.

Then Marie recounted the time she was thirteen and wanted a microscope, knowing her parents couldn't afford one. She had brought some of her out-grown clothes to a consignment shop, made a few other pieces too, and kept bringing more in, though it took almost a year, until she had enough money to get herself a microscope. The department store clerk had given her a hard time when she finally did go in to buy one, asking her if it was for her brother. "And when I said I didn't have a brother, he wrapped it up. But you know what he said when he handed it to me? 'Don't break it.' Can you imagine?" She wanted, she told Sonya, to study living forms, see how they are put together.

What Sonya could imagine was a younger version of her mother bent over a microscope, sitting in the yellow glow of a lampshade, peering in to find first the squiggled lines of worms moving across the slide, then, when her mother said "living forms," trumpet blossoms, silver-blue fish, and the pink coral reef she had just read about, floated out from under the slide and lit up the dim air around the instrument, beyond the lampshade, growing around the arched back and curling around the knob in her mother's hand. When her mother adjusted the knob, the geometric shapes on the slide all fit together, circling smoothly as gears. Then, looking up, the younger Marie discovered that the flowers had begun to grow up her arms, dangle over the lampshade, spreading its yellow glow to color the whole room.

"Grandpa looks at things that close." When he took the girls out on an excursion, he called it "finding the day," and they anticipated that second when he found something, leaf, shoot, insect, bead of water balanced on a stem, to show them.

"That's right. I learned it from him. That's why I want to teach it."

"How come Grandma doesn't look at things like that?"

"It might be because she has always been sad."

"Is that why she doesn't do stuff with me and Lois like Grandpa does?" On their recent summer visit, a few months before, she and her sister had offered to set their grandmother's hair, but she had been insulted and said that her hair was fine as it was.

"Yes, I think it is. Most of the time she can't enjoy herself."

"My eyes don't feel heavy anymore."

"Come help me make a salad." They went inside.

So when, a few days later, the daily tensions in school persisting, Sonya was singled out for her unsocial behavior, it was the younger version of her mother leaned over a microscope that she thought of. During lunch the math teacher, Mr. Philips, patrolled the rows of tables in the cafeteria scanning in particular for errant behavior. When he spotted someone to punish, he pointed first to the kid, then to the front of the room. When he had a few of them nervously assembled, he flicked the lights three times, commanding silence.

Sonya was about to take the bubble gum out of her mouth and wrap it in her napkin when Mr. Philips signaled her to get up. He pointed again to the front of the cavernous room where two other fifth-graders already stood silently facing the crowd. She walked up, reluctantly, and stood beside them.

He flicked the lights. "These three people," Mr. Philips began, elongating the sentence with his authority, "have broken the rules. Let's see which rule it was." He pointed to Sonya and to the boy beside her. "Take it out and put it on your nose. And leave it there for the lunch hour." They took their gum out, stuck it on their nose. "And our third miscreant has been throwing his food instead of eating it." That meant Sonya was one, too; what was a "miscreant"?

"Each one of them will write for me 'I will not disobey the lunchroom rules again' one hundred times on lined paper. By tomorrow. Let this be a lesson for the rest of you." He told the three to return to their seats.

Sonya finished her lunch with her head tipped down, wad of gum on her nose, and imagined she was her mother at thirteen bent over a microscope, concentrating not on the whispers of those around her, but instead on the wonder of the squiggled shapes before her, darts of light.

At home that evening she stretched out on the bedroom floor with her notebook to write out her lines, first numbering the margin. Then she tried to remember if the line started with "I will obey" or "I will not disobey." She figured it was probably the longer one. She had just written out the sixth line when Lois came in and flopped down beside her.

"Hey, what are you doing?" She pushed her red-brown hair off her shoulder.

"This stupid thing." Lois had seen what had happened, but Sonya had not wanted to talk about it at school.

"Don't do it, Sonya." She took a piece of paper and a pencil and began drawing a figure. "Let's draw Mr. Philips."

"I'm supposed to do these, Lois. He might do something worse if I don't."

"I don't like him." Recently Sonya observed that her sister had begun to move her mouth slightly before she actually spoke, sometimes, as if practicing, or choosing her words partly by the shape of them in the air, by the way her mouth would have to move to form them, feeling them out. And though a stranger might not notice this, or might think it the sign of a mild affliction or that she was about to sneeze, Sonya realized that Lois did it when she was about to say something especially significant. Her mouth moved that way now. Then she said, "Don't do what he told you. He was mean to you."

Sonya put her pen down. She watched Lois drawing for a while, then pushed her notebook out of the way and picked up a pencil. "Let's give him three legs."

Lois had already made his arms twice the usual length and given him extra hands, twisted and pointed in many directions. "He is always pointing." She rotated the paper so that she could work on the dragon's breath coming out the top of his head while her sister detailed his legs.

When they were finished with the figure, they wrote the title, *Monster Man*, across the top and tacked it on the wall above the desk they shared. "There," Lois said.

After English class the next day, the girl whose father owned the sole steakhouse in town asked Sonya if she had written her one hundred lines.

"No, I didn't."

That afternoon she was called over the loudspeaker to Mr. Philips' room. When she opened the door, he stayed at his desk and gestured for her to come over. "I heard you have not done what I have assigned," he began.

Lois had advised her what to say if this happened. "I've been chewing gum since I was five. I have never stuck it on any furniture. I was about to wrap it in a napkin so I could eat."

Mr. Philips, not expecting this, first adjusted his tie clip, then reached out and patted Sonya's arm. He smiled tightly. "Listen, sweetheart. These are the rules. You don't chew gum in a Norwich school. If we make an exception for you, we'll have to make an exception for everyone, and then what good would the rule be? Hmm?" He waited for her agreement. She looked down at the scuffed toe of her sneakers.

"We could chew gum at our old school." Lois had told her to say this if it seemed that he hadn't listened to what else she said.

"This school has rules," he supplemented with a condescending sigh. "Do it this once. It will take you half an hour, and the others will learn by your example. That will be your reward. Do you understand?"

She pictured the squirms of light struggling under the thin sheet of glass, pressed to the edges of the sharp slide, pinned, and she nodded.

"Now return to class."

Without looking at him again she left the room.

As soon as her father got home, late that afternoon, she gave him a full account of what had happened.

"Philips? Is he one of those men who leads with his paunch?" He pushed his belt down, drew in a gulping breath, and extended his stomach as far as he could over his belt.

Sonya said, "Dad!" as she held her stomach and laughed, wiping her eyes. She thought a button might pop off his shirt.

"I know the guy, he's not that big. But he could look like this."

He ran his hand over his broad expanse and walked around the kitchen in an exaggerated step. Then he told her that she did not have to write the one hundred lines and that he would take care of it.

Later that evening she sat at the kitchen table to listen when he dialed.

"Hello. I am Mitchell Hudson, Sonya's father." He nodded a few times and said, "I see." Then he said, "Well, that isn't her explanation of what happened, and I would not describe her as 'surly.'"

There was a pause. Then, "No, she will not. She's already explained why."

He hung up, looked over at Sonya, and when he said, "Don't give it another thought," the curved petals and striped fish, loosed from their flat gears, billowed out from under the slide, coloring the air as they drifted upward.

The next day when Mr. Philips passed her in the hall he ignored her.

"The sun, the clouds. The sun, the clouds."

Sonya went into the dining room when she heard her father's voice. He was sitting at the corner of the wooden table that he had made from an old door. A clay vase-like object stood on the table, its handles like arms poised at its hips. He held an empty brown quart beer bottle up, between himself and the sculpted clay, his back to the sun. When he tilted it to intercept the late afternoon light coming in the windows, it cast an amber shadow over the clay, and he said "the clouds." When he tilted it so that the sun shone fully on the red brown vase, he said "the sun." He did this over and over, until he heard Sonya approach him. He turned to look up at her, sun on the side of his face, and said, "Sweetie, come here, come sit with your father." Sonya pulled a chair beside him and sat down.

"Watch what your old man can do." He smiled.

He moved the bottle again, more slowly this time. "The sun and the clouds, all from these hands."

Sonya scanned the clay for what he saw.

"Terra cotta," her father said. "Baked earth."

When it was dark, it was mountains tucked away in slanting rain. When it was light, it was red streaks of making, a quick fire. Looking at it, she could smell the way heat moved up its curved base, through its handles, and rippled out its narrow neck.

He put the bottle down on the table and faced Sonya. "With these hands," he said, "just the two of them." He turned them over a few times, marveling at them as he did. He looked up at his daughter, picked the bottle up, held it in his lap, sun lighting his eyes. The hazel mesh of them, like marbles lit up. While he did not blink she knew he was somewhere else, but she did not know where. Green of fields, she thought, or of many leaves flipping in the sun at once. Fields and trees are here, and gray of slate and rain, but he is not. A word from her rock book was what she wanted, something tangible in her mouth. Malachite. Jade. But no word was quite right for those shades, or for the distance she saw in them. He blinked.

"I'll go help Mom with supper."

Her father smiled. "That's my girl," he said.

And sometimes she heard the distance. They could feel the argument coming from the kitchen before they actually heard it, taut air strung from that room to the girls' bedroom, where after dinner they lounged on the floor drawing. The familiar voice both surprised and did not surprise Sonya, as she had noticed the empty beer cans lining the kitchen counter earlier in the evening.

"I'm Mr. Nickel's son," her father said, as he rummaged around the cupboards, maybe for snacks to bring along. Maybe he was going out again. "Nickel the Younger. That's what I know, that's what he knew."

Lois and Sonya looked at each other, wondering who Mr. Nickel was.

He continued in the same slurred voice, wind-driven, forlorn. "Tell them I'll write."

They heard the jangle of keys, the back door slam, their mother yell "Christ, Mitchell!" Then the car door, the sound of the motor driving away. Sonya speculated, too, how far a trip it was to Australia. But he couldn't drive there.

They ran into the kitchen just in time to see their mother pick up from the sink among the salad scraps a knotted celery heart, grip it firmly, arch her arm back and let it sail. The chunk whizzed across the room in a blur, then smacked so squarely, precisely, into its target of the doorknob, that bits of celery flew into the air as the cluster of stems burst apart. When Marie realized the girls stood watching, she urged, "It's late. Go to bed please." As they turned without speaking and walked to the bedroom, though they were startled by their mother's anger, having never seen her throw something before, most impressive to them was the incredible speed with which she had thrown the heart and the remarkable accuracy of her aim that blew it apart.

After they returned to their bedroom, put away their paper and markers, they slipped into bed and lay in the dark quietly for a few moments. Then Lois said, "She has a much better throwing arm than he does." And though their mother would have, over the next few years, not nearly the practice of their father, she would remain more gifted, graceful, at it. They would come to realize, too, from just the handful of times they would see such an outburst from her, that she was not only more judicious in her choice of missiles, never breaking anything of value, but was also each time, as with the celery heart, more precise in her aim and in her form, pegging her target plumb with no wasted movement.

That night Sonya listened to her sister's steady breathing, watched shadows on the walls and puzzled not over her mother's display of anger but over the name Nickel. Was it someone who lived in Australia? Or Portugal? And younger than who?

After what felt to her like hours, she heard a vehicle pull into the driveway, heard the back door close, listened for the clump of feet through the house, then heard crying, though she couldn't be sure which parent it was or if it were both of them. She covered her ears and finally slept.

The next morning her parents' words to each other were polite but brief. And their father barely acknowledged his daughters, but instead sat at the dining room table leaning forward slightly, holding his head in his hands as if it were heavy. Or maybe his shoulders were heavy, or his heart.

One night in late autumn Sonya woke to the sound of crying. It was muffled and low, and she knew it was her mother. She heard her father rumbling around in the house, heard him slam the front door, heard him pace up and down the gravel driveway, cursing. She lay on her back, this time covering her ears with pillows before she could hear any more of his words, and watched the shadows of trees the streetlights made on the wall. There must have been a slight breeze, because the few leaves left and the branches heaved slowly on the wall, horses moving underwater, trying to ride faster. Sonya felt underwater, too, and thought of the soundless world of a sunken ship, where cups and plates floated weightlessly and darkness tried to fix everything in its beam. She would open her mouth in that world, but no sound would come out. She closed her eyes. People floated toward each other and away, their mouths gaping soundlessly, drifting. Was there a box of lucky stones on the ship? Bright speckled fish swam in and out of the sunken hull with ease. The fish did not need to talk. Faces drifted before her, mouths open without sound, opening and closing like flowers in the time-lapse film she had seen in science class, but without beauty. Opening with no words coming out, and closing again, swallowing more gray emptiness. She switched her light on and fell asleep.

The next morning she watched her mother at the stove cooking eggs. When her mother looked at her, Sonya saw clouds in her eyes. Her parents barely spoke at breakfast. Afterwards, when her mother washed the dishes, she picked up a towel to dry and asked her if she was all right. Her mother nodded, said, "I'm fine."

When they drove out of the driveway for good in November, the girls' father and Lois rode in the U-Sweat, their mother and Sonya following in the car. Though the windows were rolled up, Sonya smelled the cold metal of the gravel pits on the edge of town and the dry weeds and brown grass of the fields, ready for winter. They took the county road to the interstate. In the four months they had lived in Norwich she had not gathered any stones or shells for her box, nor did she leave one when they left.

6

The Warm Air, The Singing, And The Fields

Here there were tree-lined streets of houses with bay windows and green or black shutters, trimmed lawns and orderly flowers. Some of the houses had brass doorknockers. Almost all had neat blacktopped driveways leading up to spacious two-car garages. Though this town was a mere couple of hours from the last place they lived, it was different so substantially it might as well have been in another state. The suburb of Harpur Springs sprawled northwest of the capital. And though the last district he had worked for had not been enamored of Mitchell Hudson's ideas for their school, the centerpiece of which was a woodworking course for girls, maybe this one would be. A friend had told him about the job to fill an unexpected retirement, and he had applied right away. Mitchell was optimistic about the place not solely because of the favorable response to his application, but because here, he said, at least the girls could attend a school that wasn't made up entirely of white kids, as the last place had been.

The house on Hightower Road was modest beside the others in the area, and its bushes and lawn had apparently been neglected. A woman had lived there for the forty-two years before the Hudsons rented it, and had recently become unable to care for the place. It was set back from the road, and two strips of dirt led to the garage. It had a splintered wooden fence around it, with a sagging gate on one side of the house leading to the rolling backyard, ample enough that Sonya and Lois could build forts out of leaves and run around in them, and their mother could plant vegetables and bulbs.

And though they moved in when the ground had given up its color and was veined with snow, the first weekend they lived there the girls' father hung a wooden rope swing he had made in a willow along the back border near a row of forsythia bushes. Since he had a week before his new job started, he also decided to paint black shutters on the two front windows. The girls' mother did not like the idea at first and reminded him that they did not own the place. He persuaded her by saying that it would look nice, that it would be cheaper than buying shutters and probably easier than putting them on, and that the shutters on the other houses in the neighborhood were purely decorative anyway.

The following Saturday when he finished them he told Marie and the girls to get in the car. Then he drove them around the neighborhood, approaching the house from every angle, and asked them at what point they thought someone could tell that the shutters were not real. He was pleased when they all agreed that it wasn't really until they pulled into the driveway and took a close look that they could see by the subtle brush streaks that they were painted on. "I thought so," he said. And so the Hudsons settled into the neighborhood.

From the first day in school, classmates approached Sonya and Lois. On the way out of art class a girl wearing a tie-dyed shirt and ragged jeans told Sonya she thought her leather and bead necklace was "far-out." And the next day, in the cafeteria, another girl asked her, "What does your father do?"

"He makes clay objects and teaches people how to make things out of wood." There was a puzzled expression on the girl's face and, to fill the silence, Sonya asked the girl what her father did.

"He makes money." She smiled at the chance to add, "Quite a lot of it, actually." That was the whole of their conversation.

The school's formal name was after the neighborhood it was in, but everyone called it The Brick School. It had high ceilings, corridors painted primary colors by the students, spacious stairways that dipped in the middle from years of wear. The smells of chalk-dust and glue, paint and markers, permeated the place, like in any school; the tall arched windows in the classrooms and in the stairwells let in reams of sun and added an elegance not always found in suburban schools.

Sonya sat near a window when she could—the restrictive system of assigned seating had been discarded—and gazed out at the pine trees that bordered the front of the building. Sometimes all she needed was a word. In Social Studies the word might be *China*, *Holland*, or *waterway*, and her attention veered away from the filmstrip, out into the blue day beyond the arched window, where she saw the canal. Animals slow in the sun make chomping sounds along the grass the high reeds in the afternoon heat and swish of tails at flies. Slender wooden boats glistening with muscled arms pulling them over the calmly flowing water. Clay urns of earth and seed, moist darkness in them all one could ever hope to hold, sweat on the neck dipped to the river, bowl of back curved and bent down into the cool, down into the cool then up again, and water brought to the lips while tails swish at flies and the sun, we circle and circle, the sun overhead, up out of time.

Sometimes on the walk home from school in the afternoon Sonya stopped at a set of old wooden bleachers along the edge of the playing fields, climbed up a couple, reclined on her back with her head on her books, and now, since it was late November, watched her breath thread the cold clear air and disappear. The bench was hard and splintered beneath her jeans. She looked into the deep blue afternoon sky until specks of light blinked around the corners of her eyes. Then imagined nothing. She imagined all things, all houses and streets, clothes books pencils and people, dropped away from the edges. Then stepped down the history timeline that bordered her classroom. Further and further she went, down into the damp cellar of the past, before people, heartbeats, and blood. She imagined gray nothing with the world fallen aside. She felt an ache of terror in her, a fear of gigantic things, of voids, of limitless whistles of space, and then had to walk herself back up out of it, up through the damp steps of ages, past lost languages and dry riverbeds, and clothes strewn over chairs in dusty morning light, past scraps of paper thrown on desks, and meals cooking in huts, alleys and kitchens, smoke-pits, back up into the late daylight of the playing fields, the November ground, stretches of shadow across it, up into the cold air and the hard bench beneath her, back up to the heft of her school books in her arms and the rest of the walk home.

Then briefly the cold paused, and the warm returned. It was on a Saturday afternoon like this that he came roaring into the dirt driveway, beeping the horn repeatedly. Lois and Sonya emerged from their room, and their mother from the kitchen. They peered out the front door.

"Whose car is that?" Lois asked. Their father had left earlier in their old car.

"He just bought it. Grab your jackets, girls."

The three of them walked out and met him halfway to the house. "Do you like it?"

"It's cool," Sonya and Lois said together. They walked around the red wagon, another VW.

Their father addressed their mother and proudly presented his assessment. "It's got 75,000 miles on it, but the tires are practically new, and the engine sounds smooth." He knew the basics about automobiles, like how to jump start one by pushing it down a hill, if he had to.

"Did you bring him down at all?"

"He knocked a hundred off. I threw in a set of bowls and a carafe."

"That's great, Mitchell," their mother said, and squeezed his arm. "We'll have more room in the back." They stood beside each other smiling.

"Let's go for a drive," he said.

The girls climbed in the back seat, and their parents slid in the front.

He detailed the car's features for them on the way out of town. "And it doesn't have a radio either, but what the hell."

Their mother said, "When we take it on trips, you'll have to sing for us."

"Marie, you know I can't sing."

"Yes you can," she said. "I hear you in the shower every morning."

"I didn't think anyone heard me," he said, laughing. "Well, I'm not ready to take my act on the road."

They reached a county road far beyond the suburbs. There were fields on either side. Their father said, "Let's see where this goes." Since the day was warm they had rolled the windows down, and the smell of dried November fields and cut hay drifted into the car.

Their father started the song softly, as if he were talking at first; then gradually the notes rose up and over into the back seat. It had a quick beep-beep rhythm, and he tapped against the wheel to keep time. Their mother already knew the words about love and a new moon and before long joined him, a new new moon begun, and tapped too, against the dash, rocked gently to the beat, the new moon over the fields and when their life is done, they would still feel it, it would still be there, the new moon, the moon just begun.

And the song lifted so clearly to the back seat, carried there by the open windows and the warm air blowing in and blowing their hair, and blowing the fields they flew along and blowing the singing words about the car, and sounded as if they hovered just above their heads. The words held still just a moment above their heads, so they could get a quick look at them before the afternoon air washed them away, out the windows, to float out over the fields somewhere. The speed was part of it too, as Sonya and Lois looked out the windows at the fields and far trees and scattered houses in the sun flying by, all with the lovely notes attached to them, set in motion by the tapping, lifted on the warm air, sent out by their parents' voices. And it didn't matter that the car had the faint smell of a cigar, a slight tear in the back seat, and a stain on the square of carpet beneath their feet. It did not matter that it had lots of miles already on it. There was the warm air, the singing, the fields they were flying past. The earth feeling wide and smelling warm out the windows. The moon, wherever it was besides the song, the long curved road ahead, the beat to keep. There was the warm air, the singing, and the fields.

Though their father often had everyone laughing at the Friday night suppers with friends at their place, and despite his occasional singing, the girls had from a young age recognized his serious approach to certain subjects, like clay. It was around this time, when she was in junior high, that Sonya began going into the basement to watch her father work. Frequently he worked in the late afternoon when he got home from his job as a shop teacher for the high school, more often for a while in the evening or on a Saturday afternoon. Most times he couldn't concentrate, he said, with the distraction of a child watching him. But when it was all right Sonya found a wooden crate to sit on and studied him, sitting on his stool, from a distance. Moisture spun from his wheel, its motor whirring rhythmically. He seemed to do his looking with his hands, as if his hands were searching directly beneath the surface of the clay. Sometimes he made bowls, sometimes, at a work table, panels that he fit together of reliefs, life-sized disembodied heads, the faces twisted to the side, eyes maybe closed, lips parted, calling over a shoulder to someone far away or to someone not there at all, sometimes hand-sized figures, or pots, dishes, tiles. After they were fired, he would sell some of these at art festivals, others he would keep. With his set of wire tools, his strip set for edging, and his clay cutter, he could make just about anything. But even when he was making a carafe, it seemed to Sonya that he was making a face. His hands worked the outlines, his thumbs smoothed the edges, as if they were tracing a cheekbone or a mouth, his hands waiting there to catch the words when they first came out. Was he looking for someone on the other side, talking back to his hands? She wondered, but never asked. She rose, usually after an hour or so of watching, and turned away from the watery smell of the rich moist clay and of basement dust, and left him in his wheel-hum. She walked up into the tangible realm of the kitchen. And if her mother asked her to set the table or to take out the garbage or to knock the dust off her shoes before tracking it into the living room, she knew what she could do to help; the world was definable again.

For art class Sonya painted a picture of a man with lumps of clay, blocks of wood, various tools, and animals around him. The chisels and the palette knives, as well as all of his other implements, he had made sure his daughters knew by name and by function. She put the animals in, too, crickets as well as cows, because her father believed all living forms were sacred and said, "It is not our place to tell other animals when their time is up." That was why the Hudsons no longer ate meat. She didn't think a lot about it until every once in a while a kid at school would ask, "Is it true your family doesn't eat meat? How can you stay alive?" The title for her picture, *He Who Talks to All Things*, was in cerulean blue, each letter cloud-shaped hovering above the man. Her art teacher told her it was an interesting depiction of a deity, since it was wearing jeans and a plaid wool shirt. Sonya smiled and nodded but said nothing, since she wasn't completely certain what "deity" meant. Later she showed the picture to Lois who said, "That's him."

The sisters knew the language of each other's humor, too. Having had much practice by this age, Lois had learned how to make her sister lose control, particularly at the dinner table, where her goal was to reduce Sonya to rolling on the wooden bench in laughter. When she took a grain of rice, and with her tongue carefully maneuvered it until it rested on her top lip, she could say short sentences, such as "please pass me the butter," without the rice falling off. No one seemed to notice but Sonya, who would look over and discover that Lois had deftly moved it with the tip of her tongue to a corner of her mouth. Their father thought that uncontrollable laughter at the dinner table was impolite, and told her, as he sometimes had to tell Lois too, that if she was laughing so much that she couldn't eat, perhaps she wasn't really hungry and should leave the table. When this happened, Sonya assured him that she was hungry, wiped her eyes, and tried not to look over at Lois, who had pushed her red-brown hair off her shoulder and was eating in graceful bites while the piece of rice balanced on her bottom lip. She faced Sonya directly and asked, "What's the matter?" Soon both lost their composure completely and made grunting, sucking, mouth-full-of-too-much-laughter sounds.

And usually their father threw his napkin down, pounded the table with his fist, and said, "Stop laughing right now!" When the girls continued with subdued quivering, he yanked first Lois then Sonya up by her arm, smacked each three times firmly on the bottom, and threw them back into their seats.

"Mitchell," their mother said. Her voice sounded far away. "Please."

"They'll learn to listen," he said.

The rest of the meal was finished in silence, except for the teary sounds of Lois and their mother sniffling. Sonya told herself to cry later but had lost her appetite.

Later, at night, Sonya usually heard the muffled cries of her mother from their bedroom downstairs. She heard the chaos in her father's hands as he fished a beer out of the refrigerator. Then she listened for his thumping to the front door, and then the door's slam. Familiar now, too, was the diminishing sound of the motor as he drove away. She listened for the even breathing that told her Lois was asleep, and then she covered her ear with her pillow and fell asleep, too.

Before school in the morning she wanted to ask her mother what was wrong, but she was afraid to know. And why was her father in the bathroom, letting out an exasperated sigh and blowing his nose? Or, why did he sometimes call himself an asshole? Instead she asked a question like, "Was it something we did?"

And her mother smiled, put her hand on Sonya's neck, and said, "No. Don't think that." They would stay that way awhile, in the fragrance of her hand lotion, but she did not offer an explanation.

Other times, though, no explanation would have been needed; the reason for the strain was obvious. Recently, Mitchell cut out a newspaper article with a list of estimated casualties from the war. There were detailed columns with a breakdown by years of US involvement, listing both dead and injured, Americans and Vietnamese. He trimmed the edge and pinned the article on a bulletin board that he had mounted above the kitchen sink, so he could read while he did the dishes. Beside the article he had also pinned a news-magazine photograph of a group of Vietnamese children squatting together crying, a dead body on the ground nearby.

When Marie came in later and saw these, she asked him if it was really necessary to post such disturbing material where the girls would see it. She suggested he tack the clippings to their bedroom wall instead or near his work space in the basement.

He argued that it was precisely because the girls would see these every day that he had posted them in the kitchen. They had to be educated about the horrors of the world, particularly about what destruction their own country was wreaking on mankind; it was irresponsible of parents to try to shelter their children from reality. He and Marie had explained firehoses to the girls, other kinds of brutality against Black people, riots, protests they had heard about.

"Mitchell, they are in junior high, for God's sake," Marie had said, a shadow of sadness falling across her voice. "They don't need to know about napalm yet."

"This way they won't be shocked when they get to high school and they learn about atrocities in their history class." Though he had sounded a bit triumphant as he made this proclamation, his agitated voice rose precipitously as he continued. "Do you think I want them to live in a world that also has landmines in it? How do we explain that? What do we say—some guy lay awake at night, thought about the most hideous way to hurt another person? With the most deceit involved? The most unthinkably horrific thing, so kids get their legs blown off? Their eyes melted from the heat of them? Do I want them to live in this kind of world?" He grabbed a saucer he had made from the counter and tossed it into the sink, and the shatter of it was surprisingly loud for such an insubstantial amount of clay. That ended the conversation.

So the article and accompanying image stayed posted above the sink, gaped from their confining black and white not just at whoever was washing the dishes but at anyone who walked into the kitchen. That glass of refreshing juice, the nourishing meal prepared with garlic in olive oil, the early morning radio, the afternoon laughter there or slants of backyard sun spilling in, all existed in a state more fragile for the backdrop they were against, the newsprint's looming reminder of the daily anguish that others endured.

But whatever distress was developing between their parents, the girls knew uncomplicated joy with each other. As the frayed ends of one season wove into the next, there were days on which, despite what the calendar said, it was difficult to tell what season it was. There were always reminders of the one before and the one to come, inextricably knotted as they were, one color blending imperceptibly into the next like strands of multicolored cloth. Ages were like that too; Sonya and Lois, in the throes of junior high school, could one day discuss their college plans, saying they hoped they would do as well with their studies as their mother with hers, and the next day revel in throwing raisins into the air and trying to catch them in their mouths.

So it was when spring finally came and brought with it grass that was thick in their hands. Their father pushed his wooden mower with its gleaming blades up and down the yard one day in May, propelled by his graceful stride. His legs were the motor, he proudly told them. The blades made a shook-shook sound, and a fine spray of grass shot off the top of the cylinder. The girls gathered clumps of the cool grass and shaped it into two round hats. Sonya said the grass smelled like the inside of a stone tower.

"How do you know what a tower smells like?" asked Lois. "Have you ever been inside one?"

"No. But I don't have to go inside one to know what it smells like."

"To know for sure you would have to be there."

"No I wouldn't. You can know something without seeing it."

"No you can't," said Lois.

"You know the earth is round, but you never saw it all at once. You never saw its roundness," said Sonya.

"Yes I have, in pictures."

"Well, I saw pictures of a tower."

"But that's different. You can't prove something like smell with a picture."

"Smells don't have to be proven," said Sonya. "Smells just are. When we see Grandpa Blasion this summer, ask him how he knows which mint is which." The girls often referred to him by name, though he was the only grandfather they visited. All they knew of their other one was the story their father told them, short on detail. They took the outlines and filled the specifics in mythically; they did not see a parent burdened beyond relief, a wanderer who probably did not count among his few belongings a reliable map, with an old dusty bread truck for a home. They envisioned, instead, a figure setting out on a journey having all he needed with him in a shining vehicle, glancing out a night window as he drove to navigate by stars and then consult his map, any road welcoming to him.

"But everyone has a different nose," said Lois. "Yours is the shape of a garlic bulb and mine is beautiful."

Sonya grabbed a handful of grass and dove, straddling her sister's stomach, who kicked, yelled, and shrieked with laughter. When she rubbed grass on her nose, Lois grabbed her forearm and bit hard. Sonya fell over on her back next to her. They caught their breath.

"My nose is going to change anyway. All of me is."

"How much will we change?"

"I'm not sure," Sonya said. "The filmstrip we saw in health class just said we are changing. It didn't say how much."

She had learned from the filmstrip that their bodies would change on their way to becoming men and women, for example the men and women that all of their parents had become in having them, their children. There were diagrams of reproductive systems, mysterious arrows and, in the case of the women's system, curves resembling a stethoscope. In that distant and ordered land of adulthood everything fell into place, everything made sense and was exactly as it should be. That was what she and Lois and their classmates could look forward to. For now she didn't have the words to explain all of this mystery and suggestion to her sister; they could look at each other and in that silence anticipate together. They had already, over the last year or two, observed the other's shadows of hair and darkening nipples. Sonya imagined the arms of their ovaries stretching and growing outward, sea creatures reaching, as, reclining in the grass, they contemplated each other's body a moment, wondering.

"Let's wear our hats," Lois said.

"Here," Sonya said, gathering a clump of the grass, ragged with the fragrance of dirt and sun. "I'll put it on your head. What size do you need?"

Lois got up on her knees. "I'm a size eight."

Sonya knelt before her and placed the pile on her sister's head. "She Knows What She Sees."

Lois bent down slowly, keeping the pile in place, and scooped up the other round of grass.

Sonya bent forward slightly. Lois said, placing it on her hair, "She Knows Every Smell."

They walked a circle around the yard, in deliberate steps, so their hats wouldn't fall. After setting them aside, they gathered supple willow branches to mark out a moat. The forsythia bushes, too, ecstatic.

"No enemy will cross this water," Sonya said. "We will be safe."

Before they went in for supper a couple of hours later, they carefully placed their grass hats beside each other in the center of the moat.

"If this was our castle, this is probably where the living room would be," Lois explained. "We are putting them on the fireplace mantel."

"Or in the middle of the courtyard," Sonya said. "Or on the dining room table. One of those rectangular ones with twenty thousand goblets lined up and down it."

"Silver goblets."

"Yes, silver goblets. And gold plates."

Lois's mouth moved slightly first, forming the words. Then, with precision, "Golden plates," she said.

Then, after a bath each of them scrubbed a ring of grass out of the tub. They had washed the grass off their skin and out of their hair, but they had not washed away its pungent scent. In bed Sonya listened to her sister breathe and smelled the back of her hands. The sun was still in them, the grass in her skin. The sheets were cool against her legs, and the ground of the yard still firm under her bare feet. Night air came through the screen, and a net of stars was flung across the sky. Net of night sky mesh of fire and lights smell of wind from a distant sea, the sound of dogs barking aimlessly "we're here, we're here." Net of night sky entangled with the grape arbor in the yard wild geranium and heave of swishing willow vast humming down the streets of space and darkness, the sea and a field leading down to it deep grass and earth in the field soft under feet and night wind off the water cooling feet and hands the sound of water entangled geranium and wild grape. How could he when the shadows fell whatever day it was outside there were shadows to fall on him and that meant light coming into that front hallway across the banister some light some seed spinning out its years in his yard his town beyond his town some place there was that seed and its light how could he when there was that. Deep blue twilight of dream that boy who would not know voices in the distance muffled by the churning of water against the shore and would not know joy resting in the grass of the field under a net of night sky to sleep beside the sea.

When, that summer, they did make the trip to their grandparents' place, Marie brought course reading in anticipation of the following term. She stayed up in the evening, sitting at the kitchen table with a metal desk lamp she brought with them, after everyone else had gone to bed. The girls, sleeping on cots in the next room, did not mind the light; they fell asleep to the soft rhythmic sound of Marie methodically turning the pages of her textbook.

And though they had forgotten their earlier discussion of the varied scents of mints, the girls still had plenty of topics, as usual, to talk with their grandfather about. He always asked about the previous year in school, and they asked him about his plants.

One afternoon, when Herbert and their parents had gone into Mercy Hill, and Lois had fallen asleep in the living room, Glenda took Sonya aside and whispered that she had some work for her to do.

Moving aside the metal tabs that held the screens in place and then lifting the screens down without waking her sister, and carrying them out to the backyard was not the difficult part. That was Sonya's grasping of her grandmother's plan for cleaning them. When all the screens were leaned against either a tree or the picnic bench, Glenda came out with exactly the number of toothpicks that there were screens, ten.

"Use one on each. Like this." She bent to lean one toward her, took a toothpick, and poked it through the tiny top square of wire, then the next square and then the next. "But you will do this for each opening, each row, until all the screens are clean." She had been complaining of the dust build-up, especially in the summer, on the screens, and of how at night, with the windows open and a little breeze, dust drifted into the house while they slept.

Sonya, trying to conjure Lois's poise and confidence, began to suggest simply hosing them off, but her grandmother delivered an exhortation on the tremendous waste of water before Sonya had finished her sentence. Setting the tin cup of toothpicks on the picnic table, Glenda then marched back up to the house without another word.

Sonya selected a toothpick, sat down cross-legged in the grass, the frame of a screen resting against her folded legs and tried to decipher the clouds. No smell of moisture in the air, no hope for rain or even wind to blow away the particles of dust. The smell of wire mesh, imprint against her bare knees, all the days and nights pressing into a room, what the wind brought with it from down the road or across the field, and all the human pressing from inside—if she could catalogue all that, the work would be less tedious. Begin with pollen or with insect wings, move to fireflies and then to moonlight, and on the other side, her grandfather pressing to meet the morning air or leaning his head against the frame at night, breathing in the wire-scent mixed with the scent from cooled earth. Or from a cave in the adjacent county, rumored to wind for miles.

Now half a row, half of one row across the top of one screen. The story Glenda told them was that the boy, at near her age now, had gotten lost one summer in the cave (one summer long ago, she said) into which, according to his friends, he had ducked during a thunderstorm. They had run back to the farm, but he had not followed. The county sheriff had assembled a team, but the combination over the next few hours of adolescent memory made fragile by anxiety, a blackening sky, and the boy's, as was discovered later, further retreat into the tunnel, made his recovery impossible. The grass at the entrance matted by torrential rain offered no trace of footsteps. Then the hours lengthened to days, and days to weeks, then to months, and his family's agony to every second of their lives.

One whole row complete, each square poked through with a toothpick, a fleck of dust barely visible or not visible at all, drifting out or evaporating out, thinning into the summer air, then half another row.

When he walked down the road, three months later, the story was, and stumbled into the front yard, an older sister thought at first that she was bringing water to a stranger. Several days passed before he revealed what he had eaten. How had dirt kept him alive, and spring water? And rodents that had also wandered into the recesses of the cave? Maybe moss too, he wasn't positive, some texture over the rocks, scraped and ingested.

How had he lived without sunlight? Two rows down, she wondered. And could he stand to full height all that time, or did he have to lie in the cool trickling to stretch out his legs? His back? And what about his voice? If he had spoken in the cave, would it have echoed two or ten-fold? Or would it have sounded weaker, rippling to him from the wet rock?

This will take a year, Sonya thought. How had he stayed lost? How far into the cave had he climbed, crawled or stepped, to be, for all that time, hopelessly distant from the sliver of light that would eventually lead him back to the field? How far inside had he disappeared? Labyrinthine, Glenda told them, and her husband agreed. A thousand squares, at least, each one would be a life in another state, each one would be a star from another year, each one could be a fleck of clay made into all the sculptures of the world— the ones that appeared in her father's over-sized sculpture book, or a shade of green from a plant her mother loved. Or every square could be someone's pain removed, punctured, dissolved, finally lifted, the burden leaving air in its place, full breathing. She would tell her grandmother, if she asked. What must the relief of finally seeing the opening have felt like to the boy?

But she didn't ask. She expressed dismay when, an hour or so later, she came outside to check the progress and saw that only half of one screen had been cleaned. She knew this not because there was any discernible visible difference between a square Sonya had poked and one she hadn't; Glenda saw that a single toothpick had been retrieved from the tin, the one still in Sonya's cramped hand as she bent over the screen at the middle of it.

"Never mind finishing," Glenda called abruptly as she strode over. "Let's get these back inside." She took a rag from her housecoat pocket, quickly ran it over each side of every screen with a crisp snap afterwards, and then hoisted a couple up from where they still leaned. Soon after all the screens had been secured in the window frames, Sonya's parents and grandfather returned from their sojourn into town, and her sister woke from her nap. It was then that Sonya understood that the nixing of the cleaning was not due to any generosity or change of heart on her grandmother's part; it was because she did not want the others to see the evidence of her coercion.

And when asked about their time spent, Glenda's answer, without even so much as a conspiratorial glance toward Sonya, had been, "We sat out in the yard awhile, enjoying ourselves." What caught Sonya's ear was the word "enjoying." How many times had she heard her grandmother say it? Had she ever? It was no more a part of her language than "relax" would have been, or "wonderful" or "beauty," for that matter. A look of knowing passed between Marie and Sonya, but neither of them spoke of it, not then, and not later, out of earshot of Glenda.

On another day that week Marie came to Sonya's room again, this time extending the casual approach she had used earlier about her daughter's drawings to a casual encouragement regarding her well-being. Though she hadn't herself, at eighteen, talked so freely with Glenda, certainly not in any way that revealed vulnerability, she could rightly take pride that her own relationship with her offspring was much healthier. After all, she, like most of her friends, had been influenced by the democratic surge of the 1960s, the exhilarating openness in all areas of life, a freer discussion of child-rearing. She had read Benjamin Spock, read passages aloud to Mitchell too, talked with other mothers who were also moved by his empathetic ideas. Surely her own teenage daughter would be amenable to the suggestion that she seek advice.

"There is no shame in needing help, in wanting to talk with someone. Lots of people talk with someone about what's on their mind. I guess I don't really have to say this because you know it already. You already agreed to see Dr. Francis, I mean—you did see him. You went to the trouble of looking through that book he gave you with the animal photographs. You tried the relaxation tape. It's not as if you haven't begun to get some help. Think of it that way, Honey. You have already started the process."

Sonya was sitting on the floor looking at a package of colored pencils. She did not look up at her mother as she said, "But I didn't get anywhere with the pictures or the tape."

"I'd go with you this time, too. We'll try someone else."

Sonya thought of getting dressed to meet with someone in an office. That would also involve being outside for a couple of hours, walking, traffic, lots of sound. Talking of course, oh for it to be translucent again on her tongue, the crystals of the sugared word her mother handed to them dissolving slowly luxuriously. It wouldn't be like that though. And then the drive home, there would be the nice turn into their street, the summer trees shading the yards, their shadows, sunlight on her arms, the safe turn into their driveway. But then the coming back to her room, changing clothes, figuring out the rest of that day, whatever was left of it to figure out, and having to figure it out around that rupture in the middle of it. Then trying the next day, too, to resume her routine, but everything would be stirred up, changed, more awkward than before the visit outside. It would be difficult to get back. How could she explain all this to her mother, waiting at the edge of her chair, with all the kindnesses she was giving away?

"I don't know." And too the earth itself, that used to feel wide and smell warm to her, now constrained her in its width, its scope and depth, those animals waiting outside. "Can I think about it?"

Her mother sighed. "Assure me that you *will* think about it."

"I will."

"OK," she said. Then she left her daughter's room.

7

Sometimes They Were Just Themselves

It was in the cafeteria the year before that Sonya first saw Veronica Simmons and wanted to be her friend. Veronica stepped through the lunchroom laughing, stopping at every table to talk on her way to her seat, her short red hair lighting the way. She was on the student council at The Brick School. Her real claim to fame though was that she had never missed a word on a spelling quiz, not even on the advanced level ones, not "parsimonious," not "squeegee." When they were both trees in a play and had to stand behind cut-out shapes six feet high, carrying them on stage by side-stepping, nearly peeing with laughter, Sonya knew they would be friends.

Soon they had a Saturday routine worked out. One of their parents dropped them off in downtown Harpur Springs in the afternoon, and they went first to Lerner's to try on bras and then to Woolworth's to have a soda and to get their picture taken in the photo booth with the gray curtain. Both of them sat on the round wooden stool leaning into the center, toward the retreating point of light, stuck their tongues out, pushed their noses up, and smiled. Four shots printed out for a quarter. They usually took eight, so each could have a strip to take home. Sonya hung hers in rows on her bulletin board beside a piece of Queen Anne's lace and a picture of Amelia Earhart. Veronica made a border for an Elton John poster with hers.

Often on weekends they slept over at each other's house. At Veronica's, they stayed up late, ate pizza and popcorn, and watched reruns of *The Honeymooners* in the Simmons' refinished basement. They had their old furniture in there: a brown nubby plaid sofa with two matching chairs, a mahogany coffee table, wall-to-wall shag carpet, and bookcases filled with glass figures, plastic flowers, and photographs. Sonya wondered why no one ever lounged in the real living room with its stiff chairs with carved

wooden backs, plush sofa, arrangements of dried flowers, and floor to ceiling three-layer drapes. Though a few of the times she stayed over Veronica's
parents had a party in this room, she thought it strange for a family to have
so much mostly unused furniture and space. Everything was gauzy cream
and pale yellow, and sometimes Sonya stood at the doorway peering in, as
though she were viewing an underwater exhibit, hushed sunlight drifting
in from above, or a life-sized magazine display. And in all the other rooms
too, their house was orderly; everything matched. Veronica had lived in
that house at the end of Nottington Lane, with her parents and black Angora cat, Spikey, her whole life. It was a life of order Sonya had always, seen
from a distance, perceived that others had.

After they watched TV and cleaned up their mess, they dragged their
blankets and pillows back upstairs to Veronica's room. Sonya slept on the
floor in a sleeping bag. Sometimes Veronica lay beside her, so they could
whisper awhile before she climbed up to her bed and they fell asleep.

Veronica liked being at Sonya's house because none of the Hudsons' furniture matched. All the pieces had been either made by her father, salvaged
by her mother from a barn or a roadside sale, or, occasionally, just a roadside, or given by their friends who had gotten new. The walnut rocking chair
complemented the pine one beside it in the living room, though they were
different styles. Also not matching anything, and the sole exception to their
other methods of acquisition, was the new brass lamp Mitchell had just
bought Marie for finishing her degree. The girls had made a card to go with
it, a colored pencil drawing of diplomas wrapped in oak leaves holding up a
globe. The lamp stood, spare in design, gleaming from a corner of the room,
its glow illuminating in the evening the various grains and shades of wood.

When Veronica slept over at Sonya's, they stayed outside until supper
and often ran back out after. Sometimes in the fall they gathered leaves in
the yard and built forts with them. They took wood scraps from the basement pile Sonya's father had collected, and configured them into whatever
they needed: miniature ships, saddles, horse whips, a banister was made of
wood the spindles where sunlight fell across the day the pieces in her hands,
or wooden cases carrying lockets from their lovers overseas. Sometimes
one of them would be the lover appearing suddenly on his horse, rustling

out of the veiled brush into the waiting arms of his beloved. Sometimes they were just themselves resting on top of the piles of leaves they gathered in the cloudy afternoon of late October, their hair entangled. They wore jeans and flannel shirts, sweatshirts and sneakers. Sometimes they were just themselves gazing at the sky, smelling of twigs and the cold ground.

Once Sonya reached over and carefully covered Veronica's face with bits of dried leaves while Veronica breathed slowly, her eyes closed, her hands folded over her stomach. Then she propped herself up on one elbow and leaned toward Veronica, gently picking each piece off her face and out of her hair. Veronica's hair was lighter near her temples from hours in the summer sun by the pool of the country club her family belonged to. When Sonya touched this spot, Veronica looked up at her, and she smiled when Sonya said, "Your hair is lighter here." Sometimes they stayed there until her mother beckoned them in or until the dampness from the ground seeped into their clothes. Then they went inside, took hot showers, or maybe did their homework in front of the fire.

Sonya's father often asked why she and Veronica had to talk to each other on the phone every evening, if they saw each other every day at school. "There is always more to talk about," she explained.

"That's just the way girls are, Mitchell," said her mother.

"Well, it ties up the line," said her father.

When Sonya told Veronica he had said this, she asked, "Is he expecting a call from President Nixon?"

Sonya did not know how to tell Veronica she loved her, so she drew her a picture, working on it for a month. Two girls rested on a pile of brown and red leaves surrounded by different scenes which hovered around them like planets: a castle, a ship, a library, a photo booth, and a playground. She titled it, in crimson because that was Veronica's favorite color, *She Brings a Sanctuary with Her*, and gave it to her in April for her thirteenth birthday. Veronica said it meant more to her than all her other presents combined, and she hung it up in her room next to the walnut mirror that hung above its matching dresser. She told Sonya she liked the word "sanctuary."

"It is one of my favorites, too," Sonya said, wanting Veronica to know that she was like a sanctuary.

That year when they received their packet of school photographs, Veronica gave one to her with, "to Sonya, my Woolworth's friend," written on the back. Sonya tacked it up on her bulletin board next to her photo booth pictures.

Lois was busy, too. One of her new friends, Nancy, played the cymbals and, without much persuasion, talked her into playing an instrument also. After considering a few of the quieter string ones, she settled on the trumpet. Marie said that that was a perfect choice for someone who came out of the womb with both of her boots laced up. And the girls' father said this might mean she would sometimes have to practice in the garage, which he reminded her was unheated. When it was obvious she was undeterred, he agreed to get one for her.

After spotting an ad in the newspaper on a Saturday afternoon, he disappeared into the basement, rummaged around, and came back upstairs with a shelf inlaid with tile, a glazed carafe, and a fruit bowl. He called to Lois to put on her jacket.

"Where are we going?"

"We're going to get your instrument." He told Marie they'd be home later, handed Lois the fruit bowl, and said, "We'll give him a choice. Let's go."

An hour and a half later Sonya and Marie met them at the front door. Their father was carrying the bowl, and Lois was carrying a black case, slightly worn and scuffed.

"He wanted the shelf and the carafe for it, but I shook on that," their father said, setting aside the fruit bowl. "We still got a good deal. Show them, Lois."

She put the case down on the living room floor, let her hands rest a moment on the top of it, a flourish of drama, and then opened it reverently. The inside was lined with faded green velvet, indented from the instrument. And the trumpet was tarnished in a few places, but she picked it up, held it to her mouth, and let out a loud excited blast.

"Isn't it cool?" Her lips formed the words in the air before she added, "I don't even care if it isn't new."

Marie and Sonya agreed that it was nice.

"We can always buff it up a little if you want," their father said.

He returned the bowl to the basement, and Lois brought the case to the bedroom, where she and Sonya took turns blowing into the instrument until their mother called them to supper.

Within a few days Lois had found some flower stickers to adorn the case, the thick wide petals reaching their spirals of color out from the central eye with almost enough enthusiasm to match her energetic blasts through the mouthpiece.

Though Lois had developed her own friendships in her grade, and could tie up the line as well as her sister could, she and Sonya often hung out together with each other's friends. They rode their bikes (their father had found matching blue ten-speeds, two-for-one, at a "midnight madness" sale) and ate apples and crackers by the bagful. Or they set up badminton in Veronica's backyard and knocked the birdie around, then cooled off with pink lemonade in the air-conditioned house where the drapes were drawn.

One night in early June Sonya slept in a tent in Veronica's backyard, where they brought out a flashlight, some Oreos, and juice. When they were settled into their sleeping bags, Veronica divided a row of cookies between them.

Veronica twisted several of hers apart, nudged the filling off each with her thumbnail, and created a pile of filling rings, each delicately placed on top of the one before it, a sugar turret on the edge of her sleeping bag. Then she retrieved the chocolate circles that she had set aside, and these she stacked in shorter piles around the central one.

Sonya, meanwhile, nibbled the trim on a few, then popped the whole middles in her mouth and took a couple gulps of juice. She watched Veronica arrange her uneaten assortment.

In the dark of the tent it was easier for Sonya to admit worry to her friend. Though she figured she knew the answer, she asked Veronica nevertheless, "Does your dad ever talk about leaving?"

"How do you mean? When he goes away on a business trip?"

"No. I mean—I don't know—leaving like he won't come back."

"He never says stuff like that. Why? Does yours?"

"Not really. I just wondered."

Sonya grabbed another cookie and twisted it apart, scraped the creamy insides off with her teeth, then ate the outside rounds. Veronica quickly chewed one too, and they took turns holding the flashlight up to each other's mouth.

Veronica said, "You're gross."

"So is that." Sonya was laughing so hard she was afraid she would pee in the sleeping bag, so she ran out, squatted in a cluster of birch trees and peed.

Veronica came out of the tent, leaned over, and spit out her chewed cookie. Sonya realized that she hadn't actually eaten any of them. And a couple of evenings recently, when she was at Veronica's and they relaxed in the basement eating pizza and watching late-night reruns on TV, Sonya noticed that her friend had begun taking a saucer downstairs with them. She first carefully dabbed the top of her slice with a napkin to draw off the excess oil, then just as deliberately selected a few olive and pepper pieces from it and put those on the saucer, setting aside the picked-over wedge. As Sonya worked her way through three whole slices with additional grated cheese, Veronica held her saucer in one hand and with the other put a vegetable bit in her mouth, one at a time, and chewed it slowly. Almost as if she were savoring them, as Sonya often watched her grandfather do with coffee grounds and apple peels, except that there was so little of it she gave herself to savor. And it wasn't after a meal; it was the meal. Now, with the cookie, she hadn't even done that before spitting it out.

Beside her in the birch trees Veronica whispered, "I hope the neighbors don't see us."

Back in the tent she said, "I'm warm now. Let's get on top of our bags."

When they were settled on top, Sonya pulled her nightshirt up. "My legs are hot," she said.

"Mine, too," Veronica said, and she rolled her nightgown up to her waist. She reached over and snapped the elastic on Sonya's underwear, who then did that to hers.

They were quiet, catching their breath after laughing. Then Veronica moved so close, whispering, that Sonya smelled the moisture of sun and grass. "Pretend your hand is a million bugs crawling over my stomach."

Sonya ran her hand along Veronica's stomach. "Does it tickle?"

"A little," said Veronica. "I'll do it to you." She ran her fingers back and forth over Sonya's stomach, then moved her hand down, past her belly button, and drew circles along the top of her legs. "Could these be dolphins swimming around an island?"

"They could be." Then Sonya touched Veronica along the top of her legs and her belly, making a circle around her crotch. "Now the dolphins could be leaping out of the water," she said, her hand briefly raising and then landing again on her friend's warm skin. "Does it tickle now?"

"Kind of. It feels weird."

"It does to me, too."

Sonya wanted to ask whether Veronica felt OK, since she had spit out the cookie, but she knew that her friend wasn't feeling sick. She wanted to ask, rather, why she had not eaten any, but, embarrassed by their closeness, neither said anything else for a while. Their hands dipped by turns for several more minutes, each holding her breath in anticipation.

Then, their hands still again, Veronica said, "Ask me how to spell 'develop.'"

Sonya was confused at first by the request. "You know how to spell it. Why do you—"

"Please, just ask me." There was anxiety in her voice, and Sonya thought she had started to cry.

"How do you spell 'develop'?"

"D-e-v-e-l-o-p." Now Veronica was crying. "It doesn't have an 'e' on the end, like envelope does."

"What is it, Veronica? What's the matter?"

"I missed it yesterday on our weekly quiz. That puts me two words behind the highest score." Her first miss had come the week before last.

"It's OK to miss one sometimes." When Sonya's attempt to reassure her friend did not appear to be working, she added, "Hey, really. It is."

"But it was one of the easier words, and I know how to spell it."

"I know you do, and next time it comes up, you will know it."

"They don't come up again. There isn't one repeated the whole year. That's Mr. Jenning's rule, remember?"

"Next time you will probably know them all, anyway."

"Do you think so?" Veronica started to calm down.

"I'm sure. Besides, everyone knows that you are the best speller in the class, even if you missed one."

"I know." She had stopped crying now. "I feel better," she said, crawling back into her sleeping bag.

Then they drifted to sleep in the safe cave of the tent, under a net of night sky, while the warmth from the only time they would touch each other that way floated up alongside forgotten words that others had spoken in the dark to join the sound of trees rustling in the yard and now and then a car driving slowly through the neighborhood.

The house was filled with wafts of cigarette smoke, and bursts of laughter poured from the dining room and rocked the house. Sonya had been at Veronica's for dinner. She stepped into the dining room, kissed her mother, and said hello to her parents' friends on her way to the bathroom. Then she took a shower, letting the water rinse completely through her long brown hair, imagining a waterfall, a gorge.

When she got out, her father called to her from his seat at the head of the table. She glanced in at the table covered with crumpled napkins, wine bottles, and, since a few of their friends smoked, full ashtrays. Everyone appeared to be in a bleary after-feast daze induced by wine, laughter, and raucous argument, the usual Friday night atmosphere of their house.

"Come here," he called again, making a sweeping gesture with his arm. She walked over and stood beside him. He slid his arm around her waist.

"Hey, you were in the shower awhile, kid." Then he elaborated for their guests. "She was probably thinking about boys. My girls are at that age, you know." He laughed. Recently he had asked Lois and her friend Nancy, one evening when she had joined the Hudsons for dinner, whether they yet had "boys on the brain," and told them that if they didn't yet they soon would. "There and elsewhere," he added with a chuckle. The girls had looked at each other, shrugged and blushed.

Now Sonya stepped away from his arm and focused her attention on a ridge of lasagne left along the edge of the plate closest to her. She felt her mother's protective eyes but was too embarrassed to return the glance. No one said anything.

Then her father said, "Want some lasagne? Grab a plate." He smacked her on the bottom. "I'll heat some up for you."

"No. I ate at Veronica's," Sonya finally said, not looking at him or at anyone, and left the room.

The next morning she overheard her parents in the kitchen, washing the last night's dishes. When her father asked what he had done, her mother said, "Well, you thoroughly embarrassed the hell out of Sonya."

"Oh, Christ," he said. His resigned sigh was audible from the adjacent room.

Thinking about it—going out, talking, wearing clean clothes, explaining, then coming to her room again, and everything else Sonya managed to fit into the category of "it"—exhausted her. But she had promised her mother that she would think of it. Think of talking to someone. To try she sat cross-legged in the middle of her floor and looked at stacks of drawings, most of them on heavyweight textured paper, around her room. She catalogued them in her head, counting really, and told herself that tomorrow she would make a permanent mental note, or perhaps even a physical, paper, one, of just how many were in each spot and not only that, but record the information in her drawing notebook with some kind of order. For now she tabulated them by number (to tabulate by color or by size would be much more involved): there were three leaned up against the closet door; there were two stacks of four each against her bookcase; fourteen prints leaning individually along the walls; and several more loosely placed at the base of her bed, beside her desk, and scattered on the floor. She would think of those numbers, how each existed in its own place now, how each in another life had been a silver curve of spoon or the strength of a snow shovel's wooden handle, the green glass of a bead that clung to Elinor's wrist, a bustled and polished tap from Lois's trumpet. That's what numbers had. She would think of these; she had promised her mother she would.

8

A Small Piece Of Blue Glass

At the beginning of June of that year a new girl had sat down beside Sonya in French class. They smiled at each other instantly, as if with prior acquaintance, unself-consciously. A few days later in the cafeteria she noticed on the table near her seat a note with her name on it. She unfolded it to find "Bonjour" in meticulous letters exactly centered on the piece of lined notebook paper. Swiveling in her seat, she searched the noisy room. A couple of tables over from hers she saw the new student, Odessa Siegler, looking at her, her thick black hair wild off her shoulders. Sonya refolded the paper neatly and tucked it in the pocket of her jeans.

"Come to my house later," Odessa said to Sonya that afternoon after French.

"Sure."

After school on the walk to Odessa's house she asked, "Where is your name from?"

"It's where my grandfather, my mother's father, was born," she explained. "He told my parents when I was born that he wanted them to name me something that would make them remember where her side of the family was from."

"Where is Odessa?"

"In the Soviet Union. A city of many lights at the edge of a glimmering sea. That's what my grandfather says, anyhow. My parents were born here, and my brother was already five."

"What did they name him?"

"Frank."

"Oh." They laughed. "Your name's pretty. I've never heard of anyone with that name."

When they reached the house, a two-story rambling clapboard, and went into the living room, Sonya scanned the boxes stacked in a few of the corners, piles of newspapers and magazines on the floor, and a number of lamps with dangling, beaded shades, some of those on the floor, too.

"Do you still have a lot of unpacking to do?"

"Actually, we are all moved in. It always looks like this."

Sonya started to apologize, but Odessa quickly added, "My parents like to collect antiques. Some of the items are just plain collectibles," her word emphasized with a chuckle and accompanied by the curl of finger quotes. "Almost antiques. This is nothing really, you should have seen our other place. They got rid of some stuff when we moved here."

In the kitchen, while Odessa poured them each a glass of juice, Sonya noticed the stacks of china and velvet utensil boxes, each slot filled, on the table, as if in preparation for a royal banquet. There was also a wooden case of several pairs of old eyeglasses, the kind with the pinch clasp for the nose-bridge, dusty and looking up.

Lining the stairway were portraits of various sizes, all sorts of painted faces gazing out from under the ornate frames. "Who are all these people?"

"Beats me," Odessa said laughing. "My grandmother got each of those on sale somewhere, and she could tell you the place, date, and price of every one."

Sonya had never seen a room like hers. From its ceiling a twisted piece of dried grapevine hung from one end of the room to the other, and along one wall on a table stood three fish tanks with rocks in a couple inches of water.

"What's in these?" She walked over and checked for any sign of movement.

"Those are my rocks."

"What kind?" Sonya had not yet met someone in school who shared her interest in stones.

"One tank is for stream rocks, one for ocean rocks, and one for field stones."

Some of Sonya's were glued neatly to the inside of a lidless cigar box and labeled with a fine-point marker. Her lucky stones were different; those were in her box along with some shells. She wanted to ask why they were in glass tanks, but she thought she could figure it out herself. Odessa anticipated her question.

"This way I can see them from over here." She was across the room, putting away her school books.

"Oh," Sonya said, upon closer inspection realizing that each tank had a piece of paper designating the origin taped to the side of it, in the meticulous lettering of her note. "They look neat in here. So you collect, too."

"Yeah, I guess I do. I like to see how they look in water."

"I believe in lucky stones," Sonya said. "I keep some in a box my grandfather gave me. Those are my collectibles."

"How can you tell if a stone is lucky?"

"You hold it in your palm and see if you can feel water moving around it."

Odessa walked over and looked at her so intently, the blue of her eyes turning the room to glass, that Sonya, a little dizzy, asked, "Will you show me your school pictures?"

She took out a photo album and they sat on the floor as she showed Sonya pictures of her family, old friends at her other school, and herself.

Later, as they stood on the back porch, Odessa reached down and held Sonya's hand.

"Thanks for coming over," she said.

"Thanks for having me over."

On the walk home her left hand stayed warm, and with that a new time began.

Frequently they went to Odessa's after school. Or they hung out in the Hudsons' backyard and talked, or took Sonya's box of stones and shells out and spread them all in the grass. Then they picked up each and assessed, one piece, one color, at a time, what they liked best about it. After studying each one, they returned them all to the box.

Whatever they were doing, whether examining rocks or lounging in the grass or on the floor discussing pictures, one of them might rest her hand on the other's shoulder or leg. It was not out of the ordinary for them to be sitting on the stairs in school beside each other one day and for Odessa to have her head against Sonya's shoulder. Both had recently begun their periods, and she had had cramps all morning; hers were worse than

Sonya's, and now she felt nausea coming on. A couple of boys from their class strode by, saw them, and stopped to look at the girls. One of them pointed and said, "Gross! Look at those two!" Odessa lifted her head from Sonya's shoulder, and they stopped talking. Then the other one said, "Oh, how sweet," and grabbed his friend's arm, tried to rest his head against it. The first one pulled away and yelled, "Hey, watch it, you horny fag!" Then they began shoving each other. A few of their friends ran by and pushed them too, and one of them shouted, "Who wants it up the butt?" The whole group stumbled down the hall, laughing. But the girls sat beside each other until they felt calm again before they stood up, resumed their day.

Often that summer they were thirteen they rode their bikes to Saginaw Lake, a reservoir in a valley where towns once stood. Sometimes they stayed an hour or two, sometimes packed a lunch and stayed longer.

"Do you think they moved all the houses first?" Sonya asked as they lounged on the sandy beach one July afternoon, after having cooled off in the water. Marie had explained the difference between a natural lake and a reservoir; though the terms were sometimes interchanged, they did not have identical meaning. She appreciated that science aimed for precision. And she wanted her daughters to appreciate that, too.

"I don't know. If they didn't, imagine all those catfish and eels and striped sunfish swimming in and out of doorways and windows and drifting in rooms."

"And think of all those tables and chairs, dressers and toothbrushes," Sonya said. She closed her eyes and imagined a lost weightless world of abandoned daily items, saw sun streaming through soundless rooms. She opened her eyes, rolled on her side toward Odessa. Her hair was so dark that sometimes when it was wet it seemed to have deep green braided into it. They wove their hands together.

"Think of all those rings, all that jewelry, and no one sees it." Among the pieces her family collected were pendants and earrings.

"All those pictures and mirrors." In the reflection in Odessa's eyes, this close, she saw clear wells, smooth steps down into a pool of sky, saw, this close, the mottled stone in her earring. She was one of only a few girls in their grade who had pierced ears.

After keeping their hands together for a while without talking, they rolled against each other on the blanket. As they drifted toward sleep, Sonya breathed in heated coconut and sun beneath the immense blue of July, limitless. How could he when there was lake water for a body to plunge into move through even clouded with sand sometimes the blue above above sifted out the speckled green the body moved in its silk the light above the body stroked how could he leave that.

"I miss you at night," Sonya told her one afternoon as they hung their bathing suits and beach towels out on the clothesline in her friend's backyard.

Odessa lifted her T-shirt over her head. "Here," she said, standing in her shorts and bra, as she handed her the damp navy shirt she had worn over her suit that day. "Put this one on and give me yours."

Sonya laughed as she took off her striped T-shirt and gave it to her friend, who put it on, then she slipped the navy one on.

Odessa reached over and straightened the hem of the navy T-shirt, kept her hands on Sonya's hips, and said, "Don't ever give that back to me."

That night Sonya spread the T-shirt beneath her in bed. She slept on it, and folded it under her pillow during the day.

She still hung out with Veronica. Occasionally they went to the mall or downtown or slept over at each other's house and whispered in bed about friends or school. But seldom did the three of them spend time together. Veronica thought Odessa was weird. "Why does she have all those rocks and sticks in her room?" she asked one day, her tone slanted toward derision.

When Sonya explained, "She wants to be closer to the world," Veronica, puzzled, didn't ask anything else about her. Their ages were, for most, at the brink of easy judgment.

Odessa thought Veronica was boring. "Their living room feels like a museum—all you'd need is one of those maroon velvet ropes," she said to Sonya one day, explaining why she had felt uncomfortable at the other girl's house for lunch the day before. "I wanted to write my name in the carpet, just to mess it up a little. A snow angel would be cool, right in the middle of the room." Sonya, with alliances to both of them, laughed at this but did not say anything.

And Odessa thought it strange, too, that Veronica had invited them to lunch but that she hadn't eaten. She poured them juice, got a glass for herself, and then retrieved from the refrigerator sliced cheese, lettuce, tomatoes, condiments, pasta salad, and bread from the breadbox. After arranging all the ingredients neatly on a board on the table, she urged the two of them to make themselves a sandwich. They assembled theirs and waited for her to sit down, but when Veronica realized they were waiting, she said, "You two start eating. I told my mom I'd clean up the breakfast debris." As she rinsed dishes and loaded the dishwasher, she questioned Odessa about her old school, her classes, how French was progressing. She finally sat down just as the other two were finishing their lunch, and she poured herself a half a glass of juice.

"There's plenty of pasta salad left," Odessa offered.

"I'll have some a little later."

"We can sit with you now while you eat."

"No, thanks. But I'm glad you enjoyed it." Veronica sipped her juice.

On the bike ride back to Sonya's, they had puzzled over this.

"Does she always do that, not eat anything at mealtime?"

"Sometimes we have snacks at her place, like pizza or popcorn at night." Sonya thought about Veronica's habit of selecting a bit off the top of a slice, but then not consuming any of the rest. With popcorn, she sometimes licked salt from her palm, but didn't actually eat much of the popcorn itself. Reflecting, she needed to expand her answer to Odessa; she wasn't certain, though, which direction to expand in.

"I guess sometimes, well, lots of times, she doesn't eat much, but she always seems to be busy with the food or moving it around her plate some-how. I know that sounds silly, but that's what it's like. Not exactly like eating, though. More like rearranging."

"Do you ever say anything?"

"A few times I've said something like, this is delicious—I talk it up—you should have some, but it has never made any difference. She has an answer for everything. Like that maybe she will later or that it's her cramps or that she has to clean up first."

"Did hers just start, too?"

"She didn't tell me when it began. She just started talking about having cramps."

"Has she always been like that, I mean about food?"

"Most of the time I've known her, but it wasn't as bad when I first knew her."

"Doesn't it seem strange?"

"Yeah, it does, I never quite got used to it."

"Maybe we should talk to her mom about it."

"Her mom's always busy. I never even see her."

"What about her dad?"

"Talk about strange. He's a bank president or something, lots of evening board meetings. Or council meetings. It all sounds very official. I wonder if he even notices."

"Well, we could ask Veronica herself directly about it." Odessa was hopeful they could do something to intervene.

"Let's try that."

Maybe it was the afternoon sun warming them as they rode down tree-lined side-streets or perhaps the joy being with each other or their anxious speculations about their friend that inspired them, after a pause, to begin talking spontaneously about food.

They had slowed their bikes to a stop at a cross street, waiting for traffic, when Sonya, catching her breath, looked over at Odessa standing so close to her that she could smell her perspiration and see it glisten on her hairline and neck, and said, "I love blueberry pie when it's warmed and a blob of vanilla ice cream on the top slides down the pie, turning purple, but the center of the ice cream stays frozen. And you don't know if you should eat it with a fork or a spoon."

"Or your hands. How about when you eat fruit with your hands, like a peach? Or never mind a peach, how about a plain old tomato with salt?"

"Salt and mayonnaise." Sonya caught her breath.

"How about when you have onion soup and you have that layer of melted cheese sitting on top waiting for you?"

"Soup? That could be tasty. What about pasta and sauce on a winter day?"

"A December day," Odessa agreed, "but then you end up back at blueberry pie because you have to have dessert on a cold day. A pan of brownies would do."

"A pan? Is that what you said?" They had forgotten that they were stopped for traffic. Sonya laughed. "A pan? Excuse me, I'll have a pan of brownies please."

"You know you could eat it," Odessa said, reaching her hand out to rest it on the handlebar of her friend's bike.

"I know I could. You'd have some with me, too."

"Who's the one talking about ice cream on the side awhile ago?"

"That too."

They suddenly realized that there was a lull in traffic and that it didn't matter. Neither one wheeled her bicycle forward to cross. Instead, they looked at each other and laughed some more. Sonya was aware, as if in clay relief announcing itself against other details, saying here, here, of Odessa's hand resting beside hers still on the handlebars. She felt the slight weight of it, pressure of it, through the bike's frame against her leg. The afternoon was warm, their T-shirts were damp, and since there was not one vehicle that second flying past, the roadway welcomed them. It might as well have been a carpet rolled out at a banquet hall, the whole extravagant crusted, creamed, stirred, ornate, and delicate event placed against some length of linen starched crisp, laid out before them for the taking. And they looked at each other and caught their breath.

Now she was less excited than usual about visiting her grandparents, because it meant being away from her friend. And some of the old car games that she and Lois had played when they were younger, like the one that involved spotting colors or the one of listing as many different state license plates as they could, no longer held their interest at all. They traded mood rings for the drive to Mercy Hill, tried cards for a while, and each wrote a letter, but Sonya still felt restless.

The first few days they were there their grandfather showed them some new plants and a few other changes since their last visit. Their father helped him build some tool shelves for one of the greenhouses, and their mother spent some time inside with their grandmother. By mid-week Lois and their mother were outside picking cherries, but Sonya wandered around the fields instead.

Her grandfather came over and stood beside her as she picked up some rocks and threw them, one at a time, into a field.

"Do you want to help your grandmother? She's planning to do something with those cherries."

"No. I don't feel like it now, Grandpa. Maybe later."

"You know when I feel sad, I think about all that water, lots of it."

"What water?"

"Lakes and rivers, ponds, or sometimes a larger body of water."

"But you don't live near any large body of water." She knew that New Hampshire had a sliver of Atlantic coast. Their parents had taken her and Lois to see the ocean a few times, extending the road trip with a circuitous return route. She knew that it was far enough away she couldn't smell the salt from Mercy Hill.

"It's all up here," he said, tapping his head. "It's all in the loft. I've got tremendous sweeps of it."

"You just think about it?" She tried to imagine a map of just New Hampshire's streams and rivers.

He nodded. "I think and think about it."

She thought of water imprints, veined aquamarine, pressed in his memory like the leaves she had collected and labeled in her science class, made permanent by two sheets of wax paper and the seal an iron gave them. "And then you feel better?"

"Yes, I do." He observed Sonya thoughtfully, then added, "Or when I was in love. I thought about it then, too."

Sonya did not ask him about love. "Maybe I could see if Grandma wants help."

He rested his hand on the top of her head as they turned away from the field. Inside, she helped her grandmother, though she did so without talking very much.

One evening Sonya, unable to sleep, got up from her cot. Lois was asleep, all the adults outside. She tip-toed to the open window and peered out to see her mother and grandmother off in the side yard admiring plants, and closer, her father and grandfather standing together, their shadows elongated across the grass, a bottle of beer in their hands.

"I'll tell you, Herbert, men are built for independence. That's what the old seafarers and explorers were about." His voice was subdued, but Sonya thought she heard something decisive in his tone.

"Yes, they probably were." Her grandfather, as always, listened carefully and was thoughtful about the ideas of another. "But you know, a lot has changed since those days."

"Didn't you feel it yourself, when you went with your fishing group up to Alaska? Couldn't a man survive up there by his own two hands, pull in a fish when he needed it, grow a line or two of beans, brew a batch on the side?"

"Well, I felt it for a day, and the rest of the trip was an adventure of course, but it stopped right there. I came back here, realized how much I had missed the sound of her in the next room." Sonya thought she saw him rub his ear scar. "It was an adventure. But survival, no, that is something else for me. That's here."

Not wanting to hear her father's next words, Sonya closed the window and slipped under the sheet. The image of her father foraging alone in the Alaskan wilderness numbed her with worry. Then she pulled the sheet up over her head, swam alongside Odessa and dreamed way out into the reservoir, with its sacs of cool water, drifted to sleep.

Near the end of the week, still preferring solitude, she took a walk along some of the more rural roads by herself. Sometimes, on a cloudy day, the reservoir had the appearance of melted nickels poured on the surface. Vats and vats, bins, barrels of nickels. Ships filled with nickels. Cargo. All melted down, then poured out over the water. Odessa would understand that. She lived in a house filled with items from ships. Sonya could see them now, the utensil trays, the beaded lamps, the decades-old journals. Stacks of albums.

By the time she returned to the house, her parents had gone into town and her grandfather had begun working out in the greenhouses. She didn't know where Lois was.

Sonya stepped into the living room and saw her grandmother sitting in her rocker with her head resting back and her eyes closed, her feet up on the brown hassock, and the shades drawn. Her purse, usually on her dresser, was on a table nearby, its black vinyl and gold clasp gleaming despite the dimmed light. It was the same purse she had had for several years. Sonya noticed that upon returning from a trip into town, her grandmother always wiped the purse off with a cloth and put it back on her dresser. Though she had never seen the inside of it, she guessed there couldn't be much in there; it still had its narrow stiff shape, no creases at all. Maybe there was a Kleenex in there, a change purse and a wallet. Maybe she carried her rosary. The inside of her mother's purse she knew well because Marie often let them, when she and Lois were younger, pour it out on the living room floor and play with the contents. They always found a lot to marvel at: not just the jar of hand lotion and the glass tube of nut-colored musk oil with its mysterious scent, the stitched leather wallet and the oval plastic change purse with the slit that opened when squeezed. She also had a pad of paper; some pens and pencils; often a county map, which changed every time they moved to a new place; sometimes a spare pair of earrings or a necklace; a slender pocket-knife; a well-thumbed field guide to wildflowers; an old throat lozenge tin which she used to carry gum; sometimes a package of crackers or a piece of fruit; paper clips; a stapler; keys on a braided ring; and, the girls' favorite item of all: two stubs of worn chalk, the chunky sidewalk variety, one blue and one green. These Marie had found left outside one day when they were drawing. She had meant to put them away but forgot she had slipped them inside her purse. She told the girls, the first time they discovered the stubs among the wondrous objects, that she decided to keep them with her so that when she was studying or later when she had an interview, and dug for something in her purse, she would see the chalk and be reminded of the lovely drawings they used to make on the sidewalk. The girls' joy at hearing this increased at each reminding, as they saw the pieces of chalk stay among the honored contents when their mother switched from the lined burlap with the flowers on the outside to the sturdy brown leather with the long wide strap.

Sonya didn't want to wake her grandmother, but she must have sensed her there, because she opened her eyes. That her purse was now on the table meant she had been about to go somewhere.

"Grandma, how come you didn't go into town with Mom and Dad?"

Glenda's annoyance shadowed her words. "It was too much to do today." She quickly added, "I don't need anything from town. I wanted to get Lois started on her work."

She explained that Lois was helping her out by cleaning some jars in the basement. Sonya offered to help too, so her grandmother went into the kitchen, Sonya following and watching from the doorway, and got her a rag and a bowl. At the sink Glenda ran the tap, holding her hand under it, waiting for it to turn hot. Drops of water splashed up along the ceramic sink while Sonya watched. Clear drops up in light and back down in the basin what was penance for? her hand turned up under the water palm up waiting and the water came down from what other day waiting for what else turned up under the water until steam rose. She filled the bowl, shut the water off, and carried the bowl and rag over to her granddaughter, watching from the doorway.

Sonya crept down the old basement steps, calling her sister's name.

"I'm over here."

She looked toward the root cellar and saw Lois standing before floor-to-ceiling shelves along one wall, wiping off a jar by the glow of the bare bulb hanging near the center of the basement. There was a bowl of water beside her on the dirt floor.

"Grandma told me you were doing some stuff for her and that I could help," Sonya said, walking over and setting her bowl beside her sister's.

"She wanted me to dust all these jars," Lois whispered, gesturing toward the shelves. They were stocked several deep in neat rows, the curves of various colored liquid shapes receding into the darkness of the back of the rows. Etched in pencil on the side of some of the shelves, and not in any apparent order, was a year designation: 1958 on one, 1963 on another. Sonya recognized faint cupped peach halves and the muted red of peeled tomatoes, a multitude of berries, suspended. She was reminded of the time the year before in science class when their teacher passed around a jar with a frog floating in formaldehyde and explained that the next year they would learn dissection, beginning with special earthworms. The prospect had made her a little nauseous. Now she thought of the sweetness of fruit to bring herself back.

When she realized that a number of jars in the front were shiny, she offered to begin the ones behind them. "We can work backwards down each row."

"I'm doing only the ones in front," Lois said, still whispering. "If she looks over here from the stairs, they will all look clean. No one can see the ones behind anyway."

Sonya covered her mouth as she began to laugh. "Lois!" Then she rinsed her rag and picked up another jar in the front of a row.

Just then they heard footsteps on the stairs. "How are you girls doing with your work? Is your grandmother going to be proud of you?" She came all the way down the stairs and walked over to them.

Surveying the shelves, she said, "The ones in front look nice and clean."

Lois began an explanation. "We are starting there and then—"

"I asked you to wipe all the jars." Their grandmother, though she didn't raise her voice, was clearly annoyed.

"With me cleaning too, it won't take much time to do all of them." With Sonya mediating, she acquiesced.

"Don't fritter away the time. Try to get them finished soon. Your parents will be back shortly and we'll need to get supper started."

"Yes, Grandma."

When she spun around and walked toward the stairs, Lois rolled her eyes to the ceiling and Sonya shrugged.

Though Glenda's back was to them, she tilted her head to the side a degree, as if so slight a movement could make visible to her, her grand-daughters' expressions. Apparently it did, because instead of heading up the stairs she walked over to a wall cabinet, opened it, and pulled down from the shelf a plastic bag. She turned to the girls, watching her.

"These I use for, well," Glenda said, gesturing a half arc up toward the kitchen, "cleaning around the house." She carefully unwound the brittle rubber band and opened the cloudy plastic bag to reveal about twenty toothbrushes, worn Pepsodent lettering on some of the handles, the faded bristles pushed apart. A scent of bleach and of dust rose up with the opening.

"The two of you could use these for the basement."

Lois's mouth hinted at moving, in a glimmer so slight only Sonya, from her thoughtful intention on her sister's beloved idiosyncrasies, would have deciphered it.

Then she spoke. "Do you use these on the basement windows?"

"I haven't yet, but I think it is a good idea. Or for cleaning the light bulbs."

The briefest hesitation was all Lois needed to formulate her compromise. "Why don't we concentrate on dusting off those jars instead?" And then emphasis on a word that she knew would appeal to her grandmother. "We will stick with the rags, for efficiency."

Glenda, after an exasperated sigh, cinched the top again with the rubber band, closing off the memory of every day begun with one of those brushes, though it might have been spent in darkness or in solitary rocking, far from the origin of the radio toothpaste jingle, kin to cigarette box-top, highway, open road for someone who might have known hope. But not for her.

And so they came to an agreement. Damp rags instead, strips of their grandfather's old work shirts, and the cleaning of only jars. An agreement on more than the method and object of cleaning. Without looking at the girls, Glenda returned the bag to the cabinet and walked up the stairs.

These now among the materials that could fill a person's mouth. Now too the chipped and faded colors of her grandmother's broken days, of days decided already by the time she brushed her teeth in the morning—the trace still in the handle, along with the bleach scent absorbed, making permanent all that speechlessness. Not an act of clearing out, of cleaning one's mouth to make way for measured words; no, instead the filling in, closing off, the mumble of clamped pain, bits of words.

They figured out a system to take turns having one of them lift and hold the jar, the other wipe it off. The holder set each one aside, and then together they would return them to the shelf when they were dry. Occasionally, to make the task more entertaining, they would think of what the fruit resembled.

When this distraction became too funny, they resorted to serious considerations, like wondering whether it mattered if they did not return the jars in the same order they were in originally in each row, and wondering why, if this stuff was in jars, the process was called canning. They speculated, too, about when the jars on the unmarked shelves had been stored, whether their mother had picked any of it, and how often their grandparents ate it.

Did 1941 have more sun in it than 1953? Were the shorter days of one year warmer than the longest of another? What month in their mother's girlhood bear the most fruit? What exact Tuesday, 1949, did this plum fall from a shaded tree branch and into their grandfather's waiting hand? Was it a Tuesday? Did he stop sometimes in his picking, lean back, devour a plum in a couple of bites, and with the juice running down his throat toss the pit in the grass and get to work again? What was it all about? How much could science measure?

After most of the lower rows were finished, Sonya went upstairs and asked their grandmother for a stepladder so they could reach the higher shelves. She was glad to accommodate this request, no longer angry about the girls' earlier deception, offering to clean their bowls and bring them fresh water.

When they were completely finished and brought their rags and water upstairs to the kitchen, she took out a plate of ribbon candy and, though it was just before mealtime, asked if they would like some with a glass of juice. They accepted the juice but declined the treat, saying they would rather wait to eat when their parents returned.

Upon their parents' return, their grandmother praised the girls' efforts and took Marie into the basement to show her what they had done. In front of her mother Marie praised them, too.

But that night when she said goodnight to her daughters she reminded them that they would soon be leaving. Then she asked them, whispering, if they had minded doing work for their grandmother.

"It wasn't too bad," they said.

"Was anything strange? I mean, did she do anything—"

Sonya said, "No, it was fine."

But Lois asked, "Like what?"

"Oh, nothing—well—you girls know she can be stern. Thanks for helping her."

And at the end of the visit, still missing her new friend, Sonya thought the ride home seemed even longer, almost tedious, this time. She and Lois talked, occasionally dozed, and took studied glances out the car window at the passing landscapes. Among the questions Sonya contemplated was how Odessa had spent her recent days, when she had last seen her own grandmother, how her family had become collectors.

How had Glenda come to be this way? The girls had seen her winter rubber boots, with the fake fur at the end of the central zipper, wrapped in a clear plastic bag in the hall closet, and could picture her out shoveling the driveway in them. She always appeared able to do the same physical labor as their grandfather could do. But the sweat of labor had not opened her, no exaltation in the sureness of muscle. Everything about her had seemed sealed away, out of reach of sunlight's bending and fading, sunlight's own work on an object or a person. Though Marie spoke fondly of her grandparents, Glenda never mentioned her own parents to the girls. They knew she had grown up on a farm. But there was a barrier to the past, a wall of stone, perhaps built by hand, through which no light came. Nor snow or rain, or any hint of another kind of day. There was but rare mention of her siblings, and never with any significant background, merely a casual detail tossed into conversation with Marie that they overheard. Always in the past tense, too. All they had with Glenda was the here and now, the wiping of the beige rubber mat she stood on at the sink, the cord pull maneuvering to get the blind rising and, later, lowering at a level in the single kitchen window, the even rocking from the living room and its hypnotic sound. What was the chaos all this was measured against? Why did she keep cleaning when everything always shone so clean already? Did it take so much of her to maintain all of that? Maybe so. But was there no other her, no extra her, for everything else in life?

Apparently all the reveling was in Herbert. But he worked too. He also whistled sometimes, or hummed, or read *National Geographic*, occasionally aloud to the girls before bed, explicating in great detail the corresponding photos, or exhaled with delight after a lengthy draught of crisp beer on a hot summer day. Perhaps the sadness that weighted Glenda down was irrevocable. Permanent, as were the hills around the town in which she lived, the predictable nor'easters, the summer cattle lounging, bristling at flies.

When the Hudsons returned home, the girls caught up with each other quickly, filling in details on daily happenings, sleeping over, riding their bikes. When Sonya stayed over at Odessa's house, they slept beside each other. On a humid August night they had just flipped the lights out, and the stars affixed to the ceiling were glowing behind the grapevine. Both windows were fully open, the sheets tossed at the bottom of the bed. Every once in a while a breeze moved over them. As she fell asleep, Odessa rolled over on her stomach and took Sonya's hand in hers. The air held the dust of screens and the shadow of rain. She thought of rich dirt, then of stepping out into the night on the edge of a grassy plain. In the expanse the darkness brought the smell of damp grass closer, and as far as she could imagine all around were stars sprinkled like salt crystals across the sky. Her father had started with those easier to identify, the Dippers, Orion. Her mother had explained the white residue on a T-shirt, the concept of salinity, the extravagance of nature, in even what it left behind. An ache of openness, exhilaration, when everything else, everything but all she needed, dropped away.

One day Sonya was relaxing out in the backyard pondering the sky when Veronica rode up on her ten-speed. She had been to a baseball game with some friends; she liked one of the players.

"Hey," she said, joining her friend in the grass.

"Hey. How was the game?"

"Quite exciting. Rob's team broke a tie in the final inning. When we celebrated with ice cream after, he told me that Tim Sanders likes you."

"Did you have some ice cream?" That prospect drew Sonya's complete attention. Not a sundae of course, but maybe she'd had a small cone or at least one scoop in a cup.

"What? I didn't have any. I had a glass of water and they had ice cream. Did you hear me? He told me that Tim likes you."

"Tim Sanders? The kid with curly hair? How does he know me?"

"He saw you and Odessa at the lake a few times and thinks you're cute."

Sonya remembered then seeing him with his friends from a distance, jumping and diving, holding each other underwater. "Oh," she said.

"Want me to tell Rob to tell him you think he's attractive, or at least cute?"

"I don't think he's cute. I don't even know him."

"Why don't you go out with him and get to know him? Maybe you'd be enthralled. Rob could arrange it."

Sonya didn't say anything, though she contemplated the use of "enthralled." She thought of complimenting Veronica, despite the exaggeration; it wasn't every day that a person could work a word like that into a conversation.

"He seems nice, guys with blond hair usually are pretty decent," Veronica continued. "Robert Redford, for one. Speaking of, we could all see a film."

Sonya resumed analyzing the cloud formations. "I'll think about it," she said.

"You think too much," said her friend, standing up. She hopped on her bike and rode away.

That night she phoned. "Plans are set for Friday night. The four of us are seeing a film at the mall. My mom can bring us and pick us up."

"Oh," Sonya said.

"It's a Redford series. Decide if you want to see *The Great Gatsby* or *Butch Cassidy and the Sundance Kid*. I favor the Newman flick; his coolness is beyond measure."

"Fine by me," Sonya said, without explaining that it was the outfits of Cassidy and Sundance, particularly their splendid leather vests, that most held her interest, that made the proposed mall outing endurable.

Veronica called her the following day, too. "What are you wearing, Sonya?"

"My cut-offs and my red striped T-shirt."

"No, not now. What are you wearing Friday?"

"I don't know."

"Wear something pretty. How about that white shirt with the embroidered flowers on it and some nice summer pants?"

"That sounds good."

"Do you want to borrow some eyeliner?" Veronica had begun wearing that shopping, along with blush and eyeshadow, and had recently suggested that Sonya fix her full eyebrows with a little painless plucking. A few minutes of extra time in the morning, a whole day's worth of benefit—echoes of what had emerged the year before in school, snips here and there overheard in the hallways.

Her response was the same this time. "No. That's OK, thanks anyway."

"At least braid your hair," Veronica said, her parting advice before hanging up. Sometimes Sonya gathered it with a rubber band or a bandana, and it hung thick down the middle of her back, though she always brushed it out first.

Tim was tall and thin, and as they rode to the mall Sonya thought he smelled leathery, maybe like a baseball glove left in the sun.

"I saw you and Odessa at the lake on Wednesday," he said. "You hang out together a lot, huh?"

"Yeah. She's cool," Sonya said. "I saw you, too. What were you guys looking for?" She had seen them searching the water after jumping on each other.

"One of the guys lost his retainer. But we found it."

At the theatre Rob put his arm around Veronica, and soon after Tim slid his around Sonya. It might as well have been a curtain rod across her shoulders, but she smiled at him.

As Veronica's mother pulled into Rob's driveway to drop off the boys, Rob said, "There's going to be a party next Friday near my house. You two want to go with us?" He addressed Veronica, who then looked at Sonya.

"Your mom would let you," she said. "Can I, Mom?" she called to the front seat.

"If you're home by eleven."

Veronica said to Rob, "That would be fun." She waited for agreement from her friend.

Sonya heard a far-away "OK" drift out of her mouth.

That night they sat on Veronica's bed with a row of Oreos. "I love Rob's hands," she said. "I feel crazy inside when he holds my hand. What did it feel like when Tim had his arm around you?" She lined up the cookies along the plate's ridge.

Sonya had twisted a cookie apart and was scraping the inside off with her front teeth. "It felt like he had his arm resting on my shoulders," she said.

"Do you want him to kiss you?"

"I don't know yet." She did not tell Veronica that the idea hadn't occurred to her.

The next night at dinner Sonya asked her mother about the party.

"Yes, I don't see why not," she said. "But be home at a reasonable time."

"Who is this kid anyway?" her father asked.

"A guy I know from school."

"He's totally cute," Lois offered, her eyebrows arching with enthusiasm.

"What's his family like?" he asked.

"I haven't met his family," Sonya said.

"You're going out with someone," his voice was rising, "and you don't know anything about him?"

"It's a party, Mitchell. She isn't marrying the guy," her mother said.

"Listen, if it gets serious, your mother and I want to check him out."

"OK by me," she said, wondering what the big deal was. She reached for another ear of corn. "Pass me the butter, Lo."

Her sister passed it to her and smiled.

While their parents were out of town, the two oldest Gallagher brothers had gotten four cases of beer, a couple of dime bags, and five boxes of potato chips. At the beginning of the evening the seventeen-year-old stood up on the couch in his cut-offs and water buffaloes and announced the rules. "Don't wreck anything," he said.

Within an hour there were cans crushed on the floor, cigarette butts littering the coffee table, and from every room in the house drifted pitches of laughter and cursing that had climbed up onto the Jimi Hendrix riffs blasting from the living room stereo.

One of the hosts was rolling joints on the dining room table, then passing them into the living room. Sonya and Tim sat beside each other on the floor in the circle that had formed. She had seen older kids smoke before but hadn't tried pot herself. This time she watched more closely to see how it was done, and when the joint came to her, she too pinched it, held it to her lips and drew it in. As she passed it to Tim, she drank a gulp of beer to ease the burning in her throat.

After a few more had gone around, Tim said to her "Let's go outside," taking Sonya's hand and leading her through the crowded kitchen and out the back door. They walked to a secluded part of the yard and stood beneath the plentiful branches of a maple.

"Put your beer down," Tim said. They put their cans on the ground near the trunk. He faced Sonya and gently urged her back against the tree. He leaned against her, his hands fumbling up her shirt. He pressed his mouth into hers. She had to pull stifled breaths through her nose. His tongue squirmed like a damp fish trapped in her mouth. He reached down and stroked her crotch through her jeans. She ran her hand along the outside of his jeans and found his penis standing up, pushing up for air. He pressed himself against her and tried to unbutton her pants. Sonya steered his hand away each time. They stroked each other, then finished their beer and lay down in the grass. The house was lit up, and the loud murmur of voices that had floated out on the warm night air hovered over the yard, wrapped in the Allman Brothers notes that accompanied them out. When Sonya closed her eyes, the notes arched their backs sauntering, stepping by twos and threes across the grass, some lifting a heel up over it, others rolling down reveling grass-stained. The guitars themselves feeling sumptuous. She listened and meditated on what Odessa was doing that moment, what she was looking at in that long, long, moment. A leaf canopy? A lamp? An engraved spoon? A case of dusty eyewear, circles around an emptiness that had been color? Was it from another century? Was there music in that room? Music that her hands lifted from its delicate paper album sleeve. Were there notes making their way slowly around the curves in Odessa's ears? After a while, she and Tim sat up, picked up their beer cans, got to their feet, returned to the house.

Later, when Tim's father stopped in front of the Hudsons' house, Tim walked her to the front door. "Thanks for coming to the party with me."

"I had fun," Sonya said. "Thanks."

"I'll call you tomorrow," he said.

In the morning Sonya called Odessa and asked her to ride out to the reservoir. She packed a sandwich for each of them using the soybean spread her father had made, in its own special container in the fridge with the heart he drew out of beans on top. Her friend liked this recipe and never had it at her own house.

The first time Odessa tried the spread at the Hudsons', she was taken with the drawing too, and asked Sonya why he drew the heart. When Sonya explained that he had made the lunch treat with love, Odessa, surprised, had asked, "Your dad talks about that kind of stuff?"

"Sure, doesn't yours?"

"No, not really ever."

"Does your father hug you?"

"No, he never has done that either. Does yours?"

"Yes, he hugs us all the time." The bear grips, at times embarrassing for Sonya, she realized, talking with her friend, were something she had begun to feel proud of. "I'm sorry yours doesn't do that."

"Most fathers don't," Odessa said, shrugging, a tinge of sadness in her voice.

At the reservoir later, as they unfolded their towels in the sun, she asked, "How was the party?"

"I liked the music, some rock stuff. Otherwise it was boring."

"Tell me all about it, every boring detail."

"There isn't much to tell. Someone threw up in a planter out on the deck. Rob got so high he ate two one-pound bags of peanut M&Ms. Those were the highlights. Veronica said the cops came by later, but Tim and I had left by then."

She considered telling her friend about hearing a couple of older guys boisterously yell "jail bait!" at them as Tim led her through the kitchen again, after they had been in the yard. And that the younger guys within earshot had laughed too. Bait? She would not have been embarrassed to admit to Odessa that it took clarification from Veronica for her to figure out the comment, the technicality of Tim's age aside. A fact lost, Veronica had said, on the witless among them. But Sonya decided not to mention any of this, not wanting the offense of it to taint their time together, seep into the absolute thrill of lounging on their towels in the heat. That was theirs completely.

"Do you like him?" Odessa asked.

"I haven't decided yet. He's kind of got a nice smell."

They swam awhile, then cooler, ate their lunches before exploring for stones.

On the return ride, a few hours later, Odessa asked her to stay over.

That night in bed she said, "You smell good yourself, Sonya," and moved closer.

At home the next morning, her mother told her that Tim had called the night before and that he said he would call again, which he did that evening, asking her to go to a matinee with him the next day. She told him she couldn't because she and Odessa had plans to ride out to the reservoir, thanked him, said maybe on the weekend, and hung up.

All day at the reservoir Odessa was reserved. Whenever Sonya asked, "What is it?" or guessed something like, "Did you and your mom have a fight?" her friend said, without even a glance toward Sonya, "It's nothing." And when Sonya told her about her mother's new job teaching science, hoping her friend would be interested and ask further, Odessa said "That's great," then got up from the blanket and dove into the water. She spent the rest of the afternoon there, sometimes floating around on her back, her eyes closed. Sonya looked up from her towel every once in a while to check on her. Sometimes she was sitting out on a flat slab of rock, or poking at the lake bottom with a stick, bent over, as if searching for lost coins.

They rode their bikes back to Odessa's without saying a word, changed into shorts and T-shirts, and hung out their suits and towels on the clothesline. They made sandwiches and took them, with two drinks, up to Odessa's room, then sat on the floor and ate in silence.

Finally Sonya said, "Please tell me."

Odessa started to cry. She took Sonya by the hand and led her over to her bed. They sat down. "My dad was transferred again. We're moving at the end of the summer."

"What do you mean?" Sonya's thoughts were jumbled.

"He has to take the job. He says career-wise he has no choice."

"Why? You just got here."

"That's how big companies work," Odessa explained, pulling on Sonya's fingers without looking up at her. "Harpur Springs is just an office to them."

"Where?"

"Somewhere in California. Some stupid town. Some town I will hate my entire life."

"Why? I don't understand." Sonya's head hurt. Her throat knotted with fire, her voice came out twisted with tears. "Don't leave," she said. "You can live with us."

"My mom would never go for that."

They flung themselves back on the bed and, weary, gazed up at the grapevine.

"Stay here tonight," Odessa said.

Sonya nodded.

Later, they cried themselves tired enough, salt endlessly spent, then fell asleep.

The next evening at the dinner table Sonya's mother said, "Tim phoned you last night. He asked that you return his call."

"I don't care," she said, staring at her food. "I really don't."

"What is it? Did he do something to hurt your feelings?"

"No," she said, tears she had fought to keep in falling onto her plate.

"Sonya's upset because Odessa is moving." Lois had lured it out of her earlier.

"Oh, Sweetie," her mother said, and reached across the table to touch her arm. Her mother's hand was warm resting there.

Sonya picked up her plastic cup, drank the rest of her lemonade, then threw the cup against the dining room wall. Her father jumped quickly around the table, yanked her up by the arm, and slapped her on the bottom.

"Mitchell, leave her alone. She's upset."

"Well, she's too old to be acting like a child."

Sonya yelled through her crying, "Then you're a child too!"

"Go to your room until you are suitable company for the rest of us," her father yelled, the veins in his neck bulging.

As Sonya ran to the bedroom, she glanced back at Lois, who was looking at their father, her mouth moving pointedly, readying, and Sonya thought she could decipher from her lips a sting encouraging their mother to throw something at him. Lois had mentioned recently, when they overheard an argument, that their mother hadn't thrown anything in quite a while. Sonya, bracing, leaned now to catch Lois's eye, and when she did, she gave her sister a look that said *Do not say it.* Then Lois closed her mouth, looked at her food again.

From the bedroom Sonya heard the click of forks on plates, and an occasional sniffle from her mother and her sister as they finished the meal in silence.

Then her father said, "I'll clear tonight."

Lois was still holding back a bit as she told him, "I think you should wash and dry, too."

"Fair enough," he said.

Afterward, while he worked in the kitchen and Lois talked with Nancy on the phone, their mother went in the girls' bedroom to talk over the distress.

Sonya sat up as her mother settled on the edge of the bed and then moved wet strands of hair away from her daughter's eyes. Then she held her.

"I'm sorry I acted that way. It was childish."

"No need to apologize."

Sonya did not know what she would do without Odessa, but she didn't want her mother to worry about her, so she didn't say that. Instead she said, "How can I help her pack?" She thought of how much she had missed her on their week-long trip to her grandparents' in July, and began to cry again.

"I know, I know. Everything will be fine. You'll write to each other, and there is always the phone."

Sonya held her mother closer as the knot inside her grew tighter. After a while she said, "Want me to help with the dishes?"

"No. Don't worry. You're feeling pretty nicked. Why don't you rest or ride your bike or have a bowl of ice cream." She kissed Sonya's forehead, then stood up and walked to the door. She turned around. "I'm here if you need me."

"Thanks."

Her mother smiled at her, then closed the door. Sonya slept.

Later she told Veronica and Tim that during the upcoming few weeks she wanted to spend as much time with Odessa as she could. Tim said he would call her again at the end of August, and she and Veronica planned to call every few days to catch up with each other's news.

Sonya helped Odessa sort through her room, decide what, if anything, to discard, and helped her pack. Odessa gave her a plaster of Paris boat she had made in school, three rocks Sonya chose from her collection, and her kindergarten picture. Sonya gave her a drawing of a stream. The water, flowing the length of the picture, was bordered on both sides by a vineyard growing up to its edge. Along the banks were various stones of many sizes and colors, some with fossils in them. Two girls on their backs on a raft drifted downstream, fish jumping around them. Across the hypnotic blue sky hung the title of the picture, in cadmium yellow light, *Stepping into a River with Odessa*.

The day before the move the two girls rode to the reservoir. They found some fishing line. Sonya took off her bead bracelet and bit the string apart, then divided the ten colored beads, five for each, and they strung them with the line, which they had cut in half against a rock. They tied their new necklaces around each other's neck, stood back and admired them.

"These are cool," Odessa said.

"Yeah, let's never take them off."

"OK." They smiled.

A few days after her friend moved, Sonya walked to her empty house in the afternoon. With a stick she dug a hole in the lawn beneath the clothesline. From her pocket she took a small piece of dark blue glass, compressed sky, that they had found swimming, worn smooth by the water, and put it in the dirt. She pushed it down as far as she could. Then she covered it up and went home.

9

The Blinding White

When the radiant arc of summer had lost its beam, the days no longer floating high and dry but slipping into damp gray-coated afternoons, Sonya knew fall was here and that she would feel better if she could get interested in school. But nothing there much held her attention. Once home though, she usually dropped her books, changed into old jeans and a sweatshirt, and retreated into the basement. Her father had cleared a space for her on a low shelf, used as a desk, along one wall. Beneath the shelf he made a drawer, attached with brackets and fitted with retooled casters. She bought a black lamp and clipped it to the side of the shelf. Above her work area she hung her color chart, with blocks watercolored in squares and labeled underneath, twenty-one altogether. Beside this she taped a piece of lined notebook paper Odessa had sent her with nothing on it but "I miss you" centered in neat script. From her work stool she often heard Lois practicing, and even in the sound of just the crisp brassy steps of her warm-up scales, Sonya found refuge from the din of school hallways.

Frequently she stayed there until she heard her parents get home and then call that it was dinnertime. The exceptions were the days that she and Lois cooked. They had decided, on the first day of Marie's job, to make dinner for their parents, spaghetti, baked potatoes, and garlic bread, all enhanced by flowers on the table. Marie had liked it so much, the girls had offered to fix dinner on designated days, and their mother said she would help them think of vegetable dishes, too. Her job was in the capital, at one of the city's high schools, and since this meant a commute and longer hours away, she was glad for their offer. But even on the days they cooked, Sonya stayed in the basement for as long as she could.

She bought some new pencils and charcoals and, for the next three months, drew what she called her River Series. It was comprised of drawings of rivers in numerous stages of storms and in different seasons. What bordered the rivers was always in charcoal, whether it was grass, a town, or a field. The rivers themselves were always in color, and sometimes there were bright spotted fish in the water, their one closest eye looking out into the world. Sometimes the riverbeds were lined with stones, neatly fit together and dusted in pastel like tiles at the bottom of a pool, or strewn throughout the bottom rinsed in the beauty of disorder. There was always, whatever the particulars of the scene and the variants of color and shadow, the figure of a girl somewhere, barely visible. She might be a line wider than a stroke of charcoal, her slender length fitting between two trees. Or she might have, instead of feet and hands, nearly transparent webs of color, digits spread through the water like drops of ink. The figure took on the shape nearest her, whether a tree or a fish, but the lean of her body was unmistakably human. For Sonya, being with Odessa had been like stepping into something already in motion, something begun ages and ages ago that would continue. When she was with her friend, she experienced the warmth of moving into this; the spiral of energy widened to include her, and closed again, so that they existed in their own heated dazzle, where every movement rippled with significance, and the larger world, unnoticed by them, sometimes dropped away. She had never known feelings quite like that.

Though she titled it her River Series, the pictures weren't serial, did not progress in any way meaningful visually from one to the next. Instead, each of the twelve drawings came out like a moment punctuated with unarticulated longing, dazed, held still by chipped colored pencils and smudges of dusted black and gray. She filed them inside a large folder in the order she drew them and decided not to show them to anyone.

Marie, when she found her out in the backyard crying one evening, put her arms around her daughter and said, "Maybe if you traveled with Veronica again you would feel better." They had not spent any time together since the school year had started.

"Maybe," Sonya said. Though not sure, she appreciated her mother's optimism.

But her father, sad these days himself, could not offer solace to her. She came home from school one afternoon to an unlit house and saw his outline in a chair in the living room; he had called in sick that morning. When she heard his tears, she approached him tentatively. "What's the matter, Dad?"

"That President."

"But you are glad he is gone." Her father had rejoiced with dancing around the house that August day that he resigned, had filled every room with cigar smoke by sucking one down to the nub, a first for him, and even bought himself a modest bottle of port, which he and his friend Leon had sung dry in no time.

"Yes. He is out of office. But my God, the grief, the lives he ruined." He sighed deeply and took a handkerchief from his pocket. "All those lives here, the parents here, in this country. He will never have to know that kind of pain. And all those thousands, I mean thousands"—his voice rising—"millions of Vietnamese lives laid waste, whole villages wiped out, all those lives ruined. For what?" He was sobbing now.

His despair threw the rope over, threw the rope in that daily place where they walked the stairs in any kind of light trying to live their lives from day to day the smell of the plastic chair coverings muting out other scents and clogging that airway, knotted it tight so no daylight leaked in, no daylight got in again.

Sonya hadn't heard that expression before—"laid waste"—and she imagined, rather than people, which was too difficult, just as it was too difficult to hear the despair of this one person in front of her, because it was her father, mounds of ruined buildings, thatch on fire that she had seen in the newspaper, crops destroyed, water buffaloes shot slumped in a field, piles of rubble everywhere. But all of it was too much.

"Do you want a cup of tea, Dad?" She had seldom seen her father drink tea, but it came to mind now to offer.

"Come here." When she walked over to his chair, he reached out and pulled her to him. He kissed her forehead, and hugged her so tightly that she couldn't take a full breath for what seemed like several minutes. "Sure. Tea would be nice." Then he released his embrace and blew his nose.

She went into the kitchen, and by the time she returned with the hot cup he had switched a lamp on and was drying his eyes.

Lois, of course, had noticed her sister's funk. One day after school in late November she came down to the basement with a plan. "I heard Tim is going out with Kara Clark."

Sonya looked up from her drawing. "Oh," she said, and resumed her sketching.

Lois scooted a wooden stool beside her and watched her draw. They didn't talk for almost an hour. Finally Lois asked if she could take a peek inside the folder of pictures.

"Maybe later."

"Dad says you better snap out of it."

Sonya stopped drawing but did not look up.

"And Mom's worried about you."

Sonya sighed and put her charcoal pencil down.

Lois picked up a marker and peeled the label with her thumb. "The Griffins are going away next week and Barb asked me to feed their cats, but I'm busy with trumpet. I told her I'd ask you."

"OK," Sonya said, looking up at her sister. "I'll do it."

Lois let out a breath of relief.

The Griffins had a side door that faced the driveway, and when Sonya rode up the driveway one sunny afternoon after school to feed their three cats, two of them were standing on their hind legs, paws against the glass door, watching her hop off her bicycle. She walked toward the door, saw the cats, one hefty and white, one speckled orange, and stopped about ten feet away. When their mouths opened and closed in the glassed silence, something inside her dropped open, and she was looking over the edge. Her heart beat quickly, and she wiped her damp hands on the sides of her jeans. She could not look at the cats, so she looked at the scuffed toe of her sneakers, she looked at the thin rattling brown of the hydrangea planted beside the house, at the green garden hose coiled around its silver holder. She tried again to look at the door. And she tried again. Whenever Sonya looked toward the cats, she felt the edge approaching, the danger of the high cliff, the bottom drop-off. There was nothing beyond it; the vast white blankness of terror had no borders, no definition. It loomed before her, huge and limitless, blinding any glimpses of rational thought and drowning out all sounds. Her ears tingled. But she wasn't on a cliff. She stood firmly on the blacktop of the driveway, walked up and down it, trying to walk off her shaking, thinking, *I have to go in, I have to go in there.* Every time she glanced toward the door, the breach of horror muscled wider, oblivious to her, and powerful.

After walking around the driveway and the yard for forty-five minutes, Sonya told herself she had to go in the house; soon it would be dark, and she had to be home or her mother would worry. As she approached the door she hesitated and thought of riding to the store, buying some dry food for the cats, then coming back and throwing it in a window. Or maybe she could pry the side door and just toss it in there, if she bought dry food. Dry food might be the answer. How many days could they live without food? Could they get by overnight at least? But people were counting on her, believing in her, knowing that she was capable of the task before her, knowing she was capable of opening that door, stepping inside, then up to the kitchen and opening the cans on the counter and scraping the wet food into the bowls on the floor. Lots of people would believe that she could do that. If anyone asked her mother, "Is your daughter able to do this chore she has already agreed to do?" of course she would respond without the slightest doubt, saying something like, "My daughter can do that any day of the week!" If her mother were watching her right now, she would say "look at her, look at her walking toward the door." Then Sonya was almost there, then reaching for the knob of the outside door, turning it, opening it, the key already out of her pocket and in her hand for the inside heavy door, and then the faint cries grew a little louder. The key was in her hand but she stepped backward instead of forward and let the outside door swing closed again. She glanced up at the sky, then down at her sweating hands and she heard *of course my daughter can do that!* Then she opened the first door, unlocked the second, shoved the key in her pocket, ran up the steps into the kitchen, and, fumbling with the opener on the counter, opened the cans as quickly as she could, and, trembling, scooped the food into the bowls on the floor while the cats cried and swarmed around her, moved in and out around her ankles, slithered against her legs, and all the while not looking at them, she threw the cans into the sink, ran out the door, slammed it shut, and, shaking, walked to her bike. There might have been a figure standing behind a closed threadbare curtain in an upstairs window, who parted it slightly and standing in shadow peered down at the back of Sonya's head, then let the curtain fall closed again and withdrew into the recesses of the room to gnaw on a plate of bones, a chunk of gristle on the edge, rancid drops sliding over the lip. Though she felt that watching on her neck, Sonya did not look back as she rode down the driveway and headed for home, the impulse to look, to be convinced she wasn't followed, nearly equal to the impulse to escape.

When she reached her house, she sat out in the yard awhile to catch her breath before going inside. Her throat was grainy, strained with the scream she had not let out at the Griffins' house still, granular and tight, tensing the muscles of her neck. Its exact beginnings imperceptible—as she had ridden up their driveway on her bike, her psyche had already been altered—a film of fear had slipped over her life, blurring its outlines, distorting its sounds. Even had Sonya *wanted* to look back over her shoulder in the yard to see where it had begun, see its dimensions, what might have followed her, no such glance was possible. But all she wanted was to be able to breathe normally. The light from the kitchen was beginning to spill onto the grass, the sky deepening toward dusk. She glanced in the window and saw her mother stirring something on the stove, watched her a minute or two before putting her bicycle away and walking into the house. That evening she did not mention to her family what had happened. Later, she phoned Veronica and asked her to ride over with her the rest of the week.

Sonya was distracted the next day in school and thought of little else except of what had happened with the cats. That evening she called Odessa and tried to describe for her the experience, saying it was like being on a cliff in a high wind, a roller coaster off the track. Something too big. Those did not seem precise enough.

Odessa described a photograph she had seen in a magazine. "Like looking at an oil rig or a gigantic ship in the middle of a sea, and the people on the boat in the picture are really tiny?"

"Yes. Yes, like that."

Sonya heard her friend sigh, then say gently, "Tell me what you are most afraid of."

She thought about it for a couple of minutes. "I don't know," she said.

Veronica offered to do the rest of the week's feedings by herself, but Sonya said no, she had agreed to the task, and that they could go together. But each afternoon at the Griffins' house she could not bring herself to actually step inside; instead, she paced the driveway while Veronica attended to the cats.

The following week when Sonya slept over at the Simmons', as soon as she stepped in the house she scanned the downstairs and asked where Spikey was. The black Angora, who for all the time she had known him was strictly an endearing pet, a name, had become a cat. Veronica said she thought he was outside.

"Can he stay out all night?"

"I guess so."

Later Veronica brought up the fear. "Maybe you were bitten by one when you were young, and for some reason you are remembering it now. And it is affecting you now." They lay in the dark in her room.

"I was bitten by a goat at a petting zoo when I was five," Sonya said. "That scared me and I remember it, but I'm not afraid of goats."

"Maybe it was worse," Veronica said. "Or it happened when you were an infant."

"But my mom would know. Lois asked her. She said nothing like that happened to me." Sonya had not wanted to worry her mother so had told only Lois about it. Her sister had then told their parents, and now they were worried. "Besides, why would I suddenly be afraid now?"

"I don't know," Veronica said. "Can you think of any reason?"

"No," Sonya said, "Nothing." It had come upon her so suddenly, a storm unseen on the weather map of daily concerns that guides a life, the pockets of shadow here and there and the dazzles of illumination, startling and expected. This was out of the realm, and she had no legend.

They listened to the sounds of the neighborhood. Over them the sky slipped its diamond covering. They ran out of words. They slept.

A few hours later when Sonya got up to use the bathroom, she cautiously opened the bedroom door and started down the dim hall, a wall night-light guiding the way. When she was almost to the bathroom, she heard the spongy sound of the carpet moving lightly. She glanced down to see Spikey's outline walking toward her along the wall, heard its cry break the hush of the sleeping house. Its yellow eyes blinked up. It watched her neck.

Sonya retreated and quickly stepped back into the bedroom, closing the door loudly enough to wake her friend.

"What happened?"

"Are you awake?"

"Yeah."

"Can you come to the bathroom with me? It's out there."

Veronica snapped on the bedside lamp and rubbed her eyes. "It? Oh, the cat." She yawned. "I guess my dad let him in. He won't hurt you, Sonya." She yawned again. "He knows you."

Sonya turned toward the door, then immediately back to her friend. "I can't—really. Will you come with me?"

Veronica sat up and, more awake, looked at her and hesitated briefly before saying, "Sure." She got out of bed and walked past Sonya to the bedroom door, then opened it. She headed down the hallway, then stopped when she realized that Sonya was still waiting at the bedroom doorway. Then Veronica turned toward her, held out her hand, and whispered, "Come on." She took her hand and led her to the bathroom. "While you pee, I'll let him out."

"Thanks."

A couple of minutes later Sonya went back to the bedroom to find the lamp still on and Veronica in bed. She returned to her sleeping bag on the floor. The pleading was apparent in her eyes and in her voice. "Don't say anything at school, will you?"

Veronica said, "I won't," and switched off the lamp. After a moment, her whispering voice filled the darkness. "I hope you can figure this out."

"Me too."

Sonya did not sleep over at Veronica's again after that night. The next time her friend asked her to, Sonya said she couldn't.

A few weeks later her father mentioned the fear to her for the first time. He came into their room one evening holding a drawstring bag made out of brown corduroy, the size of his hand.

"This is for you," he said to Sonya, but before handing it to her he explained the gift's purpose. "I don't know what this fear is about, but I know that you won't always have it. When that time comes, when you are no longer afraid, open this bag and take out what's inside. It's a way to recognize that. You'll see what I mean." As he extended it toward her, he gestured for her to take it by the string.

"Thanks, Dad." Sonya held it up and felt the weight inside it pull down the center of the bag, though it wasn't at all heavy. "So I can't look inside yet?"

"No. Listen to me." As he turned to leave the room he said, "Always pick it up by the string. It's a present. Don't poke it."

When he left she brought it over to the bookcase, still holding it by the string, and set it down. There she could daily contemplate the bag if she wanted and recall her father's words, or ignore it for a stretch of time, if that better suited her mood. She explained to Lois what it was, and her sister promised not to look inside it now.

And of the nightmares that had begun the week she fed the cats, Sonya spoke occasionally, though only to Lois. She could never fully describe the fear, and the dream-scenes were so innocuous, usually taking place in familiar settings, that they probably didn't sound much like nightmares to her sister.

"And we were all in the kitchen. I was at one end, and you and Mom and Dad were at the other. There was an orange cat between us, walking slowly toward me."

Lois asked, "Then what happened?"

"I screamed to you 'Get that thing away from me!' And I woke up that second, with all of us standing around the kitchen."

"Did it bite you?"

"No. It was walking toward me, looking at me."

"Was it the Griffins' tiger one?"

"No. I did not know it."

"Oh," Lois said. "Did I get it away from you?"

"No. I woke up before you could."

"I'm sorry."

"That's OK," Sonya said.

Nor did she tell anyone, not even Lois, that she had three or four of these every week, the fear so tangible that the next day the dull ache of horror still gripped her, the hollow feeling in her bones when everything was emptied out of them except for the huge blinding white. It was always there, either dissipating from the previous night's images, or returning, overlapping, in the next, or in the nightmare of the one after that; she could not get away from it.

One Saturday afternoon in the winter Sonya's mother said to her, "Your father and I were thinking that maybe if you drew or painted some cats, it would help. You could see them as just another animal, just something else to paint, make beautiful on paper in your own words, your own way. You could draw them as you see them." This she modified after brief reflection. "Maybe not exactly as you see them, but to find some beauty there."

Sonya thought about it a minute. The idea terrified her. "I can try it," she said.

The next afternoon, down in the basement, she selected some colored pencils to begin what she decided would be called a Dream Series. Her first one would be a kitchen scene, but before she started she sorted all her pencils and charcoals, tossed away old scraps of paper, and carefully dusted her work area. Then she took out a sheet of paper. She meticulously drew cupboards, shelves, dishes on the edge of the sink, her parents, her sister, sunlight coming in the window, herself at one end of the room, and a plant on the counter. When she picked up the gray and began to think about the cat's posture, the fear flooded her. The backs of her ears tingled. She put the gray aside, and instead drew some silverware on blue-and-white checked picnic napkins on the counter next to the plant. She brought the gray pencil again to the area of the paper where she had decided the animal would be but again felt too uncomfortable to sketch its outline. This happened each time she tried, so she left the space white and decided the picture was set. She titled it *There It Is*.

The following weekend she drew a sidewalk scene. The houses on the street were painstakingly detailed, as were the yards, bushes, and blocks of cement sidewalk. She herself was detailed crossing the street: brown hair braided back, jeans, sweater, even her watch with its macrame band. On the porch railing of the house behind her was a blank area with the house's siding in rigid lines around it. This one she titled *Its Eyes Follow Me*.

She created fourteen of these, in charcoal, with colored pencils, and a few watercolors. In none of them did a cat appear, and in none of the titles was the word "cat." She beckoned her mother into the basement one afternoon about a month after her suggestion.

"Sit here," Sonya said, pulling a wooden stool beside her desk. "I want to show you something." She held the stack of pictures close to her, and announced each title as she handed it to her mother. "And this one is called *It Finds Me*." This was of a glass door balancing far above her, unattached, a void within its delicately drawn border.

Marie smiled at the first few, but by the fourth piece she wasn't smiling. She studied each one carefully, occasionally looking up at her daughter to say, "This color here is lovely," or "This is King Street, isn't it?" Then she set it aside to study the next one. But she said nothing about the white hollow that the pictures had in common. She did not need to ask about the significance of the titles. Sonya saw in her eyes a look she had seen before. She watched the lamplight on her mother's face, her eyes cast down at the drawings in her hands. The gray of her eyes seemed to turn in on itself. Sonya saw there the inward look that meant: *You are my daughter. I don't want you to ever feel pain. I want to protect you.* That look was inward because it also meant: *I am only one person and have limits. I will place my heart between you and the world. But that is the best that I can do.* Sonya felt their love for each other accompany them in the room, straining at the edges of what was physical. She looked up at the dusty sun-filtered window casements, and they gave comfort; her box of colored pencils and her pile of charcoal sticks, though chipped, worked down, vulnerable to breaking, seemed full of every color and texture on the earth, full of possibility. She looked back to her mother and wanted to tell her all of this, wanted to say that, at thirteen, she knew the world and it was OK. She did not want her mother to worry.

"Mom," she said, and her mother lifted her head. "It's OK, really."

Her mother tucked a strand of hair behind Sonya's ear. She continued her contemplation of the pictures for a while.

"I think we should talk to someone about these," she said finally.

"Like who?"

"A psychologist. Someone who could help you with this."

"I don't want to talk to anyone about it. I'm fine, Mom. Really."

They were silent awhile. Then Sonya asked her mother which picture she liked best. She told her, and asked her daughter the question, too. Sonya picked out two. Then she put the pictures in a folder that had Dream Series written across it in black marker block letters.

"I love you," her mother said.

"I love you, too." The frequency with which the girls and their parents expressed this, and it was often, did not diminish its significance.

"Come help me with dinner. Let's see if we have enough stuff to throw together a salad."

Sonya inserted the folder in the drawer with some other folders, snapped off the lamp, and they went upstairs into the warm and fully-lit kitchen.

Though she seldom thought about why it might be true, creating artwork had become as important to Sonya as the social aspects of her life. That winter she had a charcoal drawing in the student art show. In addition to the afternoons, sometimes after supper she returned to the basement to draw. Lois was busy with trumpet and with her friends, but the two often hung out together. Veronica was working tirelessly so she could be in honor society the next year when they entered high school. Once in a while they completed their homework together or went downtown shopping or for a bike ride, but Veronica spent a lot of time with her boyfriend. Odessa and Sonya had called each other every week for the first couple of months after she moved, and they wrote each other often, sometimes enclosing pictures clipped from a magazine. Gradually throughout the winter, though,

Odessa became involved with friends at her new school, and she and Sonya talked and wrote less frequently. Sonya often dreamed about her though, woke with her sun smell still so near, a tracing on her own skin. Later in the day when she remembered the dream and saw again her friend's face, eyes closed as she slept beside her on the blanket at the reservoir, or expressive as she sat beside her talking, gesturing, laughing, the hurt flooded her again, fainter this time, the bruise slowly fading.

Just as that had become a part of her, so too did the fear, forming around Sonya's life so that there was always the limitless white terror to negotiate. She lived with it, asked before going to anyone's house whether or not the family had a cat, so if they did, she could decline the invitation or she could feel prepared, anticipate a way to avoid it. When she walked down the street and there was a cat on the sidewalk, it was easy enough to cross to the other side. But once her back was to the animal, its eyes narrowed on her neck, herself becoming prey with nothing to hide behind. She glanced back often to make certain it was not following or readying for attack. In these situations she often told herself, *I am bigger than it is,* but this did nothing to ease her anxiety. Nor would a full-throated and urgent scream have helped, had it been possible for her to let one ripple from her throat, to crack the quiet-street atmosphere, the day's schedule, the order of the neighborhood. All that helped was for her to get away as quickly as possible.

And at Veronica's, whatever they were doing, such as sitting in the kitchen with homework drinking a soda as they were one afternoon, she had to stay alert. When she asked where Spikey was, Veronica said, "He is probably upstairs asleep." But Sonya could not relax. When she asked her to put him outside, her friend said, "He is nowhere near us." It was only after Veronica saw her continued discomfort that she found the cat and nudged him out into the yard. After that, any time her friend came over she made sure he was outside.

They rambled down the boulevard at night toward their side of town, the girls drowsy in the back seat, having enjoyed the spaghetti special at the Italian place. It was a Saturday evening ritual. Their father, steeped in wine this time too, gestured as he drove beneath the cold stars, one hand loosely hold-

ing the wheel. The headlights cut a path down the street, and streetlights illuminated cars parked along the curb with snow between them. Sonya noticed
a woman up ahead, on their right, coming out her front door and walking
toward her car parked on the street. As she came around the front of it and
walked toward the driver's side door, Sonya's father put his other hand on the
wheel and aimed their car toward the woman. The headlights, now pointing
directly at her, caught her frozen that moment, her left hand on the door handle, her head up, a look of terror on her face as she stared, immobile, at the
vehicle driving straight toward her. When their car was a couple of feet from
her, he swerved suddenly away and barreled down the street. He laughed.
"What a look on her face!" He slapped the wheel.

The girls, fully alert now, sat up in the back seat, said nothing, and stared
out the window at the night sky.

Their mother said, "Mitchell, pull over. Let me drive."

"What?" Then he said adamantly, "No. I'm driving."

The twenty minutes left of the drive were passed in silence, except for an
occasional note he hummed.

For the next few weeks that blank terror on the woman's face, as she
looked out over the edge of her life, accompanied Sonya's thoughts. Terror
had consumed everything else, had taken the place of everything else. And
she assumed Lois thought of her too, though they never talked about it.
It was an occurrence too strange to bring into the light of language. But
Sonya couldn't shake her. She went to the basement several times and tried
to draw her out; each time she picked up an implement and sat before the
expanse of clean paper something stilled her. She could begin the outlines
of the nighttime street, the slope of the boulevard, the hint of dark looming
trees somewhere lined above their speeding car. She could sketch the house
the woman walked out of, its porch illuminated by a faint yellow glow
through gauzy living room curtains. The pools of streetlight encircling the
parked cars she could manage. But Sonya, every time she tried to draw the
woman, paused this side of the terror. She held her hand up, poised above
the paper, and could not get any closer. Fear she knew; she knew the blankness she wanted to illustrate on the paper, yet she could not. To make in any
way permanent the look she had seen would be to acknowledge unequiv-

ocally that her father had done such a thing; she could not make it fit. She hid her half-drawings in a folder and buried them under a pile of papers in her desk drawer. But the woman's face continued to surface in her thoughts, a sphere pale and still, unwilling to be forgotten.

10

Or Sorrowfully Away

The increasing silence between them seemed aggravated by the cold metal of winter afternoons. To the girls, their parents' questioning about each other's day turned brisk, clipped, the weight of cold pressing in on the conversation, freezing off the edges of words. Their once tangible joy obscured by the pain closing in on them.

So in the evening when they read the newspaper in the living room, the old exchange of information from articles, the old exclaiming over the horror of political events, was supplanted by Mitchell's occasional turning toward Marie to ask, "What did I do?" The stranger's pale face floated between them, suspended, looking about blankly, speechless. Now each saw the other through her, yet yearned for the finite answer that would release her from her weightless drift of fear, resolve finally that she was safe, unharmed, could settle somewhere for good. But that did not come.

"Nothing," Marie said, the word's own enormity belying the truth of its saying. Then again, softer, "nothing." Nothing to be done about the indissoluble sphere of grief grafted onto everything between them. Nor, then, about the mutual mundane annoyances, either.

One evening in late February Sonya and Lois were setting the table when their mother said, "It will be just us for dinner, girls."

They looked at each other. "Oh. Where's Dad?" Lois asked.

"He's out."

While they were eating, their mother said, "I want to talk to you about something."

"What is it?" they asked, looking up from their plates, knowing by her tone that something upset her. They figured it wasn't about her job because that was going very well.

"I have asked your father to move out," their mother began, in a voice tired, the water-logged words finding their way with effort and hanging over the table, unavoidable. Lois put her fork down and started to cry. Sonya wanted to ask something, but her throat was tight, and she was afraid of the answer. Her mother knew the question.

"Yes," she explained, "we will be getting a divorce," her words having no place to hide from the brightness of the dining room. "Please don't worry about him. He will be fine." She reached over and held their hands as if to say *we will be, too.*

After doing the dishes in silence, Lois withdrew to the bedroom, and Sonya walked around the yard for a while through the crusted snow, looking at the vast spaces between the stars and thinking about nothing. She leaned against a tree under the sky swept with cold, looked up at the ragged branches forked above her in the dark, watched her breath drift up. While they walked in the woods once with their father, sun had flooded the leaves, and the floor of the woods smelled of dirt and bark. Lois had pointed to tree after tree, asking the name for them. "Pine. Birch. That's an oak," he had said. Eventually she pointed to one whose name he didn't know. He said, "Whatever it's called, a tree is a metaphor." They had looked around them puzzled, but knew that the word was significant. Now Sonya knew what the word meant, and thought again about what her father had said. She stayed outside until she was nearly numb from the cold, then went in. That night she dialed Veronica.

"Guess what?" she said. "My mom is getting me some new mat boards, and my parents are splitting up."

Veronica, unsure what to say about that, told Sonya about some early spring sales at the mall, and asked her to join her on Saturday to get a new bracelet and to see a matinee.

"That would be fun," Sonya said.

Their father did not come home that night but stayed at his friend Leon's house, as he did for several nights after that.

On another evening shortly after, Lois was in bed reading, and Sonya sat in the dark in the living room listening to the stereo with headphones on, watching the red and orange lights of the monitor flicker with the shifts in bass. Their parents had gone out earlier, they said for dinner, but the girls guessed more importantly to discuss their separation, and were back rumbling around the dreary tension in the house. The globe light above the sink cast shadows into the living room, when Sonya saw movement in the semi-dark of the kitchen out of the corner of her eye. She turned her head then, fully toward the kitchen to see her father down on his knees before her mother, his hands clasped before him, his mouth opening and closing around words Sonya could not hear, mouthing his heart's oblivion. Her mother stood before him looking down, one hand at her side, the other resting on her hip in the incongruously casual gesture that spells despair, the bright daily world holding on when a larger, darker one momentarily slams into it, shuts a person down so that she says, "would you like a cup of tea?" or "I just can't remember *where* I left my comb."

As Sonya turned back to the stereo, she remembered the story about Mrs. Stanley, an elderly woman her mother had known as a child. While a few neighboring men, one sunny afternoon, cut her husband down from the barn rafters where she had found him, she went inside and made two silver trays of cucumber and butter sandwiches, cut them neatly into quarters and set them in the parlor with a pitcher of iced tea for the men to enjoy when they were done. Sonya thought of Mrs. Stanley, how she must have concentrated, then concentrated, on the apple blossom pattern engraved on the sides of the trays and on the play of silver glint in the afternoon sun. While her parents talked in the kitchen, the stereo's pulses of red and orange continued beating up and down their narrow lines within the restricted range of measurable sound.

During the weeks that followed there was very little movement in the house. The air was thick with accumulated loss, and Sonya and Lois stepped quietly in the morning, and placed their school books quietly in the afternoon when they returned home, as if too quick a movement or too loud a sound would break the world. They spoke softly, and heard no music.

One evening Sonya lay on her stomach in bed, her French book open to the next day's vocabulary list, trying not to think about much except for the column of words in her notebook. When Lois came in and settled beside her, Sonya smiled at her and kept writing. They did not talk while Sonya completed her list.

Then Lois rested her head against Sonya's shoulder. "I'm scared," she said.

"Me too," Sonya said. "But everything will be OK. We'll be fine." She tried to focus on her homework so Lois would not see her upset. "We have to keep up with our school stuff so Mom won't worry about us, all right?" Writing, memorizing, knowing.

Lois nodded. "Can I sleep here tonight?"

"Of course."

They slept against each other, warm and comfortable, as they had sometimes when they were quite young.

The wintry night through her screen and streetlight in, and above far above, the avenues of space, drifting as she slept. Vast spaces, dark beyond adjective, language fumbling in the mouth. In a name, Budapest seen from a train or across an ocean, a place she did not know, known and unknown becoming the same, distance bridging them, until the avenues opening on dark and dark above her became known. Far above her, then into the room, the spaces of empty rooms, the furniture forever moved, dust marks behind for proof, but no words. Things forever moved. Only the avenues, the crystalline darkness above, permanent. The night air became too much. She dreamed of an elegant landmark from the train, an aqueduct, a statue, a cathedral, and then the sun, at the skyline, doing its slow shine, its here and now. Where the new day began.

The soft light from the kitchen had them fooled, sifting around the outline of their father sitting at the table on a cloudy afternoon. Then a loud sound finally came. When he heard the girls come in the house, he called out an enthusiastic, "Hello!" and said, "Come see my plan." He gestured toward them broadly with his arm. They knew he had been drinking when they heard his voice and were not surprised to see the line of empty brown quart bottles along the table like statues, all the labels facing out at them. The girls stood beside each other, five feet away, holding their school packs. Their father had a world map spread before him on the table. It was studded with brightly colored push pins. He picked up a pin from the pile on the table and held it poised for emphasis.

"And next, the very *next* place I will travel after I round the Horn, will be here!" He plunged the pin decisively into the map. "The women's breasts are like melons and hang freely and people eat fruit plucked right from the trees in their yards. Drink wine out of hollowed gourds and make instruments out of tree limbs. What do you think?" He turned again toward the girls, who were standing noticeably still. His eyes had the distant float of inebriation in them. He did not wait for a response before grabbing another pin.

"And then, then," his voice rising, breaking when it reached the ceiling, raining back down on them, "I will journey—do you like that word? Do you know its roots?" His eyes fixed briefly on them. "It comes from the Latin 'diurnus' meaning 'of a day'—then I will journey to Cameroon, where the sun is going to shine right out of my ass and the clay is so rich I can dig it out with my own hands by the ton from the riverbank."

They heard the front door open and turned to see their mother come into the kitchen.

"Hello, Marie!" He greeted her with an expansive voice. "I have been discussing my plans with the girls." He addressed them. "Isn't that right?"

Their mother looked at the table, then said to the girls, "Get in the car." They hadn't taken their coats off. They said nothing as they left the house, still carrying their school bags.

Their father followed them to the front door, yelling out as they were getting in the car, "Well, fuck you! Fuck you if you don't want to hear my plan! You can go to hell!" He slammed the door.

"There is nothing we can do," their mother said as they drove out of town, Lois in the front seat, Sonya in the back, each staring out a window. They drove to a county highway. The rain-slick road unraveled for miles in front of them, with fields of blackened stubble on either side. They drove and drove.

What did all of it mean in this rain? This rain, of a day. He had explained the word from a newspaper article about Vietnam spread out before her and Lois at the table, saying it meant dead or wounded. Could it refer to people in villages as well as to soldiers? Yes, to all of them. *Casualties.* She recalled how strange it had sounded to her, not seeming to fit what it described, as she struggled to understand where the casual part came in. Her father's definition had brought to mind images of soldiers resting against a rock or a stump in a field, holding their guns on their laps, legs leisurely crossed at the ankle and eating a bunch of grapes, even though their uniforms were covered in blood, even though someone was screaming for them nearby, even though they may have stopped breathing several days before. Why was that a casualty? How could there be one word for all of that?

Once in a while their mother said, "Look at those Canada geese" or "Look at that milkweed," and offered a detail about habitat, a lovely scientific detail, precise and tangible, which she hoped would help distract the girls. And they glanced toward a pond or a marsh and said, "Yeah" or "It's pretty." But each word, a shard struggling its way up to the conversation. They looked out at the occasional town with one gas station and a few people about doing their errands. Commonplace, unpained, errands.

"Let me know when you get hungry," their mother said. But the girls were not hungry.

This rain so diurnus, this rain so in its ash falling slanted falling across the field where they lounge against a rock falling across the day, this day, the day of their casualty the bunch of grapes splattered with their: where is it now, their day? What would close the wound, what would be the word for close the wound for getting up from the stump and brushing off the dried blood for gathering his belongings and walking away whole for eating ordinary grapes again rinsed glistening in tap water for not screaming anymore? For no wound in yelling anymore but yelling just to feel his throat still alive. For no wound in humming as he walked across the field or humming with the wheel of clay-spin, for humming to see something diurnus take shape in his hands.

Late in the afternoon they pulled into a state park. "Let's hike," she said.

They got out and walked to a two-mile trail through mossy woods along a stream and followed it. They watched water trickle down the moist sides of spongy cliffs, and saw bits of shale crumbling down muddy steeps. They stopped and listened to the stream, then hiked some more. Eventually they walked back to the car, slid in, and reclined in their seats. The three of them closed their eyes and slept for about half an hour.

When they woke, the filtered charcoal of dusk surrounded them, heavy with drizzle that had fallen most of the day. The trees in the park were still and black against the March sky. It took them a bit, coming out of their sleep, adjusting their seats, to remember where they were.

Then Lois said, "I'm hungry."

"Me too," Sonya said. "I'm starving."

"That sounds like my girls. What do you want to eat?" Their mother started the engine, and they wound their way out of the park.

"I want something fried," Lois said. "How about French fries and spaghetti?"

"Sonya?"

"Sounds good to me."

They drove into town and found a place named the Parkside Inn. Starting with bread and butter, they then moved on to fries and pasta. The girls drank a milkshake while their mother sipped a cup of coffee with her meal.

Afterward she asked, "Do my babies want dessert?"

Sonya blew her cheeks like balloons, and Lois held her stomach.

Their mother smiled. "Maybe later. Girls," she sighed. "You know he loves you. What is happening isn't because of anything you did. You know that."

"I know," Sonya said.

"Lois?"

"OK, Mom," she said. "What will happen to him?" Her mouth shaped the words in the air first. "Where will he go?"

"Your father will be fine. He has lots of friends who will help him. Don't you two worry about him."

The girls nodded. Lois rolled and unrolled her straw wrapper. Sonya sighed.

"Let's go home," their mother said. She took care of the bill, and they walked out to the car. By now it was night.

"It's your turn to sit in front," Lois said.

"You still can if you want," Sonya said.

"No, you go ahead." Sonya climbed in front, and Lois in the back. She leaned forward, between the two front seats, and asked, "How much farther to home, Mom?"

"At most, about an hour and a half. We'll be there soon."

Lois stayed leaning forward, and the three of them talked about movies to occupy themselves most of the way home.

"Is there really a place called Transylvania?" Lois said that if there is, she would like to live there.

"That's Transylvonio, my dear Fronkensteen. With a castle for you."

The girls tried to muster the childlike dimensions of their humor so that now, as in past periods of distress, unfettered silliness could rise spontaneous and boisterous to buoy them along.

When their talk shifted to *Billy Jack*, and Lois started to hum "One Tin Soldier," their chatter faded away. She trailed off after only a few passages of the song, the three of them quieted by reflection on the overwhelming violence in the film.

Lois acknowledged this by saying, "Well, never mind that one." Her pointed declaration did give them a chuckle.

Marie, chuckling, too, was nonetheless cognizant that the three of them were sad at the thought of not just this song, but lately, of music.

The house was unlit when they pulled in the driveway. They went in, switched on all the lights. The beer bottles were still neatly lined up on the table, but the map and push pins were gone. Their father left a note on the table saying he was at Leon's house.

The girls got ready for bed. "Let's leave the bathroom light on tonight," their mother said.

The day their father took his clothes out, Sonya was home sick from school. She rested on the couch and read *National Geographic*, several old issues her grandfather had given her piled on the coffee table, trying not to hear her father in the bedroom slowly open and close dresser drawers and fold his clothes into canvas duffle bags. He tossed his shoes and boots into boxes, where they bumped against each other as he carried the boxes through the living room, out the front door, and loaded them into the back of a borrowed car. He came in, walked back into the bedroom, and next she heard him ask himself, "What have I done?" She heard the shrill metallic pitch of change pouring into a tin container. Then he came into the living room with the leather tobacco pouch he had kept his coins in.

"You could use this for your pencils," he said.

"Sure."

He put it on top of her stack of magazines on the coffee table. Then he left.

She picked the pouch up, pulled it open with the tabs, and smelled its yellowed cracked lining. Must of Italy. Dust of commerce and clank of markets. Hollow of a pocket, a vacant square, chairs stowed up on tables and shutters closed. Footsteps a block or two away, everyone gone. The pouch so hollow in her hands that she closed it. She would feel better when she could fill it with her charcoals, colored pencils, and erasers. She returned it to the table. Later in the afternoon, tired, she picked the pouch up again, smelled it, put it beside her pillow and fell asleep.

With his clothes, books, and other personal items carried out in bags and boxes, only their father's work was left to move. Every Saturday he came by in the afternoon to load a couple of pieces into the old red wagon, which Marie had told him to keep, and bring to Leon's house. Sometimes, if a piece was particularly substantial, the girls helped him. First they dusted it off, then wrapped it in a camping blanket and carried it carefully up the basement steps, through the garage and placed it on the back seat. Sonya thought of the profiled reliefs under the cloth, an eye looking blankly upward, or sorrowfully away. The busts, which had seemed at times almost as if they had a voice, coming as they had from baked and seeded earth, were silent now in the gloom of the blanket, mouthing their unheard *O*s, empty of possibility. Their whispers would be drowned anyway by the rattle of the car for the half-hour ride to the house where their father, with the help of his friend, unloaded and carried them up the stairs to the spare bedroom. Neither of the girls asked him why he took only two or three at a time, and their mother never pressed him to remove the pieces more efficiently. Gradually the dust marks on the basement shelves and floor were pronounced. Within a few months he had removed everything, even, with Leon's help, his wheel, except two clay pots bordered with squares of red and azure tile that he had made the first year they were married. Marie had always liked these. He left them standing together on a wooden window shelf.

Soon after the last load had been moved out, he asked the girls if they would like to see his new place. They had asked a few times earlier, but he had said each time that it would be better if they just waited to see it when all of the move was finished.

It was upstairs, in the rear corner of the house. When he had told them earlier that it was nice, the girls, knowing the house was in an old city neighborhood, had pictured a spacious painted room with a lot of windows, a high ceiling, and his sculptures featured prominently. But the pale green wallpaper, curled and torn in a few places, gave the whole place the appearance of neglect. They looked at the double bed with its dingy white chenille bedspread, but briefly, not wanting to think about that space beside him. Reclining then against a rock the banister how could he when some were trying to survive the pain so diurnus. And though there was an old pine dresser against one wall, with a mirror leaned on its top, there were bags of clothes on the floor beside it and a box of shoes. He saw his daughters glance down at these.

"I still have a few things yet to unpack."

They didn't say anything but continued to survey the room, noticing his comb and a clay bowl on the dresser, but that was all.

"Where is all your work?" Lois asked.

"In the basement."

"How come it smells like a camp in here?"

"The window was painted shut." The girls inspected the window, then Sonya glanced out beyond it at the tar-paper roof of the garage.

"At least Leon could fix it for you so it opens." Sonya had thought this too, but Lois was the one who expressed it.

"Hey, he's busy. He has his own life, you know."

"I'm hungry," Lois said. "Can we go out to eat now?"

Their father hesitated a moment, then said, "By all means. Let's go."

He brought them out for sandwiches. They did not talk at all about his room. Instead, he asked Lois about her music practice and Sonya about her drawing. They told him about some of the pieces they were working on in these areas and about projects in school, mentioning exclusively the more positive aspects, not any of the usual difficulties, both deciding, though without discussing it, that he had enough other worries. And he was willing to follow their lead, telling Lois that if her music teacher hadn't yet played Miles Davis for them, then he ought to hurry up about it because, as far as the trumpet goes, Davis knows "what for." Rather than explain what her teacher had said about Davis' tonal quality, Lois was content to listen to her father describe hearing him for the first time on the radio at a friend's house, the two of them sitting on the floor so mesmerized that they forgot, for the length of the piece at any rate, to light the cigarettes they had stolen from his friend's father.

Nor did Sonya talk to her father, then or at any time, about her fearful dreams. She did not know how to account for them, and a description of them would sound foolish. In a recent one, she had been named, for some reason that was not explained, Final Judge at the International Cat Show. She stood in the center of an arena packed with twenty thousand people, a row of ten cats sitting before her, all watching her. She told herself that she had to tell someone there, a show official, that she was not the person best suited to be the judge, but she did not see anyone there she could tell. The crowd was attentive as a booming voice methodically announced the origin of each over the sound system. "Number One is from Spain." Event regulations required her to scrutinize thoroughly each cat as it was introduced, and all of them would be before she could bestow the prize. "Number Two is from Canada." They were various sizes, shapes, and colors. She wanted to bellow "Number One" so she could leave but instead, since that was not acceptable, tried to determine where the exits were without people noticing that she kept averting her eyes from the animals. As the announcer continued talking, he spoke more haltingly. Could any of the spectators see the sweat dripping down her back?

By the time Sonya woke up and kicked all the covers off her bed, the collar of her nightgown was ringed in sweat. She got up and switched the desk lamp on, then lay back down, closed her eyes, and listened to Lois turn over though she was still asleep. To dispel her fear, she tried to focus on the specks of yellow beneath her eyelids as she turned toward the light.

They had just gotten out of the water and flopped down dripping on their towels, feeling the sun pull the drops of moisture from their skin. When they closed their eyes, Odessa had said, "See the spots of light? It's like we're looking inside our bodies. Those are some of our atoms floating around."

"There are so many, it's impossible to count them."

"We have a lot of them."

Sonya detailed other phrases they had spoken that day, what they wore and ate, what the sky and water resembled; she thought of hair and skin, her own, Odessa's, of the faint lotion lingering on them, and of their mouths, eyes, and gestures, atoms and cells, tried to imagine everything they were made of. This calmed her enough that, though she left the lamp on, she finally fell asleep an hour later.

In late spring the girls' mother drove them one day after school to a house on the other side of Harpur Springs and pulled up in front of it.

"Do you like it?" she asked. The two-story bungalow with broad eaves was sided in unpainted cedar shingles.

"It's nice," they said.

"I thought we might like to live here, so I bought it for us."

When she had come home, a few weeks before, driving a powder blue used Bug, she had said that there had been a lot of recent changes, so why not leave some things the same. Besides, she said, she was familiar with VWs. The new house was a significant change.

The girls jumped out of the car, ran around the yard glimpsing in all the windows. They chose bedrooms before they had seen them and, later that night, planned where to put the new furniture they hadn't yet found. All framed against the woodwork in the grained sun of a day not yet arrived.

A few weeks later, after they had packed the last box and readied everything for the move, Sonya picked a striped shell from her old box of stones and shells and brought it out to the end of the yard of the house on Hightower Road. Its smooth curve of inside reminded her of a larger one through which, at a souvenir shop on the New Hampshire coast, she and Lois had heard the ocean. Their father had explained the echo, held in the seamless shell-cave, as sea-talk still moving through from the days before humans emerged from water, when they shared it with fish and coral. He said that was why people liked to listen to it. Lois had whispered, as they stood holding the shell close between them, "Maybe it's calling us back." Their father had hugged both of them and said they were his "smart sweet babies." The one in Sonya's hand now was not large enough to hold such a sound but, though no music issued from it, she liked its curved body, memory of that sound. She dug a hole in the grass with a sharp rock, placed the shell in the dirt, and covered it up.

11

Stealing Butter

"**S**he seems in a bad way." One early morning that summer, after they had been settled into their new place for a month or two, Marie received a frantic call from her father. He didn't reveal many particulars, but Marie knew they had to go.

All she could tell the girls after hanging up was, "It's Glenda."

The next day they were packed and on the road, the first lengthy drive in the recently acquired second-hand VW. The girls no longer reveled in the same sense of adventure they had as kids making this trip to Mercy Hill, though generally they still enjoyed it, and, as always, anticipated with great excitement visiting their grandfather. This time, however, the anxiety of the unknown cast the journey in dread.

"What do you think it is?" Sonya asked.

"She isn't dying. She's too mean to just die," Lois said. "She'll probably find some way to take the neighbors with her when she goes."

"Lois." Sonya deferred to their mother's anxiety.

"You know it's true." Lois shuffled around in the back seat. "Maybe she has finally wigged out completely. The other day I read about a woman home from her honeymoon licking fresh paint off the walls of her new apartment. Her husband found her and—"

"Lois, please." Marie glanced in the rearview mirror.

"Sorry." She leaned back and flipped through the copies of *Ms.* magazine her mother had tossed in next to their picnic basket. The rest of the drive was at a much lower pitch.

As was his custom, their grandfather met them at the driveway, embraced the girls and Marie. They could tell that he hadn't been getting enough sleep and that he had been crying. "She's asleep now, so let's be quiet going in."

They brought their bags in while he prepared a pitcher of iced tea and some cookies. "Let's sit out in the backyard."

At the old picnic table he explained to them what he was concerned about. "One day last week, in the afternoon, she went into the bedroom to lie down, and she hasn't gotten up since. To use the toilet of course, but she hasn't gone into any other room."

"Has she been eating?" Marie asked.

"Yes, some, but not much. I've been bringing food in to her."

"Did she say what it is, Grandpa?" Sonya asked.

"Nothing to explain it. She keeps saying 'remember the time such-and-such,' and fretting over everything with such detail, events I'd forgotten years ago, conversations. It's as if she bumped her head or something, and all these memories came loose." He sighed. "Or she's taking a last look over her shoulder on her way out of a room, right before hitting the switch, if you know what I mean. She's taking inventory of everything in there. That's what it's like."

"Oh, Dad," Marie said, as she rested her hand on his arm. "She's probably not going anywhere." She hesitated, then added, "But have you dialed Dr. Edwards?" They had had the same physician for many years.

"She says she doesn't need help and refuses to see any doctor." He stroked his ear scar as he described his frustrated efforts. "I ignored that yesterday, called Edwards over here, and she threatened to throw an egg salad sandwich at him and closed the bedroom door. He shrugged and said to call him again if her condition worsened in any visible way or if she agreed to see him. But it's not like she has coughed up blood or anything." Then his hands drafted a resigned gesture before him. "I thought maybe you could talk to her."

"We'll see what we can do," Marie said, looking to the girls.

"We'll help," Sonya said, and Lois nodded her agreement.

Marie made dinner that night, and Glenda still had not woken by the time the girls cleaned the kitchen afterward. They went to bed early, on cots in the living room, but their mother and grandfather stayed up late in the kitchen talking in the sink-light cast across the table. Sonya overheard him saying to Marie, "Well, dear, it is probably for the best, as I've said, for you and for the kids. But I know it's hard."

She heard his coffee cup occasionally clink against its saucer, and she knew that, having finished the liquid, he was now chewing on the pinch of grounds at the bottom of the cup. It was one of several ways he had of squeezing more daylight out of something, as he liked to say.

Then he said, "I phoned him last week, when all of this started. I wanted to see how he was doing anyway, my usual check-in. We talked awhile. He said he would send something."

"I know Mitchell appreciates hearing from you."

She drifted to sleep with them continuing to talk quietly about the divorce.

The next morning while they were finishing breakfast Glenda yelled from the bedroom, "Marie, is that you and the girls? I thought he might have called you."

"I'll clean up, you go on in." Their grandfather began clearing the table while they went into the bedroom.

"I didn't mean for that to happen." Glenda was in bed and, though it was summer, reclining beneath a blanket she had made of crocheted orange and yellow squares. Marie took up a seat beside her, and the girls found metal folding chairs their grandfather had arranged earlier near the end of the bed. The room's floral wallpaper, pine dresser with Glenda's purse on it and a dish of clip-on earrings, a silver cross displayed on the wall above, and bed with an iron headboard were unchanged each year the girls saw them. The room still smelled of geraniums.

"For what to happen?" Marie and her mother looked at each other.

"Those times in the store, the winters of '41 through '44."

Marie, puzzled, said, "I remember sometimes you took me shopping, but I wanted to go with you."

"I shouldn't have made you take that butter."

"What butter?"

"I slipped some inside your coat."

"I don't remember that."

"Or a bottle of cooking oil, or a package of meat—I don't know now what kind it was—or a can of tuna."

"Mother, I don't remember that. I remember shopping with you, and you lifted me up sometimes to read the labels on the higher shelves. Please."

"We had nothing those years. It was so cold."

Sonya and Lois listened. They knew their mother's childhood had had some rough times, but Marie had always talked to them about what she did have, not what she didn't. Would she want them to know all this? Sonya leaned forward to catch her mother's eye and asked with her eyes whether she and Lois should leave the room. Marie's eyes, earnest, as silently said *stay*.

Glenda addressed her granddaughters. "She always behaved. She never said a word of complaint, never refused what I asked." They had rarely heard her speak with such emotion or so freely. "I asked too much of her, I know."

"Really, don't." When Marie started to cry, the girls did also.

"What is this?" That was the tone to which they were more accustomed. "If you are all acting this way, you might as well leave and let me have some peace." Glenda rearranged her sheets and blanket, not looking up at Marie and the girls as they left the room and closed the door.

That afternoon, sitting in the yard, Sonya mulled over what her grandmother had said. And her mother's frugality, which was increasingly in sharp contrast to the extravagance of the suburbs around them, made more sense. Whenever possible, she salvaged a discarded thing, always seeing the potential for beauty that others had missed. This helped them furnish their new place, since Marie had given their father some of the living and dining room furniture, had given some to a women's shelter, and some of it, now old and chipped from numerous moves, she had lugged out to the curb with the garbage. Occasionally the disposal of something was needed for primarily symbolic reasons. So they had spent a few weeks, after the initial refreshing of the painted white walls, acquiring pieces new to them, though not necessarily new. Some items were rescued from others' curb discard piles, the three of them scanning the nearby neighborhoods and wedging into the car once a dinged dresser and another time a scratched end table, "junk-jacking," as Marie called it. Any found pieces they stripped and re-stained or varnished, Marie urging the girls to consider their work with pride and not to worry that a neighbor might drop by and recognize a transformed item. Likewise she was pleased with the bedroom curtains she had stitched from burlap snapped up at a remnant sale. All of this inspired Lois to create some table runners and wall hangings in her introductory weaving class, and in several weeks' time the house was just about complete.

It was one of their mother's many gifts to be able to find objects that had some beauty and invariably had some purpose. She would not, unlike their father, buy something simply because it was going cheaply and might have some as yet undisclosed purpose. Sonya recalled the time when he was inspired, after a spring cleaning, to donate the bowling balls he found in a box in the basement to a library fundraising tag sale. He came home, however, with parts of a mannequin from which he planned to later make a hat stand. The limbs rested on a bookcase in the living room for months, until he finally got rid of them after numerous pleas from Marie to get them out of the house. He was frugal too, but Marie was far more efficient than this, wanting nothing to go to waste. Sonya understood better now why this was true. She had already known that her grandparents had always grown much of their own food and, in earlier years, killed their own chickens. The stringent necessity behind this way of life was becoming evident to her.

Herbert retrieved the package from the afternoon mail, and they all went in to give it to Glenda. "You woke me up."

"Well, dear, I think this will be worth it. It's from Mitchell," her husband said, handing her the rectangular box wrapped in brown paper.

They resumed their earlier places, Marie beside her, the girls at the end of the bed on folding chairs. Herbert stood beside the bed.

Glenda sat up and leaned against her pillow and the headboard. She unwrapped the box and then lifted from the enclosed crumple of newspaper an oblong clay piece. She pulled a three-by-five card from the box and read the message aloud: "Glenda, for your rosary. Love, Mitchell." She passed both to Herbert, saying, "Put this on the dresser."

Glenda did not linger over the sentiment of the gift; her quickly moving to drink from her water glass on the nightstand was an indication of her feeling for the gesture. The force of her emotion often propelled her away from the subject at hand and into some other territory, perhaps of the seemingly petty daily tasks or of an inconsequential discussion.

"I dreamed about shoes," she said, abruptly drawing their attention away from the gift by taking a look inward, unusual for her. Herbert placed the dish and note on the dresser, left the room, and quietly closed the door behind him.

"What about shoes?" Marie asked.

"There was a sale display, with rows and rows of them, all in bright colors." She opened her hand and waved it about like a Chinese paper fan. "When I looked at the tags to check the sizes, they were all my size, seven and a half. Every single tag. I couldn't believe it."

On the dresser Sonya recognized, turning away from her grandmother's account to glance at the gift, in the curved edge of the piece her father's decorative streak, the way he sometimes, with a wire, laced the outer lip of clay with a defining row of crescents. The ridge of inlaid red and blue tile shards, just below this, she also would have known as his, his signature love of broken color, of each chance for a surface to catch the light and bring it into the clay. This dish, elliptical for a string of beads to lie in, would extend, when held, beyond two cupped hands. That her father was not one to talk up the attributes of organized religion underscored for her the kindness he showed toward her grandmother.

Though she missed the fuller description of the shoes, she turned back in time to hear Glenda emphasize, "And every single pair on sale."

When her grandmother took another sip of water, Sonya noticed that the pair of praying hands napkin holder, always on their kitchen table, was now on the bedside stand. It hadn't been there earlier. She figured that her grandfather must have put it there. The carved hands stood, devoid of their usual purpose, pressed together. When she was younger she used to puzzle over them: What were they praying for? More napkins? But what about the set of hands and the figure in the Rambler? She wondered as she grew older, as she struggled to formulate an answer, was it just to stay on the dashboard, fastened to its beige vinyl and watching? Now she understood their purpose.

Looking directly at Marie, their grandmother said, "I'm sorry about the yarn balls," and returned the water glass to the nightstand.

"I don't remember the story of the yarn balls."

Sonya and Lois looked at each other, again wondering if they should hear this. Again Marie silently said *stay*.

Glenda directed her narrative at the girls. "We had money for only one pair of shoes, and children's feet grow so fast. So I bought a pair that I knew was too big for your mother's feet, thinking she could grow into them. I stuck a cluster of yarn, matching colors, into each toe, so they wouldn't slip when she walked."

She brought her fingertips together as she said "cluster," mirroring something picked or gathered, a group of flowers.

"Turns out, it took two years for her feet to grow into them completely. They fit awhile. And then I think she wore them tight a year or two after that."

"It was just a pair of shoes. I never went without a coat, whatever size."

Glenda, still turned toward the girls, continued. "When your grandfather was a boy he had no shoes. His feet nearly froze doing chores on the farm in the early morning. You know what he did?"

They shook their heads.

"He stood awhile in fresh cow dung to warm them up. There was always plenty of that! He could tell you stories."

Sonya saw him young, the mist on the fields and the steam rising from his feet. Maybe the feeling of lake muck between her toes was how the dung had felt to him. And though Sonya knew that both her grandparents had grown up on a farm, neither one all that far from Mercy Hill, she had never thought of them struggling as children. She could imagine her grandfather young, but young and happy, not desperate and poor.

"Do you girls know what his scar is from?"

"Mother, I don't think they need to know."

"They are old enough." Glenda was determined. "When he was a young boy, he had a terrible ear infection. There was no doctor around, and nothing they could have paid one with anyway. His mother knew that if the abscess could be cut to drain that the ear would be able to heal."

Sonya and Lois listened intently as her story gained momentum, and they detected their mother's discomfort.

"She took him into the kitchen one day and soaked his ear in whiskey. Then she took a knife and dipped it in boiling water and held him down against the table. She cut the infected part out. Then she poured more alcohol on it. It bled for two days. But it healed after a while and the infection was gone. It left that scar."

Glenda was the only one not crying, but she reached again for the water glass, took a draw from it, and held it awhile before returning it to the bedside stand.

Again that afternoon, several stories later, as had happened earlier in the day, Glenda drove them from the room, this time saying she was tired.

And that evening soon after the dishes were cleaned and stacked away, Marie and the girls went to bed, fatigued from their day of witnessing, listening to resurrected instances of pain, seeing Glenda's hardships suspended before them in the air, their damage done for so long. Then, that circumstance dissolved like dust, she beckoned another one to form. The girls, whispering, speculated how many more days they would spend like this one. As her sister drifted to sleep, Sonya pondered how her mother endured the taxing rhythm of it.

What would it be like to be unable to leave a house or a room, confined by some inward constraint that no one else could see or name? She imagined the range of scents available to Glenda in that room: the musty haze of summer heat settled in the bed-clothes and on her skin, the faint smell of moth balls, mixed with the smell of geraniums, lingering in their closet and sweater chest in the winter, dormant now but there nonetheless, beneath the heat absorbed by the green-speckled linoleum and the braided area rug. The nearly scentless water glass beside the bed, odorless condensation marking it. Maybe the smell of heat trapped in the stained pine dresser, in the loops of faded shade pulls, resting too. What would it be like to live solely in this range, to have the only variation orchestrated by slight shifts in wind or temperature, by the steadiness of night and day, by the changes in one's own sweat through a day resting, standing, sitting, looking, smelling, resting, waiting as if resting, waiting?

The earth felt wide and smelled warm to her, and outside she experienced its dimensions, its width and breadth, depth, not as confinement but as what to live among. She reflected on what it would be like to have to give them up, to live in fear. Was that what her grandmother had, or was it depression? But Sonya did know fear, though not to be paralyzed by it. She could be out in any day, go anywhere, hold the day in her mouth with a hum. The underside of wet stones, of leaves deep on the floor of the woods, the shadowed movement of fish her grandfather saw pulling themselves back home—it was all within reach. The scent of towers she and Lois had conjured, of the mossy streambanks they wandered, of book seams, some village in that book—it was all here, in her. Even so, that night she turned to the outline of her sister on the cot next to hers and listened awhile, drowsing, to her steady sleep-breathing. How could he leave a brother, how, when someone wounded could find balm in a string of pale beads.

And on the second day, resuming their listening posts, the girls learned about the extent of their mother's childhood isolation, and Marie attempted to keep those pains healed over, sealed out of reach, that Glenda was determined to disrupt. That Marie had spent a lot of time alone they knew, but now Glenda acknowledged that there were times when she couldn't accept the needs of a child, particularly one upset or lonely.

"Sometimes I just closed her door," she admitted to her granddaughters. "I knew she was in there. She might be sitting on the floor crying, or looking out the window, wondering if I would come in. But I couldn't go to her. I could barely get myself through a day, let alone help a child through one. Especially one of mine. I know it sounds awful."

Sonya and Lois glanced at Marie, who with several passes had tried to derail her mother's narrative, the rawness beyond what she wanted to reflect on now. "Really—"

Then they looked at each other, unsure of how to negotiate this awkwardness.

Finally Lois said to their grandmother, "You know, she's been pretty good to us. When she locks us in the garage for a few days, she has a valid reason—like we didn't clean our room or we let our grades slip."

Marie's shocked expression was brief, because as soon as Glenda let out a relieved crackling laugh, she laughed too.

Sonya hit her sister on the arm. "What about the thumb screws? Want to tell her about those?"

"And the hair shirts?" Lois added. "Actually, we call them hair tank tops."

"Yeah, we could tell her about those, too."

Much to the surprise of all of them, Glenda was still laughing. So unusual was the sound, especially of late, that her husband came to the door of the room, opened it and peered in at them. "Hey, girls."

"Come join us, Herbert."

He walked over and stood beside the bed, held his wife's hand. "It sounds like you are tickled up," he said.

She looked earnestly at him. "I'm still old and mean. A couple of laughs aren't going to change that."

"I'll take them anyway," he said.

That night when Sonya was in bed, again listening to her mother and grandfather talking in the kitchen, she heard optimism in his voice. She heard her mother say, "This does seem to be helping."

But on the third day Glenda still was not interested in an excursion, despite the efforts of her family to bring her out. Several times that morning she said, with a wave of her hand, "I've seen it all before," referring perhaps to the yard, the garden, the town, her life, or to all of it.

And that afternoon Marie as well learned something, as the girls had the days previous, got a more searching glimpse into the struggles of a life with which she was already intimate.

"I was twelve when my mother became pregnant again, her sixth child, the one she lost."

"You mean the one that was stillborn?" Marie had heard this story before and had told her own daughters about it, too.

"She brought it here in the early winter. Then all that snow and ice came. Everything froze. We had lard for sandwiches. There was ice on the inside of the windows. She got sick and her milk dried up. There was nothing else to feed the baby. I saw it getting thin and almost sallow. One morning she hadn't gotten up yet and she was always the first one up. I went into their room—he was outside working already—and there she was still lying in bed, holding the baby pressed to her nipple. I went to her. The baby was blue. Maybe just from the cold I thought, but I was wrong."

"Do you mean—?" Marie started. The girls sat very still. "I thought—"

"And then she grabbed me and pressed the baby to me, said maybe I had some milk for it. But I didn't. I was twelve." She let out an uneven breath. "Her baby did not have life. It was dark after that day." How could she herself then, the anguished question lay before her all these years, *did not have life*, a stingy splinter of sun across the stone floor as she knelt and glanced up at it briefly to accentuate the coldness of the stone beneath her knees.

Then they were all quiet awhile, Glenda with her eyes closed, Marie blowing her nose, the girls on the folding chairs, transfixed. All of them confounded by sadness.

When she opened her eyes fifteen minutes later, she said, "I need to rest some. Marie, why not take the girls into town? Maybe buy them a new blouse."

"Sure. We'll let you sleep."

But no one was keen on driving into town. Instead, in the hot afternoon, the girls stretched on their backs in the grass, Marie sat with her father at the picnic table.

"Why didn't she ever tell me that? Or you?" Marie, having told him what she and the girls had heard, first tried to step gingerly.

"All that shame," her father said. "And going back to when those black days started. It was too much for her." He put his arm around his daughter's shoulders. "Many times I urged her to share it with you. I told her it might help explain things."

"What did she say?"

"She said there was nothing that needed explaining. You know how stubborn she can be, like a tree root. I hoped that someday she would tell you, that somehow it would become easier for her to say, whatever it might explain. Or maybe just less hard."

"But *you*," now not delicately at all, "Why the hell didn't you ever tell me? I mean, ever? There wasn't any way, *ever*?"

"It was hers to tell."

Marie shook her head, gathered herself to return to calmer breath. It took some doing, her forehead pressed into her open hands. Then, after a while, lifting her head, saying, "Finally she could."

"We can be glad for that," he said, and he kept his arm around her. "She got a cloud without any lining, but she made the most of it."

Glenda slept the rest of the day, and Marie and the girls helped Herbert with yard work, all of them glad for tangible, definable tasks with immediate results.

The following day was declared, without anyone saying so, a day of rest. Everyone was exhausted from the catalogue of minuses, Glenda reliving it, as if each day, all that expelled darkness for her, drained those hours of daylight from her listeners, all of them traveling back through the bleakness and sharing it with her. Glenda did not call anyone in, Marie and the girls tried to relax in the yard reading copies of *Reader's Digest* they'd found in the house, and Herbert sat with them, refilled their glasses of iced tea now and then. They had brought out an issue of *Popular Mechanics* for him, an expense he occasionally allowed himself to indulge in, but he was too unsettled to focus on a magazine.

Sonya watched him, leaned forward in his lawn chair, stroking his earcord. He had retrieved and was chewing on apple scraps she and Lois had left on a plate in the grass, mulling them over. She realized that maybe it wasn't a casual gesture, the way other people picked lint off a sleeve or jiggled change in their pocket. Maybe when he rubbed his ear it was a way of bringing his mother's sacrifice back to him, of keeping her courage present, giving him solace, strength. He pressed the last bit of daylight from the sun-soaked apple skin, knot of seed, tang of squinched drop, as she watched him.

For the next few days Glenda did not call them in.

Finally one early morning she beckoned again. "I think you should all go home now. You have things to do besides listen to my old stories and wait for me to get out of bed."

"Mother, we're fine here."

"No, you should go."

Marie and the girls kissed her goodbye, then packed their suitcases while Herbert made them a lunch for the road.

"Are you certain about this, Dad?" They stood in the driveway with the car loaded.

"Yes, I am certain."

"I think she will be better now."

"I do, too. You girls don't worry." They hugged him. It was Lois's turn to sit in front first on the drive home. Despite Marie telling the girls on more than one occasion that they were too old for such concerns, the two of them still negotiated whose turn it was to sit in front and, on longer trips, for what portion of the drive. Not that there was any risk of argument. The reassurance they found in the vestiges of rules and behavior left over from younger years out-weighed the obvious lack of necessity to still abide by them. The three of them climbed into their seats and backed out of the driveway, looking over their shoulders at him and waving as they drove off.

About an hour into the drive Lois asked Marie, "Did you really forget all that stuff Glenda did?"

"Some of it."

"You're amazing," Sonya said.

"Yeah, you totally are," Lois added.

Marie smiled. "Just promise me you'll never think I'm perfect. I wouldn't want you to be disappointed."

"OK," they said, "we won't."

As they drove past hills drenched in midday sun, Sonya imagined her father sitting on his work stool, his hands around the finished dish, thinking he could help Glenda carry her burdens. Thinking clay carries for us our weighted counting, clay and tile take in light and carry us through our day. Through the burdens of heat and sadness. Her ceramics teacher, Mrs. Meyer, said about clay, about all sculpture, about the solidity of it: here, world, this gift, as she extracted a lump of it from the plastic-lined box it had been delivered in, held it up above her studio workbench before the class, here, beauty to ponder, beauty to get your hands around. Like the

dirt of New Hampshire fields, if grass could be peeled back and the richness underneath brought to the surface, insects reveling in it all their lives.
Rows of trees sometimes lined the fields, or rows of stones hauled to the
edge years ago. All that physical labor people spent their lives doing, now
a row of stones in a field someone glimpsed from the passing car window.
Or sorrow people labored over. And on a day in class with slides—she was
relieved no figures of the animals—more than *The Thinker*, more than the
enormous colored Os featured in a museum courtyard or in a city square,
the *Burghers of Calais* had left their mark: eyes cast downward, taking their
bronze shadows everywhere, what could close that distance between them?
That distance between them so pronounced, and nothing in their hands
but despair, despair and the one set of keys, no thing of wonder for them to
close around, no plum, no rosary.

Sometimes the life-sized art was overwhelming, but then sometimes
the object one could carry in hand was life-sized too, whatever its actual measure. Field and slope of hills beyond, as the day, lengthening itself
out, stretched to fit human need. Not so much about what her teacher
called scale, as about the feeling behind it. Couldn't any object be life-
sized, straining in its beauty at the edges of life? Or the viewer strained
in comprehension of its beauty to an edge? Comprehending other beings'
many ways to register sentience. Comprehending the smells of rich soil,
sun-soaked leaves, curve of land to watch, for us, to walk. To find comfort
in. The ceramic dish her father made Glenda, now a part of any time she
picked up or returned her rosary, the beauty of his art inseparable from
her life-sized desolation, her glimpses of relief from it, solace the string of
beads provided. His dish, comfort too.

Sonya did not even realize at first, turning her glance away from the
fields and toward her mother and her sister, that the object wasn't specified
as she said, "It was very pretty." But knew, a few words later, when she did
realize, that it didn't need to be.

"It certainly was," her mother said.

And Lois piped in, "for sure," before adding, "I liked the way the edges
curved up and outwards. Sometimes he makes edges that just turn in."

Marie and Sonya nodded their agreement. From then onward, the rest of that drive home and the rest of that summer, the rest of moments that could not fit easily into a category of hours or of seasons, the three carried with them those glints of color curving outward, not pointing away, not leaving, but opening to light, offering themselves up.

Upon their return home they settled back into some semblance of a summer routine, occasionally still picking up an item for the house at a tag sale, taking care of their new vegetable and flower gardens, and adjusting to divorced life, like the families of many of the kids Lois and Sonya knew. Sometimes they heard bits of others' family problems, about custody struggles or late payments of child support. The girls didn't know exactly what their father's financial obligations were, but they knew their mother wanted it this way, so they did not ask her for the particulars. This way, to whatever extent he failed to meet, or indeed met, these obligations, the girls would not know, and their talks with him could still be about clay reliefs, trumpet practice, or charcoal pencils.

And one day, a few weeks after their trip, Herbert called to say Glenda had finally gotten out of bed. She had wanted that morning to be taken into town. They had gone to a diner for a cup of coffee, then shopping for groceries and thread. He said he hoped she would regain the twenty pounds she had lost, and that he had bought ice cream toward that end.

By the time early October came she had indeed regained the weight and was fully restored to her daily rituals, though they still involved, as they had before, some days or parts of days sitting in the living room with the shades drawn. But now Marie worried about her less, and even mentioned to the girls that perhaps on their visit with her parents the following summer, now that she and Glenda had had a kind of reckoning, they would enjoy each other's company more than in the past.

12

Markings In A Language

At one of the tag sales they had been to Lois had gotten a pair of cross-country skis, and the evening of the first significant snowfall she headed out to the covered streets. Sonya watched from her upstairs bedroom window, opening it a couple of inches to let in the frigid air. There were no streetlights; those were a few blocks away on the boulevard. Living room and front yard lights cast their yellow glow onto the snowy ground. Lois steered cautiously down the driveway, then gradually found a stride as she marked a trail through the street. Sonya watched her to the corner and stayed by the window to look for her coming up the other way, around the block. The neighborhood was hushed with the newly fallen snow, the hush cracked by the occasional bark of a dog a street or two over, and now and then the muffled chug of a car trying to make its way through the unplowed streets. After about twenty minutes, she saw Lois's red jacket, her arms and legs swinging out of the darkness as she glided down their street past the house, slipped back into the tracks she had made, and swooshed around the corner, out of sight.

Sonya recalled pictures from the book for her World Cultures class— mothers in the Andes carrying their babies on their backs while gathering wood, a Japanese woman serving tea to a matriarch—and tried to think of an image for how much she cared about her sister. They were, by turns of necessity, the younger or the older one. They were, by their always-changing need, sometimes the protected one, sometimes the protective. They brought schoolwork home for the other when one was sick, tried to keep up with each other's gossip, swapped clothes, gave and sought advice. If need be, helped each other with designated chores. But there were subjects about which they did not speak, such as the divorce, and occasionally hearing their mother cry, and knowing the other heard her too; rarely now did she cry in front of them. With these there was an understanding that each other's pain was resistant to the touch of a word. These they worked around, and would enter gradually, as the passage of time allowed them to.

She closed the window and, at her small rolltop desk, another tag sale find, took out a sheet of drawing paper and her set of charcoals. Moving the pencils around, she made about twenty circles, in varying shades and sizes, then took out another sheet. One image becoming the next, the lunar eclipse had entered her imperceptibly, the edges of light and shade not discernible. The moon was first in full light, then partial, then dark, then again emerging from the earth's shadow. *Penumbra*, her father had handed them, slowly unwrapped by its definition, magically, held up by its root, almost shadow; orbit and sphere they knew. After three hours she titled it, in neat block letters along the top, *Lunar Eclipse: Sometimes One, Sometimes the Other.* She left it on her desk. The next day she gave it to Lois, who smiled, said, "It's great," then mounted it on poster board and hung it on her bedroom wall.

Now not as likely to venture out or to take risks as her sister was, Sonya had declined her offer to try the skis. Since her fear began, she was usually cautious outside, especially when she was by herself. This time, though she had taken a glance around the bare winter hedges that bordered the yard, she had not seen a cat as she walked across the crusted snow to the hedge along the rear of the yard. She cut a handful of the bright stems of the bittersweet plant, whose red and orange drops were like a constellation against the snow. Turning around she saw a black and white cat stopped in the snow about fifteen feet away, between her and the house. The cat was surprised too and watched Sonya closely. She met its yellow gaze, then immediately averted her eyes from it, to the snow reflecting afternoon sun. But this meant to be vulnerable, giving the cat a chance to leap at her. Because she had to be aware of what it was doing at all times and of where it was, she glanced quickly back to the animal, and then away again to a bush, and then back, but she could not maintain a prolonged look at it. The animal was not moving. Then it let out a cry. When she saw its pink cave of mouth, it was as if she saw, behind its row of teeth, another mouth, a bit smaller but with the same shape and color, inside the first one, echoing its sound. Then as the second one opened immediately after the first, exposing a second row of teeth, she saw yet another mouth within that one. The image echoed backward, a mirror seen in a mirror. She could not think clearly enough to figure out how it had fit all those other mouths inside its first one. And what else was in there? Was there a shred of faded cloth snagged on a broken tooth somewhere? A chip of bone lodged in fat that had wormed its way up behind one of the yellow eyes? That prowl in the abandoned house, no doubt, had given the animal its strength and its appetite for forlorn, discarded, flesh, its gums bleeding and tearing. A shoe left in one of the otherwise barren rooms, the smell of wet fur. Something there, its shadow spilling from behind the partially opened door. It could spring just as easily from a base of snow in a backyard, find a vein and rip it out, threaded by skin and hanging to freeze in the winter air. It planned these assaults with its extra mouths, where to embed its teeth. Its eyes said as much, intent on her, pinned as she was by its stare to that spot on the snowy ground. She did not know how long she had been standing there. Having intended to run out momentarily, she had not put on a coat or gloves. One hand gripped the cutters, the other the bunch of bittersweet. Then a truck door slammed, and the animal darted off through the hedge. Sonya walked around the imprint it had made in the snow on her return to the house.

One Sunday morning in late February, when the sky was the slate of impending snow and the snow along the streets was dirtied with exhaust, Marie retrieved the wicker picnic basket from a basement shelf and cleaned out the dust. She beckoned the girls to the kitchen. "We're having a picnic. I'd like cheese," she said, handing them the sandwich ingredients. While the girls prepared the food, she washed out the thermos and made coffee. They put the items in the basket.

"Where are we going?" asked Lois.

"You'll see. You should dress warmly."

They bundled themselves in long underwear, jeans, turtlenecks, wool sweaters, laced their boots, packed the car with the basket and a blanket, and then left.

After an hour and a half of driving they pulled into a state park. The girls recognized it as the same one they had gone to a year earlier on a rainy afternoon after finding their father in the kitchen drunk with his map. The road into the park was closed, so they parked near the entrance and carried in everything they brought.

"Let's find a table," Marie said.

They hiked across the expanse of snow-covered lawn in front of the park. In the distance, bare trees bordered the woods crisscrossed with hiking trails and a stream. All the tables leaned chained against the trees. They found one that had slipped partially down and wriggled it near the base of the tree, still chained. They drank the steaming coffee and ate the sandwiches, fumbling with wool mittens on. Now and then a cross-country skier greeted them with a hello or a wave.

"Are you freezing?" Marie asked. "Should we stay?"

"We'll move around after lunch," Lois suggested. "That'll warm us up."

"I keep thinking about all that snow Glenda had, and relentless cold. It's no wonder she stays in for the whole winter." Marie had hoped that, after their conciliatory talk of the previous summer, this winter would be different for her mother who, though she hadn't retreated to the bedroom again, had resumed her reclusive habits. She checked frequently with her father for any change. There hadn't been one, however; those days of clarity and openness, when a door was pried ajar and an evanescent lantern beam swung into the room, had been frustratingly brief, one luminous sweep and then murkiness returned.

"Did she always do that?" Sonya asked.

"Yes, every year for about five months. It was as though she had retreated so far inward she went to another place." Marie took a sip of her coffee. "Something in her stayed there, too, and what emerged was all that harshness. At least last summer she talked a bit. You know how unusual that is for her. That's what is worrisome, a person withdrawing so distant that others can't pull her out by the shirtsleeves."

"But you forgave her," Lois said. "Glenda knows that now, so it's cool."

"Yeah, we were there," her sister added, "You did forgive her."

"Forgiveness doesn't take away her darkness though. I guess it can't do that."

"But it still matters," Lois said. "Especially to Glenda, even if she doesn't exactly say so."

"It does, Mom," Sonya insisted. "We do what we can, that's what you say. And we all have limitations, right?"

"Yes, you girls are right. I know. You two are getting awfully smart." She smiled at them, pausing. Then she said, "Let's get warm." They packed up their lunch and got up from the table.

Across the field they found the playground area, where the swings were tied around the steel sides for the season but were still hooked at the top. A few spins clinked loose the chain ropes. The girls each climbed on one and began to pump, then tilted their heads when they gained some height, and saw spinning the sharp outlines of trees, the massive woods around the park. They listened to their shouts and laughter echo over the snow and through the frozen woods. They watched the trail of their breath hover before them at every backward dip of the swing; their momentary forward plunges seemed to bring them perilously close to the immeasurable gray sky, but they swung back quickly. Then up, up, to the other side, spun up to threads of blue beyond it, blue blue day, cobalt bursts of joy, suddenly theirs, startling them. Could this be yelling humming of a day to feel whole? "Look!" they said, "Watch this, Mom!" They were soon flushed and warm with the heat of their movements in the unmoving slate of woods and sky and February snowfield.

He did not feel whole threw the rope over and looked up at it briefly pulled measured got the metal kitchen chair thought about it not too long long enough to think about his body's weight there the weight of his despair. Or not thinking about it that moment the decision was made it may have been about the weight of his body then just that and the rope and knotting it so no daylight leaked in cutting off from him the rest of that place would not know joy it was more than the smell of thick plastic to tie off from him his father and his despair.

When they were done swinging, having swayed slowly toward the hard flat ground, they hiked through the trees and studied the frozen stream.

The leaves engraved in ice and the scattered tracks of animals were like markings in a language they bent closer to as if to hear. "Look at these," their mother said, leaning down and tracing with her gloved finger the pronged imprints of a raccoon. They all looked down. They did not talk until they got back on the trail.

After walking until a late afternoon dark had crept from the woods, and the profiles of trees blurred into the muted sky, they left the woods, picked up their basket at the table, and climbed into the car.

On the way home, with the day's laughter echoing in the car, Lois suddenly declared, "I'm going to ask Kaplan why he never plays any women trumpeters for us."

"He might say he doesn't know of any," her sister offered.

"Then I'll tell him he better go find one for us."

"A teacher likes a challenge," her mother said. "Research is part of the job. You tell him I said so, if you need to." Music was returning.

With that Lois smiled, then fell asleep in the back, and Sonya drowsed in the front seat. Several minutes later, she opened her eyes momentarily as she turned toward her mother and saw her rub wet eyes. But Sonya was not concerned; she could tell by her mother's slightly wind-burned face and her yawn that her tears were not from sadness. They were from relief, and from having been made tired by exuberance—some of her own, watching theirs.

13

The Chaos Beneath Conversation

What characterized this time, in the house on Sumner Street, were the rituals the three of them had adopted, almost without noticing. Frequently on weekends they tried a new recipe, and often on Sunday afternoons they carved out a couple of hours and went for a walk or a drive, sometimes with one of Marie's friends. Individually they had rituals, too. Lois had trumpet practice most afternoons; Sonya continued drawing and thought vaguely of college around some aspect of her art. And Marie had begun a graduate program, with evening courses at the state university. On those days she stayed in the city and did not get home until late at night. This also meant much weekend time with her course work. But all of this order, even when scheduling constraints made their lives hectic, contributed to a sense of contentment in this house.

The girls had routines with their father, too. He had not asked them to his new place again after that initial visit, and they never mentioned it. Instead, he would come over on a Saturday, the red wagon rattling into the driveway, and beep the horn. Usually he had to push aside old newspapers, Styrofoam cups, and articles of clothing to make room in the back seat for one of them. It was on one of these outings that they realized he was growing his hair out. It still had dark reddish brown through most of it, though the sides were streaked in gray. When they asked him about the length, which they noticed was now slightly over his shirt collar, he said that he hadn't had a ponytail in the 1960s, so he was working on one now. The jeans and plaid flannel shirts hadn't changed much, but the string ties were new.

One Saturday after he took them out for sandwiches he stopped inside a bar for cigarettes, he said, though they knew he didn't smoke, leaving the girls to wait in the car. Half an hour later he stood in the doorway and gestured generously toward them. "Come on," he called, "meet my friends," then disappeared through the door.

The girls got out of the wagon and walked hesitantly, neither one wanting to enter first. As their eyes adjusted to the dim surroundings, they saw their father at the bar, friends around him, a pitcher or two before them. "This man here, Ernest," he said, hand on a friend's shoulder, "makes the best spaghetti sauce I've ever had. Ever." The enthusiasm that accompanied alcohol consumption was a familiar hallmark. The girls stood beside each other as he gestured toward them. "And these are my kids," he said to his friends. "They are nervous. Aren't you, girls? That awkward age." He laughed. "Don't frequent bars much, but they will loosen up in a while." He asked the bartender to bring over two sodas.

As they sipped the drinks, turning the straws, he asked, "Are those cold enough? You can get some chips, too, if you want, anything you want." He called to the bartender to bring them a bowl of potato chips. "Nicest kids you'd ever want to meet," he said.

In another hour or so he was talking about the divorce. Another of his friends, Jim, who was currently settling one, began talking about his wife needing space; all he had left was space, he said. He studied his napkin. "Hey, buddy," the girls' father interjected, "take it from me. It won't mean a damn thing in a month or two. The outside, maybe three. But it hasn't changed my life, not one fucking bit, and you can count on that."

Back out in the bright still daylight, a couple of hours later, he stumbled to the car, the girls following. "Get in," he said. "I'll take you beauties home." Both girls squeezed into the back seat. He said he would take them the scenic way. They sifted out of traffic and wove down tertiary roads, bumped past farms on the outskirts of town, flew past clothes drying on lines, chickens running through yards. Their father drove with a kind of abandon, and Sonya was reminded of a couple of times riding with him at night when he turned the lights off, and they sailed along in the darkness, nothing to mark their way. Then a few moments later he turned them on again, thrilled to discover that the car was still on the highway, the danger averted, feeling the exhilaration of luck afterwards. Now he expounded from the front seat with a broad sweep of his hand. "At any moment the world could change. And THAT, that's what keeps us going, despite all the wars and the terrible, terrible pain."

As he pulled into their driveway an hour later, he leaned over the seat and kissed each of them. He smelled of beer and smoke. "I love you guys," he said in a watery voice.

"We love you, too. Thanks for lunch," the girls said, and got out of the car and walked up to the house. He beeped enthusiastically as he drove away.

"How's your father?" their mother asked, meeting them at the door.

The girls did not look at her. "He's OK," they said, as they hung up their jackets.

But while some aspects of her life had changed, what hadn't changed was Sonya's persistent fear. The nightmares, still a few every week, usually took place in a room, perhaps the living room. The morning washed all surfaces clean, illuminated the plants and the polished wood chairs. A calico cat walked slowly toward her. She screamed to Lois and to her mother, who were on the other side of the room, "Get that thing away from me!" But she woke up then, at the frozen instant. The words, still in her mouth, tasted as if her stomach were lined with wet copper. She heard water running, or the radio low, or someone singing downstairs in the kitchen. Morning rays gleamed in. People walked their dogs. Papers were delivered. Buses ran on time. The suburbs were aglow with efficiency. Yet the chaos beneath conversation, she had gotten accustomed to, the daily tingling behind her ears, the edge-of-a-precipice sweat, grown around her life. It became another emotion, flew alongside longing and love, sadness and worry. It was something to draw about, or with, in all the illuminating detail around that hollow, but not to speak of.

Sonya's silence on the subject did not diminish her mother's concern. One Saturday afternoon in the spring Marie went into her room and sat on the bed. Sonya was at her desk drawing a shadowed mountain range like the one she had seen in a travel magazine her father gave her. The sounds of Lois's trumpet drifted in, a *Sgt. Pepper* piece she was working on, muted by her closed bedroom door.

"Honey," her mother began.

"Yeah?" Sonya continued drawing.

"I want you to talk to someone."

Sonya turned around, pencil in her hand. Her mother rotated a silver ring on her finger. "What do you mean?"

"I see the way you walk around them outside," she said, not specifying which animals. "I see it at people's houses. I can see it in your eyes." She paused, looking down briefly, then back up. "It has been three years now, Sonya. I can't stand to see it anymore." She had first urged her then to talk with someone about it, but Sonya had refused. And a few times since she had mentioned it again but with no success.

Sonya listened to Lois's fluid notes and watched a line of sunlight cut across her desk, fallen on her fingers folded around the pencil.

Her mother continued, "There's nothing wrong with talking to someone."

Marie was as strong a person as her daughter knew.

"I can live with it, Mom. I mean, I do. I can handle it." Her throat tightened as she remembered the day the door of terror first swung open while she stood in the Griffins' driveway.

"But you shouldn't have to. I don't want you to. I know what fear does to people. It can make them go to seed." She did not elaborate.

"And not come back?" Sonya was glad that her question made her mother smile, but she knew she was serious.

There was a protracted silence.

"OK," Sonya finally said. "I'll go."

Her mother walked over, bent down and kissed her on the forehead. "I'll arrange it," she said, and closed the door behind her.

When the day finally came, two weeks later, Sonya and her mother did not talk as they rode the elevator up to Dr. Francis's office on the fifth floor of the complex in downtown Harpur Springs. When the ding signaled the stop at their floor, Marie reached out and rested her hand reassuringly on her daughter's arm.

In the waiting room Sonya flipped through a few magazines, tossed them back on the round glass table and glimpsed out at the threads of traffic in the street below. Her mother read an interior design magazine, showed

Sonya photographs of furniture arrangements. "Our living room might be featured in a magazine someday," she said, laughing.

Sonya would rather that moment be at the Army Navy Surplus store, rifling through racks of dusty wool pants and faded flannel shirts, but she didn't say this. Instead, she nodded.

Marie's effort to amuse her daughter hadn't worked. "Just tell him what you feel. Don't worry."

Sonya nodded again, looking down at the toes of her shoes placed evenly beside each other on the abstract print carpet. "I will." Trying to decipher a design, and imagining her own modifications to the existing one, kept her occupied awhile.

The receptionist led them to the office, chatting about the March weather. "Dr. Francis, this is Marie Hudson and her daughter, Sonya." She closed the door.

Dr. Francis stepped forward, firmly shook first Sonya's hand, then her mother's. His full graying beard moved slightly when he smiled, and the rest of his face was ruddy like a mountain climber's. "Please sit down." He gestured to two armchairs facing his impressive wooden desk, his furniture not as casual as he, in a blue wool cardigan and unbuttoned shirt collar. "Would you like a cup of coffee or tea?" His eyes also spoke his sincerity.

"No, thank you," both said as they sat down. Sonya observed the prints on his walls, elegantly framed in carved wood, and the row of windows that faced the street. Her mother admired the jade plant.

Dr. Francis glanced toward it. "It seems to like the window," he said. "I had it out in the hall before, but it wasn't doing well there. It's much livelier now." He smiled. He put on his half-glasses, looked at a folder he had opened, and took out a pad of legal paper and a pen.

"Sonya," he began, looking up at her, "your mother told me on the phone about your fear of cats, what we call ailurophobia. Why don't you tell me about it? It would be helpful for me to know when you first encountered it, and it probably was like an encounter, right? Like an awful and tense conflict." Here he raised his hands, facing each other as they gestured, grappling. "And the situations now? Is the discomfort worse in certain circumstances than in others? I would like to know the day-to-day workings of it." He picked up the pen, poised ready. "Take your time," he said. "I know this won't be easy. Tell me whatever else you want me to know about it." He leaned back, his broad frame filling his brown leather chair, and smoothed his beard with his left hand.

Sonya told him about the day she was first confronted with it at the Griffins' house, describing, with her heart pounding loudly, having seen two of the animals look at her out the side door. As she detailed the sweaty hands, heart beating rapidly as she walked up and down the driveway, he took notes, leaning forward again and looking up now and then to encourage her with "I see" and "What else?" She told him it took her forty-five minutes to enter the house, and that a friend rode over with her after that and fed the animals, unable herself the rest of that week to go back inside.

She told him about her fear at someone's house, how, if there is one, she has to first determine where it is, then decide on staying or sitting down. Here, she was thinking primarily of all the negotiating she'd managed at Veronica's. She explained how she feels on the street if there is one on a porch or on the sidewalk. "But it's not that bad then," she added. "I can always cross the street."

"What else?" he asked, still writing. "Do you ever dream about them?"

"Sometimes."

"How often would you say? Frequently? Once in a while?"

"Once in a while," Sonya said.

"Once in a while," he said, jotting it down.

Then she added, "No, I guess frequently, three or four times a week. Would that be called frequent?"

"Yes, it would be." A pause, then, "Would you like a glass of water?" When Sonya nodded no, he continued. "Do they threaten to harm you or actually harm you in your dreams?"

"They are sitting in a wicker basket or in a chair, and then they get up and walk toward me."

"Then what do they do?"

"Well, they look at me. I ask someone to take it away, but then I wake up."

"I see." He lifted his pen. "So you wake up before anyone can move the animal and before it makes any contact with you?"

"Yes."

Then he wrote a minute or two longer. "And who are the people in your dreams? Does that aspect vary?"

"Usually it's my mother or my sister, sometimes my father, a friend or someone else I know." He jotted something down with each new detail she revealed.

Then he stopped writing, removed his glasses and held them in his hand. "This might be a tough question." He waited a moment before asking. "There is some difficult work ahead for you. Are you prepared to let me help you with it?"

She looked out to the blue sky, saw afternoon sun slant across brick buildings along the street. The sun was sharp on the rough brick, clay of domes, of monuments, home to wanderers and grate-walkers, star-followers, clay dug from rich black earth, from streambeds beneath crisp light. And then, later, the moon came into it, river plains flooded in light, richly textured land awash in muted white. And the song of what was buried rose, indiscernible from the sweet-smelling night wind above the water, rose and wove itself around the willow notes, the night-bird notes, the dark-tree-being notes, one lullaby hovering above the land, song filled with longing, the frame of one body rocking to hold it, the song weaving loose, full-throated, heard now just below the daily strum, heard soft and low, song of somewhere such beauty the atoms full, choir of night sky and water and animals rejoicing, rejoicing. She looked from the brick buildings in the sun back to Dr. Francis, waiting for her answer.

"Yes," she said.

"Very well then." He stood up, walked over to a bookcase and selected a book. "Here's what I want you to do." He sat back down. "This is a book of photographs. I want you to flip through it and mark the pages that distress you the most. You can put a slip of paper in. I'm sorry to have to ask you, but this will give direction to our initial inquiries here. Bring this to your next appointment. And we'll see what you've marked and go from there. How does that sound?"

"That's fine," Sonya said, but she was wondering how she would manage to carry it.

Then they all stood up. Dr. Francis handed the book across the desk, and Sonya took it without looking down. They all shook hands, and he walked them to the door.

"Goodbye," he said. "I'll see you again in two weeks."

"Goodbye," Sonya and her mother said. "And thank you."

Dr. Francis nodded and smiled.

When they reached the elevator, Marie said, "I'll carry the book."

Sonya handed it to her; she hadn't yet looked at it. "Thanks," she said, wiping her hands on her jeans.

On the drive home her mother asked gently, "Why didn't you tell me you had bad dreams?"

"I didn't want you to worry."

"Sonya." Her mother gestured as if she would say more, but that was all she said.

Having told Lois that evening about Dr. Francis's task for her, Sonya was followed around by her sister the next afternoon carrying the book.

"Come on, I'll help you do it."

"I can't right now, Lo. I have a bunch of things I have to do, but thanks anyway."

"Wouldn't it be better just to get it out of the way though? Then you don't have to think about it for the next two weeks." Lois was persuasive, but her sister's anxiety held more sway.

"I'll do it soon," she promised, closing the bedroom door on their conversation.

This was the answer Sonya gave a few more times over several days, until finally, the afternoon before her appointment, Lois's urging prevailed of necessity.

"Here are some index cards. We'll use these." Lois took a pack of them from a kitchen drawer.

"I'll cut them into strips first," Sonya said. She lined them up neatly, and meticulously cut them into strips of equal width. "This should be enough to start." She brought the stack over to the couch.

Lois took the over-sized book, *1,000 Photographs of Feline Favorites*, from the kitchen table, brought it into the living room and sat beside Sonya. "Give me the markers," she said. "I'll turn the pages. You tell me where to mark."

She opened the book and began turning the pages. The white breach looming just below, Sonya tottered above, heart pounding. On the third page was a picture of a robust cat with one blue eye, one green.

"That one," she said, pointing toward it, her head tipped slightly away. Lois marked that page with a tab.

Each page had several glossy prints of cats, each a different size and color. Some were in baskets, some in fields, some on laps. Some pictures were nearly full page, some thumbnail portraits. Sonya kept her head turned to the side, looked toward the book out of the corner of her eye. Every other page or so, with no particular pattern, she pointed and said, "That one." Twice she got up to cut more markers, walking around the room awhile before sitting again. Her fear kept a constant pace, easing only when Lois finally closed the book an hour and a half later and put it down on the other side of her.

Lois glanced at the binding. "Lots of pages marked, Sonya."

"Yeah," Sonya said, and leaned against her sister, head on her shoulder.

Then she stood up slowly and walked to the bathroom. After closing the door, she lay down a while against the linoleum, its coolness keeping her from throwing up. The cool somewhere to get the rope to pick that place to cut the daylight off close all sound how could he when there was coolness beneath bare feet the smooth floor relief sunlight from somewhere knocking on the moon's door how could he when there was that.

"Are you OK?" Lois had put the book away and was still listening several minutes later for her sister to emerge from the bathroom.

"I'm all right, Lo," she called through the closed door.

When they returned for the next appointment, Marie handed the book to Dr. Francis, who greeted them at the office door, and said, "I'll wait out here," and she went to the waiting room. He urged Sonya to take a seat across from the desk.

Dr. Francis came around the desk, sat in his chair, and flipped through the book, carefully so that the slips would not fall out, pausing a few times to study a picture. Then he closed it, placing it beside Sonya's folder open before him, and contemplated the book crammed with enough markers to split the spine. While looking at the ceiling, he lifted his beard up and scratched his chin through it, then stroked it back into place while he ruminated, his other hand resting on the closed book. Then he faced Sonya, asking, "Would you like to tell me about school?"

"It's not bad, actually."

"Your mother tells me you like to draw. What sort of drawing do you prefer? Portrait? Still life? Landscape?"

"Different scenes. I don't have any special subjects."

"She says you are talented. Do you feel you are gifted at it?"

"Drawing relaxes me."

"What else was happening in your life when the fear started?"

"I was just going to school."

"What about your friends?"

Sonya briefly thought of Odessa, but she said, "My friend Veronica and I hung out together then."

"What was that like?"

"We had fun."

"Do you still get together with her?"

"Sometimes."

"I see," Dr. Francis said. Then, "Did you have a boyfriend? Do you have one now?"

Sonya shrugged. "Sort of then. Not really now."

"Are you close to your sister?"

"Yes."

"Your parents' divorce was after your fear began?"

"Yes."

"What was the divorce like for you?"

"I don't know," she said.

He smoothed his beard again, then added, "Is there anything you want to tell me about?"

Sonya shrugged again. "No, I can't think of anything."

Dr. Francis jotted a few notes, stopping now and then to consider as he did. Then he walked to the door, opened it, and invited Marie in.

When they were all seated, he said, "As far as the phobia is concerned, in cases such as Sonya's that do not appear to have sprung from a precipitating event, adaptation techniques, such as relaxation exercises, have proven to be an effective way for a person to manage the fear. They can help diffuse the feeling of imminent danger. I recommend that we start with these." Addressing Sonya, he asked, "Do you have a favorite place?"

"I like the ocean."

"Great. Sun, sand, waves, boats, birds—imagine what is for you the ideal scene and then situate yourself in it. What many people learn to do is to imagine themselves in a relaxing environment when they feel anxiety or panic coming over them. The scenes should be as convincing, as realistic, as you can make them, and you should be able to call them to mind fairly quickly. For instance, a woman in her eighties is afraid of elevators. Well, she suffers from claustrophobia. Her daughter lives on the third floor of an apartment building. The older woman broke her hip and can no longer take the stairs, so she uses visualization when riding the elevator up to her daughter's apartment. Do you have any questions yet?"

"It works for her?" Sonya asked.

"Yes. Without it, she would have difficulty even entering the building, anticipating having to ride the elevator. Now in your case, what you'll have to learn to do when you encounter the animal is to close your eyes, visualize yourself at the beach, and let the calm you feel there come over you. You will relax and be able to function in that setting. I should say though, that this response won't come automatically. Developing it will be a challenge. It will take a concerted effort and perhaps much practice for you to fully incorporate the technique into daily situations. But I'm confident that you will do so in time."

Marie's profound frustration was evident. "Will the phobia eventually dissipate? Or at least let up somewhat? It can't be like this indefinitely." She held her purse on her lap, and she had twisted the leather strap twice around one hand, and was now pulling on it gently with the other, a gesture

Sonya had not seen before. "That's it? Hell, that's all you can tell us? She's got it, and that's it? I just can't accept that."

"Your concerns are understandable. These fears are sometimes difficult to predict, as you have seen regarding the onset." Dr. Francis spoke deliberately. "But they don't usually simply resolve on their own. I wish they did." He opened a desk drawer, pulled out a cassette, and turned to Sonya. "We have a relaxation tape of beach sounds that I can give you. Play this as you fall asleep; it may help rid you of the nightmares. Let's meet again in two weeks, so we can see how the tape is helping. And if you have any questions about any of this in the meantime, please don't hesitate to call. If you think of anything else you want to talk with me about, keep it in mind and we will get to it next time." He handed her the tape and then closed the folder of notes.

As he walked Sonya and her mother to the door, he added, "Good luck. See you in two weeks."

They thanked him and left.

When they settled into the car for the ride home, her mother asked, "Do you want to talk to someone else?"

"I like him. I'll try the visualization and the tape. Can I let you know later?"

"Of course."

Neither of them spoke the rest of the way back. Sonya felt comforted when they pulled into their street; its tree-lined neatness gave order to the world.

During the day Sonya practiced the visualization technique. Or, more accurately, she prepared to practice it. In the safe confines of her bedroom or the living room, she could sit for an hour or so after school, close her eyes, and imagine herself in the salt-filtered aura of the beach, sun and wind on her face, her feet immersed in warm sand. The scene indeed relaxed her. But any time she also brought to mind the reason she was supposed to practice the visualization in the first place, the calm quickly dissipated and her heart pounded. If she shut out the thought of those animals, she was fine. She figured she would work on the visualization at home first, before actually trying it in the presence of one of them.

And only one night did she turn on the tape of sonorous beach sounds. Realizing that the patterned caw-caw of seagulls distracted her from being attuned to stray sounds outside, she clicked the tape player off before it had played half a minute. Perhaps later she could try that again.

The next time she saw Dr. Francis, two weeks after, and he asked about her progress, she could genuinely say she believed it was going well.

"You've etched the scene firmly in your imagination?" He leaned forward at his desk, enthusiastic.

"Yes, I can see it all very clearly."

"That's great. Now what happens when you are outside and you encounter an animal? How long does it take, approximately, for you to relax after you start the visualization? Are you reasonably comfortable with it?"

"I—I haven't actually—I mean, I can see it all vividly. But I haven't tried it outside yet with one of them. I will, I will try that soon, but I had to make the image complete and set first, before I use it outside."

"So you haven't—? That's all right. We'll work with that." He leaned back in his chair and thoughtfully smoothed his beard.

"You asked about my drawing, so I brought you one," Sonya said, reaching into her backpack.

"Wonderful." He leaned forward again.

Sonya took out the drawing, an eight by ten, from a folder and handed it to him across the desk. "It's of one of them, from a series I did about it."

He contemplated the drawing, which she had titled *On the Sidewalk*, depicting, from the vantage point of someone walking under shaded trees, a stretch of slate squares diminishing into the distance. They fit neatly one after another until, about halfway down the stretch, a hideous black hole loomed where a square of sidewalk should be. It could not be breached with a leap; anyone approaching would have to safely cross to the other side to avoid the slipping sidewalk, curving down into the ominous cavern.

After Dr. Francis concluded his solemn study, he put the picture on his desk and folded his hands together, but he kept his attention on her rendition.

Sonya, nervous from his prolonged silence, said, "This is what it's like."

"From everything I've heard, from others as well as from you, this indeed illustrates what a phobia must feel like. May I keep this?"

"Yes." She had meant for him to keep it.

"Thank you."

At the end of the appointment he encouraged her to attempt the relaxation method outside, in the presence of one of the animals, now that she could so readily call the image to mind. And to keep trying the tape while falling asleep. This would help them know where to go from there. This time he set the next visit in a month, since that would give her ample opportunity to practice the techniques. He said that by then they would have quite a bit to discuss, and that he was looking forward to hearing about her progress.

Sometimes when she walked in the woods at the far end of their street, Sonya remembered her grandfather's stories of salmon running. Only once in all the years he lived there could he afford to leave the hills of his town to go on the fishing trip with his friends. He had told her and Lois many times when they were young, and visiting during their annual summer trip, that the salmon in the Alaskan rivers were at least five feet, and some over six, from end to end. He couldn't even show them by extending his arms. Their color he described as orange-pink like a sunset, and said that they were so abundant "you could walk across them like a tile floor, one huge ripple of them," making a sweeping gesture with his hand. "As far as the eye could reach," he always said. Then he took out a black and white photograph of himself and his friends in waders standing on a riverbank squinting and smiling, holding up colossal fish, mountains in the background.

In the woods she saw leaves, rocks, branches, flowers, and sometimes thought of the salmon. She smelled the bark of birches, rolled acorns between her fingers, held leaves up and examined their network of veins. In the dusk, she looked for the first star as she walked back up the street. She listened to the sound of her shoes on the pavement, felt the pull of muscles in her legs, and thought of the fish pulling themselves upstream, their pink muscled flesh glistening in the sun. She wondered where they came from and where they were going. "As far as the eye could reach," her grandfather always said.

14

This Heated Aspect Of The Air

Above the tape's primary sound, a sonorous low surf, the patterned cry of seagulls was meant to blend in almost undetected. When Sonya first played the tape it sounded pleasant enough, but with the lights out and her eyes closed, she had become accustomed to keeping an ear on neighborhood sounds and to sleeping in the succor of the house's hum. She could not be alert, could not hear stray noises, when the beach tape played; her first attempt to sleep to it had been unsuccessful. The next time she tried it with the volume lower, then with it, gradually, the lowest it would register, and still the gull sound was distracting. After a few weeks of trying to sleep to the tape, she closed it in a desk drawer.

Frequently in the month that followed Sonya's last visit to Dr. Francis she had the chance to try the visualization technique he had suggested. The first time she tried this she was walking down a sidewalk, having gone to the store for milk, when she saw a white cat dozing on the front steps of a house. She began to cross the street, then heard Dr. Francis's voice encouraging her, and turned back toward the sleeping cat. But she quickly discovered that closing her eyes to visualize the beach scene would make her vulnerable. What did the sea wind and warm sand matter, if the animal should open its steely eyes and fix them on her? Next she attempted to imagine the scene with her eyes open, while rooted to that spot on the sidewalk, but before she could hold them firmly the water, wind, and boats dissolved into particles and drifted away as her brain scrambled for what she could do, such as throw the carton of milk at the cat, if it lunged at her. Instead, trembling, the grocery bag gripped in her sweating palm, she crossed the street. A few times afterward, when each successive effort seemed less fruitful than the previous one, she thought of calling Francis to ask him how long it would take for her to effectively use this method, thinking his bit of urging would help, but each time she told herself she would just ask him when she saw him.

As the date of the upcoming visit with him approached, Marie deftly slipped, "It will be so interesting to see what he suggests from here," and, "You and he will have a lot to discuss, I'm sure," and other similar rallying remarks into ordinary supper conversations.

But increasingly caught between not wanting to disappoint her mother and her anxiety about her stalled attempts with the relaxation techniques—she could not bring herself to admit to Dr. Francis that she had not made any progress at all—Sonya became sick the morning of her appointment. When she called to cancel and the receptionist offered a reschedule date, Sonya declined that one as inconvenient. The next couple of offers met with the same resistance, until finally she said that she would check her schedule again and call their office as soon as she found a suitable time.

When Marie realized, over the following week or two, that Sonya had not yet rescheduled, she reminded her daughter that she would accompany her. When that was not met with enthusiasm, she pleaded with her by saying that it would be a shame to let the momentum started with Dr. Francis just dissipate; how wonderful it would be to conquer her fear, maybe even, eventually, get to the root of it. But none of Marie's remarks, though Sonya said "Yes, I know," to most of them, had the intended and hoped-for result. Gradually Marie understood that she would not make another appointment.

Then one day she went into her daughter's room and sat down in the rocking chair. "I talked with Dr. Francis this afternoon." Finally she had phoned him herself.

Sonya was at her desk drawing and looked up. "What did he say?"

"He feels that maybe you are not comfortable yet talking openly with him, but that the visualization—he asked if you were still working on that and I said I thought you were—it should benefit you. He said, too, that when you are ready to talk at greater length, then meeting with him will be even more productive." She hesitated, then added, "And that you will let me know when that time comes."

Sonya looked away from her mother, poised at the edge of the seat with her hands folded in her lap, and turned back to her desk. "I'm sorry, Mom," she said, and began to cry.

Her mother walked over, stood beside her and, one arm around her shoulders, the other hand resting on top of her head, gently coaxed Sonya against her stomach. "You don't have anything to apologize for," she said.

Although Sonya would not see Francis, she still thought often about what he had advised. She began to practice the visualization at night, and this helped her fall asleep, though it did not reduce the frequency of her bad dreams. And in the months that followed and throughout the summer she tried many times to transfer this closed-eye-falling-asleep calm to daytime encounters with cats. But she could never close her eyes around them or make that leap of imagination; she had to stay alert. The fear would not let up at all. She anticipated that during her last year of high school it would continue to be a firmly entrenched part of everything else she needed to worry about: the daily awkwardness, anxiety over exams and over the imminent preparation of college financial aid applications, and, especially, the grueling effort of sifting through peers' relentless speculative talk about everyone else's business.

The summer before that school year had started, Sonya thought again that perhaps her grandfather would understand her fear. Despite her faith in his insights, in the past she had found it too difficult to mention it to him, painful as it was to talk about. And then, too, she did not see him often enough. It occurred to her sometimes that if it were Lois with this affliction, it might be solved by now. Lois would have asked anyone, with her gift of directness, for an opinion about it, and surely would have questioned their grandfather well before now. Sonya wasn't like that though; this time, finally, she had decided that when they visited she would ask him directly what he thought.

But when he greeted them in the driveway, hugging first Marie and then the girls, and Sonya noticed more gray hair than he had had before, she mulled over how she would bring the subject up.

"I'm getting gray, aren't I?" he asked the girls.

"You look handsome, Grandpa," they said. Elegant would have also come to mind, even when he wore his beige work shirt and carried a trowel.

He laughed and waved his hand. "You always say that."

And when the time came, later in the week, when he and Sonya were by themselves walking through one of the greenhouses, she decided that maybe she would wait and just write him a letter about it when they were home again. But about halfway down the row, as he was explaining something to her, he suddenly put his hand on her shoulder and, instead of leading her all the way down the row, urged her back the way they had come. Sonya glanced over her shoulder to see that one of them, a calico, had wandered in the other end of the greenhouse and was exploring some pots stacked on the floor.

They were so fast that it would be a matter of seconds before it would notice the back of her neck and then bore there with its bits of cut-glass teeth, puncture with wet fur, make a path through her skin with its eyes, yellow or not, whatever color in their hollow of color was the depth they sprang from their tear their craving at her neck.

"It's one of the neighbor's, and I don't much like it," he said. "Let's look at tools." He walked behind her, between her and the cat, and pointed at the shelves above a workbench near the door they had entered.

As they approached the bench, he asked, "Do you still have that wooden box I gave you?"

Sonya could barely hear him. "Yes." Concentrating on her answer, she said, "It's on my bookcase at home with some stones and shells in it."

"Hang onto that box because they are hard to come by now. Look." He took a box off one of the shelves. "They make them out of pressed wood now, like cardboard, and they are flimsy. They aren't useful for storing much, practically made out of sawdust. They're a little smaller, too. But yours is real wood."

Sonya scanned beneath nearby benches to confirm that it hadn't followed them, and when she realized it was sprawled out in the sun at the opposite end of the row, she turned back toward her grandfather and wiped her sweating hands on her shorts. After watching her, he glanced at the box in his hand, then returned it to the shelf.

"Whatever it is," he said, "someday you'll be looking at it from the other side of town. It will work itself out. It will be over with."

Sonya wanted to ask him what he thought it was and how he knew everything would work out. "Really?"

"I know it will." He rubbed his ear scar.

She focused her attention on him, absorbing more of his assurance.

"I'm old, remember? That means I've seen some knots. So believe your grandfather about this."

"I do."

"Let's go outside." Since he walked behind her on the way out, Sonya did not worry as much that the animal would follow her with its eyes and knew that if it did, it would be at least slightly deterred by her grandfather's shoulders before it could reach her.

And with her grandmother, while there was not the same intention of a serious conversation that Sonya sought with her grandfather, there was calm she found in a way of relating that was almost like talking. Back in the house, she sat at the kitchen table and sliced tomatoes while Glenda and Marie stood at the sink rinsing beans and snapping off their tips. Sonya looked up to see her grandmother, as she reached around her mother to grab another bowl on the counter, cup Marie's elbow briefly with her other hand, then resume the prepping. She found calm in the rhythmic snapping, the toss in the metal bowl, sound of the water. Soon would come the corn shucking, silks threading the air, swift hands, the yellow emerging, and all the while close by the curve of tomatoes, warm musty scent of them. The green snaps, clear rinse, the only talking.

She had felt more relaxed the rest of the visit, more immersed in the New England hills, knowing she didn't need to try to figure out how to talk with her grandfather about it. And now she understood that once when he had sent her a card saying "Everything will be all right," he was referring, not to school or to the divorce, the two options she had thought of then, but to her fear. She did not know when her mother had told him, but she was glad that she had found the words.

With her father, Sonya did not have to worry about bringing her fear into the conversation. He did it for her, asking now and then, as he did one day in the early fall when he took the girls out for their Saturday lunch, whether she had yet opened the drawstring bag he had given her.

"No, I haven't," Sonya said, though she was quick to add, "But I look at it sometimes. It's right there on a bookshelf in my room."

"Hey, that's fine. I know some day you'll open it and take out what's inside."

It was after the meal, and as he sipped a cup of coffee, their father began to answer a question the girls had asked, more than once, years earlier.

"You know, my father had a fear also. I guess I can tell you now more about what happened. You're older. Jesus, I am, too." He laughed, and Sonya and Lois looked at each other, puzzled.

This story they already had the rough outlines of, but their father, when they had tried to fill those in, had always said he would tell them more when they were older, though he'd been vague about which particular ages qualified as older. Apparently he had decided that.

"He was afraid of being with himself in one place for any length of time. Because there would be too much of him there without my mother. He kept moving so that wouldn't happen. Left Wikeegee, took us south for a while, then back to the Midwest. And then when your uncle Samuel and I finished high school, he probably figured it would be even worse, since we wouldn't be there to take up some of that space. That's when he left."

"Did he tell you he was leaving?" Lois was the one expert at pressing for specifics.

"Not in so many words. Actually, not in words at all. He started selling off furniture. A china cabinet here, a dresser there. The place emptied out. One day he came home driving a used bread truck. Still had the name, Nickel's, along the sides in worn green letters. No explanation. Just parked it behind the house, worked on it at night. He mounted some shelves and a cabinet. We'd look out the back door and see his work light."

Sonya imagined her father younger and someone beside him familiar, though it was someone who she had never seen, standing at the door looking into the yard. At the center of that dark she could see the dim work bulb, its whitish yellow spilling through the driver's side door and the round back windows, pulsing faintly with his movements like a distant signal on a sea at night.

"Then bought a cot, painted over the rear windows."

"Then he just left?" The sharp brevity of Lois's question elicited a sigh from their father.

"No, not right away. He slept in it for a week or two first. Came in in the morning to get ready for work, went out to it at night to sleep. We tried to talk with him about it, but your grandfather was not a man of many words."

"So you didn't know he was planning to leave?" Sonya realized as she was asking this that there wasn't a gentler way to ask it.

"No. We came home one day in the afternoon and it was gone. I remember staring at the four yellow marks in the ground where the wheels had killed the grass. We found an envelope in the kitchen with some money in it—he had sold his car—what was that, Buick? No, maybe a Plymouth, mammoth ugly thing. And a note saying he loved us but he had to leave. 'Be on his way' was how he put it. Then a few days later we saw a couple walking around the yard, talking and pointing. We asked them if we could be of assistance, and they were surprised to see us. Turns out he had sold the house to them. Barely broke even. We asked them if he had mentioned his trip, but of course he hadn't."

He took another sip of coffee, let out another breath. The girls had almost more detail than they could absorb.

"That couple must have thought he was the most awful man, not telling his own kids he sold the house. For a while he'd send us notes at the house, I guess knowing they would give them to us, which they did. Actually, they rented a room to us at first; maybe the old man had talked with them about that. If he had, they never let on. Or maybe he figured they would forward his correspondence if they had to. At any rate, he was all over the place and described the roads he was on and what he saw, but he did not talk about himself. Samuel and I would talk to each other about Mr. Nickel. 'Where do you think Mr. Nickel is now?' Then the notes stopped coming. Eventually we realized what sort of trip this was. Mr. Nickel didn't know any other way, he couldn't do any more than he did."

Their father finished his coffee, took out his wallet and put a tip on the table.

"So what happened after that?" As if the story had been merely a story, and not something she knew to be true, Lois was hoping for some other kind of ending.

"That's it. Nothing happened after that."

The girls hesitated.

"Wherever he is, he is finite. Just like the next Joe. He did what he knew how. He didn't know any other way."

They needed more time to contemplate all of this, but not here at lunch.

"You kids ready to scoot? I've got some stuff I need to get done this afternoon."

"Sure," they said.

They didn't talk much on the return ride to their house. But when their father steered into the driveway and waited for them to step out of the car, Lois said, "Thanks for telling us the story."

Their father looked at them, said "Hey," and shrugged as if it wasn't a big deal.

Once inside, each withdrew to her room and lay there for a while, feeling blank and stunned, the long shadow of their father's grief drifting down slowly like a lost scarf through the years since his boyhood and settling, finally, on them, clothing their hearts. Then, somewhat restored, they could get up and attend to the remainder of their Saturday. Now though they were accompanied, and would be permanently, by the dim figure of Mr. Nickel, a hazy and pained apparition who, had the circumstances of his life been otherwise, they could have laughed with and would have loved.

In the beginning of that school year there had been various notices posted in the hallways announcing the names of clubs for students to join, their meeting times and places. Though several sounded promising to her, including the Outdoor Experience and the Journalism Clubs, Sonya had not found one whose focus closely enough matched her interests. She discussed the options with Marie.

Her mother encouraged it completely, saying initially, "It will be fun," and a few days later, and then in a few weeks, repeated, more pointedly, "This would be good for you." By this Sonya knew her mother meant it was good for her to spend less time by herself, to be more social. And beneficial, too, for her to be distracted from her fear, which her mother worried would worsen somehow.

"Mom, I'm fine," Sonya often said. "It's not a growth. It can't get worse." But she worried about it, too.

And she understood that for her mother the question was not so much what group her daughter would join but whether she would join one at all.

Now that Veronica had become completely absorbed in the duties of her sorority, among them fundraising car washes on Saturdays, the two seldom got together anymore. Veronica had made a lukewarm attempt to interest her friend in joining, but Sonya did not understand the appeal of such a group, nor the practice of coercing potential members to humiliate them-selves to prove worthy of membership. A secret that had slipped out and was circulating was that initiates were blindfolded in their underwear and then surrounded by members who marked those places on their bodies in magic marker that they assessed to be in most need of improvement. Of course no older member would confirm this. There was opportunity for humiliation, indeed, even ample, for most kids, just in growing up. Why add to it? She couldn't quite figure it out.

"It doesn't mean we are vituperative," Veronica had explained.

Sonya sounded the word out to herself.

"Malicious."

"I know," Sonya said. And that was the extent of their discussion on the topic.

She wondered, too, whether any of Veronica's sorority sisters ever dis-cussed her eating habits with her. Perhaps in that group no such problem was perceived; every member appeared to Sonya nearly as thin as Veronica, though it did seem when they had talked about the club that day, that she was getting even thinner. As she spoke, Sonya observed that her jawline was becoming more pronounced. Or it seemed that way, and her wrists, pressed against the books she was holding in front of her, almost flat. Sonya didn't draw attention to these observations specifically, but she did ask, "Have you been doing OK?"

To that Veronica answered, "Yes, great," and rushing off to her college prep chemistry class tossed, "My day is one frisson after the next. Look that up," over her shoulder. It had been quite some time, anyway, since the two had had a lengthy, and sincere, conversation.

Though the initiation requirement of membership did not appeal to her, Sonya understood the desire to belong. There were a number of other students who, also seeking a group, did not find one to join and who, like Sonya, did artwork apart from schoolwork. A few of them, as representatives, approached an art teacher who then asked the principal for them whether it would be possible to find a place for an informal art club to work. Despite initial resistance, the principal acquiesced when she offered to staff it. After a couple months of arranging schedules and more budget discussion, that winter one of the regular art rooms was transformed, at least for a couple of after-school hours three days a week, into The Art Annex. The art staff rotated those days among themselves, and any students who wanted could hang out there to finish a class project or begin a new one of their choice, not for grading.

It was the no-grading policy that inspired Sonya, as well as the autonomy of the projects. Any student could stop by, grab some tools and begin working, a signature required on a sign-in-and-out sheet for equipment use. They could even bring materials home. In January she began enjoying this offer, as several other students by then had, both those known for their art skills and non-artists alike.

Though Elinor Jarett had moved to the area recently, the previous fall, a lot of people knew her already. Sonya had seen her from a distance in school and admired Elinor's ability to talk with anyone; she wasn't connected to one particular group of students. She had in those few months worked set design for a play, had helped organize a folk music festival and, occasionally, beginning that February, dropped by the Annex to talk with a friend or to make something.

From a distance Sonya also noticed Elinor's clothes. It seemed that she had dodged the customary pressures of that much-scrutinized territory.

She wore jeans and vests (some obviously home-grown), was casual in a way that signified that she was simply passing through the school on her way somewhere else. She just happened to be there that day, so she would enjoy herself. It wasn't just that she resisted the current trend of paisley and floral polyester shirts, flowing skirts and hip-huggers over platforms, pastel angora turtlenecks with thin gold chains dangling a cross or a birthstone over the collar's edge, holding its breath; many students in the school were casual. There might have been as many who wore hiking boots as wore platforms. Sonya noticed, though, that Elinor often wore an article of clothing a few days a week, when most students knew that the more new clothes they had, casual or not, the higher the status. No one would intentionally wear something more than once a week, if it could be helped. And she wore the same pair of brown leather hiking boots most days, alternated with, when the weather was milder, one pair of brown leather clogs. With Elinor it was something else then: perhaps a kind of enjoyment, a way of luxuriating in the textures of a day, of which clothes were merely one tactile aspect. They were part of that enjoyment because they were a part of her life, not because they said anything about group affiliation or about what her parents did for a living. Her father, in fact, like many fathers in the area, as an engineer in the city, could have provided amply for her material comfort, and her mother, at home, would have had time to help her daughter coordinate her wardrobe. So it seemed to Sonya, from a distance, that Elinor had some insights into life, or at least into the frequently hideous and often painstakingly negotiated snarl of high school. And despite not fitting in in that most visible, fashionable, way, or perhaps because of it, she appeared at ease in the world, as if this place had had her name on it, written in the gold-leaf of a sunny afternoon, for a measurable portion of recorded time.

It was in the Annex that Sonya first talked with her. Elinor came in one afternoon and asked students if they would be interested in signing a petition that she was circulating. She sat down at one of the work tables with others gathered around her while she explained what had happened. Apparently, there had been an incident two days before in her gym class that was deemed disruptive by their recently hired teacher, Ms. Adams, who brought it to the immediate attention of the administration. Several students had subsequently been suspended for their behavior. It started when one of them, who no one else would name, with a towel tucked around her, stuck a maxi pad to her forehead and walked from the restroom back to the locker room. A few other girls quickly ran to the machine, slid a nickel in, removed the adhesive strip, and stuck the cotton beam to their forehead. They then formed a line and circled around the lockers and began to sing, "Give me a K-O-T-E-X-X-X!" When they jumped up and flung their arms out on the last "X," some members of the cheerleading squad, who had laughed with them up to that point, thought Ms. Adams should be aware of what they were doing. By the time she got there from her office, several other girls had joined the chant, some were leaning against their locker, laughing and pointing, their hair dripping wet, one shoe on; not one student in the whole class was getting dressed after showering, retrieving her books, making it to her next class on time.

The five-day suspension of those believed to have initiated the fun Elinor thought unfair, and she was hoping that if enough others also thought so and signed her petition, the administration would reconsider. She had typed two lines at the top of the sheet: "We the undersigned think that the suspension of Valerie MacConny, Michelle Harris, Lynn Anne Menkowitz, Sue Tilmund, and Stacy Brooks is unfair. We ask that they be readmitted into school and that no permanent reprimand be placed in their files."

There were mixed reactions among the group at the Annex. When someone said he thought what they did was hilarious, another pointed out that the behavior sounded as if they were talking about kids in junior high and added that she believed the suspension was reasonable, given the immaturity the girls demonstrated.

Someone else asked if anyone had actually been harmed in any way, to which another student answered that the feelings of the cheerleaders perhaps had not been taken into account. Maybe that was what the teacher was trying to protect.

Sonya asked Elinor to clarify. "But didn't you say that at first the cheerleaders were laughing, too?"

A couple strands of her short brown hair hung over Elinor's forehead as she shifted to face Sonya directly. There was a scar on her chin, a few freckles on her face, and her eyes were a lighter brown than they had seemed from a distance.

"Yeah, they were. They might have even been among those who started it. There is talk that they may have brought it to Ms. Adams' attention precisely because they realized that they could all get in trouble for it. We weren't all back to our lockers from the shower, so only a couple people know exactly who was responsible, but no one is saying."

There were other comments and questions floated, as the group considered the petition.

"It seems to me," Elinor offered, "that the question is not whether we think what they did was funny. We can disagree about that and about the issue of maturity. But is the administration really concerned about what is 'disruptive' to an education? If that were their concern, they wouldn't suspend these students. Being out of school is disruptive to their education."

Then someone suggested that the administration was working with the idea that a disruptive environment had been created.

Sonya hadn't said much yet, but now she added, "This incident did make the class laugh, or most of it. You could say that humor enhances an educational environment, couldn't you? Maybe their definitions should change."

This was seconded when someone said, "And a petition might help do that."

By the close of the discussion, Elinor had all their signatures but one, and she took suggestions about where to circulate it next and advice about the question of number of signatures collected versus the benefit of expediency submitting it to the administration.

"I'm thinking about heading out," he said casually, as if he didn't mean leaving.

"What do you mean?" Lois asked. The girls' father had taken them out for lunch, and the three of them were enjoying lasagne specials at the Rosebud Cafe.

"I can't stay in that room at Leon's forever. Bhutan," he said, and sipped his wine.

"Where is that?" Sonya asked, though she didn't want to know the answer because it sounded far away.

"It's a mountainous country near China. Some pretty rough terrain, but lots of mountain scenery and places to stay for twenty-five cents a day. You kids could come and hang out there with me in the summers. How's that sound?"

"How are you going to get there?" Lois asked. "How will you make a living?"

"Maybe people there buy clay work?" Sonya asked. They wanted to know about his daily life, some tangible aspect of his plan they could hold onto.

"I know a guy who runs a chartering business, and he can get me inland passage in exchange for work. I'll find something."

Passage sounded so serious to the girls. Sonya imagined a grainy black and white film clip with people waving out of time, leaving their forlorn countries, then, weary from their journey in the steerage, arriving, stumbling off a steamer ship. And someone knew the coiled rope the wet deck in dark rain he had known the weight of the rope, the texture in his hands, the smooth metal chair the weight of his despair who was leaving whose journey.

"Do you know anybody there?" Lois asked. Serious to her meant she needed more answers. "And what about your job here?"

"I'll manage."

"Have you told Uncle Samuel about your trip?"

"Who?"

Lois's mouth found the words in the air first, and Sonya braced for the question. "How come you two did not stay in touch?"

"Sometimes people drift apart. Sometimes they lose what they had."

"But how come you two—"

"You girls want some dessert today? I was thinking we could drive over to Percy's Homemade and have a sundae."

"I could eat one," Sonya said.

"OK," Lois said, though reluctantly. No amount of pressing would give her the answers that she wanted.

That night the girls opened the atlas, as they had many times when they were younger.

"It's way over there," said Lois, pointing at a speck of mountainous green on the other side of the sweeping wash of Pacific blue. "It's so far. Do you think he'll go?"

"I don't know," Sonya said. "Things are different now. Maybe. Bhu-tan," she said. Then again, rolling it around her tongue. "My dad lives in Bhu-tan." She said it with her head tilted to the side, and when Lois appeared still worried despite the attempt at caricature, she glanced down at the spread of countries before them and asked her in a distorted voice not approximating any recognizable accent, "Where does your dad live?"

Lois consulted the charted blue and green and said, "My dad lives in Alberta."

Sonya said, "Well, my dad lives in Tangier."

"My dad lives in Siberia."

"My dad lives in Buckeray."

"Where is that?" Lois asked, and laughed. "My dad lives in You-Made-That-Up."

"Then my dad lives in Switzerland."

"Hey, mine does, too," Lois said. "Maybe they know each other."

"Yeah? What's he look like?" Sonya flared her nostrils, and tucked up her top lip so that it stayed folded, her gums showing.

"You look ug-ly," Lois said.

Sonya grabbed her sister's foot and, after pulling her shoe off, tickled it until Lois begged her to stop and threatened to bite her.

Then, making the most of their spontaneous and childish giddiness, they threw themselves back on the floor laughing, the expansive open atlas, with its delicate hieroglyphics, all that distance in its rounded fruit-colored mountains, islands, and countries, for the moment forgotten at their feet.

Sonya stood at her locker gathering materials for her next class when Elinor walked over.

"Hi."

"Hi. That's a neat vest." Sonya admired the beadwork along the fringe of Elinor's gray knit garment.

"Thanks. I made it from a kit."

"How is the petition response?" When Sonya looked at her this time, standing that close, she realized that they were the same height, in the average range, and probably in the same range for weight, also about average, though she generally didn't take too much heed in that category.

"I've got a lot of signatures, but I don't know if it will make a difference. I'll let you know on Sunday. They should give me an answer on Friday afternoon."

"Sunday?"

"Oh, I meant to ask, do you want to go for a walk on Sunday?"

"I'd like that. Where do you want to walk?"

"We could meet at one of the fields at the college campus. That's a nice place to wander around."

"Sounds great," Sonya said, closing her locker.

"How about around two o'clock, over by the baseball bleachers?"

"That's fine with me."

"See you then."

Sunday morning Lois stood in the doorway of her sister's room brushing out her hair and watched her rummaging through dresser drawers. "Why are you worrying about what to wear? You'll just be walking around a field."

"I know," Sonya said, pulling out her gray sweatpants. She took her blue ones off, put the gray ones on. "Do these look too baggy?" She couldn't help but ask, despite Lois's critical observation.

"They all look the same. Sweats are sweats," Lois declared, and walked away.

Sonya was sensitive in particular to her feet. Folds of cloth rumpled at her ankles, making her sneakers appear dainty, petite. She put the blue sweatpants back on.

In the afternoon she rode her bike to the campus and slowed to a stop at their designated meeting spot, the ground a little muddy, March grass beginning its shine. Glancing around, she saw Elinor at a distance turn from the side street and ride her bicycle onto the field. Sonya watched her approaching, the image like a photographic plate, more defined with each successive dip in a rinse, until finally she rode up right beside Sonya and her hair, face, deep green sweatshirt and every detail was clear, radiant, in the afternoon sun. Then, rather than greet each other with words, they just looked.

"Let's lock our bikes up over by the bleachers and walk around a while," Elinor suggested, as she caught her breath.

"Do you play any sports?" Sonya wondered why she had picked the field to walk in.

As they locked their ten-speeds, Elinor said, "No, I'm not any good at sports, but I like hanging out in the field. It's pretty over here and fairly close to my house. Do you?"

"I like to ride my bike, not exactly a team sport."

They stretched before walking, and Sonya looked over at Elinor's neck, the muscles relaxed with her head back, then watched as she swung her arms wide, bent over and touched her toes. Not wanting her staring to be perceived as impolite, she twisted her sides as she glanced at the field and then at the road. She thought she could feel Elinor looking at her. It didn't feel like someone watching to see if she was stretching enough or to check her technique; it felt like someone looking at her without judgment, at the way she moved, at the sway of her braided hair out from her back, at the look of anticipation on her face as she squinted up into the afternoon sky. Her stomach registered the watching.

Then Elinor said, pointing, "Let's start out with this field," and they headed out around one of the baseball fields.

"What happened with your petition?"

"We reached a compromise. Since I collected almost a hundred signatures, Wilkins said he would shorten the suspension to three days."

"That's great." Their principal was known for being somewhat rigid, but he was also respected for his efforts to be fair-minded. "What about their files?"

"He agreed not to have any permanent reprimand written in any of them, because for all five of the students this was their first 'altercation' with him."

"That seems reasonable. So circulating the petition didn't get you into any trouble?"

"It didn't seem to." As Elinor sketched out meeting with him and his assistant in his office, working through an official agenda, Sonya listened closely to the specifics while she thought about the way the afternoon wind rippled their sweatpants and sweatshirts as they walked into it. Their hair blowing about while they stepped blade over blade shadows lengthening behind them in the warm grass stretching against the green blade over blade over green shine and blade.

"Maybe they admired you for following through with it."

"I'm not sure they would use that word, but thanks for the thought."

"Did they keep the signatures?"

"Yes, they were very official about all of it. They secured them all in their own special file, and they told me about two other successful petitions from a few years ago."

"Just two?"

"Two recently, that doesn't include all the ones from the previous decade."

"What were the recent two for?"

"One was because the girls' softball team used to have to pay for their own uniforms, but the boys' baseball uniforms were free, the school paid for them."

"Was that one successful?"

"It was, partly because the students knew about Title IX, and that put some pressure on the administration."

"It's cool they won."

"Yeah, it is, isn't it?"

Sonya nodded her agreement. "What was the other one?"

"The other one involved an art student who wanted his sculpture to be displayed in the front flagpole area during graduation week."

"That doesn't sound like too much to ask."

"They agreed to that one, too, and kept it up even though some of the parents complained about it."

"Why? Was the piece a nude or something?"

"It didn't sound as if it was, from what Wilkins said. Some kind of configuration welded from metal scraps—he was thinking way abstract. But the parents didn't see it as art."

"It seems like students have succeeded with petitions here, especially if the administration is willing to stand up to parents like that."

"It does," Elinor said. "At first I thought he was just telling me all that to make himself sound good, but actually, I think he was sincere. Probably there are lots of times they do what parents want, but I think it's great that they support students in conflicts like that, too. This place is better because of that."

While they walked several loops around the field they started from and around a few adjacent ones, Elinor told Sonya about the school she had attended the year before, in New Jersey, in a much more conservative district, and about some of the tensions there between students and administrators, among other limitations. That place did not have anything resembling the Annex, and even if it had, likely would not have permitted a silkscreen project like the one currently underway of T-shirts sporting the Zig-Zag rolling paper graphic. Though some whimsical liberties had been taken with mustache length, the portrait was nonetheless a convincing likeness that gave its creators a reason for playful boasting.

Shortly after they were finished with that topic, a gust of wind came up against them and blew them back a bit. As it subsided, Sonya realized that she was walking by herself, and she turned around to find Elinor walking tilted backward, her head tipped back, her arms slack and flapping behind her like windsocks, stepping to the side as if still buffeted about by a strong wind. She kept a serious expression, until Sonya let out a loud burst of laughter and then she gave in and laughed, too. "I love doing that," she said.

When their legs were tired from walking, she suggested they rest on the bleachers.

They walked over to their starting point and Sonya slowed as they reached the seats, but Elinor sprinted to the top. "Come up," she said.

Sonya climbed to the top. They lay down on their backs, their heads together. They bent their knees up, hands on their stomachs, gazed into the immaculate afternoon sky, and caught their breath.

"I bet from the field we look like an enormous insect perched up here," Elinor said.

"Something out of a sci-fi film." They flailed their arms around, kicked their legs, watched the shadow below on the grass, laughed, then brought them to rest again. Elinor reached her hand up to scratch her head and inadvertently pulled a strand of Sonya's hair.

"Sorry."

"Oh, no problem."

They were quiet a few minutes, looking up into the blue.

"I heard you and Veronica Simmons used to be close friends," Elinor said.

"We did."

"You two seem so—you know—from different planets. I can't picture you hanging out."

"That was a year or two ago, before Veronica discovered a sorority. Everything kind of went to hell, as far as our friendship anyway, when she became involved with it."

"Was that tough?"

"Do you know how it is?"

"Yes. When I was a freshman my best friend moved away, so it's not the same situation. But I was a total drag. I didn't laugh or talk much for months, just sulked around."

"I can't quite imagine that—I mean, you sulking. But the painful part, yes. I'm sorry." She thought of her own funk when Odessa moved away. And then, the thought following, shooing it along—maybe later, some distant afternoon, when she and Elinor were talking earnestly again, she would bring Odessa into the conversation.

"My parents were so worried that they tried to distract me with guitar lessons and when that didn't seem to work, they sent me on a canoeing trip on the Delaware River."

"Did anything help?"

"No, not really," Elinor said with a soft laugh. "I gradually became more involved with other friends and returned to my usual self, but my usual self was changed."

"I guess people come back to themselves when they are ready, you know? Even come back changed." Perhaps her own changes could be part of that distant conversation.

"Yeah," she said. "Sometimes I still miss her, though. Do you ever miss Veronica?"

"Yes," Sonya said. "When I see her laughing with her new friends I remember stuff we did. We used to go downtown to Woolworth's and take our picture in the photo booth. We'd laugh until we nearly peed. They always came out so goofy. Her mother would say, 'Can't you take at least one serious one?' But every time, all four would be of us crossing our eyes or pulling our noses up or covering each other's face. We were always silly."

"Some people don't grow out of that."

"I can see that you haven't."

"You either," Elinor said. After a pause she added, "You notice how it's easier to talk this way, when we're not looking at each other?"

Her directness surprised Sonya, and her face heated with a blush. "Yes." It was easier; she hadn't thought about it until Elinor pointed it out. And even though she hadn't revealed the upheaval of Odessa's leaving, still, she had felt herself exposed in their declarations. A layer or two peeled away, a vulnerability acknowledged. "Why is that?"

"Maybe it's like a confessional. It's easier to talk to a voice." She sat up and swung her legs around. "My back is sore. Is yours?"

"Yeah," Sonya said, bringing her legs around, too. They looked out over the field.

Elinor said, "I think it means we trust each other."

"I think so, too."

"Would you like to come over?"

"Do you have any pets?"

"No, why?"

"I just wondered. Sure, I'll come over. That would be nice."

At Elinor's house, a few blocks from the campus, they drank sodas while they stood in her room and pored over pictures on the wall above her desk, their shoes tossed on the floor behind them. "There I am," she said, pointing into a sea of smiling glossy faces from her previous school. "Class trip to New York, the first time some of my friends had ridden the subway. They took photos of everything that day." She offered background on other trips, landscapes, various groupings, photographs she had taken as well as the work of others. There was a knock, and they both turned as Elinor's mother peered around the door.

"Hi. I thought I heard you come in." Though she smiled, what struck Sonya was a formal aspect that Caroline Jarett had; maybe it was the silk shawl over her knit cream-colored sweater, or the dangling gold earrings, the meticulous hair. Her style, and that of their roomy split-level house, was in dramatic contrast to Elinor's. The thought that came to Sonya's mind was that maybe her mother had just been to the opera, though she didn't have any direct evidence of this and could only guess what people wore to one, never having been to an opera herself. Her own parents hadn't been to one, though both were known to join in an aria on the radio, humming, now and then.

"Hi, Mom. This is Sonya."

They greeted each other. Then Elinor's mother asked, "Do you girls need anything?"

"No, we're set. Thanks." Her mother closed the door.

"She seems nice."

"She is," Elinor said, both of them turning back to the pictures on the wall.

As they stood beside each other for a while longer talking, Sonya was aware that Elinor had a salty windy smell from their afternoon outside. It was spring again, and the pungent scent of new grass had come inside with them. Elinor told her a few stories about the years she had been at her old school and also showed Sonya framed photographs of her relatives on a shelf above the desk.

As she looked at these, Sonya noticed a tin box on Elinor's desk with an index card taped to it marked Lionel House Fund. Elinor saw that she pondered what it was, but she didn't offer any information until Sonya asked her directly about it.

"The Lionel House is a women's shelter in the city."

"Do you do fundraising for them?" Sonya didn't know how Elinor would have found the time to.

"Actually, that is a clothes fund I started last fall. My parents give me a generous amount every month for clothes, but they said I can do what I want with it. Most of it goes to the shelter."

"What made you decide to do that?"

"I read a newspaper article about the place, specifically about a woman who came in after she had taken her kids—four of them, I think—away from an abusive father. She didn't have any money for school clothes for them, so I was thinking, well, they can have mine. That's when I started making donations to the place, and I kept doing it every month."

"That woman must have really appreciated what you did."

"I hope it helped her out," Elinor said, "but the women there didn't tell me. I do it all anonymously. They said it is safer that way, so that there is no direct link to me, or to anyone who gives them donations, in case we could become a target or be linked to an abused woman. They have to prevent the abusers from using donors in some way to harass the women they are after. Or from tracking them down in any way through us. They said that happened once, and they have to be absolutely certain it never happens again."

"It's so good that you do that."

"No, it's not," Elinor said. Then when she realized that Sonya was taken aback and maybe hurt by her remark, she explained. "I mean, I know what you are saying. But I feel like it is not really even a sacrifice to me, you know? What could I possibly need? I have everything I could want, my parents have made my life very comfortable, so it feels like this is the least thing I could give away. Some of those women have nothing. I mean, nothing but anxiety and fear to deal with. Lives that are totally perilous."

Sonya nodded, listening.

"I'm sorry if I sounded rude a minute ago."

"No," Sonya said, "You didn't. Well, at first—"

"Just at first?" They laughed.

"Maybe a little, but I understand now what you mean." They paused, contemplating. Then Sonya glanced at her watch, noted that it was later than she thought, an hour passing since they had gotten to Elinor's, so she said, reluctantly, "I better get home to dinner."

"I'll ride you halfway."

Since she lived only a few miles away, Sonya thought she should say, "You don't have to," but instead she said, "That would be nice." They gathered their shoes, went outside and got on their bicycles.

After several minutes of riding Sonya said, "This is about halfway." They slowed to a stop. "Thanks."

"Sure," Elinor said. "I'll see you tomorrow in school."

"Bye."

"Bye."

When Sonya was part way down a nearby avenue, she looked over her shoulder to find Elinor returning her glance. Again her stomach reacted as they waved.

That night she wrote "thanks, I had fun" on a rectangular piece of paper. She began a detailed border of orange trumpet flowers, the ones that had rooted up the side of one of her grandfather's greenhouses, considering their shade and proportion. The flowers reminded her of the times when he had taken the girls on a dig. He would pull on his boots, throw his pail and shovel in the trunk of the Rambler, and off they went. In the startling blue of summer they wandered the fields and roadsides until something caught their eyes. It might have been a tall stubborn lupine or a plush cattail. They would dig up a sample of it, put it in the pail with some dirt, and bring it back. Occasionally Lois or Sonya had spotted a spiky weed and when they pointed it out, their grandfather said, "That might be interesting. Let's have a closer look." Those they brought home too, and he found a place for them in a field beside the greenhouses. Whatever it was, he told them something about it, either about its root system or how much water it liked or maybe the span of its blooming. Of all the variations growing there, she and Lois had especially liked the orange trumpet flowers. Now, too, she thought about their color and abundance; there was so much of them to give away. When she finished the drawing, she tucked it in an envelope.

The next day she slid it through a slot of Elinor's locker.

Her friend came up to her later in the hallway. "I had fun, too." She smiled. "Did you draw the flowers?"

"Yes."

"They're neat," Elinor said. "Can I see more of your drawings?"

"I'd be glad to show you," Sonya said, "if you want to see them."

"I do."

That afternoon in the Annex she sat at a workbench contemplating a package of clay when she heard someone come in. A friend of Elinor's was leading her to a shelf of jewelry supplies. They put their packs down, picked up a few tools, and found a place across the room. Elinor might have sensed her watching, because after a minute or two she looked over, and they smiled at each other. Sonya experienced their acknowledgment as another kind of presence in the room. The environs were the same as they were every school day afternoon. It was March; the playing fields she could see out the row of windows were as wide and as muddy. The sky, clean, vast. Far off on one end was a street, woods bordered one side of the fields, and a distant row of backyards bordered the other. She saw these almost every day, but today she perceived them as particularly beautiful, so sure in their places. And when she looked nearer, across the room toward Elinor, she felt something like tension, except that it was pleasurable. It was as if this presence would magnify if they walked toward each other; it would spill out from them and cover the others, cover the workbenches and the plastic supply boxes, cover the bulletin board with leaves of colored paper tacked joyously, casually, and the black and white Thomas wall clock, cover the fields, the streets, and the woods. The air hummed with talk; the room whistled and laughed. In this group, loosely together and by chance, Sonya wondered if the others saw that she was changed by this new gleam on the surface of things, this heated aspect of the air. And she wondered, in her transparent joy, if she acted any differently because of it. But no one seemed to notice.

15

Her Hands

"What is your father doing in Ohio?" Marie asked, after seeing the card's postmark.

Lois had gotten home first and opened it, then showed the card to Sonya when she got in. A photograph of farmland, idyllic, serene, graced the front.

"He says he's visiting friends and will call when he's back in town," Lois explained.

Sonya asked their mother, "Who does he know in Ohio?"

"I don't know. Maybe someone he knew in school." There was no return address on the envelope. "Did he say when that would be?"

"No. He just says 'see you soon.' Lois, did he mention this to you?"

"No. You either, huh?"

"No."

"I'll call Leon tonight, see if he knows your father's schedule."

That evening the girls stood by the phone when their mother called.

"Hello, Leon, this is Marie. How are you?" She nodded a few times, then said, "Yes, fine. Their father sent them a card from Ohio. I'm calling to see if Mitchell discussed his schedule with you, or if he at least said when he would return." She said "hmm" a few times, then, "Oh well. Thanks anyway. Let us know if you hear anything." She hung up and clarified for the girls. "Apparently he didn't tell Leon very much. But all his furniture and other belongings are still in the basement there. He seems to have taken only a few clothes, so most likely he'll be back soon." Recognizing the concern in their eyes, she added, "And I know that he's fine."

"Yeah," Sonya said.

"Yeah," Lois said. They hadn't told their mother about his mention of Bhutan.

"I think I like this one the best," Elinor said, pointing to trees and a stream, "but it's hard to decide." It was Sunday after they had gotten together again to go for a walk. They sat in Sonya's room looking at a group of her drawings spread out before them on the wooden floor.

"That's where we used to live. The stream was near our house."

"Does it have a title?"

"No. Sometimes titles occur to me, and sometimes they don't. This didn't have one."

"How about *Where I Used to Live*?"

"That fits." Sonya liked the suggestion in it that she had lived in the trees or in the stream. So many of her afternoons had been spent there. At her desk she pulled out the notebook in which she kept a list of her paintings and drawings, then sat back down. There was a short description of each, the kind of pens or pencils or paint she used for it, and sometimes, heft of paper preferred, and a title, if there was one. She found her description of the trees and the stream, and jotted Elinor's title in the space beside it.

They were drinking hot tea. Sonya was aware of Elinor's hands, now raising the cup to her mouth, her cotton sleeve against her arm, now lowering the cup to hold it before her again. As Sonya picked up her cup and took a sip, again the presence was manifest, now heat on the back of her hands, drawn toward Elinor's hands. The pictures before them gave her something to focus on.

She wanted to ask Elinor if she felt it too, but she couldn't put it into words. So instead she told her about the time Lois brought home a salamander from that stream and left it in the bathtub, filled with an inch or two of water, where she thought it would stay while she was at a friend's house. By the time their mother got home in the late afternoon, it had found its way into her fig tree. Sonya heard her gasp as she watered the plants.

"Did your sister get to keep the salamander?" Elinor asked.

"No. We brought it to the stream that afternoon, watched it wiggle away."

"Was your mother mad?"

"Not really. They used to let us run around in the rain with no clothes on in that yard since we didn't have any neighbors, and wander around the woods and the stream—I mean, we had clothes on then. It was strictly in the yard that we could go without them. It's not like we were feral or anything."

They laughed at this distinction. "It sounds like they gave you and Lois a lot of room."

"They did in that place. I heard my mother tell my father once that she wanted us to have lots of longitude growing up—she laughed when she said it—because she hadn't had so much as a kid."

"Your mother seems pretty cool." Elinor had met her when they came in from the walk.

"She's the best."

Then Elinor set her cup aside, turned toward Sonya sitting cross-legged and put her hands up, palms outward. Sonya turned too and touched her hands against Elinor's. They lined up the base of their palms, measured at the tips. "Your fingers are longer than mine," Sonya said.

Where the new day began, orange blossom yellow-orange from the center spinning out into the flushed red of surprise, sudden and sometimes expected. Here, and then again here, and then here, singing out from green and balancing on the edge of green, out into the day. Then everything newly grown brought in. Spiral pulls a person in and holds her there, soaked in the ripeness of July, imagined from spring, called to the center and held in its arms, known and wonderful.

"By a bit," Elinor said. She curled the tip of her fingers part way over the end of Sonya's fingers. They brought their hands down kept loosely together, focused on them.

"If you did a drawing of me, what would you call it?" Elinor asked.

Sonya's face warmed. "How about *Her Hands*?"

"I like that."

"If you did one of me, what would it be called?" Their eyes were still cast down.

Elinor thought for a minute. "*Someone Who Understands*," she said.

Sonya did not ask what it was Elinor thought she understood, but she smiled.

They looked up at each other. Then they looked at each other without smiling; they looked and looked.

That night Sonya had trouble sleeping. She went to the window and glanced out over the hushed street. There were just a few outside lights on, and new leaves around them cast shadows over the front lawns. The sky was cloudy. She opened the window and knelt before it, heard some leaves flapping. The musty spring smell of rain coming and rich mud brought to mind the stream in Bridgeville. The bank had oozed clay where she and Lois waded on that summer day, a moist seam from the shoulder-high steep, a discovery. It slid down thick, gray, and textured in their hands. The day before, shopping with their mother, they had read an ad for a facial mud-pack in a woman's magazine at the grocery store. After discussing the possibilities, they put their sneakers aside in the grass and reached into the mud-clay swath with both hands. They began at their knees and applied it in substantial slabs, hands full, heft and smell making them giddy, until they were covered from the neck down, even their shorts and T-shirts. They eased themselves, sitting first, then onto their backs in the sun along the bank and waited for it to dry.

"If it's for our bodies, then it isn't called a facial, is it?" Lois asked.

"No, I guess not. I don't know what it would be called."

When the clay had lightened and cracked, they dipped into the stream, held themselves up leaning back on their hands. They felt it slip slowly from their skin, rinse through their clothes, and watched the clay filter away, cloud the water.

"It tingles," Sonya said.

"Maybe that's our pores juvenating," Lois said.

"Rejuvenating," Sonya remembered from the ad.

They retrieved their sneakers and walked home, their clothes dripping silt, and were surprised their mother could not see the difference in their skin.

"We can feel it."

"We look so new."

Their mother still did not see the difference, and, somewhat annoyed, hoping their clothes would not be stained, said, "Get in the shower."

Now Sonya smelled the back of her hand, air through the screen, and thought about the smell of mud. All streams becoming rivers, all rivers sifting their banks gradually over flat beds out to a sea someone lived along. The *mouth* of the river, that was the word, the opening, the confluence, joining and then moving forward renewed into a larger body of water. In every civilization people bending to the river, to water, bringing it to their faces, calling it home, so rich it was with possibility. A tent by a sea someone had, and lay awake at night and listened, smelled the water, filled with longing. Then she slipped into bed and fell asleep.

Returning from a museum trip in early April, Sonya saw daylight still faintly in the sky along the horizon, out the window of the darkened bus, though it was evening. There had been enough interest in the Annex that an occasional weekend field trip had been organized, to visit one of the several galleries or museums in the capital, all art enthusiasts welcome. Sonya and Elinor rode together on this Sunday excursion. Some of the students talked quietly, some were asleep, some were admiring what they bought at the museum. Elinor had been up near the front talking with someone, and when she was through, she returned to her seat beside Sonya. Then she took her denim jacket off, crouched down in the seat and covered her knees, up against the seat in front of her. Sonya crouched too, their knees at the same height up before them, reclining in their seat. Sitting beside Elinor like this, turned slightly toward her, with their shoulders leaned together, she could faintly smell salt, like salt water, or some lingering scent from the city. Sonya thought of the back of her neck, how her hair would feel at her hairline. Elinor reached over and took her hand, held the back of it against her stomach under her jacket. She rubbed her palm, ran her fingers up to Sonya's fingertips, then across her palm to her wrist, and then to the tips again. Against her hand Elinor's stomach rose and fell as she breathed, calmly at first, then more rapidly. Sonya heard her own breath quicken, too. Then she held Elinor's hand tightly, and they fell asleep. Into some lulled otherness, not yet defined, but theirs, drifts of other Sundays brought here, gathered and redone in a heated now. Then all was jarred as the bus braked to a stop, the lights came on, and Sonya and Elinor woke and moved apart.

In her dream that night the realtor was driving, and she taxied up the overgrown driveway and stopped in front of the house. She got out and led Lois and Marie up onto the generous front porch with the wooden swing. Sonya noticed the cats peering out the windows, perched on the railing, watching from the roof, sleeping on the steps. Sweat poured down the back of her neck. Instead of getting out of the car she rolled up the windows and locked all the doors. The realtor spun around toward her from the porch and urged, "You have to come in, too. The house is free, but on the condition that all of you tour the inside." Sonya wanted Lois and her mother to explain the situation to the realtor, but they had already entered the house and were talking excitedly about it. The realtor waited. Sonya realized the woman could not hear her through the closed windows, but she mouthed the words nevertheless. "I'm not walking in there," she said, but the words echoed, rippling into her ears, and the realtor stood on the porch, arms crossed in front of her, tapping her foot. She was still standing there as Sonya woke.

The first afternoon in the Annex after the field trip, Elinor was already working on something when Sonya came in and studied the supply shelves. She glanced a few tables over to see her bent over a bead tray, an earring wire in her hand. Sonya attended again to the items before her, voices in the room surrounding her, and could not focus on any particular idea of what to do. She thought of Elinor's hands reaching slowly, thoughtfully, pausing over rounded agate or polished onyx or tiny ordinary silver bulbs, engraved or not, selecting carefully and threading, picking up the tool for bending and clipping wire, holding all that color, one shape so close beside the other, and she left the room.

"I talked to Veronica today," Lois said, coming into the living room when her sister got home. It was later in the week.

"Oh, how is she?" asked Sonya, dropping her books into a chair. She walked to the refrigerator and took out two sodas, handed one to Lois who had followed her into the kitchen.

"Her usual hectic." Lois said nothing else. She looked at Sonya.

"What is it? What are you looking at?"

"Veronica asked me something."

"What?"

Lois's mouth shaped the words silently. Then, "'What's with Sonya and Elinor?'" She looked away.

Sonya felt dizzy and a little nauseous. "What did you say?"

"I said she should ask you, it's your business."

Through an open window floated the sounds of robins in the honey-suckle hedge and, further, a couple of houses away, the rhythmic dribbling of a basketball.

"Sonya?"

"Yeah?"

"What is with you and Elinor?" Lois's voice was gentle.

"What do you mean?"

"Veronica said someone said you two are dykes."

"Why? Because we get together on Sundays?"

"I guess because you hang out a lot."

"Who said that?"

"She wouldn't say."

"You know what? You are right. It's my business. And Veronica—she can't even let herself eat a whole fucking orange!" Sonya put her soda down on the counter, picked up her books in the living room, and dashed upstairs to her room, leaving Lois standing in the kitchen, eyes stinging from the curse, drink in her hand. She closed her bedroom door, threw her books on a shelf, took off her school clothes and left them in a pile on the floor, and put on her sweatpants and sweatshirt. She closed the curtains, crawled into bed and yanked a blanket up over her head. Curled up on her side, she pulled herself into a knot and cried. She couldn't stand the thought of her sister standing alone in the middle of the kitchen with her unanswered question dangling in the air. Her throat was tight with sadness; sorry she had been rude to Lois, she cried until she fell asleep.

Later, during dinner, her eyes no longer red, she tried to chat easily with her mother and sister, to ask casual questions about their day. But she avoided prolonged eye contact with her mother; Marie could tell when her daughters were upset by their eyes, as if the trouble were written there transparent, scripted in light and unrolled from their retina, a scroll that she alone could read. Sonya was relieved when Lois started talking about trumpet practice and a sale at the mall.

"Let's go Saturday," their mother said, "see what's left of the deals. Sound good? I'll call Donna tonight and ask her to join us. She mentioned the other day over lunch that she's been hunting for some sandals. And I could use another pair of dress slacks."

"I need a shirt," Lois said, "and maybe a new pair of clogs."

"Sounds good," Sonya agreed.

Later that evening, just before she went to bed, Sonya knocked on her sister's door. "Can I come in?"

"Yes."

Lois was in bed reading a mystery by the beam of her dresser lamp.

"I'm sorry about before," Sonya said from the doorway.

"That's OK," Lois said, putting her book aside. "It's your business."

Sonya walked in and sat down on her bed, noting the brown burlap dresser scarf Lois had made, illuminated, a blue ceramic earring dish from their father shining like a planet against the darker cloth. "This is cool material. I like your design."

"Thanks. Was there something else you wanted to talk about—I mean, besides the dresser scarf?"

As always, her sister's unflinching probing inspired Sonya's admiration. And this time, along with her smile, a pointed sigh. "The thing is, to answer your earlier question, I don't know."

"Well, Kathy and Leslie were talking about it the other day because they think Leslie's older brother is gay." Lois was referring to two girls in music with her. "And then they checked through this list of other people who they think might be and they said you."

"Why did they say me?"

"I don't know. Leslie and Veronica have been hanging out together lately. Maybe they talked about it."

"What else did they say?"

"They said with two men, one is always the woman. They were trying to figure out what her brother would be."

"What about with two women?"

"They didn't say. I guess one would be the man."

"But they are both women."

"I know," Lois said. "It doesn't make much sense."

Sonya pushed the cuticle on her left thumb back with her right thumb, then the right with her left.

"Sonya."

"Yeah?" She didn't look at her sister.

"I don't want people talking about you."

"I know." Her throat burned. "Just ignore them."

"Leslie said if people keep saying it, no guys will ask you out. I said if her hair was any bigger, a bird might land in it."

Sonya looked up and laughed. "You did *not* say that!"

"No. I told her she should worry about her own stuff. She mimicked me like I am an idiot."

"You aren't an idiot," Sonya said.

They didn't speak for a few minutes. Then she stood up and walked to the door.

"Sonya." Her sister paused. "It's OK not to know."

"Thanks, Lois," she said, turning to consider her a moment before she left the room.

The postcard that arrived a few weeks after the first one had "Sandusky" looped across a photograph of the Sandusky River.

"He's still in Ohio," Lois said. "What's he doing there?"

"I don't know," Sonya said. They sought a hypothesis from their mother.

"I couldn't begin to guess what he is doing. You know your father wanted to travel. God knows why he picked Ohio."

"What about his job?" Lois asked.

"Maybe he is using some of his vacation time," Marie suggested.

"Do you think he's in trouble?" Sonya asked.

"Believe me, girls, if he were in trouble, he would let us know."

The card read: "Been walking the river. Lovely this time of year, like a soul made visible. Love, Dad."

"Where do you think he's headed next?" Lois asked.

"He'll tell us," Sonya said. "But he might just be back soon." She had hoped to ask him about a project at the Annex. A group of seniors had decided recently that as a gift to the school they would create a mural in the room, a permanent feature with their names on it somewhere. It was to be composed of all of their talents; those who favored photography could contribute photographs, the jewelry makers something out of silver or pewter, raised, the sculptors a relief portion. Those gifted with acrylics would also add a section. And two of them had offered to make a frame for it. What would make it unique, the students had agreed, was not any overall theme that the whole piece spoke to, but that it was a collage of individual voices, a mixed media wonder. Sonya had hoped to show her father the completed work and to hear his opinion of it. But now she speculated whether he would return in time for her graduation in June, still several weeks away, though she didn't mention this.

That weekend she took out her charcoals and drew an endless highway, flat and broad, the barren hills sloped into the distance, along the otherwise undistinguished horizon. She drew a figure in the foreground, full of life, young, with a pack on his shoulders smiling at the viewer. She drew the figure repeatedly, each successive depiction smaller, turned further away, and older, more bent over as he made his way down the highway. In the last, and smallest one, his face was not visible at all and his limbs were blended with the surroundings, so he could be a scrubby highway brush, a patch of Queen Anne's lace growing along the road in late August, or an upturned and weathered root. She titled it *Sandusky Highway Traveller* and did not show it to anyone.

Ohio, flat and wide, land of open, land of highway and thoroughfare, people on their way somewhere, land of almost Midwest, meat-packing industry, Chicago, land whose name is an almost-sound, big round hollow, hollow of a word.

16

The Colorful Verge Of Expression

They lay on their backs at one end of the field of early May, the atmosphere filled with mud-thaw, spring rot, and bloom. On Sundays, after Sonya and Elinor walked, they sometimes stayed in a field and talked, then often went to one of their houses. This day the sky was cloudless, and now and then they heard a small plane buzz over or saw a jet's exhaust banner across the sky, curved against its dome.

With their heads resting on their bunched sweatshirts, they rolled toward each other. Elinor held one of Sonya's hands in hers. "I'll give you a letter, and you tell me something you want that starts with that letter." She traced a "J" on Sonya's palm.

Sonya thought for a minute. "I wish I had a glass of juice, pulpy, so that when I've drunk it all, there are still some bits of orange stuck inside the glass that I could scrape out with a spoon." She traced an "S" on Elinor's palm.

"I want a pair of brown tie shoes with a hard leather bottom, so I'll make some noise when I walk down the hall." She made a "P" in Sonya's hand.

"I need a new set of pencils, some sienna shades." Next Sonya made an "E."

"I want a painted egg, a red wooden one, with three smaller ones inside."

They did this until they could not remember which letters they had already used.

Then Sonya said, "I want to be able to walk through a neighborhood with my eyes closed. I don't know what letter that would be."

"I don't know either. Why do you want to be able to do that?"

"I'm not sure I can explain it."

"No need to, then." Elinor did not ask anything else.

As late afternoon passed and Sonya said her hands were getting stiff from being chilly, Elinor took them, one at a time, and attentively rubbed them between hers until they were warm. Sonya closed her eyes.

"Does that feel good?" Elinor asked.

"Yes." They leaned against each other in the grass.

Though Elinor had asked Sonya one night during the week if she had an answer yet to her question, it wasn't until the following Sunday that Sonya gave her one.

"Are you afraid of thunderstorms?" Driven by a downpour and rumbles of thunder, they had gone into a bus shelter to sit out the storm. When they had begun their walk the sky was cloudless, but now the rain fell before them in slants, the road glistened.

"No," Sonya said. "I like the movement of them, but when I feel safe, can look out a window at the rain and watch. Are you afraid of them?"

"No, they don't bother me either."

"How about snakes? Most people are afraid of those."

"They're pretty. Our old neighbors had a couple. When you watch them for a while, it's as if they are moving through something else, more than just that line of space. More than where their actual bodies are. Something magical happens. If that makes sense."

"I never thought of them that way. But it does make sense to me."

"I'm afraid of regret though," Elinor said. "My mom wanted to go to school, she wanted a career, but she married my dad instead, and sometimes I think she regrets it. Not that she regrets us so much. Maybe in a couple of years when my brother is in high school, she can do what she wants—my dad likes having her home now. I hope it won't feel too late for her then. I know sometimes she feels like she made the wrong decision, though she would never say so. But I can tell, and it makes me sad."

"But maybe it's not possible to live without some kind of regret."

"Maybe not. It's just scary. Not ghosts scary—upsetting scary."

"I know."

"What are you afraid of?" Elinor asked.

"Nothing really," Sonya said, quickly, deflecting the directness of the question. After listening to the sound of the rain against the bus shelter for a few minutes, she added, "Actually, I'm afraid of cats," wishing she could have told her without having to say the word.

"Cats? What do you mean? A phobia?"

"Yes." It embarrassed Sonya. Her fear had no nobility.

"My dad doesn't like heights. When he decided on engineering, he avoided certain areas, because he didn't want to have to work with bridges or tall structures of any kind," Elinor said. "What's it like for you? Is it bad?"

"It's not that bad," Sonya said. She yawned to appear nonchalant about it.

Elinor reached over and rested her hand on her arm. "Sonya, tell me."

Sonya sighed. "It's horrible."

"Describe it for me."

"I can't describe it."

"Try to. Take your time," Elinor said. She extended her legs, rotated her ankles.

"It will sound too weird."

"I don't care. Please. I want to know."

Sonya described her sweaty palms, racing heart, trapped feeling around the animals. She tried to describe the terror. "It's like I'm at the edge of an opening, about to slip in. It's an endless pit, and once I fall in I'll be bitten and attacked. They are out to get me." She ran her hands over her jeans, her ears tingled. "I can't even look at pictures of them."

"How often do you feel this?" Elinor asked.

"Every time I see or hear one, or smell one, and when I dream about them."

"How often do you dream about them?"

"A few times a week."

"My dad said once that his fear is like a soul allergy. Bridges totally wig him out. Whenever we come to one when he is driving, he has to pull over and ask my mom to drive across it, and he holds his breath and looks straight ahead the whole time. No one says anything until we are on the other side. Is that what it's like for you, a soul allergy?"

"That's a good way to describe it, because it begins in the deepest part of me and then goes everywhere else, my knees, arms, hands, all of me."

"When did this start?"

"When I was about thirteen," Sonya said, sounding unnecessarily vague, as if she did not know the precise hour, age and all, when the rattling brown hydrangea and the garden hose around its silver holder tried to keep her from the abyss facing her out the side door of the Griffins' house. She stood up and glanced out at the rain. "I think the storm is letting up a bit."

"I shouldn't have asked, I didn't realize. It would be like asking my dad to describe walking across the Golden Gate Bridge. He had enough trouble just driving out of New Jersey, and I wouldn't ask him to describe that for me."

"That's all right," Sonya said, sitting back down. "It's not that I mind you knowing—more that I don't like thinking about them. It is hard for me to talk about."

"Is it the closed-eye thing? To be that fearless?"

"Yes."

"I want to know everything there is to know about you," Elinor said.

"I want to know everything about you, too."

They watched the rain, now falling in a sheer mist. Neither spoke for a few minutes.

Then Elinor slipped her arm around Sonya's shoulders and pulled her toward her. "I'm sorry you have to live with that."

Sonya rested her head on her friend's shoulder. "Elinor," she said.

Although Sonya could not sleep that night, she was calmed by the moon's slow ticking across the rain-washed sky. Its light was first on her sill, then moved to the dresser, then across the floor to her bookshelf, and then to the other window. Where the sea washed and rolled, there she reveled. Where the bent sea grasses whispered to each other, swept in their nutty root and stem, that place she put her head down. And where the round earth of the cliff, its lull of hill, colored the air with salty haze and rolled in its fingers the heated kernels of the sun, there she slept at last. When she woke and thought about the sea from her dream, she held the day in her mouth and hummed.

That morning she drew, with colored pencils, a young woman standing at the edge of a cliff, the sea below rough and wild. The cliff was piled in luxurious meadow grass at home above the richly textured water. In her arms was a basket of suns, Georgia rich, overflowing the young woman's arms, weighing her down with their abundance. Sonya titled it *She Tells Me That She Dreams About the Sea*. Like her grandfather with his water imprints, she dreamed about the sea, though she had never lived near it. Veins of water and leaf-print sealed into memory.

Her dreams were only one aspect of her life that made her want to draw. Sometimes when Sonya rode the bike path for a few miles, turned off and pedaled up Sackett Hill and then came all the way back, she felt as if she could ride for days. Now and then she watched the lines of muscle in her arms move slightly when her hands worked the brakes or the gears. She felt the heat of exercise rise along her neck, rise to the surface of her skin, her shirt dampen. Her legs pumped, and she rode imperceptibly onto that plateau, almost stilled time of complete concentration, the air singing itself into wind at her ears. And here and here and here, she thought, how beautiful, as she rode past cattails along a swamp, past horses scattered up a hill and cows grazing in fields their slow shine, chewing through their day. Past fields of rich May mud, humming rivulets and green green. When she saw such color, she wanted to paint the veins of perception that ran just under her skin, apprehended in her hands, the elusive tangle inside her raised into form, as if the structure were there already waiting to be pressed onto canvas, to be made visible by her strokes of color over it. She stroked shapes into being, raised them to the surface, called them to their color, joined with form, made whole, made here, on textured material, spoken at last.

And when thoroughly exuberant on her bike ride, she could mull over other considerations, too, as this day she thought about how she had confronted Veronica that week at school. When Sonya saw her coming out of her chemistry class, she remembered their earlier conversation and anger, to which she was not much accustomed, swelled in her. She called to Veronica, who tensed her mouth slightly when she turned to see Sonya but left her group of classmates anyway to come over to her.

"How are you?" Her gesture was perfunctory.

"I didn't look it up." Sonya got right to the point, drawing strength from her long study of Lois's model.

"What? Look what up?"

"'Frisson.'"

Veronica looked at her blankly. Apparently she had forgotten her comment.

"You told me to look it up."

"Oh. And?"

Though the confrontation itself was spontaneous, Sonya had thought hard about this, about the way Veronica used words. She had so many and they all seemed to glitter; Sonya imagined what it must be like to close her eyes and see thousands to choose from, all sure of themselves, all precise, all ready for her to use so easily. And it wasn't about excelling, because Veronica excelled at every subject, yet she did not use other knowledge this way. But for her words were like gold coins she tossed, though not to give away or even allow others to admire; they spun at her feet glimmering and others scrambled after them. But before the coins could be retrieved and made currency by another, she grabbed them and returned them to her purse, their hollow sheen dissolving in a puff. This time, Sonya would not let her do that.

"I'm giving 'frisson' back."

"What?"

"I'm giving it back to you."

"You can't. One doesn't give words back."

"Well, I am." It was probably the first time Sonya had been indignant with her.

"That's because you're weird." Veronica glanced at her watch. "I don't suppose you'll need to look that one up."

"Thanks." Though she didn't elaborate, Sonya was thinking that she would like to be weird, if it was meant as a contrast with Veronica and her new friends. Even without having said all that, she wasn't above feeling satisfaction from Veronica's confused expression when she heard the word "thanks."

As Veronica said nothing and turned around and walked away, Sonya told herself that she would never, not even if she entered a lottery and knowing the definition meant winning a million dollars or it meant saving her drawings from a fire—maybe then, maybe for her drawings she would—but not for a million dollars would she look up that word.

And on the rest of her bike ride home, as she approached the suburbs, she felt some sadness as she wondered whether Veronica's new friends could speak through the turret of words she had stacked around herself. But she also experienced satisfaction still. Then she slowed as she wheeled into her neighborhood, breathed more slowly up the street, caught her breath, and coasted into the driveway. And often, as she did this day, after she put her bicycle in the garage, she lounged in the backyard on her stomach with her head on her folded arms. She liked to feel the ground beneath her, her breasts pressed against the earth, smell the grass and, occasionally, close her eyes just a moment or two, though staying alert for one that might wander into the yard, before going inside to shower.

"I'll be outside putting the sky on my head," their mother told them on a bright Saturday morning on her way into the yard dressed in old jeans and a denim shirt, her straw garden cap in her hands.

When the sun had begun its climb down, ready for its afternoon pause, Sonya saw her mother through the kitchen window kneeling in her bed of bulbs. She was clearing away soggy spring rot, preparing a border of flat stones the girls had helped her gather at the reservoir.

Sonya watched her for a few minutes. She wanted to tell her mother that inside her something was changing, that when she was with Elinor colors magnified. She wanted to tell her mother that the world, after all, was filled with people who stretched, stepped out in the morning with handsome baskets on their arms and stopped at the market for pomegranates, crusty baguettes, blocks of salty cheese, jugs of sweet cider. And more than that, with their baskets weighted with the world's richness dangling from their arms they laughed, they yelled to each other. They talked to each other, maneuvered as if by dance steps and reeled in spirited music, flinging themselves brightly up and out, riding the day's back, gesturing wildly. They were fearless in their joy.

Sonya wanted to tell her mother about these people, about what was new, about the round earth singing, each day like no other. She put on her sweatshirt, tied her hair in a bandana and went outside, walked over to the garden and stood, hands in the pockets of her jeans, beside her mother.

Marie sat back on her heels and adjusted her straw cap. "Do you think the glads would look better along the wall of the garage?"

Sonya considered what their height and their color would soon be. "Their height would be nice by the wall, but that red looks beautiful over here."

"That's the dilemma exactly," her mother said.

"How about hollyhocks or something taller along the wall, and leaving the glads here?"

"That's a perfect solution."

"Mom."

"What?"

Sonya didn't say anything.

"What? You want to do some weeding? Grab gloves from the garage."

Sonya got a pair of gloves and knelt at the other end of the rectangular garden.

"Remove the rotted leaves if you can, and any of these hucksters." Her mother held up a bristled weed with a stringy root. "They are already starting to take over."

They worked in silence, each at one end. From time to time Sonya observed her mother bent toward the garden as she placed the stones and leaned toward fragrant bloom, calling it up. She thought of the fine lines from smiling in the corners of her eyes.

"Hey, Mom."

"Yes, Hon?"

Sonya didn't answer right away. Her mother looked up at her. She looked back.

"What? Do I have dirt smudged on my face?"

Sonya smiled. "The mural project is totally amazing."

"I'm glad to hear that. Your sister and I will want to see it when it's finished."

She did not know how to tell her mother what she wanted to tell her, not even about Elinor's perfected delving into new techniques with wood-block prints. Thinking about that gave her such joy. "I feel good," she said finally.

Her mother rested on her heels again, tilted her head slightly to one side. She searched her daughter's eyes and saw calm, almost behind her eyes. Then she smiled, too. "Do you want to tell me about it?"

Sonya fidgeted with the soiled fingertips of her gloves. Her heart pounded loudly. "Maybe later."

"I'll be all ears." They resumed their work.

An hour later Sonya went into the garage to get a basket for the leaves, finding one near the back and lifting it off a wall hook. Then she turned and saw one of them. Apparently asleep on a camping blanket, waking when she came in, it was now watching her calmly and stretching leisurely. If she threw the basket at the animal, it might become agitated and lunge. But there was no time at all for Sonya to think out a strategy, or to decipher, behind its pale yellow stare, the slippery workings of its menace or that image of what it buried. There was instantly the horror of it, a scrap of cloth stuck to the bottom of the root-cellar door, a rose stain dried on it. Perhaps a bit of hair. Had someone run, did it rip off in her running? The door had been closed. Something reeked of decay. What was latched behind those eyes? What might spill forth if it should vent its mouth toward her? She knew she had to be quick about it, but she could not move.

When her daughter didn't return within a few minutes, Marie checked to see if she needed help finding the basket. She saw Sonya standing uncomfortably still near a wall with the basket in her hand. She also saw, across the garage, the black and white neighborhood cat that often explored their yard positioned between Sonya and the door. Then Marie walked over, picked the animal up and brought it out to the neighbor's yard, where she nudged it away. She clapped to make the cat run off, before returning to the driveway.

Sonya walked quickly out of the garage and, trembling, handed her the basket. "I guess I'll go in and get something to drink."

"Bring your drink out here. There are a few more projects I wanted to finish today. We need to start the vegetables soon too, and you can help me."

Sonya looked briefly over her shoulder and said, "I really can't. I have stuff to do."

As she stepped toward the house, her mother touched her arm. "You'll tell me when." It was an urging more than it was a question.

She knew her mother was referring to when it was time to try Dr. Francis again, or someone else. She nodded. "Don't worry, Mom," she said, and turned again toward the back door. Then she went inside.

"There's one for you and one for me," Lois said, peering into an envelope the girls' father had sent them. She pinched out two crumpled five dollar bills.

"Where's the postmark from?" asked Sonya.

"Toledo."

"What's he doing in Toledo?"

"Here's a note," Lois said, unfolding it. A few grains of sand spilled out. "Girls: I'm writing from the lakeshore. I've found some beautiful beach stones. When immersed in water they become landscapes, mountain ranges, forests. Magnificent. So don't forget to keep your eyes open. Look for those ranges. And remember, always recycle—it's starting to catch on. Love, Dad. P.S. c/o General Delivery, Toledo, OH 43610."

They sat down on the living room floor, took their shoes off, and read the letter to themselves taking turns, each a few times.

"That's what we used to do at the reservoir with rocks, remember?" Lois asked.

"Yes," said Sonya. She remembered that they would look for the outlines of hills and valleys in wet rocks. "Then when we got tired, we would flop on the blanket and sometimes look for spines in the jet trails."

"Or animals in the clouds. Why is he telling us that?"

"Just giving us advice, I guess. Why doesn't he tell us how long he will be there? Do you think he wants us to write to him?"

"I don't know," Lois said.

"That's some vacation he's on."

"Or whatever it is."

"Yeah, whatever it is." Sonya echoed her sister's indignation.

They sat awhile without talking, having wrung as much of their father as they could from the letter, turning it over in their hands.

"Well," said Sonya finally, "I suppose you could write and tell him about those two new jazz pieces for trumpet you've been working on."

"And you could tell him about having your drawings in the student display case at school," Lois said.

They noticed—but did not talk about—the affection that had developed between them, so when Sonya rested her hand on Elinor's when they talked, or Elinor put her leg over Sonya's when they lolled about on the floor and sketched ideas for earrings, or for any art project, or lingered over photographs to discuss technique, they were aware that the warmth between them accentuated the joy of whatever they were doing. Or when they were doing nothing but relishing Janis Joplin's range by imagining themselves having been on stage with her. Even so, they touched almost absentmindedly, as automatically as some other daily gesture or action, like smiling when they saw each other across the hall in school or laughing at the Annex while they helped each other out.

Given this, it was not unusual for Sonya, one Sunday afternoon when they had returned to Elinor's, tossed their sneakers in her room, found celery and peanut butter and stood beside each other at the kitchen counter eating it, to have her arm resting loosely on her friend's shoulder.

Because they were talking as they ate, they did not hear Elinor's mother when she first came to the doorway. They turned when they heard her say hello in the voice with which she usually greeted them. But next, instead of asking if they needed anything, her customary question, she glanced at Sonya's arm, then up into their faces briefly. Her expression, now one of dismay, no longer matched the "hello" still sounding in their ears. And rather than come all the way into the kitchen, which it had seemed to them she was about to do, she spun around and walked away.

Sonya brought her arm down, tucked it under her other arm. "Sorry," she said.

Elinor looked toward where her mother had just stood, then to Sonya. "It's OK."

They quickly finished their snack.

Then Sonya whispered, "I suppose I better go." They retrieved her things from the bedroom, and Elinor walked her to the door.

"Talk to you soon," Elinor said.

"Definitely." Sonya stood in the doorway. Neither one reached out to hug the other as they usually did when saying goodbye. Instead they beheld each other sadly, as if, having stepped across a threshold into a new dimension of anxiety, they were observing a moment of silence.

Sonya felt desolate as she pedaled away on her bike. On the ride home she decided that it would be best if she didn't go over to Elinor's anymore; for the following Sunday and the Sundays after that they could lounge around at her house after their walk.

Not all of her decisions were that clear-cut; there were questions about drawing that Sonya had to figure out again and again. How could she draw the lakeshore her father wandered and capture the vastness of the water when the edges of the paper were finite? She wanted to draw that lakeshore, the tumble of stones smooth in his hands, each with its potential water-drawn landscape. But that made her sad. Instead she thought about Elinor's hair smelling like wind, and of how to draw that. With sharpened colored pencils she drew herself and her friend in a field, except the field was an outdoor marketplace. There were wooden stalls set up displaying, in descending rows, eggplants, tomatoes, and squash, and then mangoes, pineapples, kiwi, and the star fruit she'd seen in a magazine. There were rounds of pale cheese, slopes of glistening salmon, knots of bread dusted with flour. Beside these there were tins of slender almonds, plates of half-moon coconut meat, and, off to the side, a barrel stuffed with chestnuts. There was a merchant behind each display, but no one else was there except Elinor and Sonya. They stood beside each other in the center of the field, the merchants and their goods all around them, with mouths slightly open as if about to say "Look at this fish!" or "Look at that mango!" Their lips parted on the verge of expression spoke their wonder. Sonya titled it *At the Edge*, though if someone had asked her, "The edge of what?" she would not have had an answer. But there it was on rough-textured paper in sharp, precise, lines of color, muted here and there with the haze that glows around a beautiful thing.

However there was one decision about drawing that was easy, though she had not thought about it deliberately but rather had come to it gradually. She would do, as she often did these anyway, only jewelry or some other art form in school and her drawings exclusively at home. The thought of working on one of them at the Annex, though she had a few times in the spring, now made her feel too conspicuous. And when she leaned this new finished drawing against her bookshelf and stepped back to look at it from across the room, she realized there were several others already placed along the walls.

17

The Root Of The Tree

At a backyard picnic organized by one of the studio group, when two students described an argument that week over supplies, a third made the screech of fighting cats, and a few of the girls clawed their hands toward her and laughed. All of this prompted one of them to ask if anyone had heard about the woman who was attacked by a wild cat out on Dearborn Road recently. No one had heard about it, and the chorus of questions encouraged her, standing, to jump into the story full stride and gesturing.

"The woman goes out to her barn, and she's standing right below one of the beams and when she bends over to get something—"

Elinor, sitting next to Sonya at the picnic table, shot out, "You are making this up, like the time you told us about that motorcycle ride," but her attempt to cut the story short was unsuccessful.

Having waved her off with "no way," their classmate continued the narrative, describing the bat-like swiftness with which the cat reportedly lunged from the rafter and the screams the woman emitted as it clawed into her neck. Her son had heard her, came running out of the house and scared the animal away with his BB gun. A few of the others said "fuck" and "gross" and excitedly related stories—all embellished with the graphic detail inspired by spontaneity—about wild pack dogs and predatory birds.

Sonya did not hear these other stories because there was a dizzying rush behind her ears that blocked out sounds as distinct as words. Sweat rolled down her underarms and into the bottom ridge of her bra. She had uncrossed her legs and placed both feet decisively on the ground to maintain her sense of balance, hoping no one would notice her strained effort. Elinor's hand rested on her knee under the table, where she had slipped it at the beginning of the story, and Sonya concentrated on it to keep herself securely connected to the world, keep the world upright, keep the yard from spinning out of orbit. The conversation had quickly moved from camping in the woods at night, to telling ghost stories around a fire, to food, and, brought back to the present, the others heaped their plates with more potato salad and beans, but Sonya lost her appetite.

A couple of hours after getting home from the picnic, she phoned Elinor. "Hey, I couldn't say so earlier, I mean, with that crowd, but I do want to say thanks."

"For what?"

"For helping me out today."

"I'm glad I was there."

"Me too." Sonya was also glad they had the hum of the phone to register their embarrassment, and not the immediacy of talking in person.

"Want to go somewhere with me tomorrow night?"

"I'd like that."

"I don't want you to get tired of me," Elinor said.

"I don't think that will happen. Where do you want to go?"

"It's a place I found for us to walk. I'll drive us there."

When Sonya had first seen a couple of cars parked in the Jaretts' driveway, she had wondered whether they had company visiting or whether, like many families in the area, they owned two vehicles. Later she realized that extravagance was theirs, too. Elinor picked her up in her mother's car, and when Sonya first got in, the glowing instrument panel, in its beautiful precision, called to mind an airplane cockpit or some other conveyance much more complicated than an automobile. Was elegance always this far beyond necessity?

"What are all of these for?" She gestured toward the various dials.

"Well, I know the gas gauge and the speedometer," Elinor laughed. "My parents go for this sort of thing."

"What is it?"

"It's a Saab. When I first heard of one, I couldn't understand why anyone would name a car after a kind of crying. It didn't seem like an ingenious way to sell one. Then I saw how it's spelled."

"Oh, right. I think I have heard of this company or maybe seen an ad somewhere for their cars."

"At least she bought one that was a couple of years old." Then, still embarrassed, Elinor added, "It all seems a bit fussy, if you ask me. But it suits Caroline." Referring to a parent by the first name, to emphasize a point, gave them a chuckle.

"It feels like we are in a space capsule or something."

"Actually, the silvery finish also makes it seem like one, doesn't it?"

"It does."

"I will think of that too, whenever I am in this thing."

They drove a few more miles, then turned onto a curving entrance road. "This is the arboretum," Elinor said, as she parked. They stepped out and looked around, beneath the sound of the car doors closing some leaves stirring, tree branches creaking, a few other vehicles pulling out and driving away. The May night was getting cool, but the day's warmth was still with them. The sky faded pale blue becoming deep ceramic blue on its way into dark. Elinor led Sonya over to a grassy hill, where they sat close enough to each other to link their arms together at the elbow, and observed the town lights below scattered across the evening.

"Those lights look like tiny glow-fish in murky water," Sonya said.

"And those like portholes," Elinor said, pointing to the distant lights of the city. "We are looking at them from our ship. If this could be any city, any time, where would you want it to be?"

"Would you be there?"

"No."

"I'd want it to be here."

"What if I would be there?"

"I'd want it to be somewhere in Greece, with all that sea around us."

"We could swim in it," Elinor said.

"I'm not a very proficient swimmer. I mean, in the reservoir I am, but not the sea."

"I'll show you. It's easy."

"I can float on my back." Sonya stretched out in the grass, kicking her feet.

Elinor lay down beside her. "It's primarily a matter of getting the rhythm," she said, flailing her arms somewhat erratically, parting water. "Do you like my technique?"

"It's lovely," Sonya said.

"Is this as much exercise as walking?"

"Why wouldn't it be?" They laughed. Then Sonya said, "I really wouldn't want to be anywhere else but here right now."

Elinor leaned on her elbow, rolled toward Sonya, and pressed against her. "Me either," she said. "I've never felt this before."

"I'm happy it's with me."

"I want to kiss you, Sonya."

Sonya was so moved she couldn't speak. Her brain became a cloud. She reached up and rubbed one of Elinor's ears.

Elinor leaned down and touched her mouth to Sonya's. Their mouths were warm and soft, new, familiar. Then Elinor pulled herself back up on her elbow as they looked at each other through the twilight, sighed. She lay in the grass and looked up, and then they laced their hands together between them and caught their breath. Neither of them spoke for a few minutes.

Then Sonya said, "I can't think of what the sky looks like."

"Sonya," Elinor said quietly, and quieter they stayed.

For another hour or so they lay beside each other, and they did not say much on the drive home, both feeling bewildered. After Elinor dropped her off, Sonya stood in the front doorway and followed her car's tail lights threading through the spring trees all the way down the street, and the street seemed to move with her, aware, transformed.

Having been distracted the next day in school, she sat at her desk as soon as she got home with the bedroom door closed. She had intended to draw, but rather than take out her paper and drawing pencils she thought about Elinor. Closing her eyes, she put her head on her folded arms and imagined again their bodies together the length of them, the other leaning over her, their mouths warm and together. She felt again the whole length of her, her body opening toward another, drawing her in, their sighs mixed. An image of a spring breeze blowing across rectangles of color came to her, but she sat at her desk for an hour listening to her own breath, overwhelmed and unable to draw.

"Hi." Sonya heard Elinor's voice.

"Hi," she said. Elinor stood next to the locker the following morning, her backpack in her hand. Sonya felt her watching her get books out and glanced over. When her eyes met Elinor's, she attended again to her locker. There was something else with them. Sonya experienced it outside when they walked, when the space of field and sky could absorb it, and yet it was between them. Now the presence was even more tangible. Again they looked at each other, as if longer studying would reveal exactly where this presence resided. Would others notice it? The hallway had become narrow to her, hotter, more confining than before, the voices surrounding them too near.

"Hey," Elinor said, "I was thinking we could—"

"What were you thinking?" Sonya whispered.

"Maybe Saturday we could see a movie, and then."

She didn't finish, but Sonya said, "I was thinking that, too." They looked away, fumbled with their grace.

"I guess I better get to class."

"See you."

"See you," Elinor said.

When Saturday finally came, Sonya encouraged the evening to come sooner by beginning early in the day trying to decide what to wear. She hand-washed, dried, and ironed three shirts.

Lois saw her putting the third one on that afternoon and said, "At the movies you can't see much of what people are wearing anyway."

"What about your new shirt with the snaps?"

Lois studied her sister thoughtfully, affectionately, clearly contemplating more than just her clothes. "Smart choice, I'll go get it." She returned to Sonya's room a minute later and handed it to her.

Sonya tried that one, too. "What do you think? Maybe with my flowered jeans?"

"That would work. Hey, they all look nice."

When Sonya decided on one of her own, Lois lent her a silver bracelet.

"Tell me what you feel," Elinor whispered, as they wrapped themselves in a wool picnic blanket, their arms and legs tightly entangled, on the grassy hill of the arboretum.

"I close my eyes," Sonya said, closing her eyes, "and I can feel every cell breathing."

She held her face against Elinor's, who had closed her eyes briefly too, breathing in the warm salt of her hair and neck.

They had planned to watch the sun drift down and then to see a movie. But when the time came to get back in Caroline's car and drive to the mall theater, neither one wanted to leave. For certain, they would be disappointed if they did; nothing currently showing could measure up to *Norma Rae*. When they saw it earlier in the spring, they decided it would be the standard against which they would assess all other films.

"The air smells like a tadpole," Sonya said.

"What does a tadpole smell like?"

"Like we're in a little sac of pond water. That's the smell of summer coming."

"What should we do this summer?" Elinor asked. "Maybe we could plan some sort of an adventure."

"This is an adventure."

"Maybe we should stay right here like this."

"Let's," Sonya said.

"Yes, let's."

"What would we tell people?"

"We could say we are studying the growing patterns of the trees," Elinor said. "We have to come here at night because the patterns are connected to the stars."

Sonya laughed, then said, "Actually, that sounds plausible. We have to be together because one of us has to watch the subjects while the other one records the information."

"That's right. Later we can write up our findings."

"We'll have a lot to write," Sonya said. "Lots of data. Enough for an Earth Science textbook. But not the faded kind with scuffed covers and pictures of forgotten canals."

Elinor understood. "Those are sad," she said. "It would have to be a clean, crisp book, with images of newly discovered frog species and plants that would make you want to sketch them. Besides weed, of course." They laughed. That leaf structure did not have the same allure for them as an artistic subject as it did among some of their classmates at the Annex. They had accepted that enjoyment, though, from time to time when offered it.

They listened to the trees awhile, new leaves moving in the night current.

"Elinor?"

"Yeah?"

"Do you worry that people might be talking about us?" Sonya had not mentioned to her Veronica's question for Lois.

"I try not to. What about you?"

"I try not to think about it either. I think mostly about how much I like being with you. Have your parents said anything?"

"The other day my mom said, 'You have been spending an inordinate amount of time with Sonya lately.' Her exact words. There was a question in her voice, but she didn't ask it. She gave me a strange look though, sort of like the one in the kitchen that day."

"Let's not worry about it right now."

"I like being with you," Elinor said.

"I like being with you, too," Sonya said.

They talked and drowsed for a while. By the time they climbed into the car to leave, the sky was nearly the deep tile of midnight.

Elinor called the next morning to say she couldn't meet Sonya for their afternoon walk.

"Why not?"

"I'll explain later," Elinor whispered.

"Are you all right?"

"I'm fine," she said, but Sonya could tell by her voice that she had been crying.

"What is it?"

"I can't talk now."

They hung up reluctantly. Sonya stood by the telephone a few moments, as if lingering there would help her adjust to the need for a furtive conversation. An image came to mind of a newspaper photo: a time capsule recently dug up, from which was retrieved a list of signatures of the junior high class who had buried it decades before, three preserved stamps, a beverage bottle with an outdated design, a couple of spinning tops, newspaper articles of the day, a local diner menu, among other gadgets and goods. The current adult commentary, from those who had gone back and dug the capsule out of their old schoolyard, posing now with the contents, mixed with the echo of their corresponding child-voices, inseparable, marking time no less dramatically than the sleek metal canister. Floating now, floating like a song hummed in the flurry of a market, or heard by a passerby out a music-room window, the same notes over, over, or a radio carried on a train, floating now, sounds inseparable from what carries them, these mixed-age voices, notes.

A couple of hours later Sonya's mother peered into her room. "How was the film?"

"We decided not to see it after all," said Sonya, sitting at her desk.

"Oh. What did you do?"

Her face warmed. "Just hung out."

"At the mall?"

"No."

"Oh." Her mother came in the room and sat down. "Where?"

"At the arboretum."

"You two were out there until eleven thirty?"

"Yeah."

"Wasn't it chilly?"

"We had a blanket."

"I see." Her mother rotated the silver and turquoise ring on her finger. "Sonya, your sister tells me that some of the kids at school are talking about you and Elinor."

"I know what they are saying."

"Do you want to tell me about it?"

Sonya's embarrassment kept her from looking at her mother. "We like hanging out with each other." That was all she could manage to say. Her heart rocked against her ribs.

"I think it's wonderful that you two are so close. But people are sometimes—what is the word for it? Unfortunately, some people—" And here, though her intention was to be honest with her daughter, she stalled a bit, not wanting to articulate the conclusion that the first half of her sentence pointed toward. "People are sometimes cruel."

Sonya's throat tightened when she heard the word "cruel." She leaned her head in her hands on her desk, not having colors enough or words enough to show her mother what her feelings meant or how much hurt the word contained. Her head ached. She did not want to cry in front of Marie but did not want her to leave. If she could take a cross-section, like a strip of filament paper, of what she felt, she would hold it up to the window, point to all the layers of startling design, the wild and intricate patterns made tangible by the wash of sunlight coming in her window. "Look," she would say, "this is it; do you see what I mean?" Her mother's observation, close, searching, was protective. The words, choked in Sonya's throat.

"Elinor's mother phoned me a little while ago."

Sonya looked up. "What did she say?"

"She is concerned that you two are spending too much time together."

"What did you say?"

"I said I was glad you have become such great friends. I'm very fond of Elinor."

"Did she sound mad?"

"Somewhat, yes. Troubled even. I said I would talk with you, and she is planning to talk to Elinor today, too."

"Mom," Sonya said, her hands turning before her, though the gesture was not accompanied by any other words. Then her hands came to rest in her lap, knotted around each other tightly.

"You are my daughter." Her mother walked toward her, seemed to move slowly, as if the air had grown heavy with Sonya's unarticulated thoughts. When she reached Sonya, she slid her hand under her chin and tilted her face up. "All I have to say to you is that I trust you."

Sonya closed her eyes to say, "Yes, I know."

When her mother left the room, Sonya put her head in her hands again and hit herself gently over and over on the sides of her head until her tears finally started. She thought of the dark-haired girl on the bus in third grade who rode a couple of seats ahead of her, lunchbox poised on her lap, her hair wild in the afternoon light. She thought of others marked along a time-line. There was a girl once at a fair in town who worked one of the concessions. Sonya paid admission every day that week to watch her negotiate the crowds of people, the world, staying calm, her hair tied back, then stood a few feet closer when the crowd thinned. They did not talk but regarded each other with interest from a distance. Sonya did not go on any rides; she hardly noticed the hawkers and sweet foods and loud music. She bore the other's gaze and then walked home. When the fair rumbled on to the ad-joining county, her mother had asked, "What's the matter with you? Why are you wearing that sadness?" Sonya had shrugged and said, "Nothing's wrong." Images came to her of being at the reservoir with Odessa and in bed with her on summer nights, the constellations overhead, whispering into sleep. And of braiding each other's hair. The images floated up like leaves on a pond, were suddenly there, each one singularly beautiful. Each one kept her tears coming, until at last the tightness in her throat eased. She got up from her desk, took her sneakers off, grabbed a blanket from the bed and curled up under it on the floor. Then she extended it over her head and fell asleep.

It began many years ago, in the first love of shadows. The first knowing of the body's dark, the curve around its shape holding darkness. Calling it-self back, it recalls water. Forms shape themselves around water. Coral and color become one. So that now, millennia later, centuries later, the shapes that made themselves in water are still here, knowing their making. She feels them as she lies there warm around her, the membrane pulsing. The inside of the body singing what it knows of making, singing that it knows making.

It began in the smell of skin, in the gesture, the root of the tree, smell of bark, back along the river, the voices distant and holding song. In the smell of hands were the new day, the urge for holding. In the smell were the river and the sun.

To hold is to hold a tree, the hollow that while filled, arms around and head tipped, looking up at the sky. Neck muscles, elegant, stretching up like lines of bark, mouth open near the sky, mouth and the green top of the tree both singing, to be that close to the sun. Neck given, and the other's mouth is on it, warm and soft, slow working the muscles of song slow bringing out into light, voices rising. And then they sing, released in the green forest of heart. This hollow of arms to fill with a solid tree, held into light.

She lies there, drowsing out of sleep, the voices along the river or downstairs in the house on its quiet street. Her arms around, she dreams or thinks of her, sighs for what she has discovered, suddenly, always there. And she rolls in her sleep-awakeness and sighs, too, for all that is new: for the other's voice on the phone, for the startle of seeing her at the door, for the way her sweater sleeves hang down over her hands, for her quick laugh, for the weighted lull of her body holding them to the earth, for the light brown of her eyes deepening with desire. She dreams or thinks of these things and of the magnificent rhythm of breathing.

When the doorbell rang after dinner that night, Sonya looked out her bedroom window and saw Caroline Jarett's vehicle in the driveway. While a feeling of panic swept over her, she tried to think quickly of what she might say. Then she was relieved to hear just Elinor talking with her mother downstairs. She heard, "Yes, go on up. She's in her room," and listened to Elinor's feet taking the stairs two at a time. The door was ajar, and she knocked on it as she came into the room.

"Hi," she said.

"Hi," Sonya said, still standing near the window. Elinor closed the door and walked over to her, standing a couple of feet away. Then Sonya opened her arms and Elinor stepped into them. They held each other tightly without talking.

Finally Elinor said, "She says once we leave home we will be more than busy enough managing all of the academic challenges of a university curriculum." Elinor's mother knew, of course, that her daughter was exceptionally well prepared to undertake her studies—in regard to both her intellectual ability and her temperament; in fact, the path to social work made sense to her. But concerns about her daughter's emotional well-being and romantic involvements were another matter entirely. And they influenced her reasoning.

"What did you say?"

"I told her I care about now more than I care about then, but that made her angrier."

"Did she say she doesn't want you to get together with me?"

"Yes, she said she would rather that I didn't, which is the same for her as saying that I can't. That's why I couldn't meet you for a walk. And I can't use her car anymore to do something with you. I'm supposed to be at the store right now. I can still use it for that, but she is considering taking away my driving privileges—her phrase—completely."

Their embrace loosened as they contemplated each other. Sonya touched the sleeve of Elinor's T-shirt, faded teal, rubbed the cuff.

"Did she ask you about last night?"

"Several questions. All my answers were vague though, because I didn't know what to say—or how."

"Me either," Sonya said. "I ended up saying I like hanging out with you—I think I may have said it over and over. I do. I was a bit flustered."

"That's what I told my mom too, but she kept asking other questions, like wasn't I interested in someone, and didn't I know what people would say. How could she ask me that now? When I didn't respond to these, she kept saying I'm not using my head very well. She was pacing in the living room making me so nervous, she might have been chain-smoking."

"Your mother doesn't smoke, does she?"

"No, but she acts as if she will begin the habit any day now. She's doing everything else that goes along with it. Maybe I should be working on tacky ceramic ashtrays at the Annex, instead of the prints—in case she starts."

"What else did you say?"

"Nothing that helpful. I didn't know how to tell her what I wanted to tell her. I guess she knows anyway how I feel, because otherwise she wouldn't be wigging out this way."

"My mom knows too." Since they hadn't yet articulated either to themselves or to each other exactly what their parents were deliberating, Sonya and Elinor spoke now in imprecise wanderings, their words sifting around them like pollen clusters.

"But she didn't yell at you?"

"No, she isn't angry. She seems to be thinking about it all, I mean thinking about me and you spending time together, like we're a problem she is figuring out. But I mean problem in a positive way; that's why she loves science, she loves figuring things out."

"My mother keeps saying that right now I should be concentrating on my final exams coming up next month. And thinking of nothing else but those."

"You always ace everything, though. Why does she worry about that?"

"That's her stress talking." Elinor faltered uncharacteristically, searching for a phrase. "They've done everything for me." Then, "It's painful to see her so upset."

"Maybe we shouldn't get together on Sundays until classes are over. That might ease her mind," Sonya suggested.

"I hate the thought of that."

"I do, too."

"But it probably would help for now—until school is over. Maybe by then she will have calmed down. She knows we see each other every day there, but I guess it's different because she knows there are other people around."

"Just until June," Sonya said. "By then, we will figure out a way to have that day again. I'm with you regardless. Let's think of it like that."

"I'm with you, too," Elinor said, then added, "I better go."

They walked to the bedroom door. Neither one reached for the knob. Instead they turned to each other, and Elinor put her hands deep in Sonya's hair, rubbed her head, then touched her cheek against Sonya's. Leaning together, renewed.

They walked downstairs. Elinor called goodbye to Marie, who poked her head through the kitchen doorway and said, "See you later, Elinor."

"I'll see you tomorrow," she said to Sonya.

"See you tomorrow." They were smiling.

After Sonya closed the front door, her mother came out of the kitchen. "How is everything?"

"Eh. Could be better. But I think it will be."

"Elinor's mother, isn't it?"

"Yes," Sonya said. Her mother took her by the hand, led her to the couch, and they sat down. "Maybe you could talk to her, ask her over for coffee, explain that you don't have a problem with us spending an afternoon together."

"Sonya, parents always want what is best for their children. Caroline doesn't want to see her get hurt."

"I won't hurt her, Mom."

"I know. But sometimes society throws challenges our way. She wants to protect her daughter, and I can understand that. I don't think my talking with her would help, especially not while she is angry. And I have to respect her parenting skills, because I think she has raised Elinor to be a marvelous person."

"I know. But how come you—" Sonya hesitated, caught on her words, "you can understand, and she can't?"

"I don't know if I do as well as I could, but I know you, and that's what counts. I know that you two—" Marie paused, too, choosing carefully her added phrase, "love being together." She did not look at her daughter, knowing she would feel embarrassed. She waited a few beats, then she looked at her as she said, "I've also been thinking lately about something—actually, someone—from my childhood."

"Who?"

"Do you remember your grandfather's stories about Alice, the woman who helped him with some of the planting?"

"Isn't she the one who killed the chickens for you when you were a kid and were afraid to do it?" Sonya remembered seeing a picture of her in her mother's box of photographs.

"That's right. She spent lots of time with another woman. In fact, they lived together. They had a farmhouse that the other woman had grown up in. They—Alice and Roselyn—had a tremendous garden, grew vegetables, had flower beds and fruit trees. There was a covered stand there, like a lean-to, where they sold the produce. I think sometimes they also sold to the market in town."

"But I don't know about a life like that," Sonya said, disrupting her mother's narrative. "That's not necessarily us, not necessarily me."

"All right." Marie knew that now was not the time to say, "Sit your ass still awhile and let me tell you," so she waited a discernible moment before asking, using another angle, "Do you want to talk about Elinor?"

Sonya knew her blush was more visible than typically, shook her head.

Her mother patted her on the leg. "Well, another time then."

After a few minutes of not talking she said, "There's an arts and crafts fair later this week downtown. We could go Saturday afternoon."

"That would be fun, but I better not. I need to do some work here."

Sonya knew her mother's look of disappointment but didn't say anything else.

Friday evening Sonya flopped down on Lois's bed, watching her sister get ready to go out with friends. Earlier in the week she had invited her to join them, but she declined. Lois had just gotten out of the shower and stood naked before her dresser, drying her hair with a towel, then brushing it out.

"What are you going to wear?"

"Maybe my striped jeans with my black boots and a turtleneck. What do you think?"

"It's not that cold out."

"It might be later though."

"Are you staying out late?"

"We might hang out at Nancy's after the movie."

"Did you tell Mom?"

"Of course. She said that's fine with her, she just wants to know where I am."

"Your navy blue turtleneck would look good with those jeans."

"That's what I was thinking, too."

Sonya watched as Lois finished drying her hair and put on her bra and underwear. Then she took a jar of lotion off the dresser and, with one leg up on a chair, she applied the moisture first to her calves and then to the back of her knees. Working her way up to her thigh she gently massaged the lotion by the palmful, deliberately, not missing an area of her leg. She applied it just as attentively to her other leg, and as generously, what seemed to Sonya like enough lotion for several people, or at least for two.

"What are you doing tonight?"

"Oh, finishing up what I was working on earlier."

"You could still come with me, throw something on and you'd be fine."

"No, but thanks. If I don't work on it tonight, I might forget what else I wanted to do with the drawing."

Now Lois moved as if he were standing beside her and she had taken his hand and put it under her own as she moved it over her body, guided his hand saying this way here, over here this is the way to touch, as she rubbed the lotion on her forearms, thoughtfully, lingering next over each elbow, then massaged another bulb of it into her upper arms.

"Tell me again who he is. I know you told me before, but I can't remember."

"Milton. That's his first name. His name is Milton Alden."

"How could I forget. That makes him sound like a very serious person. A head of state or something. Does he carry a briefcase yet?"

"Actually, I've been distracted by some of the less serious things about him." Lois laughed as she returned the lotion to the dresser and walked to her closet to pick out her clothes. "We both decided that if we had two turtles they would be named Aretha and Miles. Certainly not Cuff and Link. Not dignified enough. Isn't that amazing? We picked the same two names."

"That's neat. And that you two like the same music."

"But we'll get to the serious stuff, too. So you think the navy would work?"

"I do," Sonya said as she got up from the bed. "You're cool, Lo." She turned around when she reached the door. "I'm getting back to my drawing. Have fun tonight."

"Thanks."

In her room with the door closed, she sketched for a while at her desk. Later she said goodnight to her mother and then went to bed.

Sometime after midnight she was awoken by a car in the driveway, the front door opening and closing, the sounds of Lois coming upstairs, then closing her own bedroom door.

When she could not fall asleep again, Sonya sat at her desk for a while, looking at nothing in particular by the gleam of the lamp.

Then she grabbed a blanket off the bed and, moving a couple articles of clothing out of the way, curled up under it on the floor. Tears on the back of her hands where the smell of the day's heat used to be. When was that? How long had it been since she had smelled that, dreamt in it? Lingered in a day any day to have that, to have a day with lotion in it and all its lingering over touch. To be free to wander anywhere in any day and bathe herself in lotion clothe herself in reveling and holding, holding to that day. And to that deep night darkness of skin and singing it on another's skin Lois could do that in any night star-filled or not the pleasure was still hers in any day.

He had bolted a seat beside his, so that when they visited he could take Lois and Sonya for rides on the old green tractor, finding the day. The ground was bumpy, and always wondrous was the sweet thick texture of the tall grass or stubble they ploughed through. He held her on with one arm around her shoulders, the other hand firmly on the wheel. Above the chug and loud blur of the motor her grandfather leaned toward her and yelled, "Look." He always found something to point at, no matter how many rides they had taken, either grasshoppers jumping aside as they passed, or a cluster of wild farm dogs in the distance roaming another field, or the rising dust of dried yellow bloom before them, clouding the air briefly as it dissipated. When the girls had reached about eight and nine and had become too big for the tractor seat, their grandfather took it off and hung it in a greenhouse beside the tools he used every day. And then sometimes he walked his granddaughters through a field, still bending toward them, saying "Look," and pointing to a graceful stem, a pungent bloom, or an animal imprint held in the dirt.

18

A Fragment Of A Song

Sonya took one of her mother's anatomy books off a living room bookshelf and brought it up to her room. She studied the detailed drawings of the heart for a while, then reshelved the book. In her room again she took out some colored pencils and paper. She began a group, all with a feature of the organ placed in a landscape. In one of the drawings was a mountain range with tiny cottages buried in the trees. An atrium mirrored the top of the mountains, filled the length of the whole range, filled the sky. In another was the sea seen from above the earth with continents in green and a ventricle, sketched in veiny-red, sailing alongside Africa. Fertile plains bordered with plateaus, in shades of yellow and grain, sprouted aortas high as the pale day-moon observing from a corner. The heart, the kidneys, the liver, all the others, even in their precise scientific rendering, had the hint of sloping, hint of land. At the end of the week, when the last nuances of lines and of shading were all complete, Sonya, realizing the spaces around her room were already taken, leaned two of the pictures against the wall in the hallway between her room and Lois's room, and tacked one up in the bathroom.

The next school day after Sonya had finished these drawings she began carrying an unsharpened green drawing pencil with her to school. The green had a marble pattern with flecks of gold in it. In her room one afternoon she had held it up vertically in the sunlight, brought it close to her face, and squinted her eyes. The pencil became a marble column, and courtyards were there, with some kind of music in the distance and, over at the edges, beyond the frame of the courtyard and column, some kind of ordered life. Another day, when the pencil was horizontal and she looked at it the same way, it was a jade river moving through gold time, with bloom along the banks and out of the frame. She didn't always think precisely of these configurations at school. But she could reach down into the zipper pocket on her pack, feel through the pens, pencils, and scraps of paper, and without looking know by its flat end that she was touching this drawing pencil. It waited for her there, ready to be anything she wanted it to be. Usually it was enough as a pencil, ready, within reach, that she could search out with her hand and touch as she walked from one class to the next, and that she could think about as she sat at a desk, an object glowing among the other objects tucked into the black nylon of the backpack beside her feet.

There were other concerns, though, that Sonya did not give as much thought to. The decision in mid-May to stop participating in the Annex was not one she had particularly deliberated over. One afternoon after her last class, when she usually headed to the studio, she thought of her desk at home and realized she would rather be there. She told Elinor that she wasn't feeling well, and she went home. The following day she felt the same way, and this stretched out into a week. Elinor said people were asking where she was, and Sonya told her to just say that she was tired. Sonya tried to avoid questions about it during the day, but when she was asked one, she answered vaguely. By the end of that week the prospect of returning was utterly draining to her, and it had become comforting to dash home immediately after her last class, sit at her desk and sketch. When one of the art teachers, Mr. Peters, called on Friday to see if she was all right, Sonya finally said simply, "I have too much work to do at home." He accepted her reason, but he expressed his disappointment regarding her unfinished contribution to the mural project.

Answering Elinor's concerns was considerably more difficult. She stopped by that Saturday afternoon on her way home from the store. They sat on the floor of Sonya's room, and she tried to explain what she was doing, but since she hadn't articulated it to herself completely, her explanation was not the least bit satisfying.

"I have stuff here I want to get done," she said. "I've started a list." She nodded toward the wall above her desk, where she had written Don't Forget, underlined in pencil. Beneath this heading a few phrases were jotted on the wall.

Elinor looked over. "You are writing on the wall?"

"Why not?"

"No reason not to, I guess." Elinor stood up to peer closer and studied the phrases. *Fragile shred of moth wing. Hands gluing a broken pot. Colored shards,* among them. "I will be curious to see these. Will you show me when they are finished?"

She sat back down, and Sonya held her hand while turning her bracelet of silver and red beads around and around her wrist. "Of course. This is a nice bracelet."

"Sonya." Elinor was exasperated. "I don't understand. You have been doing other art along with the studio work since the winter, and all spring. You could still do that."

"Have you started a batik project yet?" One of their teachers had recently given a workshop on the technique, and Elinor had been keen on attempting it.

"You're avoiding my point."

"It just feels too hard." She did not know another way to explain it.

"And what about the mural? We can't have someone else sculpt the rest of your relief." Though she didn't have a lot of experience with clay, Sonya had decided to create a botanical-themed piece, hoping her father would recognize that section as hers when he saw the mural. And Elinor was honing her design of a wood-block print, birds on a lake.

"I guess fire that part and say that's all I contributed. Or someone can work over what I started. Or expand into the area where the rest of my piece would have been. All that means is that I won't have my name on it."

"I want to see both of our names on it. And I like being with you then. I'm worried I won't be able to see you enough, especially if my mom keeps feeling so stressed."

"But maybe if she knows we won't be together those afternoons, she will relax a little."

"That's true. She could use less worry, and I know I've been adding to it."

"Besides, soon it will be summer, and we will have more time to be together then."

"For real?" Elinor had not often needed such reassurance, but lately she did.

"Hey," Sonya said, as she pulled Elinor close to her and kissed her ear, "I can't wait until you show me how to be an Olympic swimmer."

"Olympic? You're funny."

Sonya went out into the hall and picked up her drawing of the ventricle, brought it in and gave it to Elinor, who held the drawing and looked up at her and then at the picture. Sonya sat back down beside her.

"Do you know what I mean?"

"Yes, I do," Elinor said, a catch in her voice.

The feeling of security that Sonya had in coming home right after school and sitting at her desk was also what prompted her to stay home one evening, a couple of weeks later, instead of shopping at the mall with Lois and their mother. After dinner they tried to persuade her to join them.

"It's a pre-summer sale." Lois explained the May event. "I'm hoping to find some new shorts, and I might look at tops for Saturday. Milton and I are going either to the movies or maybe to dinner."

"I'll bet we could find a nice deal on a graduation dress for you," Marie offered. "Maybe a pair of steppers, too."

"I think I'll stay here. I can clean the dishes," Sonya said, clearing the table.

"Leave them," her mother said with a wave of her hand. "Come with us."

"There is a lot I need to work on."

When they edged out of the driveway and spun off down the street, Sonya went into her bedroom and closed the door. She took all of her colored pencils, some in plastic cases in her desk, some in the basket on her bookshelf, some in the leather tobacco pouch her father had given her, and put them, about forty, in a pile on her floor. Running her hand over them she rolled them out, then arranged all the pointed ends facing in the same direction. She studied the shades awhile, then selected the darkest one and put it at the top of the row. The next darkest shade came next, and then she carefully chose the others in order of their shade, and placed them, darkest to lightest, in one continuous column before her, making the blunt ends flush with each other. When this was completed, she mixed the pencils all together and sorted them again, but this time with the lightest one at the top and the darkest at the bottom, displayed like a spectrum against the grains of the wooden floor. There were other ways she found to sort them, too: by length, by brand, and then by shade, the greens together, the reds, the yellows by themselves. She was startled when she heard her mother and Lois come in the back door a couple of hours later and call to her to come down and see what they had bought at the sale.

Lois took a pair of shorts from a bag and held them up. "Aren't these funky?" They were khaki and had two generous front pockets.

"Those are great," Sonya said, rubbing the material.

"Did you get a lot accomplished here?" Marie got a pair of scissors from the kitchen to cut the tags off a shirt, then handed the scissors to Lois.

"Yes, some stuff."

Marie looked at her expectantly, but since Sonya did not offer any more information, she did not ask for more.

Though the sound was subdued by the closed door, Sonya knew it was her sister crying. Lois had come home from school a while before and had gotten the mail, as she did every school day. Sonya was usually first home but the routine she had developed of retreating to her room directly and working at her desk as soon as she got in precluded checking the mail, watering the plants if needed, retrieving the empty garbage cans from the end of the driveway and returning them to the garage. Among other tasks she used to do, even fairly recently, without much intention. She knocked on her door. "Can I come in?"

"OK."

Sonya walked in and sat on the edge of the bed. Lois was turned away from her, her dark brown hair, with streaks of red, spread across the pillow.

"What is it, Lois?"

Lois handed her a postcard from their father. It was a picture of the Ohio River.

"He likes water. What's wrong?"

"He's not coming back."

Sonya flipped the card over and read: "Girls, thanks for your letter. Keep up the grades, but don't go nuts over them. Lots of fish here. Write me through June c/o General Delivery, Blue Creek, OH 45616. Love, Dad. P.S. Just sold two tile pots, a 1 ft. x 2 ft. relief and some carafes."

She read it again. She turned the card over and looked at the glossy blue river rippling across the Ohio countryside, the sky spotless. A few fishermen waded in the distance.

"Lois, he doesn't say that. He'll be there until the end of June."

"Yeah," she said, sitting up. "Then at the end of June we'll get a card from Toledo again. Then in July we'll get a note from Youngstown. Then in August we'll get a note from Columbus or Mt. Nowhere. What the hell is he doing anyway, just milling around the whole state of Ohio?"

Sonya pictured Ohio, a monstrous O, swallowing him whole. The card appeared in her hands far away and insubstantial, as if viewed through the wrong end of a telescope.

"I don't know," she said. "Since when does he notice stream stocks anyway?"

"God knows," said Lois. "He doesn't even eat fish."

"Want to write to him and ask him what his plans are?"

"So he can write back and say 'Have a good summer'? No thanks."

They reached the pause they usually did when talking about their father.

Then Lois said, "You know he will most likely miss your graduation."

"Well, maybe I can send him a picture of me in my gown."

"Don't you dare. I won't let you, Sonya. If he can't get here himself, forget it. I'll be pissed at you if you do that."

"I know," Sonya said. "I know. I won't." When she thought about it, it did feel strange. She would be standing there in black, smiling into her mother's Instamatic camera. The picture would be glossy. She would slip it in an envelope, mark it c/o general delivery, send it into a black hole. The thought of a piece of herself wafting out to an anonymous spot made her feel lonely. And though it would be reaching their father, she was afraid he would take the picture from the envelope and look at it from too great a distance; her smile, her enthusiastic look out at the camera, would be rendered blank. The thought scared her.

"I see what you mean," she said to her sister. "I won't."

Sonya felt sad then too, so she went to her room and looked through her clothes. She weeded out the articles she no longer wore and some others she just wanted to give away and carried the armful of them back to her sister's room. "Let's do clothes," she said, dumping the clothes on the floor.

Lois jumped up and reached into her closet, yanked items off hangers and tossed them over her shoulder onto the floor. "This shirt has *got* to go. And this." She rifled through the stack of sweaters on the shelf above the hanging clothes, and she pulled out a few of those. "This one, too."

When Lois finished tossing hers out onto the heap, the two of them rummaged through it, trying each other's clothes on. Every item they pored over, saying, "I remember you used to wear this with your denim skirt" or "That sweater is great, but since I bought that rag wool one I just don't wear it anymore."

An hour and a half later, each had an armful of wardrobe updates, and this meant a closet of new outfits, mixed and matched.

Spontaneous activity inside with Sonya was still possible, but with activity outside, increasingly difficult for her, Lois and Marie, without intending to, had developed different strategies. During the week Lois casually mentioned her plan a few times, hoping that if her sister had enough time to think about it, she would agree to do the trip outside by the weekend. Marie, concerned that her daughter was spending too much time inside, tried a more impromptu method. "Honey," she would say, "do me a favor. Go out and make sure I closed the garbage cans tightly. I think I heard a raccoon in the garage last night." And Sonya would check as quickly as she could and come back inside. Neither of these efforts had a lasting effect on Sonya, but they helped momentarily, though minimally, to ease Marie and Lois's worry.

Lois was pleased when Sonya agreed to a bike ride with her and her friend Nancy, though she had insisted that she did not want to be gone more than an hour. When Sunday afternoon came around and the day was warm and sunny, the three of them left the Hudsons' house and headed for one of the town parks to swim. Once they were near the park, Nancy suggested they ride the five miles out to Helen Granger's to swim in her pool instead. Lois tried to lure her sister into going. "Let's. There won't be any crowd."

But Sonya slowed and braked to a stop. "I better get home. I just remembered something I have to do today, but you two go ahead, have fun." Lois, disappointed, watched her sister turn around and ride back down the street.

When Sonya heard loud bursts of laughter coming from a yard she rode by, she turned to see two young boys diving in the grass with a couple of guinea pigs crawling on them. She remembered that a neighbor of her grandparents in Mercy Hill had brought the kittens over in a shoebox, having found the litter in his barn. Lois and Sonya had stretched out in the thick grass of the backyard while their grandfather snuck up and put the kittens, one at a time, on the girls' legs and backs. They rolled in the grass laughing with the animals jumping around them, kicked off their flip-flops, picked all five up to rub and kiss, and gave each one a number of names before putting the kittens in the box when their grandfather said it was time for him to return them.

As soon as she got home and wheeled her bike into the garage, Sonya went up to her room and closed the door. She sat on the floor near a window, tucked her knees up and wrapped her arms around them. How had this day begun, gripped around her as it did, when just then she was in the grass? It was fine and pungent, around her people laughing and animals' fur against her skin, their timid cries in her ears. Their grandfather and mother above, watching them laugh. "Marie, you've got some gems here," he said, joining their laughter. The grass quickly in their hair, then on the animals and swirling in the green air of summer. No need for shoes. Name anything, she thought, and they could do it; they believed in trees and the quick climb, in bugs and the catch, summer storms, a run through their sounds, the quiet after. Stretching out on the floor she remembered rolling in the same heat of early June and grass that they had now, tired from laughing.

Now when she cried she could not say it was for any one thing, not just the fear that singed her ears and palms when she thought of having kittens climb over her, or the worry that her grandfather might be disappointed that she was still afraid, or the wave of effortless joy that overcame them in the tall grass then and that she longed to have washing over her now. It was for all of these.

When she fell asleep, her grandfather was behind her in the aisles of a greenhouse, both drenched in the aroma of red and pink geraniums and mottled light, urging her forward down the row and giving to everything around them as they passed, whether tall, knobbly, or squat, with round or pointed leaves, pale variegated green or star-burn yellow, a handsome name.

During the ceremony Sonya blurred her eyes to the sea of black shiny bobs, parts of an animal slithering as one up across the stage and then back down to rejoin the bright camera flashes, the groups of relatives. The murmuring, the calling out of names and the tears. Despair retrieved the rope from who knows where and threw it over and it fell over his father and his mother too and would never stop falling on them more than a shadow all that weight his despair on them no matter where they were after that, no matter what piece of paper or stained cup or old shoe worn unevenly in the heel they were look-ing at, no matter what year it was or might be after that there was with them his despair. All that murmuring and tears, and then the calling out.

The parts bobbed and shimmered, scaled and crawled, incongruously gelatinous, she thought, against the formal speeches and brisk clapping, the contrived music and plush red auditorium chairs. Thinking of all those people as one form made it easier for her to sit among them. Light, move-ment, the vicissitudes of form, the intricacies of formlessness, these were subjects she had sharpened an understanding of and appreciation for in high school. And now they helped quell her anxiety being at so public an event. She felt anxiety, too, about seeing classmates who had worked on the studio project; she knew it had been irresponsible to ditch her part. When her mother and sister had asked to see the mural, she deflected their re-quest, so disappointed was she that her name would not be on the piece with the others. Better to not even look at it, and it was best for her if they left the ceremony as soon as it was possible to do so, which they did, just as the last speaker was bringing his final sentence to a decisive out-into-the-world-now-with-all-of-you close.

She had not even wanted to take time to say goodbye to Veronica. Not that she would have, even if they had lingered in the hallways afterwards. Sonya had seen her from a distance in her cluster of Honors graduates, completely absorbed by their company. For one instant Veronica had turned away, and she was like a sail tacking in the wind; she had become so thin, moved with such sharp intent, and was whisked along by an invisible propellant. Yet her body seemed distorted, as if there were not enough heft to it to sustain the power that drove it forward. And though their early laughter on warm nights in the yard was indelibly a part of them, a leisurely conversation now would have been impossible.

Elinor and Sonya had earlier in the week declined a graduation party invitation from the studio group, though Elinor told her parents she was spending the afternoon at this party. Instead, afterwards, at the picnic table set up near the hedge of blooming honeysuckle bushes in the Hudsons' yard, they ate soybean salad, corn on the cob, potato salad, chips, and drank quarts of lemonade.

Sonya went in to get more napkins, came back out and saw her mother and Elinor standing with the white wall of the garage behind them. Elinor looked over and smiled at her, while her mother's calm sweet voice explained her plan for the flower bed, in the distance floated the sound of Lois at the table; Elinor's eyes held still the warm murmur of the afternoon. Then there was another, unidentifiable, time suddenly inside Sonya; she experienced its moment, its heat, the sadness of its passing, other garages and other overgrown backyards, and a flood of other smiles in other June ecstatic heated moments, other laughs breaking out in the still air, and the feeling in her, though all these details were elusive, was familiar and comforting. The times transposed—were they in that other time, and some light from that time brought here? And the meshing of the two fixed for that instant, fixed by their acknowledgment. There they were and it was OK, it was sweet, a thrill to be eating delicious food and drinking something so satisfying. And, while holding Elinor's gaze, the phrase, unattached, *remember how beautiful*, came into her head like a fragment of a song someone else had sung earlier that she had picked up without knowing.

After they ate, they took pictures in the yard. These moments, too, were stilled time. Looking inside the camera, focusing on Elinor, Lois, and their mother smiling, Sonya remembered when she and her sister used to look through their mother's cedar box of black and white photographs, first laying aside the watch and then lifting the photos one at a time. She remembered her explaining to them one day that she had planned to marry the young uniformed man in the picture, her high school beloved, but that he had gone down over the North Atlantic during a routine maneuver. It was a few months after this that Marie had packed her botany and chemistry books, put her photo album and rosary into her matching suitcases, and boarded the bus for the city of Putnamton. How could the girls when they were young absorb such information? They listened and, after that first time, held his picture by the edges, briefly, and always placed it carefully back in the box, so as not to crease it more or as if their holding it would do him further harm. And then they lay the watch back on top of the photos. But while holding it, Sonya always tried to figure out what their mother's words meant. She could see her school ring, which he had worn on his right pinkie finger, at the bottom of the sea nestled in weeds and glittering fish, its blue stone shining. Yet she never imagined him crashing or imagined his body falling. She thought of him sitting in the cockpit of the plane as he was in the photo, at the wheel of a convertible, their mother's arm around his neck, both looking out at whoever took the picture, smiling. She thought of him over the North Atlantic, beaming out at the world below, hovering in the air like a god, like possibility.

But now, viewing Elinor through the lens, glints of sun in her short brown hair, on her pale red cotton shirt and her shorts, she meditated on how her mother had endured such loss, that stillness beside her. She never talked about it; the handful of details Sonya and Lois had was all they knew. Now Sonya wanted to take those she loved inside herself, to keep them safe. Did adults feel all the time that constant need to protect? Was it possible to go through a day and not be gripped by it? Her finger pressed the button; the shutter clicked like a box lid. She took two more exactly the same in case the first one didn't come out.

Late that afternoon when Elinor got home, as Sonya found out a couple of days later when Elinor phoned her secretly, her parents suspected she had lied about where she was that afternoon and, though it was an otherwise celebratory occasion, did not talk with her the rest of the evening or, for that matter, the next day.

When the pictures were developed, after the girls first admired the ones taken in the yard, all of which did come out, Lois picked the photograph from the ceremony least likely to have any one person recognizable. With a black pen she drew a circle around a turned head amid the blur of smiling graduation faces bobbing above the robes. She drew an arrow from the circle and wrote on the back "Your daughter." She stuck the picture in an envelope, wrote out their father's name and general delivery address, sealed it, and dropped it in a mailbox. "There," she said triumphantly.

A week later they received an envelope from their father with a coupon in it for sandwiches and salad at a chain restaurant. He had written across the top: "Got the picture. Happy Grad. Meal is on me. Love, Dad."

"Maybe we could go Tuesday afternoon," Sonya suggested, though with immense effort. Any Saturday afternoon some gesture over the table the day held up to the window or swung around by its arms laughing. That's what he saw and the lovely narrow utensil that texture of a meal its color heightened by their laughing.

"Sonya." Lois sighed at her and frowned. She tore the coupon in half and threw it away.

Their mother, one step out the screen door, had overheard this, and now peered in the kitchen as Lois walked away, and watched Sonya turning the envelope in her hands. Sonya looked up and recognized the fleeting, before-cry, pause in expression on her face, then looked again at the envelope. Marie said, "I'll be outside."

19

Falling Landscapes

It hadn't made sense to him at first, having come in the back door, to be walking through the kitchen and then into the living room after work looking toward the stairway and to see his son's black sneakers dangling above the floor. How could there be a pair of sneakers there? Lloyd Duncan, not an introspective man, nonetheless hesitated at that question. His mind spun out then, looped out wide to a field where he hunted rabbits, turkeys, and pheasants. When he was young, when the smoky smell of the shot lingered in the air commensurate with his shot of adrenalin at having gotten it, the target squirming in the grass or thunking from the sky as he and his friends ran toward it. Now something held him still, the urgency and rush of it burned in him again, his heart tearing through him.

Something held him there, looking at Andy's sneakers, as he felt as if he were being watched from above. Never in his life did he move slowly or with indecision, but that moment that was not a moment, and that would be without time for the rest of his life, he hesitated. His eyes moved slowly up the leg, the slender leg, two legs, up to the shorts and T-shirt, the white T-shirt, and then to the face, the eyes he had felt on him looking off, seeming to be locked on a spot in the living room or, closer, on the ceiling light fixture near the stairway. The rope had squeezed the skin on his neck, it must have scratched his skin with its rough fibers. Lloyd Duncan thought he heard the kitchen wall clock ticking.

Then he stretched behind him and reached for the end table near the sofa, carried it over, pushed aside the fallen kitchen chair, and placed the table beneath the sneakers, the legs moving a little. "Wait right there," he said. Then he took the quick steps up to the top of the staircase, and loosening with great effort the several knots his son had made, the rope woven in and out and around among the posts of the banister, he lowered him down to the table. The body slipped down to the table, rigidly slanted across it, and Lloyd said "Don't slip" as he lunged back down, went around the newel post, and met his son, arms hanging out, legs shooting off, at the end table.

Then he tried to gather the limbs, the whole body, to himself, pull the stiffness to him, and as he did he looked at the two framed prints on the wall below the banister which were now askew because first the hanging body then the lowered body had knocked them. If he studied these prints, which his wife had gotten at Murphy's department store, he would now notice that all the farm animals in one painting were falling, the large red barn falling, the house also, falling, soon the animals would be one on top of another and they would be desperate for sure footing, scrambling, crying, heavy on top of one another, suffocating in the pasture meant to be their life that now was where they would die. The girl with the flower basket in the other picture was spilling too, the cut blossoms she had worked so hard to gather would soon be strewn on top of her, all falling through their frame and through the other one beside them, all tumbling down the pasture sloped beyond balance, beyond the broken frames that had held them.

Lloyd held his son with one arm and with the other hand unbuttoned his work shirt, struggled to slip off first one sleeve, then shifting arms, the other. His own body odor, pungent, mixed with Andy's. Or was it just his own? He then covered Andy's head with the shirt, and that was when his wife came in the back door, calling to him.

She dropped her handbag on the kitchen table, saw through the living room, saw the back of her husband's undershirt, saw the legs projected out one side, her husband bent over him. As she approached she saw the rope dangling off the end table, coiled loose near her husband's feet. Though she screamed, her husband did not turn around. She walked to his back and pulled at him, grabbed his undershirt and wrenched her face into his back, both of them moaning, wailing. There had been other wailing in Laconius, and now the Duncans' pierced voices drifted up and out, over the sidewalks, stoplights, housetops, over the fields, first blended with the wailing from that week, the sounds dovetailing, then blended with the cries that came surely from within the past year, then drifted all the way back through every year, even before the town was surveyed, and finally sifted into the cries from the first peoples, at one thousand, two thousand years past, the oldest, first, cries, the ones so long dissipated.

They were not thinking of the sounds they made, nor thinking what to do next, nor thinking at all, Lloyd unsure, if he'd been asked, whether it was sweat or urine now dampening the inside of his thigh, his trouser leg.

Afterwards, after Paul from across the street stopped in, having walked by and heard them, and made the call for them, after the ambulance came, the crew had taken him from the house, after the call to Ben, when they sat on the couch where they would stay beyond dusk, staring at the rug, she said, "But he just doesn't weigh enough. He is too light. I don't see how it could work."

As the first few shovelfuls of dirt were measured in, several days later, Ben reached into his back pocket, took out his wallet, opened it thinking he would retrieve and throw into the ground his driver's license, but then he closed the wallet and instead tossed the whole thing in. He watched it become completely covered with soil, its black leather, all the pieces of paper inside, all he knew of commerce, the daily paying his way in the world, everything he knew of how to negotiate, the bills he never gave much heed to, tossed in now above his brother's folded hands, the coins that bought him a quart of beer, pulled now from his pocket, above his closed eyes.

20

A Band Of Fire

In Sonya's nightmares her voice was thick and slow as mercury and, as she stood facing the cat approaching her casually, she *thought* of how to say, "Get it away from me" faster, make it more direct. She thought of how to say it so one word would snap out after the next like a crisp shirt on a line in the wind; her mother or her sister or perhaps someone else would come from another room, pick up the animal, and put it outside. Then she would breathe with the relief of rescue. But the words, the clear line that hung like an illuminated sign across the inside of her forehead, came out of her mouth so slowly that people moved as if underwater and never got the thing away from her. "You must wake up," she heard the diminished alert part of herself tell all the rest. When she woke with the sluggish muscle of drowned language working through her mouth, she whispered to herself, "Get it away from me," just to hear herself say it. But it didn't matter so much in the morning late in June, already the buzzing sounds of neighbors' innocuous yard chores drifting through the window. She had to work, she said, to work on saying that command in her dream, to be able to say it in the underworld of sleep as directly as she could say it now, in the calm of early morning. She would concentrate harder next time.

In a city dreams shimmer; where all day light strikes up and down the avenues and water runs underground in dank unseen passageways, dreams have urging all around them. There, over grates and shuffles of feet, loud indistinguishable voices, dreams float, rise up out of their longing for meaning and hover above the scattered tops of trees, knowing they will be noticed. In Vienna, no, in Amsterdam, no, in crowded Bombay, all days press into clear being, concentrated form, and under the weight of every-one's feet float into the sky as one song. But here, as she sat and wondered out the ordered window and over the hushed street, were mouths wrapped in wax, voices sunken in entangled thoughts. It was exhausting, all this straining on chords for a word. How would she draw that?

The rings were shaded in gray and spiraled up the sheet of textured drawing paper, filled its height. There was something over them like skin, a protective covering. There were spots that suggested freckles or marks of age or perhaps scars grown faint. Maybe it was a throat; was the head tipped back, the throat extended? Or was it constricted? No matter what item in the grocery store what price did it matter his despair was between them and the box or can as they reached for it was there between their lungs and the air they took in between their bodies that had come together and the clothes touching them his despair was there. There was nothing below the charcoal rings, nothing above. No scale to indicate the delicate veins of a throat that might have arched back laughing or singing, heard beside someone's ear or from another room. It might have been a tree trunk with its circular pattern of years, or the loops where it grew around pasture wire and the spots marks on the bark, or indentations where animals burrowed to make a place. Perhaps what hovered below, out of sight, looked up now and then wide-eyed at a fragrant canopy of bloom and leaf that might have floated, branched, above. Its design was obvious; its sound unknown. Sonya rested it against the wall with the others beside her desk.

Sitting on the floor and looking at pictures' edges, the way one angle dropped off into another like a lost afternoon or folded itself into another like the protective crease of an envelope, she heard her mother downstairs on the phone.

"I don't think we can this summer, Dad, not now anyway. She just isn't up to it at all. Well—"

In the pause of his unheard words she leaned into the blue well of scent, steadied by her mother's hand, leaning too.

"Not really, she doesn't leave the house much except sometimes, very briefly. But that's an effort. I know, Dad, I'm trying—"

When the voice broke in tears, all the salt water spilling down, flooding down and filling the stone basin, she strained not to hear the rest of the conversation.

Instead she heard the water splashing down and heard the finger dips of people touching it on their way in. Her grandmother had been upset that Sunday when she returned because he hadn't joined her in the morning, hadn't walked the stone floor with her.

"It wouldn't hurt you one day a week."

"I'm there with you most Sundays."

"Every Sunday makes up for the other days of the week and helps you remember it all besides."

"I don't forget a thing from week to week," he had said, smiling, though he knew she was serious. "I know not to rinse my face in the holy water and not to bring my own wafers."

Marie had laughed with her father at this, but Glenda had not shared their amusement.

Visible when she closed her eyes, each word lay so long unused, transparent disc, if she could just move it to her tongue open her mouth where it lay glittering the word waiting waiting to come to life in her throat. The round moon-mint with its pale solace made a moment whole in the summer backyard, the tongue knowing its faint color, visible when she closed her eyes.

Sonya wiped her own tears now as she remembered his irreverence and was comforted. "But he is spiritual," she would have said to her grandmother had she thought of it at the time and she said now, out loud in her room by herself. The high panels of glass were there, shimmering by day and by night webbed with starlight, his wax seals of water and his overgrown trumpet vine, and she was comforted.

As Sonya's excursions outside the house were ever more seldom, Elinor tried to make the most of them; one afternoon when she had persuaded Sonya to go shopping with her, she also tried to persuade her to work where she did, at an Italian restaurant in town. She had gotten the job the week after graduation, hoping to both increase her donations to the women's shelter and to put aside some funds for her first year of study.

"We can waitress together," she said in the clothing store, while she lifted a shirt off a rack and studied it to appear casual about her suggestion. She didn't typically have the inclination to shop, but she had hoped that so mundane an outing would entice Sonya. "How would this look with my striped navy vest, or maybe with one of my gray ones?"

"I can't, Elinor, it's too much." She didn't know how else to explain what she meant.

"Too much what?"

"All those people," she said, "all those details to keep track of. I wouldn't be any good at it." She thought of all that movement. It seemed too much in the world to her.

"I'll show you. I don't know it all either—this is my first time waitressing. I'll learn and then I'll show you. It would be fun." But she knew her attempt fell short.

"Besides, Caroline would not be too happy if we worked together." Although significant, Sonya knew that this wasn't her primary reason, and she knew that Elinor knew it, too. "I better get home," she said, turning toward the door. They had been in town barely half an hour.

"But Sonya," Elinor said, as they headed for the car.

Neither one spoke on the drive back.

When they pulled in Sonya's driveway, Elinor reached over and took her hand. She held it tightly, rubbed her thumb against Sonya's.

"I'm here when you want to talk."

Sonya smiled. "I'm fine," she said, then stepped out of the car and went inside.

That night there was a band of fire around her throat, and it burned the words to ash before they could reach the air. That dazzling Alaskan blue, fragrant with spring blowing along the banks of the river. The breeze nipped her face as she stood on a dock scanning the river thick with cats swimming toward her. Her grandfather and a couple of his friends were in a fishing boat a few feet from the dock, talking amongst themselves and readying the bait for their excursion. They didn't seem to notice Sonya, her mouth open, no sound coming out. It would have been difficult, if not impossible, for them to hear her above the constant cries of all those animals. She thought she might wet herself. When she woke, she snapped a lamp on, heard the cries of cats fighting out in the street. Then downstairs, she made certain the front and back doors were locked. Before returning to bed she closed and locked the windows in her room. Then she covered her ears, his scent of tobacco leaves drying in a cool dark shed in a field of light drifting over her, and watched the pattern of paint strokes on her ceiling before finally falling asleep again.

"Come for a walk around some of the old neighborhoods and pick out houses," Elinor said. On the return from one of the museum excursions into the capital, their art teacher, Mr. Peters, had directed the bus through various neighborhoods, pointing out differences sometimes by century, sometimes by period name or decade. Thanks to him, they could now not only appreciate the obvious architectural influences in large swaths of Harpur Springs. They could also, much to their delight, easily toss comments like "cool finial" and "definitely pre-war" into a conversation.

It had been two months since they had, one afternoon, picked out which houses they would buy and discussed what they would do—detailed renovations, then give them away. The few other times Elinor had recently asked her to venture out on another house-walk, thinking that having a specific task would make it easier for her, Sonya had said she couldn't interrupt what she was doing. This time, too, would not be convenient for her.

"Then I'll come there," Elinor said. "I miss you."

"I miss you, too. What about your mother?"

"I'll tell her I'm going for a bike ride. She can't take away that privilege."

Though they tried to talk to each other on the phone every day, sometimes this was not possible because they had to do it without Elinor's mother knowing, which often meant that she dialed from a pay phone. But they hadn't seen each other since their brief trip into town a few days earlier.

A while later, sitting at her desk, Sonya heard a bike slow in the driveway. She heard Elinor talking with her mother in the backyard about some plants, then heard the screen door open and close, steps through the kitchen and up the stairs. Elinor came in and closed the door, stood a few feet away.

"Hey," she said.

"Hi," Sonya said, standing up and reaching out her hand. Elinor took it, and they leaned against each other.

"Tell me what it is."

Sonya rested her forehead on her friend's shoulder. "I don't know. There is so much out there."

"So much what? What's out there?"

"All the people." Elinor was so good at it, and never had to think about it; she could talk with anyone, joke with strangers in the checkout line, wave to kids she didn't know and they'd wave back.

"Just walk through the neighborhood with me. Think of what is out there that you love to see, think of all the yards and all the flowers and plants in bloom right now. We can talk about that instead of about the houses if you want."

Sonya thought of all of them waiting to catch her off guard, to trap her. "I can't."

"Why not?"

"It's just too much."

"Too much what?" Then, almost pleading, "Tell me, Sonya."

"I don't know." She began to cry and moved further into Elinor's arms tightening around her.

"I believe in you," Elinor said. Sonya cried harder.

After a few minutes Elinor went into the bathroom and returned with some tissues. Sonya blew her nose and wiped her eyes.

"Stay here awhile."

"Will you show me what you've been working on?"

There were drawings in various stages of completion propped against her bookcase, her dresser, the bed, and along the walls. Sonya led her over to a stack leaning against the wall by her desk. She cleared a space on the floor by picking up a few plates with dried pieces of sandwiches on them, and piled them to one side. Then they sat down cross-legged, held hands. While Sonya, with her other hand, pored over her prints deciding which recent ones to share, Elinor glanced up and noticed that the list of ideas penciled on the wall was expanding, spilling out beneath the heading on either side. She wanted to say, "I will help you, I will help you remember your ideas, describe for me all of your inspired images, let me help you so that you don't forget. Tell me, or write them in my hand." But instead of commenting on this, she focused her attention back to Sonya, who was ready with the first selection to show her.

First was the drawing of the rings, which she titled *Gray Chords*. Elinor said, "The chords seem to move up and down at the same time."

"I'm glad it looks that way."

"Or maybe they are moving out, like the rings of a tree."

"My dad says a tree is a metaphor."

"For what?"

"He didn't explain that part, but I think I know what he means. These rings could speak for something much larger than they are. Does that make sense?"

"Yes, it does," Elinor said, then admired the next one, of a rib cage huge and circular at rest in a mist on the edge of an expansive body of water. "Is this the hull of a ship or a rib cage?"

"It's a rib cage, but it could be both."

Elinor picked up another one. "This is max." In the spring someone at the Annex had started using that word, and soon everyone else there had also used it to refer to a piece at the furthest edge of impressive.

"It's the arboretum." The hill on which they sometimes walked was ringed with rays of leaving sun, and the town lights looped below, the city lights dimmed in the distant horizon. Nebulous stars becoming visible in the evening sky. "You know when you close your eyes part way in the sun and it looks like there are rings around everything? That's what I was thinking of."

"They all have circles in them."

"Hey, you're right, they do."

"What does that mean?"

"I'm not sure."

They contemplated the pictures a few minutes longer, then returned them leaning against the wall.

Elinor lay down on the floor on her back, stretched out her legs. Sonya lay beside her and said, "Talk to me about small things."

Elinor thought of some. "Friday nights are generally busiest, like seven to ten, which is chaos. Then we mellow out a bit. Last Friday a bowling league was in there, seemed like all one hundred and twenty-seven teams.

Our manager is patient though; she helps keep everything moving smooth-ly, even with a lot of customers. Or when we run out of a dish."

"Do you get to eat the food there?"

"Whatever we want. Sometimes on break I eat. Their antipastos are fab-ulous. Once in a while I take a piece of something home, like the lasagne. Most of us eat that."

There were some topics Sonya wanted to talk with Elinor about, such as the postcard she and Lois had recently gotten from their father, another with farmland on the front. This one had a brief note that said they could call him, at the number given, through the end of the summer. But he did not explain exactly what place the number belonged to. The postmark was from Greenfield. She had not found the energy to dial the number, and Lois had refused to call. Though Sonya wanted to hear Elinor's interpre-tation of the note, thinking about it brought to mind enormous sweeps of deserted highway, images of industrial lights and abandoned lots at dusk that made her tired, so she did not mention it.

Instead, she said, "Tell me more," rolled on her side, and watched Eli-nor as she recounted stories the waitresses had told when they sat around talking after the restaurant closed. Sometimes they had a couple of beers together to unwind, or a cigarette and coffee, and talked about that shift or about their lives. Most of them were older than Elinor was, and some were working to support kids.

While she talked Sonya watched the creases near her eyes move, especial-ly when she smiled. She thought of what comfort it must be to watch some-one age. She thought, too, of the sound of Elinor's laughter from another room and of how it would be to always hear her somewhere in the house.

"One of the waitresses makes up names for all of the regular customers— like Mr. Cheese Food and Mrs. Side Dish. Then sometimes I'm worried the name will slip out when I wait their table."

Sonya reached over and touched the thin silver hoop through Elinor's ear. She sighed.

"I could tell you about my paycheck. That's a small thing, too," Elinor said. They laughed.

"You always make me feel better, Elinor." Sonya noted her blue and green Indian cotton shirt and tan shorts. She herself had lately been wearing an item over several days, though sometimes she turned a T-shirt inside-out to wear it again, or alternated right-side-out, inside-out, then right-side-out until it seemed time to add the garment to the pile of laundry on the floor. But she looked at Elinor and thought of how bright her clothes were. She thought, particularly, of the cloth against her skin. Oh, to linger there. "You look nice."

"I want to take you somewhere tomorrow night. Can I pick you up around nine?"

"What about the car?"

"I feel bad lying," Elinor said, though she had resorted to it recently, "but I could tell my parents that I'm working an extra shift this week so I need the car. My mother would let me use it for that."

"Where are we going?"

"It's a surprise."

"Does it involve other people?"

"No, just us."

She didn't say anything.

"Sonya, it will be all right. Trust me."

"I do trust you."

"It will be nice."

"Is it far away?"

"No. It's close, don't worry."

"OK," Sonya said. But she still felt nervous.

Sonya got out and stood by the car in the dark. Elinor came over and took her by the hand.

"Let's walk up the hill," she said.

The unlit paths of the arboretum were familiar to them, as dense leaves rustled in the night air, their green absorbed by the dark. Fragile night bugs lifting then closing their shades, lifting then closing their shades.

"It's like being on a moving ship," Sonya whispered. "How does the air stay this new?" She tried to think about that to help herself feel calm.

"I never thought about it quite like that," said Elinor, whispering too.

"It's like a living thing we're walking through. We're walking through its body."

Elinor found a spot, and they sat close on the grassy hill overlooking the town.

"What if one comes out of the trees behind us? They step so quietly that we'd never hear it," Sonya said.

"There's nothing here with us but trees and stars. We have never seen one here before, and we won't see one now."

But Sonya could not relax.

"This is one of your favorite places," Elinor tried. "You always like coming here."

"I feel like I'm drowning," Sonya said, "and I can't see anything clearly."

"Do you want to go home?"

"I'm sorry." She started to cry.

"I feel terrible when you cry."

"I'm sorry, Elinor."

"Please, you shouldn't apologize." She held Sonya's hand tightly and led her to the car.

They did not talk on the return drive. When they reached her house, Sonya stayed in the car in the driveway.

"I'm glad you're here," she said.

"I'm glad you're here, too. Can you see me clearly, Sonya?"

"Yes."

"Don't lose sight of me."

Sonya turned and held Elinor for a long long moment. Then she said, "I won't."

"Talk to you tomorrow."

"Definitely." Then Sonya stepped out, closed the door, keeping her hand on the handle briefly, then went inside.

The blue of the water itself was drowning, rippling and running, leaking down the crumbling steps under the surface of the sea. The little figure on the steps, stick-like with hardly any substance or hands to grasp, was reaching after it, trying to pull the color back into the water. But the color was below it, near the bottom of the steps, tumbling down, moving faster than the ill-defined figure. The water with no color still moved like water, washed around the steps, swirled its particles downward. Above was a narrow strip of robust figures on the shore, reddish and blustery spots beneath their colorful umbrellas. Did it take on its own life his despair robust because it was always with them did it breathe as more than a shadow from their eyes in the room in the still house at night did it take on its own kind of life after they lost the daylight of his did it take on its own the umbrella they lived under after they lost the color of his. But everything below them, the rest of the drawing, was slipping downward, and the sole color there, the blue, was leaking out the bottom. When the drawing was finished, Sonya leaned it against some others along the wall in her bedroom and sat on the floor looking at it for an hour, then tried to think of a name for it.

21

The Tangle Of Words

She could think of mottled starlight, mushrooms in a warm field—that was doing something—and someday she would feel them again. It wasn't always what her mother asked; she had given up asking the social errands, driving to the grocery store, the mall, any place in town with her. That was over. But her method of asking Sonya to do minor tasks, most of them unnecessary, just to get her outside, continued through the early half of the summer. Marie would say, "My hands are full. Carry that planter out after me, will you?" And Sonya would bring it out behind her mother, look around, set it down beside her in the grass and head back inside before she heard her mother's urging. That she couldn't bear.

But inside, she was doing something—she had notes written on the wall for proof of that—there would be one in colored pencil of lemon trees. Did lemons grow on trees? And one in charcoal of a rainstorm, whose edges she could almost think about, almost see, moving across the reservoir. One, too, of a figure in a salvaged vehicle, perhaps a truck, sweeping across a highway in the dark, though there would be some starlight or some planet-light—were those the same?—to guide him. Maybe that would be in paint.

Then one day in mid-July her mother knocked on the bedroom door. She had come in several days recently. This time, too, Sonya called from her desk but continued what she was doing. Marie, still wearing her straw garden cap, came in and sat down in the rocking chair.

"Sonya, I can't stand this anymore."

The urgency in her mother's voice frightened her. She looked up from her desk.

Her mother was surveying the room, in more disarray each time she saw it, especially the past month. Now there were sketches and half starts, sheets with smears of color and with smears of gray, and finished drawings and paintings too, all shuffled together in no order that she could discern leaning against the bookcase, closet door, dresser, against every available section of wall space; others were tacked up, covering much of the walls. There was a pile of broken and dulled pencils on the floor behind Sonya, a piece of cardboard with swaths of dried paint, and the notes, phrases, penciled on the wall above her desk in an ever-widening arc. She saw her mother look over at these and at the accompanying underlined heading Don't Forget.

"So that I won't forget what to do next," she said. Lately, she had told her mother this every time she came into her room. Marie didn't say anything.

After a pause she started again, "I'm glad you've been working so hard, but I really think that—"

"You see why it's pretty much impossible for me to do other things right now," Sonya interrupted. "I have to stay in to get this stuff done."

"Listen," her mother began again, her hands turning, trying to speak further for her.

"You see," Sonya continued, as if she had talked openly about it all along, "It's not that I don't want to help you with things, but I just can't right now. I have to finish this. I'm working on a circular series. Elinor pointed out to me that they all have circles in them, and most of them have water. I didn't mean for them to at first. They came out that way. But now that I see it, there is so much more I can do with this. I have a lot to do. But I *am* thinking about what you said—" All her calculations with numbers, all the figuring she'd been working on, figuring all those numbers' other lives and all that light she'd kept track of on the wall. And not just her bedroom wall, but the walls of the outdoor cafes, too, because the people there had been too distracted by their delicate cups to notice. But she could, in her room, she could take note of things and she had, she had been thinking hard of all these—it wasn't easy, that light from elsewhere, Grecian or otherwise, but she had managed, it wasn't that she had been idly sitting there. "I've been thinking about what you've been saying these past few days—"

"You mean weeks, months."

"I really have and—"

"Every day I want to pick you up as if you were five years old again and put you in the car and drive you to someone, to anyone who might help. But I have been afraid to risk making you feel worse. I have been afraid of you feeling further away." Her mother let out a weary breath. "I want you to go talk to someone again," she finally said.

"I can't," Sonya said. Then a puzzled expression clouded her face, a knot came into her eyes. "I mean, why? I don't need to." The words thickened in her throat. "I'm fine."

"No, Sonya, you are not fine."

Her mother's directness startled her, the words sharp and driven.

"You don't do anything on your own anymore. You haven't ridden your bike in months. You don't go for walks like you used to. Nor do anything with people, with us, anymore. Yes, you talk to us and to Elinor, but you haven't been outside, I mean, Christ, really spent any length of time outside this house, or outside your room for that matter, in weeks and weeks. Not since you were in school, and that was only because you had to be."

Sonya concentrated on the clay cup of pens on her desk as her mother spoke, thought of all the poised and ready angles, all the ways the pens, blue, green, black, leaned and gestured in every probable direction, so decisive and angular they were, so pointed and sure.

"It hurts your sister, it hurts me, and it hurts Elinor. We are worried sick. We need help with this, and you are the only one who can help us."

Sonya hadn't heard the crying in her mother's voice, but when she looked over, Marie was wiping her eyes. Exhaustion was apparent in her shoulders now too, curved with burden, resigned. Sonya wanted to comfort her but could not move. The space of pain around each of them had created a magnetic resistance, and neither one could move closer. Her throat burned.

"Mom," she said. "Mom." She leaned her head in her hands and cried. She heard her mother blow her nose.

Marie stood up and put her hands in the pockets of her shorts. She walked to the door. Sonya could not look at her.

"Just give me a month," Sonya said through her tears. "I'll be better."

Her mother turned toward her and said, "I don't know what to do, Honey." Then she left the room and closed the door. Sonya heard her walk downstairs, step out the screen door and into the yard.

Then the crumbling began. Sonya felt all the little pieces she had placed carefully aside start to fall inward, slide downward into her like shelves of sand. She heard sifting and felt the tumbling weight move downward from her throat to her chest. It settled there. She hit herself in the tight spot beneath her breast. Poked it, hit, and pinched herself until her skin stung, too. Then she said, "I'm sorry, I'm sorry I hurt you." She touched her heart again, lightly this time, to see what feeling was still there. She got up and locked her windows and closed her curtains, then grabbed a blanket off the bed. After pushing aside clothes, notebooks, and scraps of paper, she curled up on her side on the floor, covered herself with the blanket. There in the dark cave she rocked, there in the cave of her own sounds she heard the blood swimming inside her, heard it wash against the walls of her veins, her capillaries tingling. She heard the choked pain move upward next, its animal gums exposed but teeth clenched, straining the blood as it swam up from her heart. He hung from the banister with no daylight where he was they said the two boys were together then she listened to sounds out her window then she thought how could they be together in the rope with no daylight? It is moving so slowly, why is it moving so slowly? Why is everything taking so long? It moved up her chest through the canal of frightened days, the tunnel of longing, and pulled itself toward her mouth. On the way it pushed out the sides of her ribs, threat of splintering, struggled toward her throat, pushed and strained the sides of her throat through the burning tangle of words that lay so long unused, visible when she closed her eyes. And then, in the cave of her sounds, it finally pushed up to her mouth. A choking sound came first and then the words.

"This is enough," she said. "This is quite enough." The words were clear, as if, having come from so far down, having come through that thick tangle, they were cleaned by the air. Sonya said it again, "This is enough," just to be sure she had heard it right, to be convinced she had heard herself, heard her words, that distinctly. She could picture them after they were spoken floating and sparkling before her in the air.

"It's OK, it's OK, it's OK," she said. "It's going to be OK." She wiped her eyes, stretched out her legs, and fell asleep. She slept and slept while the sun rode over, while the hours passed. While she slept, the shadows in the backyard changed shape, were maybe ship beneath a tree, maybe seahorse at a table leg as the sun rode over, washing the yard all day, and the vegetables and flowers grew imperceptibly. While she slept, the day became late afternoon, lengthening toward dinnertime.

"I love," Sonya woke up saying. "I love her hair, her smell, and her hands," she said, rolling on her back. Then she remembered her earlier conversation with her mother; she realized that it was now later in the day, that it was a summer day, and that she was on the floor of her room in a house she lived in with her mother and her sister. The back of her neck was damp, her hair was stuck to her forehead. Her eyes, sore. She put aside the blanket, stood up, and opened the curtains and the windows. Then she lay down on the floor again and listened. She heard the distant hum of a lawnmower, a car whip by, heard kids on skateboards whistle through the neighborhood, a screen door open and close. "I love her laugh," she said, "the scar on her chin, the lines near her eyes, I love her walk, all her silver earrings, and when she leans against me."

Behind this daily tumble, this ordinary mesh of sigh and gesture, and people coming and going, insidious fear had taken root and spread. Why, in this world where all things were possible? In this world, where all things imaginable already exist somewhere, in some variation. Or—unimaginable things exist. Oceans with an inconceivable amount of water. Antarctica, its five million square miles of ice. All things and people. Afternoons of steel-heat desert. Rainy villages with carts on tilted streets. Light green-blown in spring, spun around gardens, in the overgrowth of a rotted arbor. A sheet drying on a line. A voice a street away. An alley, a rusty bicycle leaning against a brick wall. Shadows on that bicycle. A tarnished bell, deep marble caverned churches in a forest. The slow descent of sunlight across a bookshelf. All objects, all animals, people, places. All fruits and plants. All cloth, charts, blue-lined graphs, green drawing pencils, forgotten brown lace shoes, useless brooms, locked cedar boxes, pocket watches, two-cent postage stamps, doorknobs. All varieties of love, all accents of human emotion. In this world, where all things were possible. Where infinite variety touched everything, every ventricle and stem, galaxy and barn. Where all things were possible, done and loved, known somewhere. And somewhere was home to a boy who cut himself off from that place; how could a father fear what feeling whistled from the hard salty body of his son? How could any love be feared?

On this huge singular earth, rolling over and over like an enormous slow blue-green fish through oceans of space, turning its fading underbelly up into daylight, then turning again its wall-eyes away from the sun, back into darkness. Over and over. Millions riding it. Sonya, in one house, pressed against its skin, her back against earth's thick green skin. Here, in her time and place, her moment of earth, she had her own love, anger, and laughter. In all that living and dying, all those individual lives, here was one person in the lonely and lovely, desolate and dream-like, sheath of a particular life. A life which she wanted, with its fears and its gifts, more than any other.

22

Honey In His Mouth

It hadn't even begun, that time, with wrestling, though it could have. The wrestling had begun out in that field, when Will had inadvertently tripped over Andy's outstretched leg as they gathered old gnarled apples from the ground to throw. In the orchard overgrown at a secluded edge of the Duncans' property, abundant still, even in neglect, were apples bitten, turned in on themselves, their gloss long shed, floated over a distant time.

For all the throwing and grappling they did there, it could have, that summer day, like the other times had, begun in wrestling, with Andy reaching around to unzip Will's fly, thinking he would slap him, thinking in jest, both of them laughing and grappling. The older boys had done that with each other. He would show his own bullying, as Ben and his friends had. But when he reached, that first time, Will pushed him quickly, rolled him backwards, and was on top of him, suddenly, suddenly Andy was looking up at him, the thick grass beneath them, taste like straw in his mouth, insects hammering nearby. He looked up into Will's eyes, afraid to look down at his penis, though he could feel it outside his own zipped shorts, his own yearning to come up and meet it, could feel the heat outside his shorts, smell its salt, and dared not reach for it.

Andy saw some quick shadowed flash at first, like the flint of fear, dart across his eyes. Then something opened first in his eyes and then between their bodies, into their thighs, burning in their groins, spreading beneath the surface of their skin, charging through them like heat lightning and in its charge they were no longer afraid, in its taking of them they rolled, hard bit like a knotted apple turning in its color, rubbed hard, skin almost pierced clean through, they rubbed raw, released, arms and legs grappling, had not discovered mouths together yet, then, punching, fell back in the matted grass.

Some smooth places on their skin, now chapped, their eyes looked away, and they did not have a word for it. The distant sheen on the apples brought back, back from its dissolving long ago in that field, in the orchard's day, back now the morning condensation lifted to their skin, brought back molecules gathered, transformed, brought back now in the beaded glistening of their skin, gloss brought to the surface, their sweat called to the surface by their beautiful urgent straining. Not one time did they have a word for it.

But this time a bee brought the grappling, a bee, done with its other sucking in the apple trees, that found Will's skin when their shirts were off and that Andy smacked away. His smacking was too late, the stinger already in Will's shoulder blade, and Andy didn't deliberate before he put his mouth on it. He just leaned, left arm thrown over Will's back, pulled him, leaned and put his mouth on the red swelling, sucked a minute on the red spreading, as he worked the stinger up, spit it out, then another sucking, more saliva to heal. That was how they discovered their mouths together, as Will turned and pulled Andy to him, first bit his lip as if to taste in the stringent heat the stinger too.

Their mouths had begun the finding outside in the remnants of the orchard and then had paused in the midday heat, the weekday heat, while ordinary summer light fell on them running as it sifted down on all sorts of other things, as it always had, on old spigots and wash basins under trees, clothes swaying a line, on slate sidewalks and curved metal yard chairs painted green. Daylight fell on them running, as it fell on someone opening a curtain, yawning on a back step, on someone slicing an apricot at the kitchen sink, throwing a ball, it fell on the two of them, running, sweating, toward the barn. And there, in the space they had discovered behind a broad post, beyond the hull of a car, the mower and the shovels, where the night's cool stayed in a pocket of shadow during the day, their mouths closed on each other's again. This time carried them all the way through their hurrying, their mouths striving to catch up with the glistening hardness of their bodies, and matching it. In that rush the oil mark here and there they would have smelled, if they were not consumed by their own salt and by the sweet dusted air lingering in that, in any, barn.

And it was there, behind the broad post, a full ten minutes or so before Lloyd stepped into the shadows to retrieve next to the coffee can of nails a socket wrench from his shelf, having misplaced the one he needed at work, there, before they hesitated in the dazed moments afterward waiting for calmer breathing, that Andy and Will had gasped so fully in pleasure.

23

Pine Trees

Sonya's goal for the weekend after the next was to go for a bike ride by herself. In preparation, she spent a good part of the ten or so days before it working on her room, broken into separate tasks, written out in a list on lined yellow paper. The first was finding old dishes and washing them. While doing this, she talked to herself about the ride, saying, "It doesn't have to be far." When the room was free of the months' worth of odd kitchenware, the pieces Marie and Lois had not retrieved, she concentrated on sorting and washing neglected laundry, including some hand wash which she had tossed in a pile in her closet during the spring. As she wrung the water out of her clothes, she kept saying, "Just to be outside will be OK."

With the accumulated clutter out of the way, several days later, she spent an afternoon organizing her drawings and paintings according to their stage of completion. The three main categories were: barely begun, halfway or so, and completed. Several others that did not fit neatly into one of these designations were also set aside in their own place. While she sorted, she thought of her old route out along the bike path that wound through town and then followed the river for a few miles before it looped back up the parkway and turned toward her neighborhood; a stitch cinched in her stomach, the pull of nerves gathered in one spot. It used to take her at least an hour to do that loop. But as soon as she heard herself say, "It doesn't have to be far," the knot eased and she could think clearly again.

And another afternoon, as she took everything off her desk, dusted the cubby-holes and the surface, she thought about their street, about riding to the right out of the driveway to the next corner and then turning left. She would pedal two blocks until she reached the street that led to the boulevard. She would ride to the boulevard and then stop. As she put her papers and drawing implements neatly back in, she decided that if it appeared too wide, the lush avenue of flourishing old trees and grass filling the middle, its houses beside each other watching, and more traffic than the side streets had, if crossing was anywhere near daunting, she told herself, she could just turn around and retrace the path to their house. But if it didn't seem unmanageable, she could ride left up the boulevard for a few blocks, then left again, and wheel down her street from the other end. She could decide, she told herself, when she got there. She would go a block at a time. She had options.

The night before her ride she flicked the outside light off and, out in the dark, took her bicycle from the garage. Pointing it toward the street, she tested the brakes on the driveway. She stood beside it awhile, hands on the handlebars, looking out across the yards faintly lit with porch lights. Closing her eyes, she listened to screen doors opening and closing, the buzz of kids in a few of the backyards, and the murmur of a radio. Mowed grass permeated the air. Sonya was outside with her eyes closed, trying to take more in; it was the most relaxed she had been in ages. How could she draw this, ages? Marked in bronze, in the changing shapes of water jugs, sketches of plowed fields, hands, hayricks.

And when, the following afternoon, she headed down the streets she had planned to, and stopped at the edge of the boulevard, she counted five cars zip by, steered left and rode up it. The trees by her side, the old and the young trees, and the swath of grass to her left, all the way along her route, were traveling the same direction she was, traveling with her. She remembered walking there with Odessa. She remembered the smell of her hair in the sun. Accompanying her. So to turn then was not so arduous, that stretch of the ride concluded. Next the cross street house by house, and to swing down to her street, steer, to come upon the house, to coast into her driveway from the other side, to have come all the way around, was not so bad. The whole ride, including the pause to count the cars, had not taken longer than twelve minutes. Then back, she slowed to a stop, walked her bike into the garage and leaned it in its place against the far wall. From the side window of the garage Sonya saw her mother refilling a bird feeder and thought of asking if she needed help with any yard work; realizing this, her eyes clouded with tears.

Her mother turned around when she heard Sonya walk behind her. "How was your ride?" Trying to ask casually, she continued what she was doing.

"It was fine." Where she rode her bike buses ran on time, newspapers were delivered.

"Good."

Sonya stood a few feet away and could feel how warm the green was beneath her, how firm the ground, could feel that the hedge of honeysuckle bordering the yard shimmered, could smell the richness of the seeds and knotted suet her mother wedged into the feeder, and knew without looking up that the tops of trees above her tangled and wove their threads. Her right hand in her pocket, her left hand hung down, the slight weight of her arm at her side; the veins in her hands held her blood so fully, exactly, perfectly. Other times, such as when she and Lois had run in the rain as kids, she had known this jubilation. When she and Elinor held each other, touch made her want to move further out into the day, further toward green, further toward sound. And now, with the opaque film that had slipped between her and the world gradually evaporating, she stood a few feet from her mother, both of them smiling, and did not ask if she needed help; to stand like this, relaxed, watching, was more than enough.

Instead, after a while she said, "I haven't done much of anything to help you lately. I'll mow the lawn soon." And make a feeder with a copper roof, she was thinking, a beacon of a roof, absorber of light, glinter of slanting rain, a monument to the lovely object, as her ceramics teacher said, no matter the size; when considering the scale of beauty, the small piece could be monumental, too. Right here in the yard. And make, she was thinking, a dome, an intricate suspension bridge, or a chair, a wooden chair pitched for reclining in the yard. And its carved side table, pedestal for a cup. Or a feeder, at least that, with its lovely roof made from a sheet of copper.

"That would be nice."

"I might visit Elinor at work. Could you bring me?"

Her mother looked over. "Certainly. She would like that very much."

"Mom."

"Yes?"

"We can talk about her sometime."

"Yes, we can," her mother said.

Then Sonya went inside.

To spiral up and outward, to rise up out of the blue well, a person could tell by viewing the outside of it that it was blue and deep inside, and there were the swirls of color to let a person know. They rose up, delicate bands unraveling into the spring air, up and out, as if fired within the well, out of sight. That was all: the stone basin, the bands of red green and blue ribboning up and out. Sometimes when Sonya drew she thought of longitude and latitude, of charted and definable points, and of the contrast with her hand that often seemed to float over these invisible and numbered lines. But how did a person know if the colors rose up and out or if, just as possibly, they dove down into the blue, out of sight? She thought of movement, of ways to lead the eye in a particular direction along longitude or latitude. She titled it *Out of the Basin* and thought that would do it.

And another afternoon Sonya knocked on Lois's door. "Hey. Are you in there?"

"Come in."

Lois was sitting on the floor reading a recent *Ms.*, a fan blowing on her.

Sonya sat down next to her. "Do you want to sit in the yard?"

"Are you going out, too?"

"Yeah."

"Sure."

Sonya dug out the old green picnic blanket from the downstairs hall closet, then poured them each a tall glass of lemonade. They went into the yard, spread the blanket, and lazed on their stomachs in the sun. The afternoon heat blazed upon them.

"I feel like a turtle stuck in mud," Lois said.

"I feel like a fly stuck to tar paper." They laughed.

"But it is good to be out here with you, Sonya. I've been scared."

"I know."

"I've been thinking a lot lately about Glenda that time she wouldn't leave the bedroom. Remember that?"

"Yeah. It was pretty scary."

"Have you thought about her, too?"

"Yes. I decided to send her that drawing, *Out of the Basin*." Sonya had shown it to her sister the day before. "I was thinking it might make her feel better if she gets that depressed again." Art, catharsis for the viewer, one of her teachers had explained. For everyone, students of art or not. For those whose work was sorrow.

"I could make a macrame frame for it."

"That would look great."

Each of them took a generous swig of lemonade.

"Do you know now the answer to my other question?"

"I think so," Sonya said.

"I still think it's OK."

"I'm glad you do."

Lois traced some water drops with her finger, making lines along her glass. "Is everything going to be all right now?"

"I think it will be. Don't worry, Lo."

Instead of coming three or four times a week they began coming three or four times a night. In one, as she and Elinor approached the hill in a car, they saw the cats running toward them from the trees. When the animals reached the hill, they stopped suddenly, about twenty of them, sat beside each other to make a border and stared down at the vehicle. After driving a few miles away, Sonya checked the rearview mirror and saw the line of them still watching. She flipped the mirror around. Though she woke up then, it didn't much help; as soon as she had woken her way out of one, she drifted into another.

Despite the taxing fatigue of the more frequent nightmares, Sonya also experienced glimpses of exhilaration at her recent ability to accomplish daily tasks. This gave her, incrementally more each day, the energy she needed to find her father's postcard and think about dialing the number he had given them.

When she eventually sat down one afternoon in the living room with the postcard in her left hand and the telephone beside her, running through her mind as she dialed were all the happenings she wanted to tell her father about. But she had decided not to question him too closely nor to push him on his return.

After a handful of rings someone picked up. "Hello. Creekview Arms."

"Who is this?"

"This is the front desk."

The desk of what, Sonya wondered. "I think I dialed the wrong number. What is this?"

"Creekview Arms rooming house."

"A rooming house?"

"Yes."

"Oh. Is someone named Mitchell Hudson staying there?"

"He has been here for a little while, yes, but I don't think he is in right now. Can I take a message for him?"

"Please tell him that his daughters phoned to see how he is doing."

"I'll let him know."

"Thank you."

After hanging up, Sonya held the phone on her lap; the rambling house was in disrepair, with worn front steps and rooms smelling of smoke, dingy yellow curtains closing in dank air. Things forever moved, messages jotted on scraps of paper lost in wastebaskets.

When Lois got home later that afternoon, they discussed the possibilities.

"Maybe he likes that town."

"Sonya. What could be so special about it?"

"I don't know. Maybe he just needs to be away from here for a while."

"Maybe. Do you think he has a job there?"

"Who knows. He didn't mention one in his note. Do you think he has a basement there? Or some other place to do his work?"

"Well," Lois said, "if he doesn't, it's his own fault. He's the one who left a job here. God knows what he's thinking."

"Do you want to call him again tomorrow?"

Lois contemplated her sister's question for a couple of seconds. "Not really. He could call us, you know."

"I know." A hesitation, then Sonya asked, "Don't you miss him?"

"No." Lois looked directly at her sister. Her mouth worked the air. "Of course I do, but I still think he should call us."

They agreed to wait to hear from him.

When they told Marie about it, she was puzzled, too.

The landscape postcard they received a few days later had a note on it almost as brief as the previous one had been: "It's just for now. I don't drive a bread truck. Lois, how's the old trumpet holding up? Let me know if you need a new case."

"It's fine, Dad," Lois said to her sister when they read the note. "I don't need a new one." The green-lined case still had a few stickers on it and now a macrame handle she had made, the instrument itself a few more years of wear than when he had gotten it for her. But she would not trade it, not even if, someday, it no longer hummed when she held it to her mouth. Not even if Miles Davis himself wanted to swap.

"How long do you think 'now' is?" Sonya asked.

"You know how he is," Lois said. "His time is different from our time. He has his own personal time zone wedged somewhere among the others. I guess he'll let us know. Let's not try to figure it out right now."

That idea seemed best to both of them. And after talking with her sister about it, when Sonya thought again about the rooming house, the curtains parted slightly, letting in a breeze—blowing off a nearby river, churn of water over stones.

Even though she was worried about her father, her happiness thinking about Elinor, more and more often, made the worry easier to carry. Early the next week she called her at work and told her she had a surprise for her.

"What is it?" Elinor asked.

"I can't tell you. It's a surprise."

"When will I have it?"

"Friday."

"What letter does it start with?"

"I can't tell you that."

"How many words? More than one word?"

Sonya laughed. "It's something that you want. That's all I can say. Are you curious?"

"Yes. Should I come over before work to get it?"

"Wait until you hear from me. I'll let you know when. OK?"

"OK."

When she and her mother pulled into the restaurant parking lot on Friday night around nine thirty, Sonya scanned the rows for Elinor's car and, spotting it, let out a sigh. Marie touched her arm as she reached for the door handle.

"I'll be fine, Mom. Elinor will bring me home later."

Their glance reassured each other.

The hostess seated her at an end of the busy dining room at a two-person table along the wall. When Sonya sat down, she remembered having been there last in the winter with her mother and Lois. Familiar were the red and white flowered tablecloths, candles on the tables and framed prints of Italy on the walls, the smells of garlic and cheese, of dim smoke drifting in from the lounge.

As Sonya reviewed the menu, she heard Elinor say, "Can I have this one? She's a friend."

She looked up as Elinor walked over and stood beside the table, put her hands in the pocket of the black apron around her waist. Sonya could tell that Elinor wanted to touch her because her hands fidgeted with the pad and pen in her pocket. Then sounds dropped aside as Sonya looked from the apron up to her face. She thought of the salt of Elinor's hair and wanted to taste it.

"This is the best thing, Sonya." Behind Elinor's words, a quick drop of relief, her breath taken away by a cold spot in a lake.

Sonya felt exposed, their love luminous in the room, as if other people could see it, as if it would spread out to and overwhelm them, disrupt their dinner.

"I would like the eggplant parmigiana," she said. The ordinariness of the request made them laugh.

"That's good," Elinor said, taking out the pad and writing down the order.

"It's not the best thing?"

"No, it's not the best thing." Elinor reached down to take the menu and rested her hand in Sonya's hand. Then she said, "I'll be back."

While Sonya waited, she pondered the curve of her elbow lifting the glass of water up as she took a sip, then returned it to the same spot on the table. She ran her fingers along the outline of the placemat, listened to the flip, flip, of the paper's edge. There were flowers pressed in the white and a thin ribbon of black bordering the sides. She sat with one leg crossed over the other, the weight familiar and comfortable, and listened to pieces of conversations, now and then a line or two rising distinct above the other voices and the assorted rock and pop jags from the jukebox. Beyond those sounds she listened to the clink of dishes and muffled yells coming from the kitchen. Each sound, it seemed, and each movement, had to be taken in and absorbed. It was like standing in the middle of a sidewalk, watching everyone come and go weighted with packages and gesturing, pushing and humming through the crowd. People did it every day, thought Sonya, every day without thinking about it. So much movement went unnoticed, so much sound unheard. When would she get to that point again—be able to go somewhere, do some simple transaction, select postcards from a rack, dig for change in her wallet, and give the coins to someone behind the counter, hear the register ring the sale in, watch the cashier slide the cards into a paper bag, fold the top over, hand it to her and say "thank you"? Then walk out of the store with the bag in her hand and turn up the street, an errand accomplished so effortlessly? Was that the goal, to function without noticing the details? She did not want to be oblivious to what was around her, nor take for granted the pleasure of moving daily with ease. But she wanted to take details in without drowning in them, without feeling them fill her mouth like sand and steal her voice. She reflected on what it would be like to move as if she were among her surroundings and not always so much inside peering out, looking behind, constantly weighing and measuring from a cave of fear.

When Elinor returned with her food she asked, "Can you stay?"

"Until you're finished."

"It'll be eleven thirty."

"I'll leave with you."

Elinor said, "I can't wait."

"Me either," Sonya said.

She ate luxuriously, telling herself that she was just another person, just another person eating her dinner in a restaurant. Each item helped ground her joy, the weighted plate and bowl on the side, the slender utensils in her hand, each bite stitching her to that time and place. She looked up now and then for Elinor and sometimes caught her eye as she carried a tray by, rushed back and forth from the kitchen. And the times when Sonya didn't catch her eye, she watched from a distance her arms, or the bend of her neck as she listened to someone, or her walk between tables as she negotiated the world. Sonya saw her new, sought her out in the crowded room, and, though she knew Elinor was there, felt a startle of pleasure to see her, as though the fact of them being in the same place precisely then was a surprise. She couldn't look at Elinor without wanting to protect her. I love that person, Sonya thought. She ate her meal, each bite nourishing, delicious, and watched.

Even public nearness, and the promise of nearness, Elinor coming over to the table an hour later when she was done with work, leaning toward her to say "Let's go," moved her. They knew without much discussion where they wanted to be.

So that now to stretch out beside her on a blanket on the grassy hill of the arboretum breathing in the rich August air, excess of summer, air saturated with the day's heat and lined with the faint pitch of nearby chestnut trees, was as much as Sonya could hold.

They could not figure out how, lying on the same hill that daily had visitors walking it to admire the trees and shrubs, the same hill they had sometimes sat on in the afternoon when wearing watches helped them keep closer track of things, now, this night, it was as if they had rolled the stone of time aside and slipped through the opening. They could not figure out how something that so ordered their daily lives could fall aside easily at night when they touched.

Their shirts unbuttoned, tossed aside, sandals off, they moved into each other's arms. And then the round of lobe, tiny weight of flesh at the fingertip, and above it curve of ear so smooth, curved to call sound in and hold it there, the voice whispered outside in the night blended with the rustle of oak leaves or a song from the back step hummed as someone came in and hung up a coat in the winter twilight or the sound of a bicycle's wheels maneuvering the pebbles up the hill to reach the wider street that would lead home. And they all fit in the curve, holding itself outward and open to the world. The individual note hovering outside it, and the closer closer sound of her moist tongue tracing the structure and then in, so far inside it seemed to run along the lining of the stomach, outline the veins' warm running and gently widen the glistening muscle of the heart. Then mouth on mouth, opening irrevocably the shell of need, and on each other's breasts and thighs, the rest of their clothes off.

Where were we, how far away were we, to have come here?

I knew you, they wanted to say, *I knew you then, along the river, but I've forgotten exactly when. The smell of your hair brings me back, the fitting of our bodies with our skin touching the length of us, opening wider and wider to take more of each other in. These things I remember.*

Yes these things I remember too, the other said, or seemed to say, *and the sounds of pleasure that you make. These too are familiar. That was you I saw, held still in the light of day by the gleaming water, wasn't it? Tell me when.*

Yes, yes, yes.

Come closer.

And closer still. Closer, closer, then the startling, green plain of being, open. Then their mouths together again and again.

So to look at their watches after, as they slowly rejoined their stretching on the hill, rejoined what held them there, was a surprise.

"Guess," Sonya said, looking closely at her watch and rubbing the top of Elinor's foot with her foot.

"Let's see. Maybe one thirty, two o' clock?"

"Four thirty."

"That's not possible," Elinor said. "It can't be. We left the restaurant about eleven thirty and drove here, and it seems like we've been here an hour, or maybe two at the most." Holding her own watch close to her eyes, tilting it slightly in the dark, she said, "My mom will have a cow." She had dialed her from the restaurant to say she was going out for coffee after work with a couple of other waitresses. She dug around for her shirt and sandals.

"Oh no," Sonya said, as she reached for her clothes, too.

But before they put them on, Elinor rolled over on top of her, their sighs weaving into the night air as their breasts came together. She leaned on her elbows, ran her hands through Sonya's hair, and kept them there, cupped her head in her hands. Sonya's hands rested in the small of her back.

"I want to tell you something, Elinor," Sonya said. "I love you."

"I love you too, Sonya. It's so good to finally say so."

They lay in each other's arms without talking for a few minutes.

Then Elinor asked, "What about your mom?"

"She knew I'd be out late, I think she knew we would come here."

And when she woke later in the day and realized it was three in the afternoon, she did not mind that so much of the day had been lost to sleep. She did not even mind that she couldn't phone Elinor at home. She rang her number right away.

"What time did you wake up?"

"Around nine."

"Oh. How come you didn't call?" Sonya knew that she could not call from home, but she felt so thrilled that it was as if, because of their intimacy, there could be, however briefly, such a mundane exchange between them, as if Elinor were not restricted by her parents' anxiety and admonitions.

"My mother woke me up at nine," Elinor explained.

"What happened? What did she say?"

"Yes."

"Is she listening to you?"

"Yes."

"You can't talk to me?"

"No, I can't."

Sonya heard some sadness in Elinor's voice. Then she heard her start to cry. "What is it, Elinor? What happened?"

"I have to go." Then she hung up.

When Sonya tried again that evening, Elinor's father answered the phone and said she wasn't home. She started to say, "Please tell her I called," but he had already hung up.

She tried for the next few days without being able to reach her. Marie said to give it some time. Sonya thought of this each instance she picked up the receiver and started to dial her number. Then she would put it down and try to think about something else, anything, for a while, to distract herself. Thinking or doing. Recent newspaper articles read again, kitchen cupboards emptied and dusted, reorganized. Finally Sonya phoned her at work, but Elinor couldn't leave her station. Just saying to another waitress, "Please tell her that Sonya called," gave her some relief.

The dreams of terror, which had visited with alarming regularity for going on six years, now, these past couple of weeks, had come more frequently with the fury of exit, as many as four in one night, a rush, come as if they needed to escape from Sonya. She had begun to think of them as bits of spoiled food, each with a slightly different cast, that she needed to rid herself of. That was the pattern of how they emerged, each one with its struggle up and out, a sweat residue left behind, the stinging taste of fear lingering in her stomach when she woke. A cat approached her leisurely, or wandered in a corner of the room, or cried, or gazed at her, and in these dreams, too, the tight knotted line of words—"Get it away from me"—twisted from her mouth. Awake, she repeated the command to hear herself say it before she fell back asleep.

Then one morning Sonya woke and realized she had dreamed about pine trees. They were cool, tall, and green. That was all. The next night she dreamed about grocery shopping and the next, no dreams came at all. She woke on a muggy August morning, having slept soundly, and said, "It's gone." The whir of a neighbor's buzz saw drifted faintly in the window. She heard her mother downstairs and Lois in the shower. The morning sunlight was dusted pale orange with the promise of heat, and she did not think— *What a miracle that I am free of it.* She thought of drinking soda in a tall blue glass with lots of ice, throwing on shorts, sandals, and a T-shirt over her bathing suit, and of riding her bike out to the reservoir to first dip her feet in the brisk water and then plunge into it.

She waited a few more days just to be certain before telling anyone. It was during supper that she told her mother and Lois about a few of her recent dreams, and they mentioned a couple of theirs. When she said, "and the next night I didn't dream about anything," both stopped eating, attentive to its significance.

Her mother asked, "How many nights has it been?"

"Over a week."

"That's great."

Lois said, "Hey, that's cool, Sonya."

Sonya wanted to share the news with Elinor but, not wanting to make her parents angrier, she had stopped trying to reach her at home. She decided it would be best to wait.

A couple of nights later Elinor phoned from work. "It's me."

"Are you all right?"

"I will be when I see you."

"What's that noise? Are you calling from work?" Dishes clanked in the background.

"I'm on break. I miss you, Sonya."

"I miss you, too." They heard each other sigh.

"How about you?"

"I'm fine. My nightmares seem to have stopped."

"Completely? For real?"

"Yes, for real."

Elinor let out a sound and then said, "Hallelujah!"

"'Hallelujah'? You never say that."

"I know," Elinor said, while they laughed. "It's the first word that came to mind."

"I love your laugh," Sonya said.

"I better get back to work."

"When can we talk about what your mother said?"

"I'm working on it." Hearing this made waiting easier for her.

One afternoon a few days later Sonya sat at her desk and glanced over at the brown corduroy bag her father had given her when her fear began. It had been in the same place on the bookcase since they moved into that house, though once in a while she had picked it up by the string, as he had instructed, and held it briefly. She returned it each time to its spot on the shelf; she had never peeked inside. Often she had wished she could, because that would mean she felt confident her fear was gone. But not until now had she genuinely contemplated actually opening the bag and taking out its mysterious contents. She walked over to the shelf, lifted the bag by the string, and then gently tugged the drawstring top open. She reached inside and felt clay, *baked earth*, then pulled out a cat, two inches wide, three inches high. It sat up, tail wrapped around its paws, and faced her, looked right at her with its eyes, inlaid bits of red tile, open wide. It had lined whiskers and eyebrow hairs, and tufts of hair etched around its ears. As she looked down at the cat and also watched her hand holding it, there was a division between her old fear and a new sensation of ease. There was a tingling in the tunnels of her brain; she concentrated on the fine points to counter her immense relief. Then she set it down on the bookcase, this time beside the brown cloth bag. The rest of that day and evening, walking in and out of her room, she intentionally did not look at it; she could look elsewhere, know the figure was looking toward her, and not have to look back.

And the next morning when Sonya rolled over on her side in bed, the first thing she saw was the cat standing in its spot. Observing it from that distance she admired it. It was simply a figure, finally an object, and not a catch in her stomach, her inside dropping endlessly away. Though there was not her old fear, there was the sensation-memory of it. As a physical wound is remembered by a scar when it rains, so she experienced the shadow of her fear, slight twinge behind the ears, still there but receding. She waited for a rapid heartbeat, but it remained fairly calm; when she put her hands together to check for sweat, there was just the round of warmth where her hands met. She welcomed the capillary tingle of perception, the soft pulse of aesthetic joy that accompanied admiration of something beautiful. What would looking at a real cat feel like now? And though she hoped the time would come soon, she dwelled on the question of when the cats of the neighborhood, going about their hunts and naps, would not notice her and when she would not have to notice them.

Later that day Sonya took the figure into the backyard.

"Mom," she called. Marie was mowing the lawn, and when she saw her daughter walking over, she shut off the mower mid-row. "I have something to show you."

"What is it?"

Sonya cupped the figure in her hands like a starfish. "This was in that corduroy bag. Dad made this for me."

"It's lovely." Her mother looked from the cat to Sonya. Then again at the figure. "He made you this."

"Yes, my own cat," Sonya said, with such reverence it might have been discovered in a cave.

Her mother had bits of grass on her clothes and in her hair clinging with sweat. "It's beautiful," she said again, smiling with relief. She pushed back her straw cap. Then she said, "He has some kindness in him. I just couldn't—" Where were those hands smelling of moist clay, holding a cup in the morning sun, the daily radio. The handsome body in the summer backyard, sweat of trembling, undone, laughter faded from the porch at dusk. The early joy in its undoing. Oh, the packing and sifting she had known would come, the lingering sadness that caught her sometimes now.

Sonya thought her mother might cry. "I know. Lois and I understand. Don't worry about that."

Her mother nodded and reached for a tissue in her pocket.

"Though Lois did say recently that she misses seeing your throwing arm."

Marie laughed softly with Sonya through her tears. "Isn't she a smart mouth."

"I'll do the lawn next time, Mom. I'll mow it the rest of the summer. I'll do the weeding, too, and clean the garage."

"I'd appreciate that," her mother said, blowing her nose.

That evening, after the supper dishes had been dried and stacked away, Sonya was sitting on the picnic table when Marie came out the screen door, walked across the lawn and sat beside her. Though dusk had begun in the cloudless sky, the air was still warm.

She asked Sonya, "Are you putting the sky on your head?"

"Yes. I see why it makes you feel better. Can I ask you something?"

"Anything."

"What happened to Alice and Roselyn?" She could not allow herself to wonder about the women during the months since her mother first mentioned them. But now she imagined directly two women living together in a farmhouse in Mercy Hill, decades ago.

"What happened? Oh, their lives? They seemed quite content taking care of their place, from what I remember. I think they had relatives nearby, probably a few close friends. A passion for gardening. Nothing devastating happened, if that's what you mean."

"Did anyone bother them?" Only recently could Sonya contemplate with any prolonged deliberation such facets of the women's daily lives.

"Not that I know of. Your grandparents wouldn't have; in fact, your grandfather never said anything, nor did your grandmother. They never talked about their living arrangement. No one did. Rather, once in a while someone would say they had 'never married.' But people treated them like anybody else in town; what mattered was working diligently and trying to help each other out, especially in tight times."

"Were they nice people, Mom?"

"For the most part they were nice. Once Alice shot at a hunter on their property—didn't hurt him—apparently he wouldn't leave when she asked him to, so she had to scare him off. And sometimes she would wrangle with your grandfather about the way something should be done, but yes, they were kind people."

"Did they live in that gray house across the road and down a little? I think it had white trim. With fruit trees out behind it?"

"That's it. It was beautiful then." Marie gazed into the yard, as if seeing those fruit trees now, recalling the beauty of the place. Then she outlined for her daughter the lives of the women, who had lived in that house for many years before it was sold. They were quite a bit older than Marie's parents. One of them, Roselyn, had died shortly after Marie started college, and since Alice could not take care of the farm herself, a nephew had placed her in the county home. She had died soon after. "Your grandfather said that would happen; neither woman was the kind to be still and let others wait on her."

Marie gestured with both hands as she continued her story, having ready all the details that she had tried to tell her daughter earlier, but that she had not wanted to hear then. It wasn't until Marie's second year away, she explained, that she had thought more consciously about Alice and Roselyn. That was the year that two young women in her dorm were accused of being lovers. "Well, no one used that word, of course. I think it was 'an indiscretion.' They had committed, or engaged in, an indiscretion and were sent home, removed from school permanently." She said their treatment by the administration would have been better if they had been caught with the till in their room. No one heard from them afterwards, and it was no surprise, given the unkindness of the other students. On this aspect of the story, she spared her daughter any elaboration with specifics.

Marie had not known the young women well, but she had often wondered then, and since, what became of them. Something happened then that had always stayed with her, and it was this part of the story she was most excited about sharing with Sonya. Several days after the two had been escorted off the campus she had had a dream about Alice in which she was in a field planting some corn. "She smiled at me and said, 'This will be grand come July.'"

"Grand? Did she say anything else?"

"No, just that."

"What did it mean?"

"You know how dreams can appear with an image of one thing, but point toward something else. I know you know that! Hell, for some reason that morning when I woke up, I understood her and Roselyn together. They were talking to me, they could have been right there in the room with me, wanting me to understand. But it wasn't about corn or their garden. It was as if they were saying, 'Look at us! Look at *our* lives! They are grand!' That was how they changed me, how I learned from them, speaking through a dream."

"I'm glad they were able to live together. And that you knew them."

"I am too. Maybe I should have tried to tell you about them sooner, I mean much earlier, but it didn't occur to me then. They were people from my childhood; I wouldn't have talked about Alice or Roselyn that often even though I thought about them now and then. And when all your distress started, I didn't know what was causing it. The longer it went on, the more helpless I felt, like my hands were in the fire with yours. This afternoon I was thinking about the clay cat your father made, and now I realize that maybe if I had given you something too, like the story of their lives, that you could think about, hold onto—I'm sorry that I—" Marie couldn't finish her sentence.

"You don't need to apologize. Even if you didn't tell me about them when I was younger, you did try awhile ago. But I wasn't ready then to hear about them. And the other story, about the girls at your college, that might have wigged me out. Besides, you did give to me," Sonya paused and looked up at the sky—gave daylight on a sleeve in the early morning gave shadow a name and globes of color a home gave breath, do now, give light and shape a place, still, always—"you did give to me, and to Lois, too, lots of ways to be in the world. You've let me imagine a life like theirs."

"These things take time to figure out."

"I felt like I was going to seed."

"But you came back." They smiled, recalling their conversation of a couple years before. "And now you have to go—I mean, go away."

Then Sonya asked, "Are you worried about me and Elinor?"

"I'm worried about how some people might treat you, but I'm not worried about you two being together."

"We love each other."

"I know."

"Why would this be so tough for people to understand? Some people, anyway."

"I'm still trying to make sense of that. But one thing I *can* tell you is that no one will expel either of you from a university for what you do. And let's not call it 'an indiscretion'—there are lots of better words for it." They laughed.

Then Marie added, "You already know what some of the rough spots might be, but trust in the love you feel. That's what counts. That's what makes the grass green and the sun shine."

Sonya burst into tears and fell against her. She could barely say, "Thanks, Mom."

Her mother put her arms around her. "Hey," she said. "Hey, hey." She rocked Sonya awhile.

24

A Passage Into Music

That far inside the sound of the mower she could make any song from it. The occasional sputter came in the taller grass, in the thicker green that got more sun, but even here was the strong bass under, the strong bass under so uncollapsed. Even here was the constant note that threaded row to row then back again; she could not hear her feet behind it. Instead she heard the sun and the red moon rising over clay. It pulled her forward along the dry wood seed smell of grass, and she followed in its path. Row after row stepping into the sun she watched her arms work, pull of muscle sure and knowing. As night followed day, and red day, day. And here, and here, and here, she worked it and she made it change.

She could be outside again, almost as easily as inside. But she hadn't, when she tracked down the rooming house address through the operator, written her father with all the specifics of venturing outside and why it was news; some would be saved for talking in person. What she did tell him in the postcard note, though, was significant: "Thank you for the cat." Her hand did not flinch as she formed those three letters; in fact, she lingered over them for the novelty of it. Then she added: "I'm so glad you have faith in me. P.S. Lois's case is still good, she doesn't need a new one, but don't stop asking."

There was more work to do inside, too. The clutter had been cleared, dishes put away, clothes washed, miscellaneous items tucked in a drawer, if that is where they belonged. Left visible about the room, still, a few pencils here and there, scraps of paper. No reason for the tidying to become antiseptic. The notes on Sonya's wall above her desk, with the heading Don't Forget, did need, though, to be accounted for. She did not want to feel like an archivist or an archaeologist, digging about and recording. Rather just a person with a drawing notebook, casually glancing at her own phrases penciled on the wall and then jotting them into her tablet.

Another, yet another, of a stream, acrylic on canvas, with *thick trees, evergreens, beside. The stream found, discovered*—how to illustrate that, the startle of discovery? That one coming sometime, when she figured it out. *Charcoal sky, storm moving across the reservoir*, that one finished. *Maybe a still life series, bowls inspired by a slide*, she had written, and the *bowl as life, as much as the fruit. Ceramic life—how to show that?* There, she had left the question mark. And the phrases for which she had actually forgotten her initial idea, these too she transferred to the notebook, phrases themselves not forgotten, even though they were mere bits of thought, a fragment now of a passing inspiration: *nickel-plated rain*; *skin of plum*; *sweat on work shirt*; *tracing in winter ice*; *fragile shred of moth wing*; *bat clung to the night screen*; something about a journey and an image for that. *Hands at a sink*, Glenda's perhaps; *hands gluing a broken pot, setting a chipped bowl*; *pieces of tile baking in the sun*; *a figure bent laying tile in a public square* (she remembered liking the choice of *square* here); and just *colored shards*. How had she imagined those?

Maybe if she checked these later, thought about them at an odd time, at times away from her desk, preoccupied with something else, then her idea, now elusive, would float back to the surface. Or if she concentrated on the medium noted—in colored pencil, an ink attempt, another watercolor version. That she had written, of that she had been certain, and of the paper's needed heft. Or, if not all of the original plan was recalled, that was OK, too. The jotting could stay there in her notebook, the mark of a passing day, of a moment her hand held a pencil against the wall of her room, her mind captivated by something she thought was beautiful. Sunlight or not, beauty nonetheless.

Erasing the notes left a smudge on the wall. She would paint over them, a wide swath with the extra paint stored on a basement shelf. That would be easy to finish before she left. Marie would agree. And every detail had been transferred to her notebook.

Out in the yard one evening, the first time they had seen each other since their night on the hill, Sonya urged Elinor to reveal the details of her talk with her mother; they still hadn't discussed what had happened. Elinor had ridden over on her bike, having recently mounted front and rear lights for nighttime riding.

Elinor hesitated. "I will tell you, but there is something else I have to do first. Tonight is the ideal time for it, and I don't know how many other chances I'll get before we go away."

"Does it involve riding somewhere?"

"No, walking. Is that OK?"

"That's fine."

"It's in the neighborhood."

The warm night air carried the scent of cut grass and faintly of apples faintly of peaches fallen from trees, the orchard distant in another year, resting in ripened earth.

"A few streets over," Elinor said, as they walked down Sonya's driveway.

"I'll go anywhere you want to go."

There were kids playing in a few backyards, their indistinguishable voices lofting up sporadic bursts of laughter.

After they had walked several blocks, Elinor said to Sonya, "It's just a little further."

"For what?"

"Close your eyes."

Sonya stopped and closed her eyes.

"No, keep walking. Here, take my hand." Elinor reached out and took Sonya's hand, and they walked more slowly in the shadows cast by porch lights.

"If it's nighttime, why do I need to have my eyes closed? It's dark anyway."

Elinor laughed. "You'll see. Well, not *see* exactly, but you'll know what I'm doing in a few minutes."

They walked over a few more squares of sidewalk, then Elinor stopped and put her hand on Sonya's shoulder. She leaned toward her and whispered, "Stay right here and keep them closed." Under the dark of the eyelids' mottled shapes, atoms floating in the unknown, then the gift of sentient light—a thousand times and ways of saying *this is for you*—the gift of opening to light, the opening itself the gift. She kept her eyes closed.

Sonya heard Elinor's continued steps on the sidewalk, then heard her softly call, but in another direction, "Come here." Then her voice sounded closer to the ground, as if she were crouching, as she said again, gently, "Come here. That's it. It's me."

Next Sonya heard a cat's cry, a solitary meow from its mouth opening nearby. She heard Elinor walking back toward her, pausing a couple of feet away, walking right past her, then, behind her, saying, "Come here" again.

She stood very still as she felt its head rub first, against her bare leg, then its fur, the length of its body. Then she heard Elinor say, "That's a good kitty, this way," then heard another cry behind her.

With her eyes still closed, Sonya let out a gasp as the Griffins' hydrangea beside the house threw itself into that autumn air, drifted down above her head dry petals buoyant here and here, some rising up a column to take the sky, drifting flakes of light sideways a bit across that afternoon, skirting down some in that place, sifting down some daylight with them to her slowly, easily, standing in that place.

She opened her eyes and turned to see Elinor crouched a few feet away, a gray cat walking toward her. Scooping it up in her arms, she stood and rubbed its head, saying, "Good kitty."

Sonya walked over to them.

"Do you want to rub her head?"

Sonya reached out and touched the cat's ears, petted the fur between them tentatively, and the animal, purring, tilted its head into her hand.

"She likes you. I've been watching her for a few weeks," Elinor said. "She is always on that porch in the evening, and she is really sweet. I've stopped to pet her several times so she'd know my scent. And I've held her, too." She put the cat down, and it waltzed up the sidewalk to the house. "She usually squirms a bit when she wants to return to her porch." Turning to Sonya, she asked, "Are you all right?"

Sonya held Elinor's forearm with one hand, and looked down at the other, the one with which she had touched the cat. "I don't feel like I have to wipe my hand off." Her heart rate was elevated, she realized, but only in part from the twinge of fear receding, as had happened, too, holding the clay cat; the other part was from her excitement at being able to touch the animal. "Can we stand here awhile?"

"Of course."

As they watched the cat settle on the porch railing and survey the street, Sonya kept her hand on Elinor's arm.

After a few minutes she said, "You gave me"—she swallowed—"the closed-eye wish."

"I've thought about it since you told me."

"That's the kindest—" She couldn't finish the sentence.

"It's OK," Elinor said.

"It's so embarrassing."

"What is? Why do you feel embarrassed?"

"It's nothing, I mean, this fear is nothing. Lots of people experience much worse fear—survive real danger or live in terrifying conditions—every day of their lives," to lift a hand to reach to rinse in tap water the wound the casualty still there, "and they never get relief from it. I've been thinking about that a lot lately."

"But what you experienced was real, too."

"I know, but cats are not the real part of it. I mean, they were not actual danger to me."

"They speak for something else though, that is real, people's attitudes."

"That part we still have to untangle. I'm so grateful for the help with it, grateful that you—" Again Sonya couldn't finish her sentence.

"That's what it's about—doesn't your mother say that?—what we give to others."

"I'm so glad I know you. And yes, she does say that."

"I'm glad I know you, too." Then Elinor said, observing Sonya's tears, "Your mood might change when we talk about what *my* mother said. That will be enough to make us both cry, speaking of attitudes." The laugh with which she said this was not meant to mask, nor could it, the distress caused by her mother's words.

Sonya wiped her eyes with the back of her hand. "Do you want to talk about it now?"

Elinor nodded. "Let's hang out in your yard."

They turned away from the cat and retraced their path through the filtered porch lights, distant voices billowing in the dark, to Sonya's street and up her driveway. They walked into the backyard and sat on top of the picnic table, their feet on the seat, looking out over the soft yard lights in the neighborhood, themselves partially illuminated by light from the house.

Elinor let out a sigh. "I think your mother understands because she saw what you went through. My mother doesn't see it."

"Or she just can't bring herself to look at it."

"Maybe that's true. Everything has been tenser than usual since our conversation, everything—walking past each other in the kitchen or both of us reaching for the phone when it rings. But if she is willing to talk about it, I know she is trying anyway."

"What did she say?"

Elinor started to cry. Her shoulders were tight as Sonya, who had not seen her cry like this before, put an arm around her, months' worth of conflict centered in her muscle.

"Elinor, what did she say?" When she realized that she could not answer, Sonya said, "It seems like your mother could try harder."

"Please don't say that. She's my mother. She's doing her best."

"I'm sorry. Here." Getting off the table, Sonya gently urged Elinor to stand up, too, then wrapped both arms around her and held her close while she cried.

They did not say anything else for nearly an hour. Sonya felt sweat run down between her breasts, their damp shirts pressed together as they stood in the August heat, the night air on their skin. Every once in a while she reached up and lifted the hair from the back of her lover's neck.

Finally, Elinor said she could sit down again, and they resumed their earlier places beside each other on the picnic table. With her composure regained, she recounted the particulars. The day after she and Sonya had spent most of the night on the grassy hill of the arboretum her mother said she was concerned. She had hoped that eventually Elinor's good judgment would prevail, but she had waited patiently enough and her daughter hadn't shown any indication that it would. This judgment, she added, was one in which she had always had an ardent belief. After much discussion with Elinor's father, who up to this point had been uninvolved, she decided it was time to have a talk with her. They were consoled by the fact that at least the girls were attending different universities and, even though both were branches of the state system, the distance between them—one in western New York, one in central—precluded frequent visits. For their part as parents they had decided that Elinor could not get together with Sonya when they were both home for their vacations. What the girls did on their own time was their business, which she acknowledged they could not monitor, but as parents, her mother stressed, they could not condone their daughter's behavior. Now that Elinor would soon be leaving she felt an obligation to make their position unequivocal, in case there had been any doubt. So there it was.

"And she said they had decided against buying a car for me to have at campus, as they had planned to do."

"For real?"

"That was the first I had heard that they were thinking of getting me one, so it wasn't a big deal."

"What did you say?"

"I said it would be a privilege—you know how much they like that word—a privilege to take a Greyhound bus to visit you."

"I can take one, too, to come see you."

They let out a breath again, then Elinor continued her account.

"Then I told her how I feel about you, which she knew already of course, but I had to say it to her. I had to be certain she heard me express that."

"What did she say?" Sonya had leaned back a little to look at her.

"She asked me if I am a lesbian."

"What did you say?"

"I said if loving you like this means that I am, then yes, I guess I am."

"I guess we are."

"It's not so bad, is it, having a word for it?"

"No, it's not. It still feels like just us. How did your mother react to that?"

"'Lots of girls go through this and come out just fine later on.'"

"What does that mean?" Sonya asked. "They get married?"

"I think that's what she hopes for. Then I realized how guilty and horrible I have felt about the times I lied to her, so I told her about some of those. She took that with some grace. Maybe she had known all along; she probably knows right now that I am over here."

And though this response had been developing all summer, and this culmination was somewhat expected, Elinor was still not accustomed to parental disapproval.

Sonya tried to find some reassuring words. "Maybe this reaction now—spelling it all out like this—is because of their anxiety about you leaving home."

"Maybe you're right. But even so I don't want to upset them. They've done everything for me." She had said this on a number of other occasions, too.

"I know." Once Sonya had said, "You've done a lot for them, too," but that hadn't helped much. And now she added, "They have to let you sort things out for yourself."

"I know," Elinor said. "But she said definitively that they will never support us."

"Never now, anyway."

"I mean, she used that word, *never*."

"Well, maybe *never* will change for her, will become longer than she realized, too much longer."

Sonya's optimism was starting to take effect. "And then what will happen?"

"She will see us differently than she does now, both your parents will probably, and who you are will be OK with them, *more* than that, it will be fine, as it is with my mother. And my father."

"According to my mother, that's because she is too casual in her thinking."

"Too casual? What does she mean by that?"

"I think she means morally."

"Morally? She said that about my mother? Like she's immoral because she's divorced?"

"Not that so much."

"Is it that she could have a lover sometime and not be married to him?" A couple of times recently during supper Marie had mentioned, though nonchalantly, a colleague, and there was something about the way she said his name and shared his remarks with her daughters that led them to speculate, afterwards, whether she might have an interest in him. They held off pressing for the scoop too soon, quite a challenge, since they were both abundantly curious.

"I suppose that possibility has occurred to her. I think that is part of it."

"What's another part?"

"How she deals with us."

"Because she understands why we're together and accepts us, that makes her immoral?"

"She suggested as much."

Sonya let out an exasperated breath.

"You just said a minute ago that you thought they would come around eventually."

"I do believe that."

"It's only because she is upset that she made those comments about Marie."

"I know it is," Sonya said. Though she wasn't entirely convinced of this, she knew now was not the time to further criticize what motivated her mother's beliefs. She looked at Elinor intently and added, "It will be all right. It's good that she is talking about all of this."

Some of Elinor's pain had entered her, now sharing their bodies. When she reached up and put a hand on each side of Elinor's face as they turned to each other, she knew it raw and cumbersome, a shadow over her eyes like a cloud shadow moving over land. Sonya closed each with her thumb, ran her thumb lightly over each lid, then over each eyebrow, as though she could shape the pain, sculpt it into something smaller, a clay bird for a shelf, something they could admire. The best she could do was kiss each closed eye, listen to Elinor's tired sigh. And though she did not say so out loud, she hoped her optimism would prove to have some wisdom in it. She hoped Elinor's father would eventually be like her own in his unconditional love for her and Lois. Knowing that Elinor did not feel that security right now, Sonya had decided not to tell her just yet about her father's quick response to her recent note. Brief as always, meaningful as he usually was, he had written: "Sonya, of course I have faith in you. Lois, I thought about what you said. Found your Uncle Samuel. I'll bring him back." They had marveled at this, on yet another landscape postcard, and soon, maybe even in a day or two, she would share their wonder with Elinor. And it was her hope that what was tenuous in Elinor's life would not be that way indefinitely, and that she herself could, this hour in the grass-laden air like no other, and next week, next month, whatever weather, next year, in whatever place, add a thousand-fold to what was good. Sonya kissed her forehead then, too, kissed her hairline near her temple, near her pulse, and kissed the salty moisture of her neck, and then she held her own face right next to Elinor's as their whole bodies rested, leaning, in their renewed breath.

She could not untie him lift him down let daylight in again bring him back to a life, make for him a life that had lotion in it had his skin on another's skin humming back to the thick grass beneath the trees with another boy to touch in daylight. Make for him a life with no angry father back to the other boy undo his despair their despair bring them back to a day with their hard salty bodies in it. Then what became of the other boy did his despair turn inward like a stone so years later the smell of the trees would be out of reach or did he get back to it. Get back to a day with touch in it even if sorrow accompanied his touch he wore it like a scarf against his skin it rippled the more for the weight that pulled it along. Did he get back to a day. Did he. With another made whole in the summer heat an apartment somewhere the sheet tossed aside the new day begun the morning radio and music, music issued from. Did he. They were together.

And when she drew them next, they were in pencil beside each other naked on their backs, not touching. They were at the top of a grassy hill looking up at the expansive sky and out at the world; they were relaxed and joyous in their looking, enclosed in the warmth that often seemed luminous even when they didn't touch, another presence with them, because the possibility of touch moved them and kept them warm. One of Elinor's hands rested on her stomach, feeling its rise and fall, the slow return to calmer breath. One of Sonya's hands rested on her own throat, tracing the trail of pleasure sounds that had just escaped her by traveling along the muscled path of her voice circling up and out, bloomed at last, from her mouth. She planned to give the drawing, which she titled *Here We Are*, to Elinor when she came over for the picnic.

Marie had told them that she and Lois would make anything they wanted for that Saturday, and Elinor and Sonya had chosen pasta salad, corn on the cob, tomato and onion salad, brownies, and iced tea. Earlier in the week Marie had phoned Elinor's parents and said she wanted to see their daughter before she left for school. When they acquiesced to a two-hour visit, Marie also invited them, but they declined the invitation. This did not surprise anyone, though Elinor was disappointed. To offset the disappointment, Marie had told them that, though they would soon be leaving, this was not to be considered a goodbye meal, and she said she would arrange a fall picnic for the four of them, wherever the girls wanted to have one. So now that Saturday had come they tried to be excited rather than sad about it. While Lois shucked the corn and their mother prepared the salads, Sonya, having finished getting the table ready, walked to the end of the driveway to watch for Elinor riding up the street on her bike.

Perhaps it was the measure of the roofs descending down the street, or the line of trees getting smaller that reminded her of the time when, a couple of days before one of their moves, their father traced the height markings they had made on the kitchen wall onto a long strip of paper. When Marie and the girls had looked at him puzzled, he said, "Some things we have to keep," but he did not explain his intentions. It wasn't until they had been settled into their next place for a few weeks that they realized what he meant. One weekend afternoon while Marie and the girls were grocery shopping he took the roll of paper from a box and taped it up in the kitchen doorway. Then he dug the old marks into the wood with a carving knife. He was working on their first names, with serifs, beside each respective height when they returned home from the store.

"Mitchell, what are you doing? This isn't our house," Marie had said.

"I know," he said, "but this will help the girls feel more like it is. I'll fill them in with putty when we move."

As Sonya looked at the trees she remembered that the markings were still there when her family left that house. She was brought back to the present when she saw, measured against the furthest tree, the distant movement of someone on a bicycle. After a moment of looking she saw emerge, like ordinary sound passing through a membrane into music, the familiar shape of a person she loved moving toward her.

Biographical Note

Jessica Jopp grew up in New York state. She holds an MFA from the University of Massachusetts at Amherst. An award-winning poet, Jopp has published her work in numerous journals, among them *POETRY, Seneca Review,* and *Denver Quarterly.* Her collection *The History of a Voice* was awarded the Baxter Hathaway Prize in Poetry from *EPOCH,* and it was published in 2021 by Headmistress Press. She has been a finalist for the Yale Younger Poets Prize, the Juniper Prize, the Prairie Schooner Book Prize, and the Honickman Prize. Jopp teaches in the Department of Languages, Literatures, Cultures, and Writing at Slippery Rock University. She lives in Indiana, Pennsylvania, where she is on the board of a nonprofit working to protect a community woodland.

CPSIA information can be obtained
at www.ICGtesting.com
Printed in the USA
JSHW021735030423
39824JS00003B/3

9 781597 099295